ASHAEL RISING

The Vessel of KalaDene
Book One

Shona Kinsella

kristell-ink.com

Hardback ISBN: 978-1-913562-26-7
Paperback ISBN 978-1-913562-27-4
EPUB ISBN 978-1-913562-28-1

Cover design by Ken Dawson
Typesetting by Book Polishers

Kristell Ink
An Imprint of Grimbold Books
5 St John's Way,
Hempton,
Oxfordshire,
OX15 0QR
United Kingdom
www.kristell-ink.com

For Brian, who set me free

Prologue

SIRION SHIVERED AND TRIED TO KEEP HIS TEETH FROM CHATTERING AS HE CREPT towards the edge of the wall. The massive building that the Zanthar invaders had built here in the mountains hurt his senses. It didn't belong here any more than they did. He hoped there were no guards at this end of the keep. The Zanthar numbers had been depleted, with as many fled as dead, but it would be wise to stay quiet. Reaching the end of the outer wall, Sirion peered around the corner. This would be the most dangerous part. To reach the camp of the winged ones he would have to cross the open ground in front of the keep he had just escaped. He ducked back and leaned against the wall, taking deep breaths. *Time to go.*

Sirion sprinted from cover, running as if a kyragua were chasing him. The Zanthar-blasted earth made for treacherous footing, sand and pebbles moving beneath his bare feet. His lungs ached with the cold night air and he fought the urge to cough, knowing it would slow him down. A cry went up from the wall behind him and he urged his legs to go faster. He could see the edge of the winged ones' camp now, tents making silhouettes against the sky. *Almost there… I'm going to make it.*

Something hit Sirion from behind – hard. His legs were still running but his feet were no longer touching the ground. A blast of wind buffeted him as a voice growled from behind.

'Do you think to spy for your masters?'

Sirion struggled against the arms wrapped around his chest, watching the earth move away from him as his captor gained height.

'Don't struggle, or I might drop you,' the voice came again. The arms around Sirion's chest loosened for a moment and he started to drop back toward the earth. It was just long enough for his heart to leap into his throat before the arms closed around him again.

'I'll ask again,' the voice said, breath tickling Sirion's ear. 'Are you a spy?'

'No,' Sirion gasped. 'I think I can help you defeat them.'

'What makes you think we need your help?'

'Your leader and Daven are matched in power. But I can change that.'

The voice didn't respond but they had stopped rising into the air. Instead, they were hovering above the ground, the creature behind him beating its mighty wings to keep them in place.

'Let us see what Ezre makes of you,' the voice said at last.

***

Sirion crouched by the fire, warming his hands and feet. The tent was larger than the others, which was fortunate for it was filled with the winged ones, all of them massive. Sirion gazed at them in awe. They appeared human but the shortest was over seven feet tall. They had wings like an eagle's growing from their backs. Each creature displayed feathers of a spectacular colour, with eyes to match. They were clustered around their leader, a tall, handsome male with wings of gold, like the morning sun on clear water. This one stepped forward now and spoke to Sirion, the firelight making his eyes gleam as brightly as his wings.

'I am Ezre, leader of the Flores,' he said. 'Who are you?'

Sirion stood before answering. 'I am Sirion, Filidh of the Folk.'

'You say you have come to help us. Why?' Ezre's voice was rich and deep.

'The Zanthar enslave my people and destroy the land we live on,' Sirion answered. 'They are a sickness that we must purge from KalaDene, but we are not strong enough to do it alone. Neither are you. I believe that, together, we have a chance.'

The golden feathers rustled as Ezre adjusted the position of his wings. 'What makes you think I am not strong enough to defeat them alone?'

'You have battled Daven for three days and neither of you has gained a clear advantage. It seems that you are evenly matched in power. Many Zanthar have fled but Daven will never retreat. Eventually, one of you will grow tired and the other will be victorious.'

'It is true that I have not yet found his weakness, but I shall,' Ezre said, his voice growing hard.

'Given time enough, I have no doubt that you would,' Sirion answered. 'But look around you. This battle is killing the very land we stand on. Daven has used all of the life force in the land stretching several days' walk in any direction. If it does not end soon, there will be nothing left to fight for but a dead world.'

Ezre looked away from the fire and Sirion waited, breath held.

'You make a good argument, Sirion, Filidh of the Folk.' Ezre sighed and pushed his hair back from his forehead. 'How do you propose to avoid that future?'

'I am what is known amongst my people as a channeler. My gift is to move energy from one place to another.' Sirion watched Ezre for signs that he understood. 'But there is little life force left in the land here and I dare not take what is left.'

'Then what do you intend to channel?'

'How many of your people do you have with you?' Sirion asked.

*****

THE SUN WAS high in the sky by the time Daven emerged from the gates at the front of the keep, a retinue of Zanthar and slaves following behind, the only difference between them being their colouring. The leader of the Zanthar was tall and powerfully built. He walked about a foot above the ground, the air holding him up as if it was solid. Sirion gritted his teeth: to use what little life force was left here for such a vain purpose infuriated the filidh. Daven's skin was so pale that Sirion could see the veins beneath, and his hair was almost white. All of the Zanthar were pale compared to the Folk, but their leader was especially striking. His magic gave him a powerful presence, drawing the eye and the will towards him. Sirion shivered. Even he felt the pull of the man, despite full knowledge of his evil.

'I am surprised to see you still here, bird man,' Daven called, halting a short distance away. 'I told you yesterday: leave now and I will let you go in peace.'

Ezre clenched his jaw but did not waste energy in an exchange of words. They both knew this could only end with one of them dead. Instead, Ezre beckoned and Sirion moved up to his side.

'I see you have something which belongs to me,' Daven said, his voice level though his eyes were narrowed. 'Very well. I shall offer it as a gift to you, a sign of good will.'

Someone behind Daven sniggered, and the mage spun around, glaring at his people.

'What is your answer?' Daven asked, turning back to face Ezre.

In response, Ezre lifted his arms and sent forth a blast of power. Daven threw up a shield of wavering energy just in time to deflect the attack, but someone in his retinue was not so lucky. Sirion wondered if it was the same person who had sniggered a few moments ago who now ran around screaming, engulfed in flame.

Daven responded with his own attack and Sirion stepped back, giving Ezre room to move. They had agreed that Sirion would do nothing until Daven appeared to tire, so he kept his eyes fixed on the Zanthar leader, watching for the first signs that he was faltering.

Back and forth the bristling balls of energy flew, Ezre's force the same golden colour as his wings, while Daven's was black as pitch. Now, up close, Sirion could see why the Flores had not yet won. Each time Daven sent forth a ball of the crackling, black force, Ezre's shield absorbed the attack, keeping the rest of the Flores safe; but each strike took a greater toll on Ezre. His shield had started out as a hemisphere of opalescent light, rippling with every move that he made. Now, the edges were ragged, and dull patches were beginning to appear, the golden shield dimming slightly after each assault and unable to fully recover before the next blast hit.

Daven, on the other hand, used his shield to deflect the spells that Ezre threw at him, endangering the other Zanthar and slaves as lightning bolts and balls of flame flew above and amongst his people. More than one of his retinue lay on the ground, moaning in pain. *He values their lives as little as ours*, thought Sirion.

Ezre thrust out his arm, his spell causing the ground to shake. Many of the Zanthar stumbled or fell but Daven hovered above in his shield, leaving his followers to the danger.

'All-Mother, hear my prayer,' Sirion murmured, eyes never leaving the fight before him. 'These Zanthar before you destroy your land and enslave your people. We Folk have done our best to keep faith during these long years, but we are not strong enough to hold the balance. We are dying. This is our last hope. Please, gracious Kala, mother of all, let this work. I beg of you.'

Movement behind Daven caught Sirion's eye, just as he finished his prayer. One of the Zanthar was circling around behind Daven. It looked as though he was trying to get a clear line of sight towards Ezre. He moved into a clear spot and Sirion saw him raise his hands and begin to mouth the words of a spell.

'Watch out!' Sirion cried, but before the words had left his mouth, the Flores who had grabbed him last night was soaring over the battle, his midnight-blue wings casting a shadow over the combatants. He swooped down and kicked the would-be attacker in the face, sending him flying backwards. Another Zanthar observer pulled a sword, slashing at those beautiful wings. Everything devolved into chaos as more Flores entered the fight with the Zanthar while the two leaders battled on. *No! They were supposed to stay out of it!* Sirion thought.

Heart pounding, the filidh watched, wishing he could join in the fight but also terrified now that the time to act was almost upon him. Daven's movements were definitely slowing, the blasts of power he sent towards Ezre not quite so strong. Sirion realised that the Flores leader was also weakening when he stumbled back under the pressure of a direct hit to his shield.

'It's time!' Sirion shouted, moving to Ezre's side.

'You can't take any energy from those fighting,' Ezre answered, raising his voice to be heard over the crackle of his shield absorbing another hit.

Sirion looked around. 'They're all fighting!'

'Then we shall have to finish this without them.'

'I can't create energy like you do. I can only channel it!'

'If you channel from them –' Ezre paused as he threw a fireball at Draven, who ducked when it passed over the top of his shield – 'it may cause them to lose their fight, yes?'

'Yes,' Sirion reluctantly agreed.

'I will not endanger my people like that. Would you?'

Sirion looked around, desperate to think of an alternative. The people inside the keep were no use; he couldn't channel through the stone walls. All of the Flores were engaged with the Zanthar. Could he take energy from the Zanthar? It was normally considered an affront to the gods to take something from another person without consent – but Daven had been doing exactly that to the Folk. Would the gods judge it a fair exchange, or would such an act make Sirion as deplorable as the invaders?

One of the Flores screamed, a Zanthar sword piercing her scarlet wing. The Zanthar fighter laughed, twisting his sword, and Sirion knew what he must do.

He closed his eyes and took several deep breaths, centring himself, before reaching out with his senses. In his mind's eye he saw a vine, questing across the ground between himself and the Zanthar. Sirion imagined this vine wrapping around the first Zanthar that it came to, connecting them. He focused on the vine, encouraging it to draw energy from the Zanthar, just as a real vine would draw water from the earth, but instead his mental vine began to wither and die, rot and disease creeping along its length toward Sirion. He dropped the vine in disgust, retching from the lingering sense of decay.

There must be another way! Beside him, Ezre fought on, sweat running down his face in rivulets, his breath coming in harsh gasps. Daven looked no better but that was scant comfort. Sirion's gaze roamed over everything, searching for an energy source. The land was already too depleted from the Zanthar's theft. The sounds of battle faded away as Sirion sought out some way to help. He raised an arm and wiped sweat off his brow, the summer sun beating down upon him. The sun! Could that be the answer? The last person to try something like that had been burned beyond saving, or so the story went. The sun was just too powerful. *I have no choice.*

Muttering another quick prayer, this time to the All-Father, Sirion once more centred himself and sent out his mental vine. He imagined it anchored to the top of his head, rising into the sky, straight towards the sun. Energy flared in Sirion, driving him to his knees before he was able to regulate what he was channelling. This was like nothing he had ever done before. The power came in waves, crashing over him. Panting, Sirion pictured a second vine, growing out of his chest, reaching towards Ezre. When it connected to Ezre, the Flores leader began to glow. He seemed to swell to twice his former size and roared as he released his next spell.

Sirion's vision was closing in, everything disappearing into a dazzling white light. He heard shouting – something about killing the slave. Then the energy was no longer just flowing through him; Ezre was actively drawing on it, pulling the power of the sun through Sirion. The filidh felt a searing heat when Ezre cast his next spell, and he collapsed to the ground. The last thing he saw was Daven, engulfed in a ball of flame, then his eyes fluttered and closed.

Chapter One

200 years later

ASHAEL AWOKE EARLY, THE LATE AUTUMN SUN NOT YET UP. THE HOME SHE shared with Bhearra was quiet. Perhaps she had awoken before her mentor, for a change. Maybe today she wouldn't feel like she was trying to catch up with the old woman all day long. Hurrying through her morning routine, Ashael swept aside the curtain separating her alcove from the main room. Bhearra's curtain was still closed. Ashael moved quietly to the hearth in the centre of the room and raked the embers around it, adding kindling to get the flames going again.

Ashael busied herself mixing tea and preparing some food then set about checking their supply of herbs in the various baskets that lined the shelves carved into the far wall. The grey light of pre-dawn began to seep through the small window and Ashael looked towards Bhearra's sleeping quarters, uneasy. The older woman usually rose first. Could she be unwell?

Perhaps someone needed her during the night, Ashael thought as she filled the leather cauldron with water and set it over the fire. *But wouldn't she have woken me?*

The light grew stronger and still there was no movement from Bhearra's alcove. Ashael had almost decided to check on her when Bhearra stepped through the entrance to their home, flushed and bright-eyed.

'Good morning, dear,' Bhearra said. 'It's getting chilly in the mornings.'

'I thought you were still in bed,' Ashael said, nodding towards the curtained-off alcove.

'Well, not *my* bed,' Bhearra answered, chuckling at the shocked expression on Ashael's face. 'I'm old, not dead.'

'I just… I'm sorry,' Ashael stammered. 'I didn't mean to offend you; I just didn't realise that you were involved with anyone.' Faces of people from the cam ran through her mind as she tried to figure out who Bhearra had spent the night with.

'Not so much "involved" as two old friends keeping each other warm on a cold night,' Bhearra said, smiling to herself and walking over to the cauldron. Ashael watched Bhearra pick up the bowl of herbs for the tea and sniff them before tipping them into the water. The elderly filidh was the oldest member of the cam, old enough that no one was sure exactly what age she was. She was tiny, too, and since Ashael was unusually tall, the difference between them made Bhearra seem even smaller. However, Bhearra's character and strength of spirit took up so much space that it was easy to forget her diminutive size.

'What are your plans for the day?' Bhearra asked, pushing thick white hair back from her bronze forehead.

'The pepper root is almost finished,' Ashael said. 'I thought I might head out to gather some more from along the stream. Maybe look for mushrooms. Is there anything else you would like me to do?'

'I had thought to work on meditation today, but we can do that upon your return. How is Alayne? I haven't seen her for a few days.'

'She is well,' Ashael answered, smiling at the thought of her pregnant friend. 'Getting big but glad that the sickness has passed.' She served the food she had prepared and settled herself on the floor near the fire.

'I expect we'll meet her little one before Longest Night,' said Bhearra, settling down beside Ashael to break their fast together. 'Perhaps I will visit her this morning, and then see Soraya. Her baby will be here any day. No babies in the cam for two seasons and then two are due close together!'

***

THE TWO WOMEN emerged from their home and, as she did every morning, Ashael touched the bark of the hollow tree that housed them and gave it her thanks. An acorn bounced off her shoulder and Ashael gave a surprised laugh. She picked it up and showed it to Bhearra.

'He gave you a gift,' Bhearra said. 'You should keep it.'

Ashael looked up at the tree that soared above her, leaves turning to their autumn colours, blazing against the blue sky. 'Thank you,' she said aloud before tucking the acorn into the travelling pouch hanging from her belt. Alayne's home was in the same direction as the path to the stream, so Ashael and Bhearra set off together across the cam.

Oak Cam was a large clearing in the forest surrounded by ancient trees. The Folk made their homes here, most in wooden huts between the huge tree trunks, though some of the younger Folk had been more adventurous and had begun to build homes high up in the mighty branches; walkways criss-crossed from one tree to another. At the north end of the clearing, two trees towered above the others. These were the oaks that gave Oak Cam its name and housed Bhearra, the cam's filidh, and Joren and Rana, the cam's two leaders.

Ashael waved at a group of woodworkers who sat together shaping some tools while another group of craftspeople sat nearby, working with stone. Young children ran around the cam, chasing each other and laughing. In the centre, close to the Heart-Fire, older children were busy drying meat from yesterday's hunt.

A shout drew Bhearra's attention as Bres, Soraya's mate, hurried towards them. 'Bhearra, it's Soraya! The baby! I think there's something wrong. Please hurry!'

Bhearra and Ashael set off after Bres. Hurrying across the cam, Ashael felt the world starting to tilt and stumbled to her knees. Bhearra stopped beside her, but Ashael waved her on. 'I'm fine. Go to Soraya.' Ashael lowered her head until the dizziness began to pass.

As she struggled to her feet, she saw a flash of a scarred face, horrendously burned, and her heart started to race. As quickly as it had come, the vision faded. Ashael found herself panting, limbs trembling with the desire to flee. *What in the All-Mother's name was that?* Knowing she was needed, she shook herself and hurried on.

Entering the hut, Ashael started to speak, but stopped as soon as she saw Soraya. The pregnant woman was lying on furs on her sleeping pallet at the back of the hut, face ashen and covered with sweat. Bres stood to the side, wringing his hands and shifting from one foot to the other as he told Bhearra how the pains had started just before dawn but had become much worse a short time ago. Soraya had started vomiting and had developed a fever.

Ashael went back outside and called to the children playing nearby. 'Soraya's baby is coming and Bhearra and I will need some things. Can you help?'

'What do you need?' asked Charis, a girl almost old enough to start learning a skill.

'We need two buckets of fresh water from the stream and new hides – the softest ones you can find. Can you manage that?'

'We'll get them right away,' answered a younger girl, Rowan.

Ashael ducked back into the hut. Soraya was groaning as Bhearra felt her stomach, the filidh's eyes closed as she listened to her other senses. Ashael went to her side, placing her hands over her mentor's. She tried to stretch her senses beyond herself, the way that Bhearra was teaching her.

At first all she felt was Bhearra's familiar presence, glowing beside her. Soraya groaned again, and with her breath Ashael felt her friend's pain deep in her own abdomen. She winced, then tried to stretch her senses further. She caught the thread of Bhearra's spirit and followed it. Finally, she sensed the baby, frightened and in pain. For a moment, Ashael felt as if she were suffocating, her breath coming in shallow gasps. Then Bhearra touched her shoulder, and she was back in herself.

'The baby is in distress,' Bhearra said. 'Soraya, I want to give you something to hasten things along, get the baby out of there. Do you understand?'

Soraya nodded, gasping in pain. Bres held a cup of water to her lips as Bhearra stood and motioned Ashael outside.

'The baby's heartbeat is weak. I'm not sure why, but it's serious. Go home and get some willow bark for the pain and springwort to speed things along. Let Joren know what's happening here. I hope the gods are with us this day.' Bhearra headed back inside as Ashael hurried off about her tasks.

***

ALL-MOTHER, YOU WHO *gave birth to the world, watch over this woman and her child,* Bhearra prayed silently. She had lost the thread of the baby's consciousness and was deeply worried. Soraya screamed as another contraction struck. Ashael wiped the pregnant woman's face with a cloth dipped in cool water. Bres paced the room. It was mid-afternoon and Soraya was exhausted.

'We're almost there now, Soraya. Get ready to push.' Bhearra squeezed Soraya's hand, keeping her voice calm, trying not to show her concern. The poor woman was frightened enough. As the next contraction arrived, Soraya pushed as hard as she could, gripping Bhearra's hands hard enough to press the old bones together, and the top of the baby's head appeared.

'I can't. I can't push anymore.'

'One more and the head will be out, and then I can help you,' Bhearra replied with a soothing voice. She pushed a little of her own energy into the woman before her. She had been doing this for some time now and did not have much more to spare. With the next contraction, the baby's head was out, face white and lips blue. Bhearra soon saw why: the umbilical cord was wrapped around the baby's neck. Another contraction pushed a shoulder out while Soraya screamed, and Bhearra was able to get her fingers under the cord, pulling it slightly away from the baby's neck. With quick, sure movements, Bhearra took the foraging knife attached to her belt and cut the cord, pulling the baby the rest of the way out with the next contraction.

The baby had not yet taken a breath. Bhearra moved her out of view. She blew into the baby's face then slapped her bottom. Still nothing.

'What's happening? Is my baby alright?' Soraya asked, gasping in exhaustion.

'Ashael can help you with the afterbirth,' answered Bhearra. 'I'm just going to get the little one cleaned up.'

Bhearra moved towards the doorway as she spoke, Bres close behind. Speaking in a low voice, she told him what had happened. Bres looked back at his mate and began to weep silent tears.

'Hush now. All is not lost.' Bhearra held the baby before her then closed her eyes, once more stretching her senses out beyond her own body, searching for the lingering spirit of the baby. *Nothing. Nothing... There!* A spark of life floated nearby. The filidh breathed this spark in and then blew it gently toward the baby's face. Nothing happened. *Please, All-Mother.*

The baby gasped and let out a great cry.

Bres fell to his knees and Soraya burst into tears. Bhearra gave a small smile, letting out a shaky breath as she moved over to Soraya and handed the baby to her.

'You have a beautiful baby girl. What will you name her?'

'Bhearrael. For the women who brought her to us,' Alayne answered.

'Sirion bless you. You saved her life,' Bres said. 'How can we ever thank you?'

'Nonsense; I didn't save her. I just showed her the way home. She did the rest herself.'

***

IT WAS ALMOST dusk by the time Bhearra and Ashael left Soraya, satisfied that the baby would be well. Ashael suppressed a yawn, tired but still elated.

'What you did was amazing,' Ashael said, looking at her mentor in awe.

'Truly, I did little,' Bhearra answered.

'I saw her, Bhearra. And felt her. She was dead and you brought her back to life.'

'It's not as simple as that,' Bhearra said, stopping and turning to face Ashael. 'Her body had stopped working, yes; but she was not yet ready to let go. I just helped her back to where she belonged. I could not have done that if it had truly been her time.'

'Can you teach me to do what you did?' Ashael asked. Bhearra could talk it down if she wished, but Ashael had never seen anything so wonderful.

'I can certainly try. Not all filidh have the same skills, though. Some of us are skilled healers, while others excel in divination and communion with the gods and spirits, like Ravena of Fork River Cam. As you further your training, we will discover where your skills lie.'

Beginning to walk again, Ashael looked towards the Heart-Fire, where Rana, co-leader of the cam and Ashael's closest friend, tossed a handful of berries into the flames, an offering to the gods. Rana turned from the fire and saw Ashael and Bhearra.

'How is Soraya?' she asked, frowning.

'She and the baby are well,' Bhearra answered. 'The delivery was difficult. For both of them. But with some rest and care they will be fine.'

'Thank the gods,' said Rana, a beautiful smile breaking over her face. 'I prepared some extra food for the evening meal. Would it be alright to take it to them in a little while?'

'I think they will be grateful,' Bhearra said, smiling.

'Until then, would you like to join me for some tea? The two of you must be exhausted.'

'That would be wonderful,' Ashael said, taking her friend's arm.

'Indeed,' said Bhearra, smiling.

***

IWAN STOPPED OUTSIDE the door to the great hall, his heart in his throat. He had no idea why they'd summoned him, but it couldn't be good. He had made light of it with his mother, trying to allay her fears, but they both knew that sometimes slaves who were called to stand before the lord did not return. The guard who escorted him shoved his back.

'Move, slave.'

Iwan took a deep breath and knocked on the scarred wood in front of him.

'Enter.' That was Meegrum's voice. Perhaps Daven wasn't there after all.

Iwan stepped into the room then stopped, staying as far away as he could without completely disobeying. The only light in the hall came from a fire halfway along its vast expanse, burning low in the hearth. A cold breeze came through the unshuttered windows, rippling tattered banners that hung high above them. Iwan shivered and took a step back, his heels now pressing against the doors.

'Come here, where I can see you,' rasped a voice from the high-backed chair in front of the fire.

Dammit, he is here.

Iwan swallowed hard and walked forward on trembling legs. Firelight danced across the scarred features of the man in the chair. The left side of his face had been hideously burned, the hair gone. Iwan looked at his feet. Slaves had been killed for looking at those scars for too long.

'How can I serve you, my lord?' Iwan asked, voice steady despite his fear.

'Tell me, were you born on KalaDene?' the voice issuing from those twisted and half-scarred lips was hoarse so Iwan took a step closer to hear better.

'No, my lord, but I've been here since I was little more than a baby. My mother was amongst those you sent to prepare the keep for your return.'

'You speak the language of this world, do you not?' Meegrum said, stepping out of the shadows at the far side of the fire.

'Yes, master, I do,' Iwan admitted warily.

'I am searching for someone,' Daven said, 'and I want you to be my eyes. You will go to the settlement closest to here and ask for shelter. You will pretend to be one of them. You will gain their trust and you will report back to me. Do you understand?'

'Yes, my lord. Who am I looking for?'

'You do not need to know.'

'How can I look for someone if I do not know who it is, my lord?' Iwan asked.

'Do you expect me to confide in a slave? I will see everything you see, and *I* will decide if it is important.'

'As you wish, my lord.' Iwan bowed low. 'I beg your pardon.'

'You will be ready to leave first thing in the morning. Meegrum will send you by portal, leaving you close to the nearest settlement. And just in case you have any ideas of betraying us...' The lord waved his hand and Meegrum stepped forward, chanting. A black mist formed in the air, coalescing into a sphere. Colours appeared, swirling together. Iwan watched the portal form. He had seen this magic before but had never been so close to it. The hairs on the back of his arms stood upright. After a few moments, an image appeared in the middle of the portal. Devorik, leader of the Zanthar guard, stood in the middle of a grassy plain, which was silver in the light of the Middle Moon. He looked like he was somewhere further afield than Iwan had ever been; the land close to the keep was almost barren. Devorik clicked his fingers and a slave stepped into view. He stood, shivering, clad only in a loincloth, his slave-brand visible on his upper chest.

The tone of Meegrum's chanting changed, turned more threatening. Iwan looked at the mage.

'Watch the portal,' Daven snapped.

Iwan pulled his eyes back to the slave on the plain, someone newly arrived from Zan. A confused expression crossed the slave's face and then one side seemed to droop. He fell to the ground, stammering incoherently, then was still.

'As you can see, the brand works at great distance,' Daven said. Meegrum stopped chanting and the portal collapsed in on itself with a rush of air. 'Should it cross your mind to run, to betray us in any way, know that you cannot run far enough. You will be discovered, and you will die. Should you decide to reveal any knowledge of our presence, we will know, and you will be dead before you can end your sentence. If, perhaps, you should decide that death is better than service, remember that whatever fate befalls you, will also befall your mother.'

Iwan grew pale, and this time he could not unclench his fists.

***

THE LORD FELL back into his chair, rubbing his eyes with a hand free from scars.

'How many more times must we do this, Meegrum?' he rasped. 'I grow weary of their stink.'

'Only two more slaves, my lord,' Meegrum answered, handing him a cup of wine. 'This would have gone faster if we had sent them all together.'

'I told you: I do not wish them to know of each other,' Daven snapped.

'Of course. That is wise, my lord,' Meegrum answered obsequiously.

Both men looked up when a knock sounded at the door.

'Enter,' Meegrum called.

A young woman entered the room, eyes to the floor, carrying a tray. 'I have your evening meal, my lords,' she mumbled, still looking down.

'Place it on the table,' Meegrum said.

Daven stood up and they both made their way to the table that lined the far wall. It could easily seat twenty and, in the past, it often had but these days there were only ever two places set.

'What has the cook prepared for us tonight?' the lord rasped.

'Pork, my lord, with apple sauce and roasted vegetables. Is it to your liking?' the slave said, trembling.

'It will suffice. Tell the cook that I will require some more of that pie she served last night.'

'Yes, my lord.' The slave started to back away but Daven caught her by the wrist, pulling her towards him and tilting her face up so that he could see her.

'You will also be required in my chambers tonight.'

She paled and her voice came out hoarse. 'Yes, my lord.'

He let go of her arm and she scurried from the room as fast she could.

'Let us eat,' he said, taking his seat, and Meegrum followed.

Chapter Two

ASHAEL WADED UPSTREAM, ENJOYING THE COOL WATER RUNNING OVER HER legs and the feel of smooth pebbles under her toes. The sun's rays slanted down through the branches, fracturing upon the water's surface. The leather bag she carried bounced against her hip, damp from the pepper root she had gathered from the edge of the stream.

Ashael and Bhearra had checked on Soraya and her baby that morning and they were both doing well. She couldn't believe how relaxed Bhearra was about what happened. Ashael had been terrified. She had felt the baby starting to slip away before she was born and there was nothing she could do about it. It was the most painful thing Ashael had ever experienced – after losing her parents, of course. Glad for this time alone to think it all through, she determined that someday she too would be able to do what Bhearra had done, to save a life that had been lost.

Ashael was so distracted that she didn't notice the stream getting deeper and her footing less secure until she fell and went under, splashing and spluttering. Water went up her nose and she started coughing, scrabbling to find her feet. Once upright again, she just stood in the middle of the stream, coughing up water. The noise she made startled the birds in the nearby trees, sending them into the air, screaming warnings to each other. Muttering to herself, Ashael finally caught her breath and waded over to the bank, pushing her wet hair back out of her face.

She froze. A stranger stood in front of her. She knew many of the people from the two cams nearest her own – they gathered for celebrations throughout the turning of the seasons – but she did not know this man. She was quite sure she would have remembered him. He was tall – a little taller than her, which was unusual. His bronze skin was not as dark as most of the people's she knew and, although she could sense strength in him, he looked undernourished. He examined her as closely as she did him; they stood staring at each other for what seemed an age before he broke the silence.

'I heard you splashing. Thought you might need help, but I see you managed on your own.'

'I fell, but I was not injured,' Ashael answered, her cheeks burning. The way he spoke was unusual, his pronunciation different from what she was used to. 'Are you from Trout Cam? Or Fork River? I don't think we have met.'

'No, my people live far to the south. I wished to see more of the world, so I have been travelling. My name is Iwan,' he said, watching her face.

Ashael put the fingertips of her right hand to her chest, above her heart, then touched her lips and her forehead before holding her hand out to Iwan in the traditional greeting. 'I greet you, Iwan, from far to the south. I am Ashael of Oak Cam.'

Iwan copied the gesture that Ashael had made but he did it haltingly and forgot to touch his lips.

How is it that he doesn't know the greeting? I thought all of the Folk used it.

Ashael couldn't take her eyes from him. He was so unusual and very handsome. She felt her cheeks warm again. A bird squawked above them and Ashael looked up, his spell on her broken for a moment. She was startled to realise how late it had become. The sun was on the descent; she would have to hurry if she wanted to pick those mushrooms and get back before it got too dark to see her way.

'It was pleasant to meet you, but I must return to my foraging before I lose the light,' Ashael said, once more looking at Iwan.

'Might I join you?' he asked. 'I have been alone for some time. It would be good to talk to someone for a while.' He looked down at his hands as he spoke and Ashael wondered if he was embarrassed by his loneliness.

'Of course,' she answered, smiling. 'In fact, would you care to come back to the cam with me? I think we can give you a meal and a place to spend to the night.'

'That is very kind,' Iwan said. He smiled but his eyes looked sad.

Ashael wondered what would make someone travel so far from their home. 'How long have you been travelling?' she asked, setting off with Iwan a step behind her.

'Since spring,' Iwan answered. 'Have you ever travelled to the south?'

'Only as far as Stoney Hill Cam. Around fifteen days' walk from here. Did you pass it on your journey?'

'Er... I may have passed by. I have not spoken to anyone.'

Ashael stopped in surprise and turned to look at Iwan. 'You haven't stopped in any cams, spoken to other people, since spring?'

'No. I, er... I've been alone.'

'No wonder you are lonely!'

'I am glad I stumbled across you.' Iwan studied Ashael as he spoke. He was looking at her as if he'd never seen a person before. Perhaps he had been alone too long.

'You must have seen wondrous things on your journey,' she said, walking again.

'Not as many as you might think,' he said.

Perhaps he's had trouble hunting enough food if he has been travelling alone all this time. I'll suggest to Joren that we invite him to stay for a few days; let him rest a little.

'Where do you plan to end your journey?' she asked, climbing over a fallen tree.

'I thought to see the mountains.'

There was something in his voice, some unspoken pain. For a moment, Ashael stretched her senses towards him. She touched on great anguish and whirled to look at him. His face was impassive; no sign of the emotional turmoil she had sensed. When she reached for him again, she felt nothing. As if he was not there at all.

Unsettled by this, Ashael didn't realise he had asked her a question until he spoke again.

'Are you well? You looked startled.'

'It was nothing,' she said, glancing up at the sky. 'We should hurry, or we will lose the light.'

***

THE SHADOWS BENEATH the trees were deepening by the time they arrived at the mushroom patch. Several trees had fallen at some point and now their bodies served as a home for several varieties of fungus. Even in death, there was life.

Ashael took her stone foraging knife from her belt and proceeded to cut some mushrooms from one of the fallen trees, kneeling beside the old wood, being careful not to take too many from one spot. Iwan had been quiet most of the way here. Ashael was desperate to ask him questions about his home and his people, but she still felt echoes of that deep pain she had touched, and she was reluctant to risk asking something that may cause him further distress. She observed him discreetly, noting his thick black hair, his broad shoulders. He had spotted some late blackberries and was picking the fruit, dropping them into the makeshift basket that Ashael had hurriedly woven from some long grass.

A hiss sounded near Ashael's hand, returning her thoughts to her task. A snake coiled on the log in front of her, its head reared back, ready to strike. Ashael froze, knowing the snake could move faster than she could.

'There are so many berries here, I wish I could carry more,' Iwan said, without turning around.

Ashael didn't want to speak in case she provoked the snake. It hissed again and made a feint lunge at her.

'Ashael?' Iwan asked.

Ashael's eyes were stuck on the snake, but she heard Iwan's movement and then his sharp intake of breath.

'Don't move,' he said in a very low voice. 'It's a split-tail.'

Ashael frowned. *A split-tail? We call them arrowheads.* Whichever the name, the snake was venomous. It had swung its head towards Iwan when he spoke, and Ashael had started to move very carefully away, but it swung back and lurched at her again, hissing and showing its fangs.

From the corner of her eye, she saw Iwan edging closer, moving slowly and quietly. A twig snapped beneath his foot and the snake swung its head towards him again, this time raising more of its body into the air. Slowly, Iwan bent down and picked up a sturdy stick from the grass near his feet. He edged closer, eyes never leaving the snake, until he was almost within striking distance.

What is he doing? He'll be bitten!

Iwan took another step, and the snake made another lunge in his direction. If he came any closer, it would strike. Ashael whistled at the same time as she pushed herself back, putting an extra foot of space between herself and the snake. It darted towards her and Iwan leaped, bringing the stick down on the base of its head., pinning it to the log. Carefully, he gripped the snake just behind its jaw, preventing it from biting him. He carried it over to some bushes and released it, hurriedly backing away.

'Thank you,' Ashael said, laughing a little with the release of tension.

'Perhaps I've earned that meal now,' Iwan smiled, holding out his hand and helping Ashael to her feet.

'We should get back to the cam before it gets too dark,' Ashael said, picking up some mushrooms that had fallen out of her travelling pouch.

Iwan went to pick up the basket and berries, and Ashael took the opportunity to look at him again while his back was turned. He had put himself between her and the snake. If Ashael had stayed still long enough, the snake probably would have realised that she was not a threat and left. Probably. Despite that, Iwan's instinct had been to help her, and he had risked being bitten to do so.

When they had both gathered their fallen items, she led him back to the cam through the dusk, hoping she would have some time to get to know him.

***

IWAN FOLLOWED ASHAEL through the forest, admiring the easy grace with which she moved. Her long legs covered the ground quickly, her dark braid swaying behind her. His heart started to beat a little faster when he thought of the snake. She had been so calm, so unafraid. She was different to any of the other women he had known, all broken and meek.

He shook his head to clear away such foolish thoughts. He must not get involved with these people. He was here to watch, that was all. Iwan was not afraid to die – that was a daily risk for him under the Zanthar – but he could not risk his mother's life.

Ashael turned to him, and he quickly tried to swallow his anger and fear – maybe not quickly enough, as Ashael faltered for a moment.

'Are you well?' she asked, concern in her voice.

'I am,' he answered, clearing his throat. 'Why do you ask?'

'You looked upset.'

'Not at all,' he said, forcing a smile.

Ashael didn't answer, studying his face in the deepening twilight. He hoped the shadows would hide his deceit.

'The cam is just beyond those beech trees,' Ashael said.

Iwan frowned. There was no sign of any habitation here. It looked just like any other part of the forest, dark and uninviting.

Ashael clearly saw his confusion for she did not wait for him to speak. 'There is a charm over the cam, keeping it hidden from the animals that share the forest with us. You have to approach it in just the right way.'

'And what is the right way?' Iwan asked, looking around.

'Do you see the beech that appears to be two trees, but the trunks are joined at the bottom?'

Iwan squinted in the gloom, moving closer until he could see what she meant. 'Yes.'

'You must step between the two trunks.'

'Are you teasing me?' he asked, a smile playing at the corners of his mouth.

'I'll show you.' Ashael took his hand in hers to pull him towards the tree. A tingle started where their skin met and worked its way up Iwan's arm. Ashael didn't seem to notice his reaction, and he was glad.

When they reached the tree, she smiled and then stepped between the two trunks.

Iwan gasped. She had completely disappeared. He moved closer to the tree and jumped with surprise when Ashael's head and shoulders reappeared, leaning between the trunks.

'Are you coming?' she asked, a smile playing on her lips. She was obviously enjoying his discomfort.

'Yes.' Iwan took a deep breath and followed Ashael through the gap in the tree.

What he saw on the other side made him let his breath out in a low whistle. They stood on the edge of a large clearing, with a huge fire burning at the centre. People milled around, some hurrying, some strolling. Around the periphery of the clearing, nestled amongst the trees, were grass-roofed wooden huts, woven together in such a way that they almost looked alive. He heard sounds from above and looked up. More huts were built on the sturdy branches of the massive trees that surrounded the cam. Walkways made of wood and rope swung over their heads from tree to tree.

Iwan had never seen anything like this place and yet it immediately felt like home.

'Come on,' Ashael said, taking his hand again. 'I should take you to meet Joren and Bhearra.'

Ashael led him across the cam, letting go of his hand when a heavily pregnant young woman approached them. She was a full head and shoulders shorter than Ashael though they looked to be around the same age. Looking around, Iwan realised that Ashael was unusually tall. None of the women he saw even neared her height, and only a few of the men did. Which meant that he, too, must look unusually tall because he was able to look down on Ashael. Would that be a problem? Would it make them question where he was from? But then, he realised, Ashael herself looked quite different from most of the people he saw. Her hair was black, like theirs, but it had red streaks through it which he didn't see on anyone else. She was taller, of course, and leaner; her skin was a deeper shade of bronze; her eyes so dark as to be almost black, while most of those he could see were lighter shades of brown or green.

Iwan snapped out of his thoughts when he realised that Ashael was introducing her friend to him.

'Alayne, this is Iwan,' Ashael was saying. 'He comes from far to the south. He's been travelling. We met in the forest, so I offered him a hot meal and a place to spend the night.'

'I would have done the same,' Alayne said, looking him up and down frankly. 'It's rare that we meet someone from so far away. You must tell us all about your journey before you move on.'

'It has been uneventful. It would make a boring tale. Until I met Ashael and the split-tail, that is,' he answered.

'Split-tail?' Alayne asked, furrowing her brow.

'Arrowhead,' Ashael said. 'Split-tail makes sense too, with the odd colouring they have on their tails.'

Iwan grimaced as Ashael told her friend the story of the snake. He had been here for less than a day and had already drawn attention to his difference. Would they believe the snake had a different name in the south or had he already condemned his mother with careless talk?

'Brave as well as handsome?' Alayne said, grinning at Ashael. 'Maybe I should go foraging more often.'

Ashael laughed. 'I don't think Gethyn would appreciate that.'

'Probably not,' Alayne said, rubbing her swollen belly, a fond smile lighting up her face. 'The fear of competition might do him some good, though.'

'I had best go and introduce Iwan to Bhearra and Joren. Will you be at the gathering later?' Ashael asked.

'I will. It's my turn to tend the Heart-Fire tonight.'

'We can speak more then.' Ashael gestured to Iwan, and he followed her as she set off towards two trees at the far end of the cam.

Iwan had never seen trees so large. They would have towered over the walls of the keep he grew up in. As they drew closer, he realised both were hollow at the base, each with a door and windows carved into them. As he watched, the hide curtain covering one of the doorways moved aside, revealing a young man around Iwan's own age, maybe a few years older than Ashael. He was tall with broad shoulders, his long hair pulled back from his face.

'Well met, Joren,' Ashael said, raising her hand in greeting.

'Ashael, good evening,' the young man responded, then noticed Iwan. 'Who is this?'

'Joren, I would like you to meet Iwan.' Ashael nudged Iwan forward a step. 'His cam is far to the south. He has been travelling and we met in the forest. I thought we could offer him a meal and a bed for the night.'

'Of course.' Joren made the greeting gesture Ashael had made earlier. 'Welcome to Oak Cam, Iwan.'

'Joren is one of our leaders,' Ashael explained.

Iwan raised his eyebrows in surprise; Joren looked so young for a leader. Perhaps that was common amongst these people.

Joren chuckled at Iwan's expression, answering the unasked question. 'I became leader only a few years ago, when I had barely come of age. The circumstances were somewhat unusual.'

'My apologies,' Iwan said, annoyed with himself for being so transparent. 'Where I come from, most leaders are much older.'

'The same is normally true here,' Joren said, offering a smile.

Iwan breathed a sigh of relief. It seemed he had managed to avoid offending the man he would need to impress if he were to find a way to stay here.

'Is Bhearra home?' Ashael asked Joren. When he nodded, she went to the other hollow tree and stepped inside.

Iwan stood with Joren, unsure of what he should do next.

'Thank you for your generosity,' he said.

Joren gave him a confused look. 'Offering you a meal and a place to spend the night is not generosity. It is no more than the hospitality required by the All-Mother.'

'Of course,' Iwan said hurriedly, 'but the other side of hospitality is being a gracious guest.' *I can't do this. There is too much that I do not know.*

'Well, you are welcome,' Joren said. 'My mate, Rana, has been out hunting. When she returns, we would be happy to share a meal with you. She should be no more than a notch.'

'A notch?' Iwan had never heard the term.

Joren nodded towards a nearby post. About halfway up, a stick poked out of the side. Notches were carved in the post, at roughly even distances. The stick cast a shadow that would move around the notches as the sun moved across the sky.

'It's like a sundial,' Iwan said.

'What's a sundial?' Joren asked.

'It's similar to your post but flat. It's what my people use to measure time.' Iwan answered, worrying that he had said too much.

At that moment, Ashael appeared with a tiny old woman and Joren turned to them.

'Of course, you must both also join us for the evening meal,' he said.

'It is a pleasant evening,' the old woman replied, her voice strong. 'Perhaps we could eat out here? If you bring that rabbit stew you were making earlier, I can roast the mushrooms Ashael collected, with some herbs.'

The woman turned to Iwan and for several moments looked at him in such a way that he was sure she could see to his heart. He tried to appear relaxed, but he felt as though she would not see more of him if he was standing there naked.

At last, she spoke. 'Welcome to Oak Cam, Iwan the Traveller. I believe we are well met.'

Chapter Three

THREE DAYS HAD PASSED BEFORE IWAN AWOKE IN THE MIDDLE OF THE NIGHT, heart pounding. Something had startled him, but he was not sure what it was until Meegrum's voice sounded inside his head.

'Report.'

'They have invited me to stay for the winter,' Iwan said, his voice low. He walked over to the window of the guest hut and peeked outside. There didn't appear to anyone close by. He scratched at the slave-brand on his chest, the itch so deep that he would never be able to reach it.

'Very good.'

The itch in Iwan's chest grew worse, to the point of being torturous, before spreading up his neck and over his skull. It was as if a thousand fire ants were crawling beneath his skin, biting and squirming as they made their way over his head, finally settling behind his eyes. He gritted his teeth against the scream that wanted to escape, cords standing out on his neck with the effort. The images of everything he had seen since arriving flashed before his mind's eye and he could feel Meegrum sneer at the kindness these people had shown to him. The itch turned into a painful burning sensation and Iwan lost all sense of time passing. When eventually Meegrum had seen all that he wanted, the itch began to recede, back down to his slave-brand, which throbbed in time with his heartbeat.

'Watch them. Listen. Learn all that you can. I will be watching.'

The itching faded, leaving only a ghost of the pain. Iwan's chest was bleeding where he had unknowingly scratched too hard, tearing the scar tissue that formed his brand. Shaking, he crossed the hut to the bucket of fresh water that stood by the hearth. He dipped a cup in and took a long drink, the cool water helping to steady him, before using some of it to wash his cuts. That done, he sat heavily on the edge of the sleeping pallet and put his head in his hands, praying to the forgotten gods that his mother would be safe and that he would see her again soon.

***

BHEARRA SAT CROSS-LEGGED in front of the Heart-Fire, the heat from the flames warming her old bones. There was something about the young man who had arrived a few days ago. He was full of secrets but also pain. She sensed a good man at his core, in the space beyond pretence. *Let him keep his secrets, for now. I will be watching.*

Bhearra tossed some herbs into the flames, an offering to the gods to watch over them, before climbing stiffly to her feet. She nodded to Rana, who was tending the sacred fire this night, and had turned for home when she heard a scream from within. She dashed inside and swept back the curtain that covered the entrance to Ashael's sleeping alcove.

Her young apprentice was sitting up on her pallet, panting, sweat making her hair stick to her face.

'What is it? What happened?' Bhearra asked.

'I'm sorry,' Ashael said, looking up, her eyes haunted. 'It was a dream. A horrible dream. I'm well.'

'Bhearra, Ashael, what's wrong?' Rana asked, rushing into the two women's home.

'All is well,' Bhearra answered, stepping back into the main room. 'Ashael had a bad dream, but she is safe.'

Joren appeared in the entrance, bare chested and bleary eyed, his hair mussed from sleep.

Ashael poked her head into the room. 'I'm sorry to have disturbed you all,' she said. Her face was drawn and Bhearra felt a stab of worry.

Rana crossed the room and hugged her friend.

Joren ran a hand through his hair and stretched. 'Do you have need of me?'

'No, go back to your rest, Joren,' Bhearra answered.

When Joren and Rana had gone, Ashael walked over to the basin in the corner of the room, where she splashed cool water on her face. 'I'm sorry to have caused such a disturbance.'

'Don't worry yourself about that. I think we could both use a cup of soothing tea.'

'Yes, please.' Ashael let out a shaky breath and went to her alcove, pulling a shawl from a peg on the wall and wrapping it around her shoulders.

Bhearra took some hot rocks from the banked fire in the hearth, placing them into the cauldron which she then filled with water. While the water heated, she took some chamomile from one of the many baskets lining the shelves carved into the walls and added it to two cups. She paused for a moment then added some lemon balm for good measure.

Bhearra studied Ashael closely. *That must have been an awful dream.* Her apprentice looked haggard; much older than her twenty summers. Her skin was ashen and dark circles lined her eyes. Ashael pulled a low stool over to the hearth and perched on it, the red light from the embers casting ominous shadows on her face.

Bhearra shivered at the sight of the aged young woman in front of her. For a moment, it looked as though Ashael had only one eye, but then she moved her head and was back to normal. Bhearra shook herself. Obviously, Ashael's fear of the dream had touched her for a moment.

The filidh handed her apprentice a cup of the soothing tea and pulled another stool up beside her. 'Tell me of it, if you would,' she said, settling herself by Ashael's side.

'I was flying, high above the land. It seemed so real. I had wings, like a bird, and I could feel how the feathers caught the wind and used it to glide. At first, it was wonderful. I soared over mountains. I felt so free.' Ashael sipped her tea.

'Then I was over the forest. Everything was dead. The trees were just blackened sticks rising out of dry, cracked earth. No animals moved, no insects, no birds. I flew over the cam, but it was gone, nothing but blackened remains.' Ashael swallowed hard.

Bhearra saw the young woman's hands shaking. She wrapped her own around them and sent calming feelings towards her.

'I flew faster and faster,' Ashael continued, 'looking for some sign of life. Anything at all. But all I saw was more death. And then it came to me: I knew that no matter how far I flew, I would find no life. That I was the only one left. That was when I screamed.'

Despite the warmth of the fire and the tea she had been drinking, Bhearra felt chilled to the bone. 'Did you see what had caused this?' she asked.

'No. I was just completely alone in a dead world.' A tear trickled down Ashael's cheek. 'Thank the All-Mother it was just a dream.'

Bhearra murmured her agreement but, deep in her heart, she wasn't so sure.

***

'HELLO?' A VOICE called from the entrance to Ashael's and Bhearra's home. Ashael put aside the fibre she had been spinning and went to open the heavy hide curtain across the doorway. It was Iwan, drenched from the rain. She glanced over his shoulder to check on the hide they had erected above the Heart-Fire to protect it from the downpour. She smiled when she saw Gethyn and Bran working together to tip water off the top while Gerod fed wood to the flames.

'Iwan, how are you? Come in and get dry.'

Iwan stepped through the entrance then stopped and gawked.

Ashael laughed. 'I assume they don't have any hollow trees in your cam?' she asked.

'No, I've never seen anything like this. It's wonderful.' Iwan's eyes were wide as he took in the large room that they stood in.

'Please, have a seat,' Ashael said, gesturing to a stool. 'Have you broken your fast?'

'I have, thank you,' Iwan answered, still standing.

'Will you take some tea then? Or water?'

'Water, thank you.'

Ashael got a cup of water and Iwan smiled when she handed it to him. The smile was beautiful, and for a moment Ashael's breath caught in her chest. 'What can I do for you?' she asked.

Iwan put the cup of water down and unfastened something from his belt. 'I was hunting with Joren yesterday and he was impressed with my sling. He said that you don't have slings here. I suggested we could make some and I could teach a few people how to use them. Joren said you were the one to see about making them.'

'Can I take a look?'

'Here,' said Iwan, holding his sling out to her.

Ashael took it, intrigued by the idea of making a new weapon. The sling was long and rope-like, made using some form of braided material. Ashael rolled it between her fingers and sniffed it. 'Rushes?' she asked without looking up.

'Yes,' Iwan answered, sounding amused.

In the centre of the rope was a sort of cradle of soft leather. Ashael examined the weave closely. 'Yes, I think I can see how it is done. How many do you want to make?'

'How many people do you think would like to learn?'

Ashael looked up and smiled. 'That depends. Will you be teaching them?'

'Yes – definitely the first group of people. Then, when a few others have got the hang of it, they could start teaching. Why?'

'Well, if you're teaching then most of the women in the cam will want to learn,' Ashael said, eyebrow raised and a smile playing at her lips.

'Oh!' Iwan coloured. 'Maybe we could start off just teaching people how to make them?'

'That sounds like a good idea. We're going to need a lot of rushes.'

'Perhaps we could start gathering them when it's dry?'

'Absolutely,' Ashael said, smiling widely at the thought of getting to spend some time with him.

∗∗∗

THE SCREAM FILLED the small chamber, bouncing off the walls and reverberating through Meegrum's skull. He nodded to the guard captain, Zekinal, who straightened, pulling the bloody knife free of the prisoner's knee. At least, he assumed it was a knee.

'You can bring this to an end,' Meegrum said, leaning his shoulder against the wall and examining his fingertips. 'Tell me everything you know of this Vessel.'

'I don't know anything,' the prisoner gasped.

Meegrum grimaced and raised a hand to his head. The translation spell that was required to speak to this thing was driving a spike through his brain, and all for it to sit there and lie to him. He crossed the room and took the knife out of Zekinal's hand, turning around and slashing the creature's chest, leaving a shallow wound that bled profusely. The prisoner howled, driving the spike of pain a little further into Meegrum's head.

'Tell me.'

'No.'

Meegrum held the blade against the breathing sac that covered the lower half of the creature's face. He stared as its eyes widened, its panic obvious even on those bizarre features.

'Please,' it begged. 'Please, no.'

'Tell me and all of this will be over.'

The creature's eyes darted from side to side, its breathing sac quickly puffing in and out as it panted. Meegrum pressed the blade a little harder against the sac and the fight went out of the prisoner. Shoulders slumped, it began to talk. Meegrum's vision went red, and his headache was intensified by the odd effect of hearing its grumbling, grating noise with his ears while hearing words that made sense in his head. This time it was worth it, though.

'It is said that she will rise when the three moons join their brother in the sky on Longest Day. The soul of all will be contained in her.'

'I hope for your sake that you know something more useful than this,' Meegrum growled.

'Agni forgive me... At the moment of her rising she will be vulnerable, and with her, all of KalaDene.'

'There. Was that so hard?' Meegrum asked as he shoved the knife forward, piercing the breathing sac. The creature bucked and writhed against its bonds, but the chains were strong. In a few short moments, its struggles were over.

'What did you do to it, sir?' Zekinal asked.

Meegrum jumped. In the intensity of the moment, he had forgotten that the guard was there. 'Suffocated it. Dispose of the body.' Meegrum handed the knife back to Zekinal and without another glance at the creature, he turned and left the room.

He strode into the great hall without knocking. Meegrum could tell there was something wrong as soon as he entered the room; his lord stood staring into the hearth though no flames burned there.

'What has happened, my lord?' he asked, hurrying forward.

'We are to report to the World-Gate in ten days' time. That little bastard, Cenric, is to wed one of the king's daughters. All of the first three castes are to attend the celebrations, which will last for a moon's cycle! By the time we return, winter will have set in, and the indigenes will have hunkered down for the season.'

Meegrum moved to the table at the far side of the room and poured wine for them both.

'I have good news at least, my lord. The rock creature finally broke: the Vessel is expected to be a woman. She will have a moment of vulnerability as she comes into her power.' Meegrum handed a goblet to his lord and waited for him to start his drink before draining his own.

'And this will happen on the summer solstice, as the Hive believe?'

'Yes, my lord.'

'At least we will have time to find her in Spring. Leave a contingent here under the command of Zekinal. Tell Devorik to get the rest of the warriors ready to move out.'

Chapter Four

S NOW BLANKETED THE CAM. ASHAEL STOOD BY THE HEART-FIRE, WRAPPED IN many layers against the cold. It was her turn to tend the sacred flames and she stamped her feet as she fed them more wood. The wail of a newborn cut through the early-morning quiet and Ashael smiled. Alayne's baby must be hungry again.

Holding her hands out to the flames, Ashael soaked up the heat and allowed her mind to drift to the warm days of summer. For a moment she could almost smell the deep green of summer grass, hear the somnolent buzzing of bees.

'I brought you some tea,' Bhearra said beside her, pulling her back to the present.

'Thank you.' Ashael took the cup that Bhearra held out to her.

'Who is taking over from you at dawn?'

'Gerod. He'll be here soon, I'm sure. He is often early.'

Ashael gazed at the flames but from the corner of her eye she saw a smile flit across her mentor's face.

'When are you and Iwan going to stop dancing around each other and start courting properly?' Bhearra asked, apparently from nowhere.

Ashael considered protesting but one look at Bhearra's face made it clear that would be pointless. Instead, she let her shoulders drop and sighed.

'It's not that simple.'

'Of course it is.'

'This is not his home, and I will never leave here.' Ashael realised her voice had become sharp in her frustration. 'Forgive me, Bhearra. I didn't intend to snap at you.' Over the two moon-cycles he had been here, Iwan had settled into the community well and had become one of those whom Joren relied upon to lead groups. Ashael often found herself in his company and she knew the attraction was mutual; she had seen the way he looked at her.

'There is so much he won't speak of,' she said.

'Many people have things in their past they would rather forget.'

Ashael stared into the fire, seeking some way to explain what she felt; that if they began courting, things would change irrevocably, but whether for better or for worse, she had no idea.

'How are you doing that?' Bhearra asked sharply.

'Doing what?' Ashael looked at Bhearra, who was pointing to the ground between their feet. The younger woman looked down and gasped. The area around her feet was free from snow and grass could be seen. Not the yellowish grass of winter but the deep green Ashael had been thinking of when Bhearra came outside. As she watched, a buttercup bloomed beside her left foot.

Ashael staggered back a step, unable to tear her eyes away from the ground. 'I'm not... I don't understand.'

'What did you do?' Bhearra asked, watching Ashael intently.

'Nothing! I was thinking of summer, but I didn't do anything.'

'Good morning, ladies,' Gerod called as he walked towards them, coming to take over the tending of the Heart-Fire.

Ashael looked from him to the expanding patch of summer at her feet. 'I must go. Forgive me.' With that she bolted as a deer from a hunter.

***

IWAN LAY SHAKING on the floor of the guest hut, sweat streaming down his face despite the cold. Each inspection Meegrum gave of his memories was worse than before. The last time, he had tried to fight it, to shield his memories, but he had lost the struggle and ended up with a nosebleed that lasted the rest of the night.

Tonight, Meegrum had noticed Iwan's growing feelings for Ashael. He had been amused, chuckling at Iwan's discomfort. He had ended his inspection with an order to 'bed her and get it over with'. Iwan pulled himself onto his hands and knees then crawled to the water bucket. He scooped a little of the water up in his hands and sipped. His stomach roiled. He hung his head and tried not to vomit. When the feeling had passed, he leaned his head back against the smooth wood of the wall and looked around the guest hut.

There was a banked fire in the hearth in the middle of the room, a bowl of fish soup that Ashael had given him lay on a table beside it. Next to his bed and freshly cleaned were the garments he had been given by Rana, as he had only one set of clothes when he arrived. Beside them were the soft leather slippers that Bhearra had given him. There was a basket of mint leaves for tea and a large badger-skin bag from Alayne. Everywhere he looked, he saw evidence of the kindness and generosity of these people. *His* people: they were descended from the same ancestors after all. How could he stay here, betraying them?

Iwan rubbed his eyes. There had to be some way out of this. He wasn't afraid to die but his death would be pointless if he had no time to warn the Folk. And the Zanthar would kill his mother. He fingered the brand on his chest as he thought, wondering how it worked. Meegrum was not privy to all of his thoughts, all of the time, but he might detect any attempt to talk about them. The lord had said he would be dead before he could finish his sentence. Could he warn them of danger without being specific? What if he did something to get himself thrown out of the cam? No – the Zanthar would just kill him and his mother and send someone else. At least he could take comfort in the fact that they didn't seem to have found what they were looking for. Maybe they wouldn't find it here.

***

'WHAT DID YOU say these are for?' Alayne asked, fingering the rush ropes that Ashael had spent the afternoon making with a group of the older children.

'Slings: the weapon Iwan is teaching,' Ashael answered. 'It sounds ideal for small game. The ropes connect to a cradle, but I've still to make those.'

'Let me know if I can help,' Alayne said. 'It sounds like something I can do when Rhys is sleeping.'

'Of course,' replied Ashael, tucking the ropes into a basket on the shelf and linking arms with Alayne. 'Shall we head out to the meeting?'

The two women stepped out into the cold evening air, breath puffing in front of them. Ashael smiled gratefully when Bres handed them mugs of steaming broth and wrapped her hands around the warmth. Alayne blew across the top of her own mug as Ashael led her to a free space on a log beside the Heart-Fire.

'I love these meetings but it's so cold tonight; I hope Bhearra doesn't pick a long story,' Alayne said, moving along to make space for Gethyn who had just arrived with Rhys bundled up in a warm wrap against his chest.

'Any idea what tonight's story is, Ash?' Gethyn asked, sitting down.

Ashael shook her head. 'We've been working on different things today. I haven't spoken to her since breakfast. Usually something suggests itself to her over the course of the day.'

'Alayne tells me you've been working on making slings, like the one Iwan carries,' Gethyn said.

'Yes, it was Joren's idea. He was really impressed with how effective they are for hunting small game.'

'Yes, I've seen Iwan hunt with it. You can count me in to learn,' Gethyn answered, sipping from Alayne's broth before handing it back.

A fussy sound came from somewhere inside the wrap and Gethyn peeled back layers to reveal Rhys, face screwed up, ready to wail. Alayne leaned over and lifted the baby out, putting him to her breast before he could cry, and Gethyn wrapped a fur around them to keep them both warm. Ashael watched the easy way the couple worked together to care for their son and felt a lump form in her throat. She had never given much thought to having a family, being content with her role as filidh, but something new was stirring in her.

The conversations around the fire began to fade away and Ashael swallowed hard, looking up to where Bhearra stood, shawl pulled tight around her tiny shoulders.

'My friends!' Bhearra called, spreading her arms wide. 'How blessed we are to meet here, in the warmth of the Heart-Fire. I'm sure I speak for us all when I thank Bres and Soraya for the broth they have provided tonight.'

Many of the Folk called out their thanks for the broth, and Bres waved while Soraya laughed and ducked her head.

'Usually, I come to these meetings with a story in mind, but today I wasn't able to settle on one. So, does anyone have a request?'

'The time the Longest Night ritual went wrong!'

'The lighting of the Heart-Fire!'

'The founding of the cams!'

'The journey over The Edge of the World!'

Bhearra smiled and held up her hands. 'Some wonderful suggestions.' She paced back and forth a little. 'Let's talk about the founding of the cams.'

'Yes, I love that one,' came a voice from somewhere to Ashael's right.

'I too, love this story,' Bhearra began, smiling in the direction of the person who had spoken. 'After Sirion helped the Flores defeat the Zanthar, our people were free. But we had been captive for three generations. We were determined to leave the keep, and the area known as the Blasted Lands, behind us, but we had no homes to return to. Before our slavery, the Folk were nomads; we followed the great herds as they migrated across the land. But we had lost many of our skills during the long years under the Zanthar. We were weak and needed to settle somewhere for a time, to recover our strength and our abilities.'

'Why is it called the Blasted Lands?' a young girl called out.

'Because the Zanthar stole so much of the life force from the land around their keep that the earth itself died. Nothing could grow there.' Bhearra paused and then, when there were no further questions, continued. 'The Folk stayed in the mountains until Sirion had recovered from channelling the sun, and then made their way down to these fertile lands which had been untouched by the Zanthar, accompanied by the Flores. The whole group spent the winter at what is now Trout Cam.'

'So, Trout was the first cam?' a boy called.

'Yes, as Danliv likes to remind me,' Joren answered, chuckling.

'There, the Folk re-dedicated themselves to Kala, the All-Mother, and her mate,

Saulas, the All-Father, and lit the first Heart-Fire as a symbol of our dedication.'

Bhearra paused and sipped from the cup of hot broth in her hands. 'The Flores stayed for that first winter. Taught the Folk how to make weapons and hunt. How to build shelters. Some of the Folk taught the Flores how to weave nets to fish. Our peoples became fast friends. When spring came, the Flores had to return to their home on the other side of the Edge of the World. We agreed to meet every eight summers.'

'What happened to them?' This time it was Alayne who asked the question.

'No one knows,' Bhearra said, sadly. 'When my grandfather was a young man, the group that went to meet the Flores in the mountains returned early – the Flores hadn't kept the meeting. For each of the following eight summers, a small group went to the mountains, in the hope that we had mistaken the passage of time and gone too soon. We never saw them again. My grandfather met them once when he was young. He used to tell me about these fantastic creatures who looked like us but had wings. I have always wished I could have met them.'

'Tell us more about the cams, please,' Iwan called, drawing Ashael's gaze. The light from the fire cast odd shadows on his face. Ashael wasn't sure, but Iwan looked emotional.

'Well, over time the community at Trout Cam grew. They knew that if they stayed together in one place, the land would no longer be able to support them, so they decided to spread out. Three small groups broke off from Trout Cam and went in search of a new home. They founded Fork River Cam, Stoney Hill Cam and Rowan Grove Cam. Each new cam took a flame from the Heart-Fire at Trout Cam, keeping the eternal flame of our devotion burning.

'Over the years, we spread further, founding new cams and exploring more of this land, eventually spreading all the way from here to the endless forest in the south; from the sea in the east to the Edge of the World in the west.'

'As long as we keep our oaths and care for the land that we live on, our people shall continue to flourish. Who knows how far we may spread?'

Chapter Five

MEEGRUM SIGHED AND MOPPED HIS BROW. THE RAG HE USED WAS COVERED IN grit and scraped his skin raw. Just one more reason that he hated being on Zan.

'How much farther?' Daven rasped from the other side of the carriage they shared.

Meegrum leaned out the door and squinted at the castle that dominated the horizon. 'Not long, my lord. An hour, perhaps.'

The lord coughed into the cloth he held over his mouth. 'Damn the dust of this place. And damn the king for forcing us back here.'

'My lord! We must be more circumspect! This carriage was sent by the king, after all; we cannot be sure it hasn't been enchanted.'

Daven made a growling sound at the back of his throat but said no more. Meegrum turned back to the window and watched the castle as they gradually drew closer.

***

THEY WERE GIVEN adjoining rooms that were so small and so distant from the centre of the castle as to be an insult. The furniture was spartan and covered with a fine layer of dust. In his lord's room, a cloth-covered tray sat in the middle of a table against one wall. Meegrum lifted a corner of the cloth, revealing bread, cheese and a small carafe with one glass. There was no such tray in his room. He was of too low a caste to warrant any hospitality; a fact that he was constantly reminded of while at court.

Daven paced the small space, fury written on his face. Thankfully he had the wisdom to swallow his rage when servants entered the room carrying their luggage. Meegrum retreated through the door to his own chamber and checked that his travelling chest had not been opened. The king would not take kindly to a guest in his castle smuggling in weapons and poison but there were no circumstances under which Meegrum would come here unarmed.

***

Meegrum let the swell of sound in the great hall wash over him, staring into his goblet as he swirled the wine within. Light from the tallow lamps flickered and shone onto the dark red liquid, mesmerising him until he realised that the chatter around him had stopped. He straightened up and found himself looking into the smoke-grey eyes of Merelle. As always, her beauty took his breath away.

'I'm so glad that you could come and celebrate my son's marriage, Meegrum,' Merelle said, her tone so sweet it was cloying.

Meegrum bowed, giving himself a moment to compose an answer. 'The king was very gracious to invite us, my lady.'

'Can I assume Daven is around here somewhere?' she asked, looking around the milling people in all their finery.

'He stepped out for some air, Lady Merelle. He will be sorry to have missed speaking with you.'

Merelle snorted. 'I'm sure he will be glad to be spared my presence, but since we are all here together for some time, no doubt I shall have the opportunity to speak with him again.'

A stout man in very fine clothing approached and took Merelle by the elbow. 'There you are. Our son has requested your presence.'

It was only then that Meegrum recognised Varald, Daven's oldest rival. The man led his wife away and Meegrum let out a slow breath, glad that Daven had not been forced to see them. When he first returned from KalaDene all those years ago, defeated by indigenes without even the most basic of weapons, Daven had been humiliated. He lost the king's favour; his lands and wives were stripped from him and given to his rivals.

Merelle had been the youngest of Daven's wives and his favourite. The king had given her to Varald, ensuring Daven's unending hatred for both men. Cenric was the result of the union. The fact that he had been selected to marry one of the king's daughters just rubbed salt in Daven's wounds.

Meegrum drained his goblet and went in search of more wine. The best way to get through this wedding would be drunk.

***

'Where have you been?' Daven demanded as soon as Meegrum entered his chamber. 'I had to attend an audience with the king without you!'

'I beg your forgiveness, my lord. I have been down at the stables. You know how Grigor can be persuaded to talk: I was gathering information for you.'

'Hmph. I hope you learned something useful then,' Daven said, sitting down heavily and waving a hand at the other chair to indicate that Meegrum should sit.

'A few things of interest, my lord. It seems that the latest batch of slaves are dying much faster than usual. That must be why the king is so impatient to have us resolve the situation on KalaDene.'

'Can't he just bring more through from their home world?' Daven asked.

'Apparently they sicken very soon after arriving here. Several trips have been made but opening the World-Gate so frequently is costly; it uses so much power that the slaves brought back are barely sufficient to replenish the mages operating the gate.'

'Remind me: who picked that world to attack?'

Meegrum rubbed his hands together in glee. 'Varald, my lord!'

'Ha! He must be feeling very nervous right now. The king may decide to geld his son instead of wedding him to the princess!'

Daven's eyes danced in the first expression of pleasure that Meegrum had seen from him for some time.

'What else did you hear?' Daven leaned back in his chair.

'Young Cenric is virile, if stupid. He's been bedding servants, slaves and minor house's daughters ever since he got here.'

'Does the king know?'

'It would appear not – at least, not publicly.'

'We shall have to see if we can rectify that…' Daven trailed off, staring into space, and Meegrum could almost see the schemes running through his mind. He may have lost much of his power and influence but Daven was a master manipulator and that could never be taken from him. After a moment, he shook himself and said, 'Anything else?'

'The king's gambling debt grows ever greater, and his gold steadily declines. It seems that he has taken to paying his debts with slaves and whores.'

'His wives will not be happy with him squandering all of his wealth. I hardly think they married him for his looks,' sniggered Daven.

'His fifth wife is with child again, my lord, but still he has no sons. Twelve daughters to provide for and no sons. People are saying he does not have the seed to make a man!'

The two men laughed and, for a time, Meegrum relaxed. All of this gossip about his enemies had served to put Daven in a good mood.

***

'LADY MERELLE, YOU sent for me?' Meegrum said, entering Merelle's chamber and looking around. 'Where are your maids?'

'I told them to leave.' Merelle's voice came from behind an elaborate screen on the other side of the room.

'Your husband would not approve of us being alone, my lady.'

'My husband is an oaf. What do I care for his approval?' Merelle snapped.

Meegrum eyed the door, wondering if Varald was due to return soon. 'Why did you wish to see me?'

'How is Daven?' Merelle stepped out from behind the screen, wearing only a thin, loose-fitting robe. Meegrum could see the shape of her body beneath it and quickly averted his eyes.

'My lord is well. He is enjoying the celebrations,' Meegrum answered, looking over Merelle's shoulder.

'You never could lie to me, Meegrum,' Merelle said, stepping in close and allowing Meegrum to smell her perfume.

'It is no lie, my lady. Only yesterday, Daven was laughing with joy.'

'Was it at the expense of another?' Merelle asked.

'Did you have some reason for bringing me here, Merelle?'

'Ah, there's the man I know; no false courtesies.' Merelle walked over to the sideboard and poured two glasses of wine. Her robe slipped as she handed a glass to Meegrum, exposing the skin of her shoulder.

'Perhaps you should put on something more suitable before your husband returns.'

'Varald has gone hunting with the king. He will not return until sometime this evening, no doubt drunk and poorer.'

'And your son?'

'With his bride.' Merelle sipped the wine thoughtfully. 'Have you given any thought to what you will do when Daven is gone?'

'Gone where?'

Merelle tutted. 'Now, now. We both know that he will not be successful on this campaign of his. He is too weak, too bitter. When he fails again, the king plans to execute him. What will you do then?'

Meegrum swallowed hard. He had faith in Daven and knew there was far more to his plan than Merelle was aware of, but to hear the future pronounced so baldly was difficult. 'Of course my lord will succeed. But if he were to fail, I am sure the king would see me executed also. He has never had any love for me.'

'Daven is your saviour and your curse. He allows you to use the Old Magic, granting you extended life despite your low caste. But in the doing, he has made you many enemies in the court.'

'You tell me nothing I do not know. Do you have a point?'

Merelle leaned in so close that Meegrum could feel the warmth of her body. 'Come and serve in my household. I will continue to allow you the Old Magic.'

'Why would you do that?' Meegrum scoffed.

'I seem to remember that not all of you is small,' Merelle said, grabbing the front of his breeches. 'It's been a long time since my needs were met.'

'I cannot betray Daven,' Meegrum said through gritted teeth, but already his body was responding to Merelle.

'I seem to remember a similar conversation when I was his wife, but it didn't stop you then.' Merelle began to undress him.

Meegrum looked into those grey eyes and saw his own desire mirrored there. 'It is a dangerous game you play, Merelle.'

'Then I hope you'll make it worth the risk,' she answered, stepping back and letting her robe fall to the floor.

Chapter Six

'I WAN?' A VOICE CALLED FROM OUTSIDE HIS HUT. IWAN FINISHED DRESSING THEN pulled aside the entrance curtain to find Ashael standing outside, sunlight highlighting the red streaks in her hair. A breeze played across Iwan's skin, and he smelled the new growth of spring. He took a deep breath, feeling the hope of the season.

'Please, come in,' he said stepping back and gesturing for her to enter.

'Thank you,' she said, stepping past him. 'You look well rested. Are you sleeping better?'

'I am,' Iwan answered. It had been almost a full cycle of the moons since the last time Meegrum had activated the brand. He was starting to think he might be free of them.

'The rain has stopped,' she said.

For a moment, Iwan thought she was trying to tell him it was time for him to move on, that winter was over, and his welcome worn out.

'I thought perhaps you could show me how to use the sling this morning?'

'Oh, of course,' Iwan said, a laugh of relief escaping from him.

Ashael gave him a quizzical look.

'Never mind,' he said, grinning. 'We should take it outside of the cam; we don't want any accidents while you practice. Somewhere with a bit of space between the trees, room to swing your arms freely.'

Ashael was nodding before he had finished. 'I know somewhere. There's a clearing near the bathing pool. Much smaller than this one, but it should give us space.'

'Then lead the way,' Iwan said, fastening his belt around his hips and tucking his own sling into its accustomed spot.

***

'IT WILL BE easier if I show you first, I think,' Iwan said, moving into the centre of the clearing. 'The movement is fast so it can be difficult to follow. Just watch as closely as you can.'

Iwan began to swing the sling in a gentle circle, demonstrating the movement for Ashael. She was watching closely, all trace of awkwardness gone now. She nodded and Iwan sped up, allowing the revolutions to become rapid. After gaining some speed, he released one end of the sling, letting the stone fly from it at great speed. The stone hit a clump of blossom on a low branch that he had been aiming at, giving the appearance that the blossom had exploded.

Ashael gave a delighted laugh as the bits of brightly coloured petals fluttered to the ground.

'Flowers are much easier to hit than animals,' Iwan said, though he was pleased at her excitement.

'Can I try?' Ashael asked.

'Of course. It's probably best if you aim for the trunk, to begin with.'

Ashael stepped up beside Iwan, her body facing the tree she would be aiming at. Iwan took her shoulders and turned her slightly so that she was almost side on. He didn't expect her to hit the tree on her first try but she should still be lined up correctly. He held her hips and turned them too, allowing his hands to linger a little longer than was necessary before stepping back.

'Whenever you're ready,' he said, his voice hoarse.

Ashael didn't seem to have noticed his arousal. She began to swing the sling, slowly at first, experimentally, as if getting used to the feel of it. She allowed the sling to pick up speed and Iwan watched how her body moved with her arm, giving extra force to the swing. She released the stone just a moment too soon and it went flying off, well past the tree she was aiming for.

'That was incredible,' Iwan called in surprise.

'But I missed,' Ashael said, her tone disappointed.

'Only just. You have the movement perfect. Well done!'

A cry came from somewhere behind them. They both turned towards the sound.

'Help! Help!'

'The river!' Ashael cried as she took off, running, Iwan only a pace behind. They crashed through the undergrowth, both making so much noise that Iwan barely heard the next shout, although they were getting closer.

His heart was pounding by the time they burst out onto the riverbank. The water had been swollen by the heavy spring rain and was running high and fast. He scanned the area, looking for the source of the shouts. A movement down-river caught his eye. A head burst up from the water, spluttering and struggling before sinking again.

'There!' Iwan grabbed Ashael's arm and pointed towards where the head had disappeared. 'I'm going in. You run along the bank; try to find somewhere for me to get out.'

Before Ashael could answer, Iwan dived into the water.

The shock of the cold tore the breath from his lungs. He took several powerful strokes underwater before surfacing. The spray that hovered just above the surface obscured his vision. He couldn't see any sign of the person he had jumped in after.

'Hold on! Help is coming!' Ashael called, and he looked to the bank. 'Grab this, if you can.' Ashael threw a large branch into the water. The current was pushing and pulling at Iwan and he rode it down-river, adding his own strength so that he was going faster than the water. He thought he heard another shout, closer now, but it was hard to tell because the water was rushing in his ears and the voice was weak.

Iwan took a deep breath and ducked back under the surface where he was able to cut through the water with less resistance. There was little visibility; he didn't see the legs until he was almost on top of them. Iwan burst up, blowing water out of his face. It was a child! A young boy, clinging to the branch that Ashael had thrown into the water, face white, teeth chattering.

Iwan grabbed the end of the branch and pulled it and the boy towards himself.

'There's a sandbank up ahead,' Ashael called, pointing to a bend in the river.

Iwan waved to show that he had heard her; he had to save his breath for swimming now – the current had pushed them to the opposite bank. He would have to cut across the river, towing the boy, and he would have to do it fast. He took hold of some protruding roots, taking a moment to prepare.

'Are you injured?' he asked the boy.

'N-n-n-no,' he answered through chattering teeth.

'You can let go of the branch now. I've got you,' Iwan said.

The boy let go of the branch and grabbed Iwan with panicky tightness, wrapping scrawny arms around his rescuer's neck.

'Not like that,' Iwan said, prying the arms loose. 'Here. Turn your back to me. Put your head on my shoulder.' Iwan wrapped his arm around the boy's thin chest, alarmed by the tremors running through the small frame. 'Now just lie back and let the water take your weight. I won't let go.'

Iwan realised that if they didn't get out of the water soon, the cold would kill the boy just as surely as drowning would have.

'Take a deep breath. There's going to be water in your face, but I'll keep you safe. Are you ready?'

The boy didn't answer at first.

'I need you to stay awake, just a little longer. Are you ready?'

'Y-y-y-yes.'

Iwan pulled his legs up, knees almost touching his chest, and braced his feet against the bank. 'Take a deep breath on three. One, two, three!' Iwan took his own deep breath and then pushed off the bank with all the force he could muster. The momentum carried them halfway across the river before the current caught hold of them again.

The cold was leeching Iwan's strength. His free arm was heavy as he struck out, pulling the boy behind him. For a horrible moment, Iwan thought they would shoot right past the sandbank, but he found a reserve of strength, kicking his legs for all he was worth. Sand beneath his hands had never felt so good. He dragged them both out of the water and then Ashael was there, lending her strength to lift the boy up.

'Rill! Rill! What happened?' she asked the boy as Iwan got to his feet, panting.

'The light, it dances,' Rill answered, his eyelids heavy.

'What do you mean?' Iwan asked.

'He's confused. We have to get him warm,' Ashael said, lifting the boy's tunic over his head. 'You should take off your wet things, too,' she said, glancing at Iwan.

He stripped his tunic off but stopped short of removing his wet trousers. 'We'll have trouble starting a fire,' he said. 'Everything is wet.'

'We need to get back to the cam,' Ashael answered. She had the boy stripped down to his loincloth now. She stood and pulled her dry tunic over her head before putting it on the boy. 'Rill, can you hold onto me if I carry you on my back?'

'I'll carry him,' Iwan said.

'You, too, need to recover. I can carry him,' Ashael said, tone firm. She turned and crouched down. Iwan helped Rill onto her back. They had not made much progress before Rill slipped off, landing heavily on the ground. The filidh fell to her knees beside the boy, putting her ear to his chest.

'He's unconscious and his breathing is very shallow. He won't make it back like this.'

Ashael bowed her head, lips moving. Iwan looked on, helpless, while she prayed over Rill. As she did so, a light began to dance over her bronze skin, all the colours of the rainbow. Iwan rubbed his eyes and looked again. Ashael had her eyes closed and didn't seem to have noticed but the light flowed over her arms and onto the boy. Steam rose from the ground around them and Iwan could have sworn there were flowers around them where none were before.

He watched, entranced, until Rill took a deep breath and stretched, as if waking from a restful sleep.

'What happened?' the boy asked.

'You passed out but you're going to be fine,' explained Ashael. 'We need to get back to the cam.' Ashael got to her feet. 'Do you think you can hold onto my back again, Rill?'

'I feel fine. I can walk.'

'That can't be. You were unconscious just a moment ago.'

'Honestly, Ashael, I feel well. Better than I did before I fell in the river.'

Iwan studied the boy. He was no healer, but Rill certainly looked well enough. Whatever Ashael had done had obviously worked wonders for the child, but, somehow, she wasn't aware of what had happened.

***

IT WAS NOON when they reached the cam. The walk had brought Iwan's temperature back up and Rill seemed well. He had kept asking to be allowed to walk but Ashael insisted on carrying him. She was breathing heavily and a fine sheen of sweat covered her bronze skin. Iwan had offered to carry Rill for her, but she'd refused.

When they stepped between the two beech trunks and entered the cam, Rill jumped down from Ashael's back and she sank to one knee. As Rill scampered off, shouting for his mother, Joren hurried over.

'Ashael, are you well? What has happened?'

'We fished Rill out of the river,' Ashael answered, accepting Iwan's hand and pulling herself to her feet. 'He fell unconscious straight after but seems well enough now. Bhearra should still check him over.'

'What of you?' Joren asked, a frown creasing his brow.

'I am well, just tired. Iwan went into the river and saved Rill; I only carried him back here.'

Iwan studied Ashael's face as she spoke, and what he saw concerned him. Dark circles had formed under her eyes and her skin looked drawn. She had looked much healthier when they had set out together just a few notches ago.

'I think it would be wise if Bhearra speaks with all of you,' Joren said, offering his arm to Ashael. She took it then turned to Iwan.

'You should get into something dry,' Ashael said. 'I'll let Bhearra know you'll be with us shortly.'

***

IWAN STRIPPED HIS wet trousers off and dropped them on the floor. The skin of his legs was pale and wrinkled from the damp clothing, so he put on a dry loincloth and stood by the banked fire, letting the lingering heat take the chill off him.

He grabbed a nutcake from a bowl beside the hearth and nibbled the edges as he thought. Should he tell Bhearra what he had seen? How could he, when he wasn't even sure of it himself? He was no healer; perhaps the boy had not been as far gone as he had seemed. Even as the thought crossed his mind, Iwan knew he was lying to himself. Ashael had done something, had healed Rill somehow, and she didn't seem to be aware of it. Whatever she had done had taken a toll on her. Should he speak to her about it instead of to Bhearra? Would Ashael believe him?

Iwan scratched absently at his slave-brand. The rough scar tissue beneath his fingers turned his thoughts to the Zanthar. Why had they not contacted him in so long? *Maybe Meegrum is dead,* Iwan thought with grim hope. Was he free? What did that mean for his mother? Was she still in the keep? Was there some way he could get them out of this?

I do not have enough information about anything. Sighing, Iwan pulled on some dry clothes.

***

'How long was Rill in the water?' Bhearra asked, studying the boy who stood fidgeting before her.

'We don't know. He was in the water when we found him. Iwan jumped in and got him out.' Ashael crossed the room, pulling the hides from her sleeping pallet and handing them to Bhearra, who tucked them around Rill, despite the boy's protestations. 'He was confused when they got out of the water and passed out after a few minutes. I prayed over him and sent myself into him to check for other injuries, and then he awoke. He's seemed fine since, but I carried him back to be safe.'

'And Iwan? Is he well?' Bhearra asked.

'He went to put on dry clothing. He should be here soon.'

'How many times have I told you to be careful around the river?' Niamh scolded her son. 'You could have drowned! Iwan could have drowned trying to save you!'

Ashael turned away to hide her smile and filled the cauldron with water, adding hot stones from the hearth. Her braided hair brushed against the skin of her back, and she realised that she was still half-naked, since she had given her tunic to Rill. She stepped into her alcove and lifted a fresh tunic from the large basket at the end of her pallet, hurriedly pulling it over her head. As she adjusted the tunic and turned, her head suddenly swam and she sat down so heavily that she bit her tongue, tasting blood in her mouth.

The scarred face appeared in front of her eyes; the one she had seen before. His lips were twisted in a cruel sneer, his eyes dancing with pleasure. A piercing scream rang out in Ashael's head. She drew in breath to scream herself and, as suddenly as it had come, the vision was gone.

Ashael's gaze darted about the alcove, seeking comfort in the familiarity of this place. She could hear a harsh gasping. It took her a moment to realise the sound was coming from her.

'Ashael, are you well?' Bhearra called.

Shaky, Ashael got to her feet and stepped back into the main room. She met Bhearra's eyes then looked at Niamh and Rill. 'I was just dizzy for a moment.'

Bhearra nodded, showing that she understood there was more to it, but Ashael wanted to discuss it when they were alone.

'Hello,' Iwan's voice came from the entrance just before he stepped inside.

'Oh, Iwan,' Niamh leapt to her feet, pulling him into a warm embrace. 'You are a guardian, sent by Sirion himself.'

Ashael laughed at the confused look on Iwan's face. 'I was just telling Niamh how you pulled Rill from the river.'

'It was no more than anyone would have done,' Iwan said, disentangling himself from Niamh's arms.

'You must tell me how to thank you,' Niamh said, going back to Rill's side. 'I could cook all of your meals for you, or make you some new clothes?'

'There is no need.'

'Let us all share the evening meal,' Joren said, clapping Iwan on the shoulder.

'That would be good,' he said, his shoulders relaxing. 'What can I do to help prepare?'

'Find Gerod,' Joren answered. 'Ask him to pass the word. There will be a celebration tonight.'

***

WHEN EVERYONE HAD gone, Bhearra insisted Ashael sit down and eat something. The old woman prepared broth for them both and sat at Ashael's side.

'What did you do with Rill?' Bhearra asked.

'What do you mean?' Ashael asked, blowing on her hot broth.

'That boy looked healthier than he did yesterday. There was no sign that he had ever been in the river and we both know the water is very cold at this time of year. He should have been worse for wear.'

'I got him out of his wet clothes and into my tunic. When he passed out, I wasn't sure what to do. I prayed over him while I was trying to figure it out and he just got up. Maybe the All-Mother has a fondness in her heart for mischievous boys.'

'Perhaps.' Bhearra studied Ashael's face for a long time before speaking again. 'What happened after you came back?'

'I saw that face again. The one I mentioned seeing the day that Soraya had her baby,' Ashael said, twisting the end of her braid between her fingers.

'Was there anything new?' Bhearra asked.

'Just the face. And a scream. A woman, I think,' Ashael swallowed hard. She did not have the words to describe the horror in that scream.

'It must mean something, to have come to you twice like this.'

'I will pray on it,' Ashael said. 'Perhaps the All-Mother also has a fondness for apprentice filidh.'

Chapter Seven

THAT NIGHT, THE FOLK CELEBRATED. A STAG WAS ROASTED, THE MOUTH-WATERING smell permeating the cam. Each household brought a dish of food to share, from rabbit stew to fragrant fish wrapped in leaves. There were bottles of lacha, a fermented fruit drink saved for special occasions. It was mildly intoxicating, and the distinctive smell always put Ashael in a good mood. It was the smell of feasts and pleasures.

Alayne and Rana turned the spit over the cooking fire while Ashael wrapped tubers in wet leaves and carefully positioned them at the edges of the fire to roast.

'Ouch!' Ashael exclaimed, blowing on the back of her hand.

'Well, you would watch Iwan instead of your work,' Rana teased. 'It's no wonder you burnt yourself.'

'I don't know what you're talking about,' Ashael responded, but the flush she could feel working its way up her cheeks suggested otherwise.

'Can't blame you for looking,' Alayne said, giving Iwan an admiring look herself. 'That is one handsome man.'

Ashael looked across to where Iwan stood with Niamh. The other woman was hanging all over him. Much to Ashael's chagrin, she found herself jealous.

'There's no need to guess how Niamh wants to thank him,' Rana remarked, her eyebrow raised.

'They're both free to do as they wish,' Ashael said, but she couldn't look her friend in the eye while she said it.

Bhearra and Joren walked over arm-in-arm, a conspiratorial air about them.

'That smells wonderful,' Joren said, letting Bhearra's arm drop and kissing Rana on the cheek.

'It's ready,' said Rana, smiling at her mate. 'Why don't you let everyone know?'

Joren climbed up on a log that lay beside the Heart-Fire. He cupped his hands around his mouth and gave a shriek, an eerie imitation of a tawny owl. Gradually, stillness settled over the cam and Joren began to speak.

'For anyone who has not yet heard –' a chuckle rippled through the crowd; news travelled fast in the cam – 'we are here to celebrate the safe return of Rill, who fell into the river this morning. It was the bravery of our friend Iwan that saved him and brought him back to his mother.' Joren paused for a moment, allowing the shouts of congratulations to be heard. 'Iwan has only been with us a for a season, but he has been of great service to us all, bringing both knowledge and friendship with him. It is the wish of Rana and I to invite him to make his home here. What say you?'

Shouts of 'aye' and 'welcome' could be heard from the Folk.

'If any person objects, speak now, make your thoughts known,' Joren said, scanning the crowd for signs that anyone wished to speak. When no one responded, Joren turned to Iwan, all eyes following him.

'Iwan, if it is your wish to continue on your travels now that winter has passed, then we will offer whatever provisions you require and see you on your way with heavy hearts. If, however, you might be persuaded to end your journey here, we would welcome you as one of us.'

Ashael watched Iwan, breath caught in her throat. Although he smiled, he looked sad. His body was tense, as if prepared to flee. *He's going to say no*, she thought, letting out her breath in a slow sigh.

'You do me a great honour,' Iwan answered. 'I would be happy to stay.'

***

MOST OF THE food had been eaten, the lacha enjoyed. Some of the Folk had drifted off to their homes while others sat in small groups. Ashael sat with Bhearra, Joren, Rana, Alayne and Gethyn. Iwan came over and sat down beside her.

'I think I must have spoken to the entire cam tonight,' he said, voice hoarse from over-use.

Ashael held out a cup of water. 'Here. Or there's lacha if you wish?'

'No, my head is spinning enough,' he laughed. 'Water is perfect.'

They sat in companionable silence for a few moments, before Iwan cleared his throat. 'There's something I wanted to ask you,' he said, looking everywhere but at her.

Ashael felt her heart skip a beat. She looked at Iwan's profile in the firelight and thought about how mysterious he was, how much she did not know of him. Then she remembered how he had leapt into the river to save Rill with no hesitation at all. Iwan finally turned to face her and before he could speak again, she leaned in and pressed her lips to his. For a second, Iwan didn't respond – just long enough for Ashael to begin to think she had made a mistake, that she had misread him. Then he cupped her face, kissing her back, hard. When they parted, her breath was coming in short gasps and her skin was tingling. Slowly, her awareness of the rest of the world returned and she laughed as she realised that her friends were all applauding.

'Finally!' Rana said, laughing. 'I was starting to think we would have to tie you two together before you saw sense.'

'Would you care to take a walk?' Iwan asked, standing and holding out his hand.

Ashael linked her fingers through his and got to her feet. 'I would be glad to.'

They set off to catcalls and laughter, heading away from the Heart-Fire and into the trees that ringed the cam.

'I am glad you decided to stay,' Ashael said, 'but what about your family? Aren't they waiting for your return?' Ashael felt the muscles in Iwan's arm stiffen before he dropped her hand.

'It is complicated,' he answered without looking at her.

'Do you have family to return to?'

'My mother. If the gods will it, then perhaps I will see her again.'

'What made you leave? Why did you decide to travel so far from home?' Ashael could feel how her questions were creating a void between them, but she couldn't bring herself to stop.

Iwan stopped suddenly and spun towards her. He wrapped his hands in her hair and kissed her, pressing his body against hers. Letting go of her barriers, Ashael's senses spread out and she felt his need, his loneliness, his fierce desire, and she lost herself in him.

She had no idea how much time had passed when he jerked away from her as if burned.

'I'm sorry. I must go,' he gasped, before stumbling off into the dark woods.

'What's wrong?' she called, taking a few steps after him. 'Iwan?'

'Please, I need to be alone.' His voice drifted back to her between the trees.

Ashael stood for a moment, fingers pressed to lips still numb from his kiss. What had happened? Why had he run off like that? Ashael took a step in the direction he had gone but stopped, hurt and confused. She stared into the dark for several long moments before turning and heading home, her shoulders slumped, tears filling her eyes.

***

IWAN LAY BEHIND a fallen tree, face pressed into the dirt to muffle his moans. He had heard Ashael move away as the burning itch raced from his brand to his skull and had then lost track of everything. A moon-cycle-worth of memories poured across his vision – everything from building a roof to hunting with Joren. Iwan fought the invasion but was powerless to stop the scroll of images.

The memories slowed as they caught up to the present. Again, Iwan heard Rill in the water and felt himself leap in after him. Somewhere in the back of his mind, he could feel Meegrum's disgust at his efforts to save the boy. When the memories showed them reaching the cam and Rill running off to find his mother, they stopped abruptly then went backwards, back to the river side. This time the images moved slowly. Against the pain and that maddening itch, Iwan tried to think. This had never happened before. Something must have caught Meegrum's attention. If there was something in his memories that could help those monsters, then he had to find a way to stop them. But how?

Iwan lifted his head up with great effort, breath coming in harsh gasps. The memories moved past his eyes, overlaying reality. He could see the rough bark of the fallen tree through Ashael's face as she knelt over Rill when he fell from her back. The memory paused. There was a sense of recognition and excitement from Meegrum. Iwan shook his head and focused on the water, trying to force them to see the surging river instead.

'Stop resisting, you fool,' Meegrum said in his mind. Pain exploded through Iwan, making his eyes water and his stomach roil, but still he pictured the river. The image of Ashael fought the image of the water, colours swirling and clashing, making Iwan dizzy. Eventually the water came to replace Ashael. Gratitude washed over Iwan along with a fierce pride, but both feelings lasted only a moment. The pain that came into his head this time was more than he could bear and Iwan passed out.

Chapter Eight

WAN CAME AROUND SLOWLY, THE SMELL OF LEAF MOULD PERVADING HIS SENSES. HE opened his eyes and watched an ant trundle across the back of his hand. Birds twittered in the trees around him and something small rustled the undergrowth nearby. Iwan lifted his head and grimaced at the ache in his neck. His vision was spinning, and he paused, waiting for it to stop, before pushing himself onto hands and knees. He was still kneeling like this when he heard talking.

'She said he ran off in this direction.' That sounded like Rana.

'Are we sure he's been gone all night?' Joren was with her.

Iwan groaned under his breath and got to his feet. He had to lean against a tree as the dizziness took him again. He swallowed hard as bile crept up his throat. *What will I tell them?*

'I went by his hut to check and there was no sign he had been there,' Rana said, her voice somewhere off to the left.

'Iwan?' Joren shouted. 'Are you out here?'

'Here,' Iwan croaked. He cleared his throat and tried again. 'I'm here.'

There were sounds of movement and then Joren appeared between the trees, Rana close behind him. Joren's jaw dropped open when he caught sight of Iwan, and he increased his pace.

'What happened?' Joren asked, concern clear in his voice.

'I don't remember,' Iwan said, wincing at the lie. Deceit did not come naturally to him, and it was becoming more difficult the more time he spent amongst these people.

Rana's eyes were wide, her hand covering her mouth. 'We need to get you to Bhearra,' she said, moving up to his side. 'Can you walk?'

'I think so.' Iwan took a step away from the tree and stumbled, landing on his knees. 'Perhaps not.'

Without speaking, Joren and Rana each wrapped an arm around his waist, allowing him to lean on them. They set off and Iwan found he had to rely on them to stay upright. It seemed his resistance last night had cost him.

'What's the last thing you remember?' Joren grunted as they negotiated a narrow gap between two trees.

Iwan's mind raced. 'The stag. We were going to have a celebration.' *That should be safe enough. I can 'remember' more after I've had a chance to think.*

'Nothing after that? What of the celebration?' Rana asked.

'I'm sorry. Everything is fuzzy.'

Joren and Rana exchanged a worried look.

'We're almost there,' Rana said. 'Do you think you could go a little faster?'

Iwan did his best to stumble along faster. *Why do they seem so worried? I must look bad.*

When they entered Bhearra's home, the old woman quickly got to her feet. 'What happened?'

'We found him a short distance away. He can't remember anything,' Rana answered as they eased Iwan onto a stool.

'Where is Ashael?' Joren asked.

'Rhys has a fever,' Bhearra answered. 'Ashael has gone to help. Rana, I'm sure she would wish to know that Iwan has returned. Perhaps you could take word to her?'

'Of course.' Rana hurried from the room.

'You remember nothing?' Bhearra asked, kneeling at Iwan's side and beginning to examine him. Joren stepped over by the hearth and stood with his arms across his chest, watching.

'Not… not really. Flashes.' Iwan's head ached, and his eyes felt heavy. All he wanted now was to sleep. And to think.

'Have you been dizzy?'

'Yes.'

'Have you vomited?'

'Yes.'

'Do you have any pain?'

'My head. My neck. Behind my eyes.'

Bhearra said no more as she worked, though she tutted to herself as she lifted his eyelids and peered into his eyes. She took his head in her hands, running her fingers deftly over his skull. Eventually she sat back on her heels.

'You have all the signs of a head injury, but I see no damage to your head. The whites of your eyes have turned red with blood and your skin is ashen and clammy.' Bhearra got to her feet and poured a cup of steaming liquid then handed it to Iwan. 'Broth. Sip it, slowly.' The tiny woman stood looking at Iwan, a worried frown creasing her already-wrinkled brow. 'There is a very rare condition, Scarlet Fugue, that causes symptoms such as yours. We do not know much about it, why it affects some people and not others. How do you feel at the moment?'

'Tired,' Iwan answered, sipping his broth. 'More than that. Exhausted.'

Bhearra nodded. 'When you have finished the broth, Joren will help you home. I would like you to rest; sleep if you can. I will check in with you later. If it is scarlet fugue, sleep should help, though it may take a few days for you to recover fully.'

Iwan was able to walk on his own back to his hut, but Joren stayed close to his side, just in case. Bhearra had given him some willow bark and it was starting to take the sharp edge off of the pain a little.

As they passed the Heart-Fire, Ashael appeared at his side. Iwan kept his eyes on his feet, sure that he would not be able to lie to her if he had to look her in the eye.

'What did Bhearra say?' Ashael asked, her voice strained.

'She thinks I might have some unusual condition, something fugue, I think. She said I should rest.'

'Rana said that you don't remember anything about last night?' Ashael's voice turned up at the end, turning the statement into a question.

The ghost of a tingle ran across Iwan's lips. 'Not really. Some flashes I can't make sense of.'

'Oh.' He could hear the disappointment in her voice. He dared not look at her; he might kiss her again if he did and he needed time to think. 'I'll sit with you for a while, if you like – keep an eye on you.'

'I thank you for the kindness, but I just want to sleep.'

'You can sleep, but it's best that you are not left alone just yet. I am speaking as filidh now.'

'If you think it best,' Iwan answered, resigned.

***

IWAN LAY ON his pallet, his eyes closed. He could hear Ashael heating water, though she was doing her best to be quiet. He concentrated on breathing deeply, trying to feign sleep. He needed to think about what had happened, but his thoughts were slow. *I managed to divert the memories, for a moment at least. But then I passed out. Was Meegrum still poking around my mind when I was unconscious?*

Ashael moved past the window and the breeze carried her scent to him where he lay. He knew that he would forever associate the smell of herbs with her. *Forever? What forever?* As a slave of the Zanthar, he had trained himself not to think about the future, not to have any hopes, because any day could be his last.

His time in the cam had changed him. He had begun to forget himself, forget the reality of his existence. He had dreamed of a future here with the Folk. With Ashael. And he had allowed that dream to seduce him.

Ashael cleared her throat softly. Iwan's heart started to beat faster as he thought of their kiss in the woods. Until his slave-brand had started to itch, it had been the best kiss of his life, all-consuming.

He remembered the first time he saw her, pulling herself dripping from the stream, sunlight sparkling on the beads of water in her hair. She was beautiful. More than that; she was kind, warm. The more time he had spent with her, the more he had come to admire her thoughtfulness, her generosity, her quiet strength.

Iwan rolled over, pulling his knees up to his chest. He felt Ashael moving to his side, leaning over to check on him. Her long hair hung down and brushed against his shoulder, lighting a fire under his skin. He had tried to convince himself that he wasn't falling in love with her, that she meant no more to him than any other member of the cam, but he had failed. *What am I going to do? I should never have kissed her.* Ashael moved away again and Iwan relaxed though he felt a pang from her absence. *How could I have allowed myself to think I could have some sort of future with her? The Zanthar own my life.*

What had Meegrum seen last night? Why had he focused on Ashael? What if she was the one the Zanthar were looking for? The only way he could protect her was by staying away from her. The Zanthar could only see what he saw, so he had to make sure he didn't see anything that could endanger her.

***

ASHAEL SAT ON a low stool by the hearth, stitching up the final seam on a new deerskin dress she had made. First Moon had gone from new to full since they had pulled Rill from the river, and during that time Iwan had been avoiding her. She brooded as she worked. There had definitely been a connection in their kiss, so why had he run away from her? And why avoid her now? He made every excuse he could to be out of the cam; going with every hunting and foraging group, unless she was with them.

She had asked him about that night, tried to remind him of the kiss, but he had run off, saying he would speak to her later. Every time she came near him, he made an excuse to be somewhere else. Ashael was starting to wonder if he had a mate back home. But then, why agree to stay?

Ashael glanced up as Rana came through the entrance

'Are you alone?' Rana asked, looking around the room.

'Yes, Bhearra is sitting with Arron. She thinks he will pass sometime tonight.'

'That must be hard for her. They've known each other for a long time.' Rana was wringing her hands together as she spoke.

'I'll be going to join her a little later, take her some food,' said Ashael, and noticed her friend fidgeting. 'Is there something wrong?'

Rana flopped down onto a stool by Ashael's side. 'I thought I might have been with child; but I'm not.' She dropped her head into her hands. 'I think there might be something wrong with me.'

'Why do you think that?' Ashael asked, rubbing her friend's shoulder.

'I stopped drinking moon tea as soon as we were mated. It's been almost two summers and still no baby. There must be something wrong.'

'Sometimes it just takes a while.' Ashael knew as soon as the words left her mouth that they would be of no comfort. She felt Rana's pain radiating from her in waves. 'What does Joren think?'

Rana snorted. 'He says that things worth having are worth waiting for.'

'He's right, you know.'

'We have waited, Ash.' Rana looked up and her eyes were red-rimmed. 'Will you check? See if you can find anything?'

Ashael leaned back from Rana. 'You should really ask Bhearra. She knows so much more than I do.'

'I don't want Bhearra. I want you. You're my closest friend.'

'Rana, I want to help you. I just… I don't know if I can do it.'

'Will you try? Please?' A tear trickled down Rana's cheek.

Ashael sighed. 'Lie down on my pallet.'

'Thank you!' Rana threw her arms around Ashael's neck and hugged her tight.

'We're only doing this under the agreement that if I find anything, Bhearra takes over. Agreed?'

'Agreed.'

Ashael knelt by Rana's side, head bowed. *All-Mother, hear my prayer. Guide me in helping Rana, friend to all. Let it be.* She took several deep breaths, grounding herself, before putting her hands on Rana's belly. She concentrated on feeling where she ended and Rana began, then let go of the boundaries. She stretched her senses, searching for anything that felt amiss.

There was a hint of pain, so Ashael followed it. It led to Rana's knee, which she had twisted a few days before. Otherwise, her friend appeared to be in good health. Ashael was about to stop when a feeling of subtle wrongness came over her. She tried to follow it as she had followed the pain, but she couldn't. It surrounded her and then was gone, only to return a moment later.

Ashael felt the ebb and flow again, twice, before she realised it was connected to Rana's heartbeat. *Something in the blood, then.* Ashael knew that she should stop now and get Bhearra, but she couldn't tear herself away. *If it's in the blood, it's everywhere. It doesn't feel like something from outside, so it's something her body has created. It's meant to be here but it's wrong somehow. How do we treat that?*

Ashael began to feel warmth spreading through her, and a shimmering golden light filled her mind's eye. She tried to ignore the light, searching for the cause of the wrongness she sensed in Rana's blood. The light grew brighter, overwhelming Ashael's senses before disappearing as suddenly as it had arrived. Ashael found herself firmly rooted back in her own body. She sat back on her heels and looked at her friend.

'I want Bhearra to take a look at you.' Ashael leaned on the side of the pallet and pushed herself to her feet. Her vision began to tunnel, and a cold sweat prickled on her skin. She hung her head and took several deep breaths.

'Ash? What's wrong?' Rana asked, sitting up and reaching to support her friend.

'Just dizzy. I think I stood up too quickly.'

'Maybe Bhearra should take a look at *you*,' Rana said, frowning.

'Why don't we both go and see her? We can take some food over.'

***

Bhearra and Ashael made their way across the cam early the next morning. Bhearra shivered and pulled her shawl tighter around her shoulders. Daytime temperatures were rising but it was still cold this early in the day. Bhearra stole a glance at Ashael. The younger woman looked pale, and dark circles had reappeared beneath her eyes. It had been a long night, but Ashael had already looked like this when she arrived with Rana, and Bhearra had her suspicions about what had caused it.

Bhearra had examined Rana, and found no trace of anything wrong with her; in fact, she appeared to be in very good health. There were only two explanations: either Ashael was wrong about what she had felt, or she had unknowingly healed Rana. Bhearra was quite certain it was the latter. In fact, she was sure that Ashael had also unknowingly healed Rill.

The two women entered their home and Bhearra went straight to the hearth to heat water.

'Some tea before bed?' she asked her apprentice.

'I wasn't planning on sleeping. Don't we need to prepare Arron for the farewell rite?'

'We can rest for a notch or two. Come, sit with me.'

Ashael sat on the floor and leaned her head back against the wall. Bhearra ground some pepper root and added it to the water she was heating.

'Rana said you had another dizzy spell, after you examined her.'

'I stood up too fast. It was nothing.'

'I think not,' Bhearra said, handing Ashael a cup of the pepper root tea.

'What else could it be?' said Ashael, frowning.

'I believe you are healing people, unintentionally, and that it is draining you.'

'How could that even happen?'

Bhearra sighed and stood in front of the hearth. 'I am not certain. I suspect it is because you care so much about others' wellbeing. I think you may be sending some of your own health to them.'

'Is that how healing works for you?'

'A little like that, but I have to concentrate in order to do it. It is not easy; I could not do it without knowing.'

'Then why do you think that's what I'm doing?'

'Rill should have been showing some effects from his time in the river, especially if he was cold enough to have been incoherent and then passed out. Yet he was entirely well when I saw him. You, however, looked ill. And now you bring Rana to me and tell me you felt something amiss in her blood but, when I examine her, she is in enviable health and again you look ill.' Bhearra paused and looked deep into Ashael's eyes. 'It seems the only reasonable explanation.'

'So, what does it mean? If you're right, that is?'

'I don't know. That is what worries me.' Bhearra leaned her chin in a cupped hand and looked hard at her apprentice. 'You seem to be developing skills outside of what we have worked on. I'm happy to see you grow, but it's important to understand how our magic works. We cannot create energy. We can only work with what is there. So, you can mend a broken arm, but you cannot grow a new one. You can make flowers grow in winter because the seed waits underground, but you cannot bring water from rocks. Do you understand?'

'Yes, I think so,' Ashael answered.

'Every time you heal someone, the energy must come from somewhere. You must be careful that you do not use more of your own than you can spare.'

Chapter Nine

ASHAEL BENT OVER THE STREAM AND REFILLED HER WATERSKIN. WHEN IT WAS full, she hung it from her belt and scooped up a handful of the clear, cold water, splashing it on her face. It was a warm day, and she was sweating lightly. Feeling refreshed, she stood and stretched then turned back towards the plain. The grass was beginning to grow again, reaching above her ankles. Later in the summer it would come up to her knees and would be more difficult to forage in. The clumps of bushes were all gaining their leaves and starting to fill out. Ashael loved this time of year – the feeling of growth and new beginnings that surrounded everything.

Shading her eyes, Ashael checked the position of the sun. Just past midday: she had only a little more time before she had to head to meet the others. She had split off from the main foraging group to look for blackweed for Bhearra. She had need of some time alone.

She hadn't healed anyone since Rana. If she *had* healed Rana. She wasn't as sure as Bhearra about what happened the night Arron died. Ashael saw movement from the corner of her eye and her heart sped up. It was the third time she had seen it since she had left the group.

'Hello?' she called. 'Is someone there?'

No answer.

Ashael stood still, scanning for signs of anyone else nearby. All was still, but the hair on the back of her neck stood up. She felt someone watching her. Her hand dropped to her belt, and she carefully unhooked her sling, pulling a stone from her travelling pouch and dropping it into the cradle. She stood like that, waiting, until her fingers began to cramp from gripping the sling so tightly. She shook her head and dropped her arms, the sling bouncing off her leg.

She had been practising with the sling and was improving each time, although she had to practice alone since Iwan was still avoiding her. Every time she tried to speak to him, he made an excuse to be elsewhere. She was hurt and angry, with herself as well as with him. Why did she care so much? He had made it clear that he wasn't interested in her.

She set off, muttering to herself, but as she passed a group of bushes, the leaves rustled. Allowing all of her frustration to come to the surface, Ashael spun around, sling already in motion. The stone flew straight into the centre of the bushes.

'Ow!'

Ashael had another stone seated in the cradle of the sling before the leaves parted. But there was no need for it: stumbling out of the bushes, rubbing at his shoulder, came Iwan.

'Iwan? What in the All-Mother's name are you doing?' Ashael demanded.

Iwan avoided her gaze. 'You're getting good.'

'Are you so desperate to avoid speaking to me that you feel the need to hide? Why are you out here, anyway?'

'I...' Iwan paused as he continued to rub his shoulder. 'I was... following you.'

'What? Why?' Ashael had been prepared for any answer but this. She took a step back.

'I was concerned about you, that's all.'

'What danger could there be?'

Iwan's eyes shifted, and he finally looked at her. 'I don't know. I just wanted to be sure you would be safe.'

'You could have done that by coming with me, instead of sneaking along at my back.' Ashael was furious but she couldn't ignore the fact she had injured him. 'Let me see your shoulder.'

'I'm fine. I should go.' Iwan turned and began to walk away.

'What did I do? Why do you keep running away from me?'

Iwan stopped, his back to her. 'You didn't do anything.'

'Then what is going on?'

Iwan turned around, his face so distraught that Ashael gasped. She took three quick steps and was by his side. 'What is it, Iwan?'

'I can't tell you.'

'Let me help you.' She cupped his cheek. 'Whatever it is, we can work on it together.'

'I can't. My mother...' Iwan leaned his forehead against Ashael's.

She could feel the pain in him, a deep-seated conflict. His closeness was overwhelming her, making her tremble. She knew that the sensible thing to do would be to step back, to insist that they talk through whatever was causing him such distress. Instead, she kissed him. Again.

***

THE MOUNTAINS REARED against the darkening sky. Ashael shivered as a cold breeze caught her hair and swept it around her face. The temperature had dropped considerably when the sun disappeared behind the mountains. She had been late to the lightning tree, where they had agreed to meet, but there was still no sign of the foraging party. *Where are they? They wouldn't have gone back without me, would they?* She wished Iwan had stayed with her, but she had sent him ahead, insisting she would be safe. She still had no idea what he thought she needed protection from. A flush worked its way up her neck as she thought of him. She could still smell him on her hair, taste his lips. There was something strange going on with him, but she no longer doubted his feelings for her.

Pacing back and forth beneath the lightning tree, Ashael took some dried meat from the travelling pouch fastened to her belt and nibbled at it while she tried to decide what to do. *They must have gone ahead without me. Even if they didn't, I have to leave now if I want to make it back before full dark.*

A chill of foreboding swept over Ashael as another cold breeze pulled at her light spring cloak. With a last look back along the trail, Ashael tightened her cloak around herself and set off towards Oak Cam.

As she walked, the feeling that something was amiss grew stronger. She knew she was being irrational but increased her pace all the same. Bhearra had told her many times to trust her instincts but, despite the gifts that had led to her apprenticeship to the filidh, Ashael often found her senses at war with her innate logic. Lost in thought, she did not notice that her legs were carrying her faster and faster of their own accord until she broke into a run. Feeling frantic now, she headed toward the cam at full speed until she caught her foot on a root and fell heavily to the ground.

Sprawled face first on the forest floor, breathing heavily, Ashael berated herself for being so careless. Climbing gingerly to her feet, she discovered she had injured the ankle that had caught on the root. Carefully, she reached down and felt it. The area was already swelling and felt warm to the touch, but she could put her weight on it. 'Fool,' she muttered under her breath, and set off again, slowly this time.

By the time Ashael approached the cam, she was limping heavily. Her feeling that something was wrong had disappeared altogether and she was embarrassed by her panic. People waved or called out to her, and she waved back but kept her course. Half-way to the Heart-Fire, Joren appeared beside her.

'What happened?'

'I know I'm late. I'm sorry, Joren. I hope you didn't send anyone to look for me.'

'Why are you limping? Where are the others?'

Ashael stopped and looked at Joren, confused. 'Aren't they here?'

'No. You're the first to return. Are you injured?'

'My ankle. I don't know where the others are.' Panic began to rise inside Ashael again.

'Let's get you to Bhearra so she can check that ankle. Then maybe you can explain to me why it is that you are wandering around alone in the dark.' He offered his arm to her, and she leaned on it, gratefully.

Joren held back the entrance curtain for her and Bhearra told Ashael to sit, immediately moving to the shelves of herbs lining the walls. She muttered to herself as she selected different plants, placing them into a stone mortar. When satisfied, she ground the herbs and added them to a cup of steaming water drawn from the cauldron in the centre of the room.

'Drink this for the pain while I take a look at what you've done to yourself. Joren, please stand to the right, out of my light.'

Ashael cradled the warm cup in her hands and stretched her leg out for Bhearra to look at while Joren moved around to her other side.

'Now, what happened out there?' Joren asked.

Ashael explained how she had been late to meet up with the group. She didn't mention Iwan. She knew, eventually, that Joren and Bhearra would need to know about whatever it was Iwan was hiding, but first she wanted to try and get through to him herself. 'I waited until it was almost dark. I thought they must have come back without me.' She inhaled sharply as Bhearra manipulated her swollen ankle: 'There – that hurts.'

Bhearra moved Ashael's ankle a few more times, then probed it with firm but gentle fingers. Ashael was aware of Bhearra's power and could feel her mentor stretching her senses into the injured ankle.

'It's as I thought; you have a small fracture. Don't worry, I can mend it, but how did it happen?' Bhearra asked.

'I tripped over a tree root.' Ashael's cheeks coloured with embarrassment.

'Wandering along with your head in the clouds?' teased Joren.

'It was dark, and I was running.'

'You were running in the dark? You're lucky it's your ankle that is broken and not your neck!' Joren shook his head.

'Why were you running, child?' asked Bhearra.

'At the lightning tree, I felt something out of place. As I walked back here the feeling got stronger and I started to panic. I didn't even really realise that I was running until I fell.' Ashael looked up at Joren. 'Do you think something could have happened to them?'

'I don't know. I can't see what would have happened to prevent the whole group from returning. There were seven people in the party. If someone had been injured at least one would have come back to fetch Bhearra. Maybe they took longer than expected and decided to make camp for the night.' Joren patted Ashael's shoulder.

'Wouldn't they have sent someone to meet me and let me know?'

'Maybe someone was there, and you missed them because you were late.' Joren said in a reasonable tone. 'Will you be alright?'

'I'm fine.'

'If you don't need me for anything, Bhearra, I have Heart-Fire duty tonight.' Joren stepped towards the door.

'I will speak with you later,' Bhearra said, sitting back on her heels and smiling at the cam leader.

Ashael leaned her head back and closed her eyes as Bhearra spread a poultice over her swollen ankle. Despite her best efforts, tears began to leak from beneath her eyelids.

'This is going to need a splint and you'll have to rest it for a few days, but the poultice will speed the healing. Now, tell me exactly what happened.'

So Ashael went over it all again. Bhearra listened closely as her hands did their work with the splint and Ashael began finally to relax.

'What do you think it means, Bhearra?'

'I don't know. This feeling of yours worries me but there is little we can do without more information. Now, you rest while I make us a meal. You'll be hungry, I'm sure.' Bhearra squeezed Ashael's hand then moved to the other side of the hearth where the food was kept.

Ashael was starting to drift off to the scent of wild onions and garlic sizzling when the curtain was swept aside, and Rana rushed in.

'Ashael, what happened? Joren told me you were hurt! Are you well?'

'I injured my ankle in a stupid fall but I'm fine.'

'Joren seemed worried, but he said everything was fine when I asked. Is there something I should know?'

She told Rana the story of what had happened but played down her fear for the foragers, while Bhearra finished preparing a stew of rabbit with wild greens and nut cakes. Somehow, Ashael's experience seemed less frightening this time and she ended up laughing over her dash through the dark. Bhearra offered a bowl to Rana, who declined then sat beside Ashael and took one of her nut cakes.

'Hey, I thought you'd already eaten,' Ashael laughed, swatting Rana's hand as she dipped the nut cake into Ashael's stew.

'I did. I guess I'm hungrier than I thought. I can't seem to eat enough these days.'

Ashael looked closely at her friend. She looked a little tired but otherwise well. 'I guess you need it then,' she said, offering Rana some of the sturdy greens which she used to scoop up the stew. 'Did I miss anything interesting around here today?'

'Well, I think Lora might be pregnant again, but she hasn't said anything yet. She's been looking green in the mornings. I'm happy for her but frustrated, too; she seems to get pregnant as soon as she thinks about it!'

'All things come in their own time,' Bhearra said. 'Have faith.'

'I know, but it's easier said than done, Bhearra. I keep praying that the gods will give us a child.' Rana paused for a moment, looking wistful. 'Anyway, Bran asked Elwa to be his mate last night. He's going to build them a home in the branches. Creon offered to help. Bran is good with wood, but Creon is the best. I'm surprised that Elwa waited so long for him – if I'd been in her shoes, I would have asked him myself ages ago!'

Ashael leaned back and listened to Rana chatter on about the people and happenings of the cam. It was amazing: she always seemed to know everything. The pain and fear of the last few hours faded in the glow of companionship and the warmth of the food. Feeling better, Ashael went through her foraging bag and sorted the herbs. She trimmed them and tied them in bunches which she handed to Bhearra, who tied them to the walls and ceiling around the room.

'I'd best be going,' Rana said, yawning. 'I'm tired all of a sudden.' She hugged Ashael gently and gave Bhearra a playful salute then ducked out the door. As soon as Ashael was sure that Rana was out of earshot she turned to Bhearra.

'Is she?'

'It's too early to be sure but I would say so. We'll keep an eye on her.' Bhearra started to heat more water in the cauldron. 'You should have some more tea for the pain before bed. I could do with something to warm these old bones myself.'

After some tea, Ashael and Bhearra went to their respective alcoves off of the main room. Ashael undressed and lay down on her pallet. The evening was warm, so she pulled only a light blanket over herself and lay staring into the dark. She was worried about the foraging party but had almost convinced herself that they were just camping out for the night. Sooner than she expected, the trials of the day overcame her, and she fell into a deep sleep.

***

IWAN PACED ACROSS his hut, the light of the fire making his shadow dance on the walls. He couldn't do this anymore. He couldn't live with the duplicity. He had been avoiding Ashael in the hope that he could draw Meegrum's attention away from her, or at least avoid giving Meegrum any more information on her than he already had, but today had shown him he couldn't keep it up. He loved her. He couldn't stay away from her. And he was worried that the Zanthar were already a threat to her.

He had contemplated taking his own life but then he wouldn't be able to warn the Folk of the danger they were in, and his death would be in vain. What's more, if the Zanthar realised that was what he had done, they would probably kill his mother. Of course, they might do that anyway, but he had to do his best to give her a chance to survive. After the time with Ashael today he had been close to doing it anyway, but he would need to find some way to make it look like an accident. He couldn't keep lying to her, putting her in danger.

Then, this evening, another idea had come to him. He had been skinning a squirrel for his evening meal when the thought hit him like a lightning bolt: perhaps he could cut his slave-brand away? After all, the scar was only skin deep. If he could do that, would he be free? Would Meegrum know what he had done, or would he think Iwan dead? This could be a way to save everyone. If the Zanthar didn't know he had betrayed them, they might keep his mother alive. And if it worked, if he was free, he could tell Ashael everything; the thought stopped him in his tracks. What would she say? What would she think of him? After all, he had come here a spy, however unwilling. What he had seen had put them all in danger, especially Ashael. Iwan put his hands to his lips, as though he could still feel her there. She might tell him to leave. She might decide she never wanted to look at him again. He hung his head and let out a heavy sigh. He would just have to take the chance. Ashael was a good person. She might find a way to forgive him. And if not... *Well, at least I'll have finally done the right thing.*

Before he could change his mind, Iwan pulled off his tunic and grabbed his skinning knife from the mat on the floor, where he had left it. *All-Father, I know I am new to you, but I am trying to help your people. Please guide me.* The brand was high on Iwan's chest. He placed the blade of the knife against the side of the scar and pressed until it pierced the skin. Blood quickly welled from the cut and began to run down his chest. It made his hand slippery, and he tightened his grip on the leather handle of the knife.

At first the pain was bearable but as he lifted the skin and pressed the knife further into the wound, he began to pant. Sweat poured into his eyes and he blinked rapidly, trying to clear his vision. He pulled at the skin and hacked with the knife. His vision swam and took on a yellow tinge around the edges. He would not stay conscious much longer. Blood soaked into the waist of his trousers, and he swayed on his feet. He made one more cut and just had time to hope it was the last one before he passed out.

Chapter Ten

MEEGRUM LED THE WAY ALONG A PASSAGE BELOW THE KEEP. THE STONE WALLS were cold and the passage dark, lit only by the guttering torch he carried. Daven walked behind, moving almost silently, only the occasional faint rustle of cloth betraying his presence. Meegrum was anxious as they neared the dungeon; so much of what was to come rested on this beginning.

'We have come far, you and I,' Daven said.

'Yes, my lord, I was thinking the same thing.'

'Our time has come again, Meegrum. We shall rise in power to exceed where we were before, and you shall be rewarded for your loyalty.'

'I will always be your servant, my lord,' Meegrum responded as they reached the door. He passed his hands around the edges of the door while breathing words in the old language. A blue light shimmered, and the door swung open, revealing a large chamber. Around the walls were spluttering torches casting a fitful light over the seven people who lay bound on the floor.

'Why are there only seven? There should be eight!' the lord demanded.

'The warriors reported they had captured the whole group, my lord. I shall summon Devorik to explain himself.' Meegrum closed his eyes and sent out a mental call to the leader of the warrior unit who had carried out the mission, while Daven moved around the room, examining the prisoners.

'It's her: the enchantress is missing.' His master's voice was deadly calm., but a shiver worked its way down Meegrum's spine. She had been the main target of the raid, the rest of the group taken only to mask her disappearance.

'My lord, I don't know how this could have happened.'

The two men waited in growing tension until Devorik hurried into the room and knelt at Daven's feet, lowering his bulky frame with difficulty.

'My lord is there some problem?' he asked, voice shaking.

'Tell me what you see here, oh mighty warrior.'

Devorik looked cautiously around the chamber. 'I see the prisoners, my lord.'

'How many?'

'There are seven, my lord.'

Daven leaned over Devorik where he still knelt. 'Can you explain to me why there are not eight?' he asked in a silky tone.

'My lord? We captured the whole group, as you ordered.'

'Eight people left that cam this morning, Devorik, and the only one you did not capture was the one I truly wanted!' Daven pinched the bridge of his nose. 'Meegrum, light a fire.'

'Of course, my lord.' Meegrum moved to the fire pit in the centre of the chamber. He used flint and steel to strike a spark amongst the kindling that was already laid.

'She must have split off from the group before we captured them, my lord,' Devorik stammered, still kneeling.

'Really? Why didn't I think of that?' Daven answered, drily. He wandered over to a table that ran along the far wall, littered with implements of torture. He picked up a thumb screw and turned back towards Devorik.

'I'll go back out now and find her, my lord!'

'Her friends have all gone missing. She will have returned to the safety of the cam by now, I'm sure,' Daven said, fiddling with the thumb screw.

Meegrum added wood to the fire and watched Daven casually toss the thumbscrew back onto the table.

'I'll wait as long as it takes for her to leave again, my lord. I will find her and bring her to you!'

Daven picked up the brand they used on slaves. He looked at Devorik over the top of it and then carried the metal rod to the fire and placed it carefully into the heart of the flames.

'Tell me, how would you punish such incompetence in your men?' Daven asked, still looking into the flames.

Devorik swallowed hard. 'Death, my lord.'

'Well, since I am a merciful lord, I will spare you that fate.' Daven looked up and Meegrum supressed a shiver at the madness in his eyes. 'You can keep your life. As a slave.'

'My lord, please, no,' the warrior begged.

Daven lifted the brand from the flames, letting Devorik get a good look at the glowing metal.

'I will get her for you, my lord, whatever it takes.'

'You have one more chance, Devorik. Fail me again and I swear I will brand you a slave and send you back to Zan! Now, get out of my sight.' Daven tossed the brand across the room. It bounced off the wall and fell to the floor with a clatter. Devorik rose hurriedly and stumbled toward the door, face pale with fear.

Daven turned to Meegrum, who was kneeling by one of the prisoners.

'This one is strong, my lord. He is fully conscious. The others linger between sleep and waking.'

Daven strode over to the prisoner and yanked his head up by the hair. The face looking back at him was that of an older man, weather-worn but apparently healthy.

'Where is the enchantress? The one you call Ashael.' The name sounded strange in Daven's rasping voice. Alien and powerful.

The prisoner pulled his head from Daven's grip and Meegrum struck him hard across the face. His lord caught the prisoner by the hair again.

'You *will* tell me. Where is the enchantress?' The prisoner stared into his captors' eyes and then spat at him. Daven grabbed the prisoner's head and smashed it against the wall behind him. The prisoner's eyes rolled back, and he slumped to the floor, knocked out. Bright blood ran down his neck from the gash to his scalp.

'What would you do with these others, my lord?' Meegrum asked. 'Shall I dispose of them?'

His master thought for a moment, gloved fingers pressed to his lips. 'No. I think not. They may prove useful yet.'

Meegrum stood and renewed the spell keeping the prisoners in their slumber and securing the room before following his master out.

As they made their way back along the passage toward the rest of the keep, Meegrum was aware of his lord's brooding silence, anger threatening to turn to depression.

'My lord, this is a delay, to be sure, but it does not threaten our goal. There is still more than a full cycle of the moons until the solstice. We shall have her in our dungeon long before then.'

'We are not yet sure that she is the one we seek. The fact she is an enchantress does not necessarily mean she is the Vessel.'

'She is the most likely candidate, my lord.'

'Indeed, but we must have her in time to be sure before the solstice.'

Chapter Eleven

I T WAS LATE BY THE TIME ASHAEL AWOKE THE NEXT DAY; ALMOST MID-MORNING, given the angle of the sunlight streaming in the window. She washed with a bucket of cold water she had drawn from the nearby stream the day before and dressed while trying to avoid standing on her injured ankle. Bhearra was smoothing a length of wood when Ashael hobbled into the main room.

'Creon gave me this wood for you to use as a staff. You're going to need it for a while. Over at least the next few days you should walk as little as possible. Sit down and let me reapply the poultice.'

Ashael sat down as requested and Bhearra handed her some more of the pain-killing tea.

'How does it feel?' Bhearra asked as she started to spread more of the poultice on Ashael's ankle.

'It's painful, but not unbearable. The itch is worse than the pain.'

'That's the bone mending. Not much to be done for that part but wait it out.' Bhearra held the ankle between her hands and Ashael felt warmth sinking into the joint. 'Joren has already been in this morning. He's going to wait until noon for the foragers to return and if there is no sign of them, he'll send a search party. '

Gethyn poked his head through the entrance. 'May I come in?'

'Of course,' Bhearra answered, getting to her feet.

'Alayne expected to be back last night. Joren said you don't know where the others are?' Gethyn said, wringing his hands.

'I'm sorry, Gethyn,' said Ashael. 'I went to collect medicinal herbs while they carried on looking for food. We were supposed to meet at the lightning tree but I was late to get there.' Ashael reached out and squeezed Gethyn's hand. 'I'm sure Alayne will be fine. They probably just got held up and decided to camp out. Where is Rhys?'

'I left him with my mother. He loves to watch her make bowls. Alayne thinks that something in the rhythm soothes him.'

'Ashael, why don't you go and visit Rhys?' Bhearra suggested. 'I'll walk over with you, and you can spend some time with him until his mother comes back. You can help Hazel decorate the bowls for the Longest Day ritual.'

Ashael knew Bhearra was trying to give her something to keep her mind occupied and she smiled gratefully.

'I'll let Hazel know you're coming,' Gethyn said. 'Then I'll be going fishing. I promised Creon I would help with his nets.' He turned towards the door and then looked over his shoulder at Asahel. 'If Alayne gets back before I do, will you ask her to come and see me? We'll be up near the white water, towards Trout Cam.'

'Of course.'

They had to pass Iwan's hut on the way to Hazel's so Ashael suggested they check on him. She hadn't seen him since they parted company the day before and she was surprised he hadn't heard about her injury and come to check on her, especially since he seemed convinced that she needed protection from something.

They stopped outside his hut, the curtain still hanging over the entrance. That was unusual; he normally hooked the curtain back through the day.

'Iwan?' Ashael called.

There was no answer.

'Iwan, are you there?'

There was a groan from inside. Ashael and Bhearra exchanged a worried glance before pushing the curtain aside and entering the hut. Ashael gasped, her hand flying to her throat.

Iwan lay on the floor in a spreading pool of blood.

He groaned again, shaking Ashael from her paralysis. She dropped to her knees and crawled to his side. A foraging knife was clasped loosely in Iwan's hand, its blade stained with blood. His chest was bare, exposing a bloody wound. Ashael gently probed at it. It was shallow, more of a slice, really – a flap of skin was still attached at one side. Blood was oozing from the wound, clotting. This had happened a while ago. His skin was hot and clammy.

Bhearra knelt by Iwan's other side, checking his breathing and heartbeat. Iwan groaned again when Bhearra lifted his eyelid, checking his pupil. Ashael grabbed a tunic from the floor and balled it up, pressing it to the wound.

'He's stable but he has a fever,' said Bhearra. 'We need to move him. You start cleaning the wound while I go for help.' Bhearra got to her feet and handed a bucket of water and a rag to Ashael before ducking out.

'You're going to be fine,' Ashael murmured to him as she dabbed the wound. 'What happened? Who did this to you?' Ashael looked down at the knife in his hand. Had he fought with someone? How had it come to this?

Iwan did not respond. His eyes flickered under his eyelids.

'What do you see?' Ashael asked, smoothing his hair away from his brow. She went back to work, cleaning the area around the wound. She moved the flap of skin back, trying to line it up. Perhaps it could be saved. Her eyes widened as she cleaned the blood away. There was a scar here. It looked like a burn scar, but it was in a clearly deliberate pattern. Someone had burned this shape onto his chest. Ashael's eyes were again drawn to knife in Iwan's hand.

'Oh no, Iwan.' The words escaped her in a rush as she realised that Iwan had most likely done this to himself. He had tried to cut the scar off.

Joren and Gerod carried Iwan to the filidh's home. Ashael and Bhearra walked just behind them, Ashael explaining what she had found in a low voice.

'Why on KalaDene would someone deliberately burn a pattern into his skin?' Bhearra asked.

'Have you ever heard of such a thing?' Ashael responded.

'Never. You said the scarring looked old?'

'Yes. It must have happened when he was little more than a boy.'

'Some sort of manhood ritual, perhaps?' Bhearra pondered. 'It is possible that his people have customs different from our own.'

'True, but then why would he try to cut it off?' Ashael asked, frowning.

'We can ask him when he wakes.'

Inside the tree home Joren and Gerod lay Iwan on the floor next to the hearth. Ashael immediately started heating water while Bhearra gathered herbs to treat the wound.

'What can we do to help?' Gerod asked, stepping out of Bhearra's way as she went from shelf to shelf.

'You have done all that we need, thank you. Ashael and I can manage from here. I would ask only that you don't speak of this until we know what happened.' Bhearra patted Gerod on the arm as she spoke.

Even in her distressed state, Ashael noticed the warmth between the two old friends, and smiled.

Gerod returned to his work, asking them to call for him if they needed anything. When he had gone, Bhearra removed the tunic that Ashael had draped over Iwan's torso and examined the wound.

'I believe your suspicions are correct, Ashael,' she said. 'It looks like Iwan did this to himself.'

Joren took a stool in the corner, careful to stay out of the way while the two women worked. Ashael brought over the water she had heated and carefully poured it over the wound. Iwan didn't react, which worried Ashael; he must be deeply unconscious.

She took his hand in hers and traced the lines on it while Bhearra ground herbs to treat any infection which she then mixed with water to form a thick paste. When Bhearra slathered the mixture on his chest, Iwan tensed but did not awaken. Bhearra carefully repositioned the hanging flap of skin over the wound.

'Should we do that?' Ashael asked. 'If he really was trying to cut it off, should we put it back?'

'The skin can be saved. It gives his wound the best chance of healing. Without being able to ask what he wants...' Bhearra shrugged and bandaged the wound.

Ashael stayed close to Iwan's side all afternoon, but he did not wake. His fever continued, despite Bhearra's best efforts. All they could do now was watch over him and wait.

That night, Bhearra and Ashael ate with Joren and Rana, updating each other on the happenings of the day. A search party had departed just after noon, while Ashael and Bhearra had been busy with Iwan. They had not yet returned. It was clear from Joren's grave expression that he was deeply concerned. As the four finished their meal, a voice called from the entrance.

'Come in, Bran.' Joren called back.

Bran entered, flushed and breathing heavily. Joren motioned for him to sit and offered him some water to drink.

'We found their bags and supplies, but no sign of the group.'

'What exactly did you find?' Bhearra asked.

'About a notch north of the lightning tree we found their foraging bags and tools lying abandoned in a circle. There were full waterskins and uneaten food. It looked as if they had stopped for a meal, but I have no idea what could have happened next. There were no tracks leading away, no signs of predators, nothing.'

'What did you do with it all?' Joren asked.

Bran gulped down some more water before answering. 'Creon and Bres stayed there tonight in case anyone returns. We left everything as we found it. I thought Bhearra might wish to see it.'

'You did well, Bran,' Bhearra said. 'I think we should go there first thing tomorrow, Joren.'

Joren paced the room in frustration. Ashael gazed at the wall, feeling a sharp stab of guilt that she had not been with the rest of the foragers when they had faced whatever trouble had happened.

'Call everyone together,' Joren said, 'We need to make an announcement.'

***

Ashael and Bhearra approached the Heart-Fire and took their places beside Joren and Rana. The soft murmuring of the Folk stilled as Joren stepped forward.

'Thank you all for coming together. As many of you are aware, the foraging party did not return yesterday, and we assumed they had decided to camp for the night. When they still had not returned by noon today, I asked a group to go out and look for them in case they needed help. That group have now returned and have been unable to find the foragers.'

Concerned voices sounded from around the fire and the Folk turned to each other in confusion.

'What do you mean we can't find them?' asked Sola, whose mate, Colm, was in the missing party.

'There were signs of where they had stopped to rest yesterday but no indication of where they may be now.'

'How can a group of people just disappear?' shouted Hazel, who was carrying Rhys on her hip.

'At this time, I have no idea what could have happened,' Joren responded.

Many of the Folk began to look frightened, and everyone spoke at once. Joren paused for a moment, allowing the Folk to discuss the situation and acknowledge their fear.

'Bhearra and I will be going out to investigate tomorrow at first light. Bran and Gerod will accompany us, and Rana will lead the cam. Are there any questions?'

No one said anything.

'Very well, then. Bhearra, would you please lead us all in a prayer for the safety of the foragers and the success of our search for them?'

Bhearra stepped forward and raised her hands to the sky. Her voice rang out strong and comforting over the cam.

'All-Mother and All-Father, we beseech you. Some of our number are missing and we fear for their safety. We ask that you protect them and guide them back to their homes and to their hearts. We ask, All-Mother, that you provide your bounty to them and keep them nourished. We ask, All-Father, that you guide them that they may find their way home. We ask for your comfort for those of us who wait for their return with anxious spirits. Tend to us, as we tend to the eternal flame that marks the heart of this cam and its people. Tomorrow we send more of our people out to search. Please let their search be fruitful. Wrap them in your embrace and bring all of our Folk back to us. Guide our feet so that we walk in balance and harmony with you.'

Ashael looked around the gathered cam with tears in her eyes as Bhearra's voice stilled.

'Let it be!' the Folk affirmed as one.

***

IT WAS JUST before dawn and mist wreathed the cam. The search party were gathered by the Heart-Fire, talking quietly as they double-checked their supplies. Bhearra strode towards them, adjusting a travel pack over her shoulder, as Ashael limped behind.

Joren joined the party and greeted them, slinging a bow over his shoulder.

'Good morning, Joren,' said Ashael. 'I brought some supplies for you: a healing salve for cuts and burns, willow bark for pain, and heiro moss to prevent infection if anyone is wounded. I also made these –' along with a travel-pack containing the herbs, she handed Joren some wooden discs hanging from thin strips of leather. Each disc had a distinctive mark scored into it. 'They're talismans for protection – one for each member of the search party and seven more inside the bag for the foragers, when you find them.'

'My thanks, Ashael,' Joren said, turning away and moving around the search party to place a talisman around each person's neck. A few other Folk appeared to see off the search party as the cam slowly came to life for the day. When the first rays of sun speared between the trees, Bhearra and Joren led the group from the cam.

Ashael paused for a moment by the Heart-Fire and took some herbs from a pouch on her belt. With a murmured prayer, she scattered them into the fire that was always burning, offering them to the All-Mother and All-Father and asking for the safe return of all members of the cam.

***

THE SUN WAS high by the time the search party reached the edge of the forest and moved out onto the plains. Bhearra walked in the centre of the group, chatting to all, telling tales and generally keeping their spirits up. Joren was pleasantly surprised at how little she slowed them down. The tiny woman had a supply of energy that appeared inexhaustible, and Joren wondered, not for the first time, how Ashael could possibly take over from her.

Joren had been thrust into leadership of the cam at a young age and had relied heavily upon Bhearra, who had been his rock. He could not imagine trying to run the cam without her at his side.

Bhearra interrupted his thoughts. 'Joren, do you mind if we stop to rest for a few minutes?'

'Of course not. There's a stream just a few minutes ahead – we can rest there and top up our waterskins.' He offered Bhearra his arm and she gave him a grateful smile as she took it. 'It's not too much farther to the lightning tree and then just a notch or so beyond,' he added.

***

WHEN THEY REACHED the stream a short time later, Bhearra gratefully sat on a log a short distance away from the rest of the group and drank from her waterskin.

She took a travel cake from the pouch at her belt and nibbled it, savouring the taste and focusing on the feeling of replenishment she gained from the food and cool, clear water. Bhearra felt someone's eyes upon her and looked round, expecting to see one of the group approaching to tell her it was time to move on, but none of them was paying her any attention. She stood and slowly surveyed her surroundings. There was no one looking at her, but the feeling of being watched persisted. Bhearra closed her eyes and extended her senses. She felt the energy of every living thing around her: the people in her group, the small animals in the bushes and the fish in the stream, the insects darting about and the plants all around, even the blades of grass beneath her feet. She filtered out each stream of energy as she recognised its source. At last, she was left with a single stream of energy that she could not place. As soon as she reached out to touch it when her own senses, it withdrew and the feeling of being watched faded.

Bhearra walked over to Joren and, taking him by the arm, led him away from the rest of the group. 'Someone is using magic to spy on us. As soon as I became aware of it and tried to find the source, they stopped.'

'What does this mean? Who could even do such a thing?' he asked, voice worried.

'Most filidh could do it. The question is: why would they bother? It uses a lot of energy to do such a thing and you need to know roughly where the person is to watch them. That's why I can't use the skill to search for the foraging party. Can you think of any reason for another cam to spy on us?'

'No, not at all. We have nothing to hide from them.'

'I'll tell you, Joren, this makes me very uncomfortable, coming at the same time as the foragers going missing. There is more going on here than we aware of.'

***

BRAN LED THE search party to the spot where the foragers' tracks stopped. They found just what he had described the night before: the foragers' belongings scattered in a rough circle, abandoned.

'This is an ill place,' Creon said at Bhearra's side.

Although she agreed with this assessment, the filidh asked, 'What makes you say so?'

'There is food, see?' Creon pointed to half-eaten food at several points around the circle, and Bhearra nodded. 'No animals have come sniffing round, nor birds. When did you last see that?'

'Never,' Bhearra replied.

She patted Creon on the shoulder and strode to the centre of the circle before sitting on the ground. She twisted her head around to Joren, who was standing at her side.

'I'm going to see if I can feel anything,' she told him. Closing her eyes, Bhearra gathered her energy and began reaching out, questing for some sense of what had happened here. She focused her thoughts on Colm, one of the older members of the group and a long-time friend. Slowly, she began to get a sense of him, sitting at the other side of the circle, sharing food and laughing with the others. She could see his crinkled smiling eyes, his weather-worn face creased with laughter. Suddenly, everything went black. Bhearra could see nothing, hear nothing, and feel nothing. She was entirely cut off from the world. She cried out in surprise and fear but could not even hear her own voice.

Chapter Twelve

ASHAEL MOVED AROUND THE ROOM, CHECKING ON THE HERBS THAT HAD BEEN hung up to dry. She had some water heating and was looking forward to sitting down with some willow bark tea as soon as she was finished. Her ankle throbbed. She had been on her feet too much today but resting was no more in her nature than in Bhearra's. Iwan was still unconscious, but his fever had broken at last. He lay on a spare pallet dragged into the women's home and placed against the wall, a light blanket covering him. Ashael had cleaned his wound and changed his bandage a short while ago. She stopped what she was doing and looked at him sleeping. His breathing was deep and rhythmic.

I wonder where Bhearra is. She should have been back by now, she thought as she checked and re-tied the last bunch of herbs. As Ashael stretched and pushed her hair back from her face, she heard a commotion outside and hobbled to the entrance to see what was happening. Bran almost collided with her. He was flushed and gasping for breath.

'Come quick,' he panted. 'Something has happened to Bhearra.'

'Has she been injured?' Ashael cried as she grabbed her staff for support and hurried out to the centre of the clearing.

'Joren has her. Hurry.'

Bran led Ashael to the other side of the cam, where Joren now emerged from the trees carrying a limp, unconscious Bhearra is his arms. She looked so small and frail that Ashael feared the worst until she saw Bhearra's chest move.

'Lie her on the ground here. Let me a get a look at her. What happened?' Ashael demanded.

'We don't know,' Joren said, carefully laying the old woman on the ground.

'Her clothes are damp; did she fall into the river?'

'We were at the place where the foragers' tracks stopped. Bhearra said she was reaching out to try and get some sense of what might have happened. She just collapsed. We tried everything that we could think of to wake her, but she wouldn't come around, so Gerod dumped his waterskin on her – but she still didn't react. I carried her back here and she hasn't moved or given any sign of waking the whole way back. What in the name of the All-Mother has happened to her, Ashael?'

'I don't know. We need to get her inside; it's getting cool out here. Bran, can you please carry Bhearra to our home? Gerod, go and ask Rana to join us please.'

When they had Bhearra safely on her pallet, Rana helped Ashael remove the wet clothing and bundle her in blankets. Ashael knelt beside her, checking over every inch of her body. There were no signs of injury or illness. Ashael sat back on her haunches and thought. Joren was waiting impatiently behind her while Rana spoke comforting words to him in a low voice.

After a time, Ashael turned to them. 'Whatever happened must be something to do with her reaching out. I need to know every detail you remember.'

Joren told Ashael everything that had happened since he and Bhearra had left the cam. When he had finished speaking, Ashael looked at him in panic. 'If Bhearra is right and there is something magical going on, then I'm not sure how much help I can be. I've only been training with her for a year. I don't know anywhere near as much as she does. I can try and reach out to her spirit, but I've only just stared learning the technique – I don't know that I'll be able to reach her.'

'All you can do is try,' Joren said, sounding resigned.

Ashael knelt beside Bhearra again and closed her eyes. She tried to calm herself and find her centre, as Bhearra had taught her. She took a deep breath, held it and slowly let it out. She did this again. Again. Again. She felt herself calming, becoming aware of the edges of her senses, where she stopped and the rest of the world began. She reached out, looking for the familiar feeling of Bhearra's spirit. Nothing. Ashael reached harder. Straining to feel even a hint of Bhearra's presence. *She's lying right in front of me. I should be able to feel something.* Frustration and fear were crowding into Ashael's mind, drowning out her sense of calm. Try as she might, all she could sense was a wall of darkness. *This makes no sense!* Ashael could feel many other spirits around herself but not her mentor's. She stayed kneeling, reaching out for a long time.

At last, Ashael had to admit to herself that this wasn't going to work. She moved into the main room and approached Joren and Rana, who were seated by the fire. Night had begun to fall, and the room was dim.

'It's no use. I can't reach her,' Ashael said, hanging her head in shame.

'There must be something we can do,' Joren said, his voice tight.

'I don't know what else to try.'

'Why don't we all try to get some rest,' Rana said. 'Often the solution to a problem comes when you're not looking for it.'

Joren and Ashael exchanged a look, neither of them believing it would be that simple, but they took Rana's advice and bid each other goodnight.

***

BHEARRA DRIFTED IN the darkness, aware of having no physical sensations. Time had no meaning here; she had no idea how long she had drifted. *Am I dead?* she wondered. *If I was dead, then surely I would be in the Summerland with the ancestors? All-Mother, where are you? Sirion, won't you come to guide me home?* She reached out her senses and probed at the darkness.

***

MEEGRUM FELT THE pull of the mind-trap draining his power. He would not be able to hold the old woman for more than a few days at most; she was too strong, and he was already depleted from the spying he had been doing. Still, it amused him to have power over her, however fleeting. He had hoped that the cam's magical defences would collapse while she was trapped but that was not the case. He had sent out Devorik and his group of warriors but although they knew roughly where the cam was, it was cloaked to them and they were unable to find it, nor even the beech trees that they had seen in Iwan's memories. It appeared that an invitation from someone inside the cam was required to allow entry. Meegrum had no idea how a charm designed to keep the cam hidden from the animals that made the forest their home could possibly work to protect the cam from his warriors, but somehow it did. *It doesn't matter,* he thought. *Sooner or later, I'll find a way through their defences.*

***

ASHAEL AWOKE SLOWLY, unsure at first of where she was. Then memories of the day before came flooding back and she sat up, urgently checking Bhearra for any change. The wise-woman was exactly the same as the night before. Ashael put her hand to Bhearra's cold brow and sobbed.

'All-Mother, please help me. Your servant, Bhearra, is lost and I don't know how to help her. Please guide me in bringing her home. Let it be.'

Although reluctant to leave Bhearra's side, Ashael had to relieve herself. She stumbled through her morning ablutions, lost in sorrow. She checked on Iwan, carefully pouring some water over his lips. He instinctively swallowed but did not wake. She leaned over and kissed his forehead, a tear splashing onto his skin. *I can't help you; I can't help Bhearra. What use am I?*

The sound of someone clearing their throat just outside the doorway pulled Ashael from her thoughts. She limped over and pulled aside the leather curtain to find Joren standing outside.

'I wasn't sure if you would be awake yet,' Joren said. 'Any change?'

'Not yet,' Ashael sighed, stepping back and waving Joren inside.

'And Iwan?' Joren asked, looking at the other recumbent.

'The same. I don't know what to do for either of them.' Ashael rubbed her face, trying to scrub away her sadness and find a solution. 'I was just going to make some tea. Would you like to join me?'

Joren nodded and Ashael's eyes scanned the baskets of herbs lining the wall, considering what would be best to make. From the corner of her eye, Ashael noticed a golden glow surrounding some of the baskets. When she turned to face them, the glow had moved, staying in the periphery of her vision. A high, sweet sound began to chime in Ashael's head. 'Do you hear that?' she asked.

'Hear what?' Joren replied.

As Ashael turned to answer him, the golden light flooded her vision, blocking out everything around her. The chiming became louder, taking on an urgent tone. She swayed on her feet and Joren grabbed her arm, steadying her. Energy coursed through Ashael's body, electrifying her nerves, sizzling through her. She felt something inside her opening up, and suddenly she knew what to do. Still blinded by the golden light, Ashael moved to Bhearra's side with quick, sure steps, almost knocking Joren over. She placed her hands on either side of Bhearra's head and saw the darkness there.

***

BHEARRA DRIFTED, BUT with more purpose now. She was pushing at the darkness around her and could feel some give. She still did not know what held her here, but she was sure that, whatever it was, it was unnatural. She had no idea if she had been here for five minutes or five days but, sooner or later, she would find a way back.

***

ASHAEL PROBED AT the darkness with her mind. Somewhere in there, Bhearra was trapped and Ashael meant to get her out. She concentrated on the golden light surrounding her, drawing it into herself until she felt she was made of light. She paused for a moment, suddenly doubtful. *What am I doing? What if I hurt her?* The light started to dim. Ashael shook her head, shaking away her fear, and the light brightened again. The chiming noise sounded again and in it Ashael could almost hear a voice. *Now, my child.* She steadied her nerves, took a few deep breaths and then pushed the light toward Bhearra. The darkness fled before it.

***

MEEGRUM WAS WALKING along the stone corridor leading to his master's rooms when the mind-trap collapsed. Golden light exploded into his mind and sent him reeling to the floor. His eyes throbbed as if he had stared into the sun, but this fire was filling his mind rather than the sky. Fire spread through his body, burning him, and he screamed in pain. As suddenly as it had come, it disappeared, leaving Meegrum panting on the floor as a servant ran to his side. He pulled himself to his feet, clinging to the wall for support, black and green spots dancing across his vision. Whatever had just happened, it hadn't been the old woman, of that he was sure.

***

BHEARRA OPENED HER eyes and sat up. Joren moved to help her, his eyes bright. 'I thought we had lost you.'

'Not yet,' Bhearra responded, her voice rasping from thirst.

Ashael hurried to get some water for her, picking up a couple of nutcakes on the way back. As she passed, Iwan sat up, stretching as if waking from a normal slumber. Ashael faltered, not sure who to tend to first, until Bhearra walked into the main room, leaning on the arm that Joren offered. Joren assisted Bhearra while Ashael got water and food for Iwan.

'Do you remember anything about how you got here?' Ashael asked as he ate.

'No,' Iwan answered, but he wouldn't meet her eyes. Ashael felt sure that he was hiding something.

'There is a scar, on your chest-'

Iwan's face took on a look of panic and he jumped to his feet. 'Thank you for everything, but I am well now, and I need to... relieve myself. I will speak with you later.'

He bolted for the entrance and was gone. Ashael wanted to go after him. She thought he may be more forthcoming if they were alone, and he shouldn't be on his own, but she had to tend to Bhearra. Sighing, she decided to let him go for now.

The light was gone and Ashael felt over-used. Her eyelids were heavy, and the room was fuzzy at the edges. Ashael took a nut-cake herself and nibbled on it while Bhearra told them what she had experienced. Ashael studied her mentor, looking for any lingering side-effects or weakness. Instead, she saw a woman who looked 20 years younger than she had. Bhearra's long, white hair was thicker than it had been and the wrinkles on her face had smoothed out a little. 'How do you feel?' she asked when Bhearra had finished speaking.

'Truth be told, better than I have in years. Better than you, by the looks of it. How did you banish the darkness?'

Ashael told Bhearra all that had happened. She struggled to find the words to explain the sense of opening that she had experienced and the way she had drawn in the light before sending it to Bhearra.

'I always knew you were touched by the gods,' said Bhearra, 'but you may be even stronger than I had thought.' Bhearra looked down at her hands, her eyes widening as she realised how different they looked. 'It would seem that you have given me back some years. It has been prophesied for many years that at the time of our greatest need, one with the power of life itself would come amongst us. It could be that you are that one.'

Ashael opened her mouth to deny that this could be possible but before she could speak, Bhearra raised a hand to stop her. 'If, indeed, you are the prophesied one, then we should take note – that person is meant to come to us *at the time of our greatest need.* If that person is here now, then we have a powerful enemy who means to destroy our people. This could be worse even than the Zanthar. We must find out what happened to the foraging party and hope that gives us some clue as to what is coming.'

***

HEAD STILL POUNDING from the explosion of the mind-trap, Meegrum dragged one of the prisoners into the great hall – a young woman who was bound and gagged, her arms high over her head as she was pulled along the floor. Daven insisted that she be conscious but restrained. Meegrum dragged her in front of the empty hearth, where his lord waited, pacing in agitation. Crouching down, Daven stroked the woman's hair almost tenderly as her eyes darted about the room in fear. She strained against her bonds to no avail, trying to shrink back from his touch. Daven twisted his hand into the woman's hair and pulled her head back sharply, her cries of pain muffled by the gag. He smiled, making his scarred face even more grotesque.

'I love the taste of fear, Meegrum, don't you?' He looked over his shoulder at his most trusted servant, who stood looking on.

'Yes, my lord. It is quite enticing.'

'Then you must share this woman with me!'

Meegrum moved to kneel at the woman's other side. Excitement fluttered in his stomach as he looked down at her and thought of what was to come. He placed a hand on her stomach, shifting aside her clothing to feel her smooth, warm flesh. She bucked, trying to dislodge his hand, but Daven pulled her head back further. Her breath was coming in short, hard gasps now and Meegrum could feel her pulse racing beneath her skin. He ran his fingers down her torso to the waist band of the loose-fitting trousers that she wore. She kicked her legs out, fighting his touch.

'I do believe she thinks we're going to ravish her,' the lord chuckled. 'Alas, there's no time for that today.'

Daven and Meegrum each began to chant, their voices sounding as one as they leaned further over the woman. Her body went rigid and her eyes rolled back in her head, then she began to twitch and froth at the mouth while the men chanted louder and faster. Suddenly her body went limp, and as it did so, Meegrum and Daven's heads snapped back as her life force surged into them. Some of the grey in Meegrum's hair turned brown again and the lines around his eyes lessened as the ageing effects of the magic he had used earlier faded. His master, meanwhile, seemed to swell with vitality, although the scars remained.

As soon as the woman was drained, both men fell back, sitting on the floor, panting and grinning for a moment. Daven stood first and made his way to the table, where a pitcher of wine awaited. He poured a goblet and handed it to Meegrum as he approached.

'I have a plan to get the enchantress. Our friend here may be useful still,' he said, gesturing to the body of the woman on the floor. 'You're going to transport her and one of the other prisoners to the edge of the forest, with this message: we will exchange the rest of the group for the enchantress. She must be at the ford of the river at the edge of these mountains, where her people fish, at sundown three days from now. If she is not there at the appointed time, we will kill the rest of the prisoners and send them back in pieces.'

'Do you believe she will come, my lord?' Meegrum asked.

'If she doesn't choose to come herself, she will be shunned by her people. What is one life against the five who remain?'

'As you say, my lord. I'll do it immediately.'

'Wait. Partially burn her body before you send them. I would have her carry the same marks that I do.'

'And the live prisoner?'

'Do you remember the time-delayed death spell?'

'Yes, my lord,' Meegrum answered, a smirk making its way across his face.

'Give him ten days.'

***

Iwan climbed over a fallen tree and slid down the other side, landing clumsily in a pile of leaves. He was fleeing. He hoped the Zanthar would leave his mother alone, but he knew his actions might cause her death... *if she is even still alive. It has been almost three seasons since I left the keep.* If the Zanthar didn't already know that he had tried to remove his brand, then they would as soon as they tapped into his memories again. They would know he had tried to escape them, and they would kill him. He saw no reason to stay in the cam, putting more people at risk. His only wish was to make it back to the keep and see his mother one last time.

Stopping to rest for a moment, he leaned against a tree, wiping sweat from his forehead. He was surprised to realise there was no pain from his wound. Cautiously, he put his hand over the area and pressed: still no pain. Frowning, Iwan pulled his tunic over his head and inspected the bandage that Ashael had wrapped around his chest. There were traces of blood where it covered the wound. Heart pounding, Iwan unwound the bandage to find that the skin of his chest was smooth and unmarred. There was no sign he had ever been injured there, not even a scar. And there was no brand. Iwan ran his hand over the skin, disbelieving. No brand. It was truly gone. He sat down heavily, the air leaving him in a rush.

How can this be? What does it mean? Am I... am I free?

Chapter Thirteen

ASHAEL AWOKE TO BRIGHT SUNLIGHT STREAMING THROUGH THE SMALL WINDOW in her alcove. She stretched her arms above her head, arching her back. Despite a good night's sleep, she was still stiff from spending the previous night on the floor by Bhearra's side. She stood slowly and began her morning routine, thinking of all that had happened yesterday. Rana had joined them and the four of them spent most of the day talking about what they could do next. The problem was that so much was still unknown. Bhearra was planning to use some blackweed to enter a trance state, during which she would reach out to the spirits of the land and ask them for guidance.

Late in the day Ashael had gone looking for Iwan but was unable to find him. Gethyn had seen him heading out into the forest with a travel pack, before noon. He could be anywhere. Ashael rubbed her temples, tired and worried. Why had he run away from her as soon as he awoke? Was it possible he knew something about what had happened to Bhearra? She shook her head. Iwan had been unconscious before Bhearra left the cam; he couldn't have any information. *All-Mother, give me strength, let me think clearly.*

She finished dressing and stepped into the main room. Bhearra was not here and the curtain to her alcove was open, showing a neatly made pallet. Ashael wandered over to the hearth where she found some tea being kept warm in the embers of the fire and a bowl of the spicy stew they had shared last night. As she sat down to break her fast, Rana called out from the doorway. She bounced into the room with her usual energy then plopped herself down next to Ashael.

'How are you this morning?' she asked, helping herself to some tea.

'Worried.' Ashael replied, sighing. 'We're dealing with something completely beyond our experience, even Bhearra's. I'm concerned that the trance work she's going to do will be too much for her mind, after what she went through, but I can't see any other way to move forward. Do you know where she is? She really should be resting.'

'She's gone down to the stream to bathe. Joren sent Gerod with her to keep an eye on things. She'll be fine.' Rana squeezed Asahel's shoulder reassuringly. 'Can you do the trance work instead?'

Ashael sighed. 'No, I wish I could. A filidh spends years cultivating relationships with the land spirits. I just don't have the connections that Bhearra does.'

'But surely it's in their interests to talk to you? If things are as dire as Bhearra seems to think, it's unlikely they won't also be affected.'

'I'm afraid it's not as simple as that. The land spirits don't think like us. They don't value the same things. Just because something is bad for us, it isn't necessarily bad for the trees or the rivers. Do you see?'

'I suppose so.' Rana put her bowl down. 'There's something I wanted to talk to you about while we're alone.'

'Of course. What is it?' Ashael looked at her friend curiously, scraping the last of her stew out of the wooden bowl.

'I think I might be pregnant. My moon-time should have been twice since the last time, and I feel different. I'm tired and hungry a lot, and my breasts are very tender... but it could just be wishful thinking – you know how much I want this... What do you think? Am I deceiving myself?'

Ashael grinned. 'I think you're going to have a baby.'

Rana grabbed her so tightly, Ashael almost toppled over. Laughing, Ashael stroked Rana's hair while her friend wept.

After Rana left, Ashael gathered up the night-soil buckets and took them to the trench behind the cam where the Folk relieved themselves. She emptied them in, throwing some loamy earth mixed with fragrant flowers over the top. She returned the buckets then headed towards the stream to bathe, hoping to meet Bhearra there. Strolling through the forest and stepping over roots and undergrowth, Ashael realised her ankle no longer pained her. In fact, now that she thought about it, she hadn't had any pain since she saw the light the day before. She picked up her pace, testing her injury. She didn't have even a twinge of discomfort. *How can this be possible?* she wondered. *I have to tell Bhearra about this.*

Ashael was so lost in the wonder of her healed ankle that she didn't notice the sounds of someone approaching until they were almost upon her. Expecting to see Bhearra, Ashael glanced around only to stop dead in her tracks. A short distance away stood Faemon, one of the missing foragers. He swayed where he stood, face pale. In his arms, he carried something Ashael could not identify.

'Faemon! Where have you been? Are you well? Where are the others?' Ashael peppered him with questions as she moved towards him. He didn't answer, his throat working but no sound coming out. It was only as Ashael reached his side that she realised what he was carrying – a corpse. She could tell the body was female, but the features were unrecognisable, the face having been badly burned.

'What happened?' Ashael asked in a trembling voice, putting her hand on Faemon's shoulder. He raised his eyes to hers, a pain-filled expression that would haunt her always, before collapsing at her feet.

'Help!' Ashael screamed. 'I need help here!' She got to her knees, pushing the corpse from where it had sprawled over Faemon when he fell. Placing a hand on his chest, she leaned over, listening for his breath. He was breathing and she could feel his heart pounding strongly in his chest, but he looked weakened. His skin was pale and dry, and his lips were cracked; he had not had sufficient food or water while he was gone.

Ashael sat back on her heels as Gerod came running up, Bhearra just a pace behind him. They both looked stunned at the sight that greeted them. Bhearra immediately started giving orders as her eyes scanned Faemon and the body.

'Gerod, find Joren. Bring back a skin of water and some nuts.' As she spoke, Faemon's eyelids began to flutter, and he moaned. 'Hush now,' said Bhearra soothingly as she knelt awkwardly to feel his brow. 'You're home and you're safe. Rest.'

Ashael went over to the body. Fighting her own horror, she tried to roll it over. When she saw the full extent of the burns, covering the woman's face and torso, she turned around and retched, bringing up her breakfast. She looked at Bhearra, ashamed to have lost control in front of her mentor until she saw that the older woman was swallowing hard and looking pale. Taking some deep breaths, she turned back to the body, swiping at her eyes to clear her vision. Ashael still wasn't sure who she was looking at; three of the missing foragers were women.

She tuned out the sounds of Bhearra murmuring to Faemon and focused on the figure in front of her. She had seen burns before – fire supported the life of the Folk, but it was also dangerous if they forgot its power. These burns looked different somehow. There was no sign of weeping or swelling such as would be normal. *Could she have been burned after her death?* Ashael wondered. *But how? Why? It doesn't make any sense.* As she continued to examine the body, Ashael noticed a discolouration on the inside of the woman's elbow. A birthmark – a kiss of the gods. It was Nela. Ashael covered her mouth and allowed her tears to flow.

Gerod arrived with Joren just as Ashael pushed herself to her feet. Faemon had come around and was sitting up. Gerod handed him the waterskin, which he sipped from gratefully. Joren looked around the clearing, his eyes coming to rest on Nela's body. He started firing questions at Faemon, but Bhearra interrupted him.

'There will be time for questions back at the cam, but Faemon needs food and rest, and we should move the body before someone sees. We should find out more before we speak to the Folk.'

Joren grimaced, displeased at having to wait for answers, but he saw the wisdom in Bhearra's words and acquiesced with a nod. He moved to Faemon's side and helped him to stand, wrapping a strong arm around the other man's waist to help support his weight.

'The body is Nela's,' Ashael stated, her voice dull as she moved to wrap her cloak around the woman, hiding her from accidental view. She lifted the body at the shoulders and Gerod took the legs, though he looked ill at ease. The group slowly made their way between the trees, Bhearra in the lead, with Ashael and Gerod carrying Nela, and Joren behind, supporting Faemon.

Chapter Fourteen

Ashael felt numb. Her gaze was drawn to Nela's body lying against the back wall of the room. She dragged her attention back to Joren, who was pacing the floor and probing Faemon with questions.

'Are you sure you don't remember anything else?'

'Nothing. It's like I told you. I remember stopping to eat and rest on the way back. The next thing I knew, I was at the edge of the forest and Nela's body was beside me. A huge man towered over us. He was dressed strangely and looked... odd. He spoke as if he was having difficulty with the words; I struggled to understand him. He told me to give you a message and said if I failed, he would find me and kill me. He said Ashael has to go to the ford at the river Donn, where we fish sometimes, or the rest of the group I was with would end up like Nela. Then he stepped into a cloud and disappeared. One minute he was there, and the next I was alone.' Faemon picked at the food Bhearra had given him but didn't eat much. At least he was drinking the tea.

Ashael realised she was staring at Nela's body again. She and Bhearra had examined it and come to the conclusion that the burns came after death, but they had no idea what had actually killed her. Ashael slid along the floor to get closer to the fire. She couldn't seem to get warm enough. Her shoulders ached and she realised she was clenching her muscles. She closed her eyes and took some deep breaths, willing her body to relax.

A hand touched her shoulder and she looked up to see Gerod leaning over, holding a cup out to her: 'Bhearra said you should drink this.'

Ashael smiled at him as she took the cup then looked to Bhearra who was moving about on the other side of the fire, pouring hot tea into cups for everyone. Faemon sat close to her, on a stool by the fire, a deer-hide wrapped around his shoulders for warmth. Joren still paced, struggling with the need to do something but with no clear idea what that should be. Bran was posted at the door to make sure none of the Folk could enter unexpectedly. He stuck his head through the opening to let them know that Rana had arrived, seconds before she rushed in. Rana saw Faemon first and ran to him, hugging him tight. It was only then she noticed Nela's body against the wall. Her face turned white, and she swayed. Joren moved to steady her, but she brushed him off and raced outside where they could hear her retching. Joren went after her.

'Why me?' Ashael spoke for the first time in what felt like notches. 'Why would they want me? I mean, how do they even know my name?'

Faemon looked at her, confusion on his face. 'He didn't say, and he wasn't around long enough to ask. I can't say I would have thought to ask even if he had. The whole experience was so strange; I don't know how to think of it.'

Bhearra cleared her throat. 'It may be that it has do with what happened yesterday, child. We haven't had time to fully comprehend what you did, and you may be capable of much more than we know. That is a conversation for another time, though.' She looked up as Joren came back inside, leading Rana by the hand. 'What we need to talk about is what we do now.'

Ashael got to her feet and moved to Rana's side. 'Obviously, I have to do what they want.'

'Obviously, you're not going anywhere,' Joren responded.

'What?'

'We don't know who these people are or what they want. All we know is that they seem to have taken a whole group of people and killed at least one of them. We can assume they are behind what happened to Bhearra. There's no way we can just send you off to them.'

'How can you say that?' Ashael snapped. 'There are still five other people who need my help. There's no way I can just sit here and let them die.' Ashael's fists were clenched at her side, and she glared at Joren. Rana stifled a sob and leaned her head on Joren's shoulder, trying to avert her gaze from Nela's corpse. Joren stroked her back and glared at Ashael over her head.

Bhearra stepped between them, speaking in a soothing tone. 'Joren is right. I know you want to save the others, but you can't just go rushing headlong into danger. We can be sure these people have a purpose in all this, and it is unlikely to be good.'

Ashael turned her back on the others and walked over to the wall furthest from Nela's body. She rested her hands against the living wood of the great tree that provided her home. She sensed the life in the tree, its great age and the slow time it experienced. It served to centre her, and she let her emotions seep away into the ground beneath her feet before turning back.

'I should have been with them,' she said in a low voice. 'If I had been on time, I would have been with the foragers when they were taken. If it's me they want now, then maybe it was me they wanted then. I might have been able to prevent all of this. Nela's death could have been avoided. I have to save the others.' Ashael looked each of them in the eye. 'I have to.'

***

ASHAEL SWAM ACROSS the bathing pool, allowing the water to soothe and refresh her. She had to get away from the others. No one seemed to understand the obligation she had to save the foragers. She rolled over in the water and floated on her back, her long hair spread around her. She thought of Rhys, Alayne's son. She saw Gethyn wringing his hands, saw how lost he was without his mate. If she did nothing, how could she look at them again, knowing she may have been able to get Alayne home; knowing their loss may have been because of her?

Gazing up at the treetops, Ashael felt a stab of fear. She did not doubt that the men who held her friends would kill her, and she did not want to die. She thought of Rana and Bhearra, Joren and Gerod. There were people here that she loved and did not want to leave. She thought of Iwan with his kisses and his secrets. If she gave herself up, she would never find out his truth. There would be no chance to explore the feelings they had for each other. She thought of the filidh and realised she would never stand with them as a full member. *Why me? What could they want from me?* Ashael remembered Alayne's face the first time she held her son. *I have to go. I have to find a way to help her.*

She rolled over to swim back to shore and saw Bhearra sitting at the side, feet dangling in the water. Ashael swam over to her, rehearsing in her head all that she wanted to say.

'Peace, Ashael,' Bhearra called as Ashael got close.

The young woman pulled herself out of the water and roughly dried herself with her undertunic before pulling her dress over her head.

'Is it Alayne?' Bhearra asked. 'Is that why you wish to go?'

'In part,' Ashael admitted, sitting beside Bhearra, long legs tucked beneath her. 'It's not just her. Losing them all – it hurts the whole cam. I can't just stand by and do nothing.'

'I understand, dear, I do. But losing *you* could hurt the whole cam.'

'It's not the same. I'm just one person.'

'What if you are the one the prophecy spoke of, the one who will rise to protect us?'

'You spoke about this yesterday, but I can't see any link between the prophecy and me. I mean, I healed you, but I didn't know what I was doing. There's no guarantee I could do it again. Truthfully, I think it was the All-Mother working through me.'

'Does the All-Mother usually answer your prayers immediately and so obviously?' Bhearra picked up a stick and began twiddling it in her fingers.

Ashael huffed air out. 'If you have any reason other than what happened yesterday to believe I might be this person, then I'll start to consider it a possibility.'

'Very well,' Bhearra sighed. 'Let me tell you a tale. One day, twenty summers ago, Gerod and I were walking in the woods, down near the stream, when we heard a baby crying. We followed the sound and found a baby girl, about three moon-cycles old, lying in a willow basket, naked and healthy in a shaft of sunlight at the foot of an Ash. We hunted around for whoever had left her there but saw no sign of another soul in the forest. We took her back to the cam and Gerod took out some others to search properly. We thought they must have run into some sort of trouble.'

'Why are you telling me this?' Ashael asked, suspicion curdling in her breast.

'Your mother and father... Well, they had just lost a baby to the fever and your mama still had milk, so she fed the baby. For days we searched for the people who had left her, but there was neither sight nor sound of them. Your mama looked after the baby the whole time and the two of them bonded, so when we couldn't find out where the baby came from, your mother kept her.'

'The baby was me? How can that be? How could I not know this?'

'There was an unspoken understanding not to speak of it, not to treat you any differently, because your parents loved you just as much as the baby they had lost. I think they intended to tell you when you were grown so you could go looking for your people if you wished. But then they died, and I guess I never thought of telling you. Others probably forgot; you're so much a part of us.'

Ashael's mind was reeling. She couldn't take in what Bhearra was saying. Her parents weren't really her parents? She'd been found abandoned in the woods?

'Maybe the All-Mother saw a family that needed a baby and decided to give you to them,' Bhearra said.

'How... How could you keep that from me?'

'I never decided not to tell you, Ashael. I just never thought of it,' Bhearra answered.

'Why are you telling me now?' Ashael asked, voice catching in her throat, thinking *Ashael, found under an ash*

'The prophecy. It is said the person who saves us will be of us but not of us. Like you.'

Ashael looked at Bhearra but had no idea what to say. Too much had happened. She couldn't take it all in. 'I need some time alone.' Ashael stood, and without another glance at Bhearra, headed off between the trees.

***

ASHAEL DROPPED ANOTHER stone into the cradle of her sling and swung the weapon hard. The pile of rocks she was aiming at collapsed. She had circled the cam, ending up as far away as she could get while remaining within its protections. Her stomach growled and she considered hunting, but she would have to calm down before she would be capable of anything resembling stealth. She almost jumped out of her skin when a someone gripped her shoulder. She spun, sling raised, only to see Iwan, looking sheepish. Heart pounding, she lowered her sling.

'Didn't anyone tell you not to sneak up on people?'

'I'm sorry. I thought you had heard me approach,' Iwan said, holding his hands up placatingly. 'Are you well?'

'No.' Ashael put her hands on her hips. 'Where have you been?'

'I… I needed some time alone.'

'How is your wound? You should have stayed and let me examine you.'

'I don't have a wound,' Iwan answered, hand going to his chest.

'What do you mean? Of course you have a wound!'

Iwan lifted his tunic. Ashael felt a flush work its way up her neck as her eyes took in his bare torso, but all such thoughts left her head when she saw the smooth skin where the wound should have been.

'How can that be?' Ashael hesitantly reached towards his chest.

'I have no idea. I thought you might know what happened.'

Ashael's hand rested on his chest, and she searched his eyes. 'Yesterday, you had a bad wound here. I cleaned and bandaged it myself.' She looked back at the smooth skin and her eyes widened. 'There was a burn here, too, some sort of pattern. Where is it?'

Iwan shrugged and stepped away, lowering his tunic.

'What was that burn, Iwan? Were you trying to cut it off?' He moved to kiss her, but she turned her face away. 'I don't know what it is that you're keeping from me, but you need to start talking to me soon.'

Iwan caught her hands in his. 'I will, soon. I'll tell you everything. I just need some time. I need to figure out how much is safe.'

Ashael studied Iwan's face then eventually kissed him, gently. 'Don't take too long.' She kissed him again before reluctantly pulling herself away. 'We should get you to Bhearra. Maybe she'll know what happened to your chest.'

***

A QUIET MURMURING came from the Folk gathered around the Heart-Fire. Joren had called them all here and now they waited patiently for him to arrive. Iwan squeezed Ashael's hand, and she squeezed back gratefully before scanning the crowd from the shadows, looking for Nela's parents. *Will they come?* Joren had broken the news of their daughter's death to them this afternoon. Afterwards, he had gone off with Rana for some time alone. Ashael wondered if Rana had told him about the baby yet. The gods knew he deserved some good news after everything he'd had to deal with today.

One-by-one, conversations were broken off and the Folk fell silent as Joren, Rana and Bhearra approached. As they drew closer and the flickering light from the fire caught Bhearra's face, Ashael heard someone exclaim how much younger Bhearra looked. Soon, others were commenting too, and throwing questions at Bhearra. She raised a hand and a hush settled over the Folk once more.

'I know that the hour is late and many of you would normally be abed by now, but we have much and more to discuss with you. I'd ask you to join me in prayer before we start.' She paused as people settled and quieted. 'All-Mother, we come before you, children in need of your loving embrace. All-Father, we beg you for guidance. There are challenging times ahead and difficult decisions that must be made. We are a simple Folk who wish only to serve you and live our lives in peace. Please help us see the path to take through this dark time. Guide our feet so that we may walk in harmony and balance with you.'

'Let it be,' the Folk answered as one.

Ashael could see worried looks on many faces as the import of Bhearra's words began to settle over the Folk. Her stomach was tying itself in knots. She had begged Bhearra and Joren to let the cam decide if she should trade herself for the foragers, arguing that the people who were waiting for the return of their loved ones had as much right to the decision as any. Iwan had argued against her plan but had refused to say anything more than that it was a bad idea, leaving Ashael to convince Joren and Bhearra. They had reluctantly agreed but now that the moment was drawing near, Ashael was starting to regret the idea to abide by the cam's decision. *What if they don't send me? I'll be stuck here, waiting for the others to turn up like Nela. I can't live with that. I should have just gone.*

Joren was speaking now and Ashael struggled to concentrate on what he was saying.

'... has returned to us. Faemon is very weak and has little memory of what happened to him while he was gone. He is recuperating with Bhearra, and I would ask that you let him get his strength back in peace, although I know you will all be eager to see him. Our gladness at Faemon's return is tempered with sorrow over the loss of Nela, who has gone to the ancestors. Faemon brought her home to be buried.' A wail cut over Joren's words as Nela's closest friend ran off from the back of the crowd. Her mate went after her and Joren resumed. 'At this time, we do not know how Nela died or where the other foragers are. It seems they have been taken by some people who are alien to us. Faemon was given a message: if we wish to have the rest of the foragers returned to us then we must send Ashael to them.' Joren paused as babble rose from the Folk. People were all asking questions at once and Joren allowed them a moment to express themselves.

Ashael lingered in the shadows as she saw many eyes seeking her out. It was almost time for her to come forward and ask for their blessing to go. Joren beckoned and she let go of Iwan's hand to step into the light of the Heart-Fire.

'We don't know what will happen, or even why these people want me,' Ashael began. 'As Bhearra's apprentice, I belong to the Folk. I ask your blessing to travel to these people and seek out our missing friends.'

'What if you don't come back?' A voice shouted from the back of the crowd.

'We have to accept that as a possibility. I am not irreplaceable. Another can take my place with Bhearra, and the cam will go on without me.' Ashael squinted, trying to see who had spoken.

'But what if they don't send the foragers back? Then all will be for naught,' Gerod said, voicing the fear buried in Ashael's chest.

'My Colm is out there,' Sola called, her voice taut. 'We have to do whatever we can to save him. I say we let her go!' Some of the others who had loved ones in the foraging group added their voices to hers.

'We have to put the cam before one group,' someone shouted.

'What about putting five lives before one?' someone else responded.

Joren stepped forward again, raising his hand for silence. 'This is a difficult decision to make. There is no easy answer and none of us can be sure of the path ahead. I'd like you all to take a day to consider this. Tomorrow evening we will meet again and put it to a vote. Before that, I would like you to hear from Bhearra, whose wisdom has served this cam for many years.'

'Many of you know I was unwell,' Bhearra began, 'yet now I stand before you, stronger than I have been in years. This was Ashael's doing. She healed me. She has gifts we have only begun to discover that may be of great use to the cam. If we lose her, we may feel that loss more deeply than any of us suspect. I ask you to keep that in your mind as you decide whether to send her into the unknown.'

Chapter Fifteen

ASHAEL TOSSED AND TURNED, HER BLANKET TANGLING BETWEEN HER LEGS. *Why did Bhearra have to say that? There's no way they'll send me now.* Abandoning sleep, she sat up and pulled on a light dress. Quietly, she made her way outside and headed to the Heart-Fire, nodding a greeting to Elwa, who was tending the sacred flame. She settled herself on the grass beside the fire and focused on the flames.

All-Mother, please guide me. I feel so lost. Let me see the path to take. Ashael closed her eyes, letting the heat of the fire wash over her. She decided to try something Bhearra had taught her – to ground herself – hoping it would calm her enough to sleep. Taking deep breaths, Ashael extended her senses down into the ground beneath her. She became aware of the life of each blade of grass, of the worms and insects tunnelling through the soil. She allowed her anxiety to drain away into the earth and welcomed fresh energy into her body. Her muscles started to relax, finally letting go of some of the tension she carried.

Sometime later, Ashael opened her eyes to discover Iwan sitting beside her.

'How long have you been there?' she asked. 'I didn't hear you arrive.'

'I didn't want to disturb you. I thought you might be talking to the gods or something.'

Ashael laughed. 'Nothing that special. Just trying to let go a bit. Everything that's happening just now is out of my hands. It's hard to accept.'

'You did the right thing – asking the cam, I mean.' Iwan had been looking at the fire, but now he turned towards Ashael. 'You're more important than you realise. I don't think you should go but the Folk do deserve to be a part of this decision.'

Ashael stared at Iwan. He seemed so earnest, but she couldn't understand what he was talking about. 'I'm not important. I'm just an apprentice and I've barely even scratched the surface of my learning. Someone else could take over if I didn't come back.'

'I know what you did with Bhearra. No one else could have done that. Besides, your value isn't just in what you can do. You are kind and loving and helpful. The cam would be a much poorer place without you.' Iwan looked down at his hands.

Is it the light from the fire, or is he blushing? Ashael wondered. She felt quite flustered herself. No one had ever said things like this to her. They sat in an awkward silence for a moment before both speaking at once.

'It's late…'

'I should…'

'You go first,' Ashael said.

'I should probably get to bed. Joren plans to lay Nela to rest tomorrow, and I offered to help get everything ready. I'm meeting Gerod and Bran at first light to collect the stones for her cairn.'

'Yes. Bhearra and I will be spending the morning preparing her shroud and getting things ready for the farewell rite.'

Iwan stood and offered his hand to Ashael, helping her up. She could feel restrained strength in his grip and her hand tingled where their skin met. Before she knew what was happening, Iwan pulled her towards him and pressed his lips to hers. Ashael's breath caught in her throat and her fingers tightened around his.

Iwan broke away first, his face flushed and eyes bright.

Ashael took his hand and started walking towards his hut.

'Where are we going?' Iwan asked, voice hoarse.

'Your place,' Ashael answered, heart pounding in her throat. 'Unless you don't want to.'

'I definitely want to, but –' Iwan swallowed hard – 'it's been a difficult time for you. Are you sure?'

'No more words tonight.'

***

IT WAS A subdued group who met for the evening meal the next day. The day had mostly been taken up with the burial of Nela and all of them felt the weight of her loss. Ashael and Bhearra had brought some food outside to share with Joren and Rana between the two massive trees that housed them all. They sat together, picking at the food but not really eating, each lost in their own thoughts. Ashael looked at Rana and realised her friend seemed pale. She leaned over, offering the last of the early strawberries but Rana shook her head.

'I can't seem to keep much down,' she said in a low voice. 'I don't want Joren to worry. He has enough to face just now, and I know it's normal. I'm sure it will pass soon, won't it?'

'It's different for everyone. Some women are lucky and never feel this way and others have it all the way through their pregnancy. There are some herbs that might help. I can make up a mix for you – just make tea with it first thing every day,' Ashael answered. 'I found some chalk yesterday; I'll add that in. It's good for settling the stomach.'

As she spoke, she found her gaze wandering from her friend, seeking out Iwan. He had wanted to talk this morning, said it was important, but she had to rush off to help Bhearra with preparing Nela's body. There hadn't been any time to speak with him over the course of the day, and in just a short time the cam would vote on her fate. She felt tense and ill at ease. Rana must have noticed her distress because she squeezed Ashael's hand before getting to her feet with care. 'I believe it is time,' Rana said.

Ashael hovered near the back of the group, shifting her weight from foot to foot. She had never been so nervous, even when Bhearra approached her about becoming her apprentice. Most of the Folk were gathered around the Heart-Fire now and Joren would begin the vote. *I think I'm going to be sick,* she thought. *What if they don't send me? How can I live with myself?* She looked up and spotted Iwan nearby, but he was looking away from her. *Will he stay here if I go? I hope he finds a mate, someone to share life with.* She remembered the night before and a smile played at the corners of her mouth.

Joren's voice interrupted her thoughts as he called the meeting to order.

'You all know why we have gathered tonight,' he began. 'You've had a day to consider the decision before us. I know that is not long but if Ashael is to leave us, she must go tomorrow. Everyone in favour of sending Ashael to meet with those holding the foragers, raise your hand.' Ashael looked across the gathered Folk and her heart sank. A few hands were raised, most belonging to people who had loved ones in the foraging group, but nowhere near half of those present. She turned away as her throat grew tight and tears began to fill her eyes.

The decision had been made, but Joren asked for confirmation anyway. 'Those of you in favour of Ashael staying in the cam, raise your hands.' Ashael saw everything in prisms through her tears. Many hands were raised in the air. Joren was speaking again but Ashael couldn't focus on his words. She stumbled away from the group until Rana stepped in front of her.

'Ash, I know this isn't what you wanted,' Rana began, reaching out to touch Ashael on the shoulder.

Ashael moved away from her friend's touch. 'I need to be alone.' She began to sob as she moved away amongst the trees.

***

All-Mother, All-Father, the cam has decided, and I promised Bhearra and Joren that I would abide by that decision. But how can I? How can I allow the foragers to die when I

could do something to stop it? Please, show me the path to take. Help me to bear this burden.
Ashael lay on her pallet, her forearm over swollen eyes as she prayed. The image of Nela's burned body kept flitting across her mind, no matter how hard she tried to ignore it. A part of her was relieved that the cam had voted that she stay, and she was disgusted with herself for that selfishness, though she knew it was natural. Iwan had come looking for her, but she had sent him away, unable to accept his comfort. Now she wished he was here. Perhaps he would understand. But how could he? How could anyone?

Ashael couldn't help but wonder if the cam would have voted the same way if more of them knew she was not really one of them, that she had just been found as a baby. They were choosing to condemn five of their own for one who wasn't. She had never felt so alone, even just after her parents died. She kept praying until, at last, she fell into a restless sleep.

Ashael felt cold stone under her bare feet and a draft swirled about her legs, flapping the undertunic she had fallen asleep in. She opened her eyes on darkness but gradually a golden light suffused her surroundings. She found herself in a stone chamber, like nothing she'd ever seen before. The stone had been shaped and fitted together to form a floor, walls, a ceiling. *Where am I? What is this place?* Looking around, she spotted an entrance to her left and slowly moved towards it. Voices came from beyond the stone archway. Ashael pressed herself against the wall and peered round the edge, trying to catch sight of the speakers. She was looking out onto some sort of enclosed stone path within the building. She felt closed in, oppressed by the weight of the stone above her.

The golden light spread, allowing her to see further. A short distance away two men stood speaking. One was short but sturdy and radiated power. Ashael could sense the energy flowing around him. It felt dark and cold to her; she had felt nothing like it from anyone she knew. The other man was huge. Taller than Joren and broader across the shoulders, he was clearly strong and carried what appeared to be a weapon at his hip. It was like a very long knife but made of some shiny material that Ashael had never seen before. They both had very pale skin, nothing like the bronze of the Folk.

The short one glanced around and Ashael pulled her head back, hoping she hadn't been seen. She had no idea where she was or what was going on, but she was certain that being found would be a bad thing.

'What is it, sir?' came a deep voice.

'I felt something.' The other voice, moving closer.

Ashael held her breath, trying not to make a sound. The short man's head appeared in the entranceway, and she almost screamed. He looked straight at her then pulled his head back.

'It's nothing. Are your men ready?' he asked his companion.

What on earth...? Didn't he see me?

'Yes, sir,' the tall man answered. Do you believe she'll be at the river tomorrow?' *They're talking about me! These must be the men who have the foragers.*

'If she isn't, we'll send all of the prisoners back like the last one, so either way your men will be needed.' The short one was speaking again, 'Make sure they're ready. The master will not be so merciful if you make another mistake.'

'Yes, sir.'

The voices began moving away and Ashael let out a slow breath. Legs trembling, she stepped out into the strange stone pathway and looked in both directions. *Which way? How do I get out of here?* The golden light that filled the air began to coalesce into a shining line flowing down the middle of the pathway, towards her right. *It looks like the light is trying to lead me somewhere.* Ashael glanced back at the room she had just left. It was in darkness now. Chewing her lower lip, she followed the light.

Ashael had no idea how long she had been wondering around this strange place. She was in a building at least as large as the cam itself. The light led her on, going dark behind her as she passed. She had seen no people since the two men outside the door when she arrived.

The line of light that she had been following ended abruptly at a massive door. Dark blue energy flowed around the edges of the door and crawled across its surface, squirming in a manner that made Ashael think of maggots. She moved forward, stopping where the golden light pooled around her feet. She could feel the short man's energy all over the door. Tentatively, she reached out and touched it with her fingertips. A buzzing filled her ears like a swarm of bees, and the taste of blood flooded her mouth. She jerked her hand back, reeling. Her skin crawled from even that brief contact with the short man's power.

Ashael squatted for a moment to rest and gather her thoughts. *What now? The light brought me here so there must be something I'm supposed to do but I can't pass.* The light pooling around her flowed over her skin, tingling. She remembered using the light to help Bhearra, how she had breathed it into herself. No sooner had the thought crossed her mind than it began to happen again. The light moved into Ashael, infusing her being. An image began to form in her mind, and intuitively Ashael knew it was the scene on the other side of this door. Another stone chamber, huge and dark, with shapes around the edges. As the image became clearer, she realised that the shapes were people. *The foragers!* Her attention closed on Colm, a close friend of Bhearra's and someone Ashael had grown very fond of. He was unconscious, as they all seemed to be. Dried blood crusted the side of his face and turned his white beard a rusty reddish brown. Ashael cried out in anguish at his suffering and the image fled from her mind.

Ashael woke, panting, safe in her bed. *What a horrible dream.* Throwing off the hide blanket that covered her, Ashael sat on the edge of her pallet. Staring her feet, she tried to ground herself until she realised that her feet were covered in dirt and dust. *Not a dream, then. Was I there? How? How did I get back?* None of this made any sense. She sat there for a long time, her mind desperately trying to come up with answers that didn't seem impossible.

If it wasn't a dream, then I must have been there. Somehow. Which means what I saw was real. Those men. The foragers. Colm. They really are going to kill everyone if I don't go. Ashael took a drink of water, the fingers of her free hand drumming restlessly against her thigh. Could she go against the wishes of the cam? She had promised to abide by the decision. *I can't just leave them there to die in that awful place. I could never live with that choice. Neither could the families of those lost because of me. I have to go. I have to.*

Mind made up, Ashael quickly dressed and collected her travelling pouch. Moving quietly, she went into the main room, which was lit by the embers glowing in the hearth. She put some food into her pouch, as well as a foraging knife, then collected her cloak from where it hung from a protrusion of wood near the entrance. She stopped for a moment, looking around this place that had been her home for the past two years. She knew that once those men had her it was likely she would never see the cam again. She looked towards the curtain closing off Bhearra's sleeping alcove. *How can I leave her without saying goodbye? After everything that she's done for me, I sneak away in the middle of the night. But if I tell her what I'm doing, she'll only try and stop me.*

'I love you Bhearra. Thank you for everything,' Ashael murmured under her breath before she turned and walked out.

Silent tears choked Ashael as she moved quickly and quietly across the sleeping cam. She knew she was letting Bhearra down, letting the cam down, but she had no choice. As she passed the Heart-Fire, she thought of Iwan. If only they could have had more time together. She hadn't even had time to tell Rana about their burgeoning relationship. *Rana! She'll be so hurt that I left without telling her why. I didn't have time to make up those herbs for her. Bhearra can do it but… All-Mother, All-Father, please look after Rana. Let her pregnancy go smoothly. Let her realise I had no choice. I have to go.*

Ashael reached the path leading out of the cam just as she realised that she would never get to meet Rana's child. That drew her up short and she stood leaning against one of the trees that flanked the path, heart heavy with loss. *I don't know if I can do this.* She stood that way for a long moment, trembling. She was not afraid to die. After all, she would be with her parents in the Summerland. It was the loss of those she left behind and the grief her death would inflict on them that made this so difficult. She felt torn in two, between what she knew she had to do and the life she was leaving behind. Then Colm's face, covered in dried blood, flashed into her mind. She straightened her spine and strengthened her resolve then started down the path leading away from the cam.

***

FROM THE DARKNESS between the trees, Iwan watched Ashael leave. He had been worried this would happen. He had known she would not be able to live with the cam's decision. He glanced over to the far side of the cam where the tree that housed Joren towered into the air.

I should wake Joren. Tell him what's happening. But he'll drag her back and the others will be killed and Ashael will never be the same again. There's only one thing to do.

Iwan stole away into the night, following Ashael.

Chapter Sixteen

BHEARRA AWOKE SLOWLY, STRUGGLING OUT OF SLEEP THE WAY SOMEONE WHO IS drowning claws for the surface of the water. Before she was fully awake, she sensed something was wrong. Terribly wrong. She hauled herself upright, spilling her blankets to the floor. Her heart was pounding but she wasn't sure why. She hurried into the main room and looked towards Ashael's sleeping alcove. Empty. Her heart sank. Still in the undertunic she had slept in, she headed out to see Joren. The morning dew felt cold and unpleasant on her bare feet as she hurried over to the next tree.

'Joren! Joren! Are you awake?' she called as she reached the entrance to his dwelling. Rana pulled the curtain aside, eyes widening as she saw Bhearra in her undressed state. Joren stood up from the stool he had been sitting on by the hearth as Bhearra hurried inside.

'It's Ashael,' Bhearra blurted as soon as she saw him. 'She's gone!'

'What do you mean? Gone where?' Joren asked, taking Bhearra's arm and guiding her to the stool he had just vacated.

'I woke up and she wasn't there. I'm sure she's gone to exchange herself for the foragers.' Bhearra looked up gratefully as Rana wrapped a blanket around her frail shoulders and pressed a cup of warm tea into her hands.

'She could have just gone for a walk. Or be down at the stream, bathing,' Joren said in reasonable tones.

'Don't placate me, Joren, not now,' Bhearra snapped. 'I know she's gone. I can feel it.'

'I'll go find Gerod and Iwan,' Rana offered and Joren nodded gratefully at her as she headed for the door.

'I'm sorry, Bhearra,' said Joren. 'We'll start a search for her as soon as the others get here.'

Joren gathered some food and offered it to Bhearra. 'Here, you should eat something, you need to keep up your strength.' He looked around the room, hands balled at his sides, frustration showing in every taut line of his muscular frame. 'Why did she go? And why sneak off during the night?'

'I don't know why she went. When I saw her last night, she was upset but she seemed resigned to the cam's decision. Something must have changed. As to why she would sneak off, I'm sure she knew we would try to stop her going. We have to catch up to her, Joren, bring her home.'

'We'll do everything we can, but we don't even know how much of a head start she has. Do you think she took the usual route, to the river?'

Bhearra thought for a moment. 'I wouldn't. If I thought people would come looking for me, I would stick to the trees for as long as I could before moving out into the open.'

'Is there something you can do to find out where she is?' He looked to Bhearra, but she clearly wasn't listening to him. He was about to ask again when she stood abruptly and headed for the entrance.

'There is something I can do,' Bhearra said, 'but it will be difficult, and it might not work. I have to go and prepare. Bring the others over in two notches.' With that, she hurried back to her own home.

***

BHEARRA WAS FINISHING her preparations as Joren, Rana and Gerod arrived. She glanced up at them from where she sat on the floor.

As Joren entered, he said, 'I know you said Ashael would likely stick to the trees, but I've sent a group to the river by the main path – they might get lucky.'

'Is that why Iwan isn't here?' Bhearra asked.

'We can't find him,' Gerod replied,

'Could they have gone off together?' Joren asked. 'Perhaps we're worrying over nothing. They could be perfectly safe and just having some time alone.'

Bhearra pinched the bridge of her nose while she considered the possibility. 'No. My instincts are certain that she has gone to them.'

'Iwan has always spent time on his own,' Rana said. 'Perhaps he has done that today and knows nothing of Ashael's disappearance.'

'Perhaps. Wherever he is, I wish he were here.' Bhearra said. 'He's a skilled tracker. Make yourselves comfortable while I explain what I'm going to do.'

Rana took a stool by the hearth while Joren and Gerod squatted either side of Bhearra.

'This is an old magic. I have heard it spoken of, but I have never seen it performed. I'll be using blackweed to enter a trance state and then I'm going to try something that I haven't done before. There have always been stories of those who could join with the creatures of the forest. It is rare because it is dangerous.

Such people can get lost in the mind of the animals that they join with, never to return to their true form. Which is why I need you here. I plan to try and join with a hawk, use its speed and sight to locate Ashael.'

'Do you think this is wise?' Joren interrupted. 'After what happened before? If you get lost again, Ashael isn't here to bring you back.'

'I know that, and I am aware of the risk. What happened before was unnatural. I don't think it will happen again, but you're right, I can't be sure. What I am sure of is that we must find Ashael before she hands herself over to these monsters, whoever they are.' Bhearra looked at each of the three gathered before her.

'What do you need us to do?' Rana asked.

***

BHEARRA CHEWED THE blackweed, letting the bitter taste of it fill her mouth. The root was tough and woody, requiring a lot of chewing to get it pulpy and release its juices. The others sat nearby and Bhearra could feel them watching her, though her own eyes were closed. She could sense disapproval rolling off of Joren in waves and trepidation coming from Rana, like a cold draft. Gerod was closed to her and Bhearra was grateful for the barrier she had erected between them. Her old friend was unlikely to be happy with the risk she was taking. As the bitter juice of blackweed trickled down her throat, she spat a mouthful of pulp out into a bowl by her side. She could feel the plant having an effect already, as her muscles relaxed, and her thoughts began to drift. She felt herself beginning to detach from her body, her spirit form floating free, and she called to the spirit of the hawk just as her body slumped to the floor, empty.

***

THE HAWK SENSED Bhearra in the back of his mind. At first, he had resisted, flapping about and screeching, trying to knock her loose, but she had sent calming energy pouring through him and he had quickly accepted her presence. From their spot perched on one of the highest branches of her tree, she surveyed the cam and marvelled at the acuity of the hawk's sight. Gently, she nudged him to take flight and exalted as he took to the air. Bhearra could feel the air currents beneath his wings holding them aloft and understood how one could lose oneself in such an experience and forget to return to their own form.

She guided him over the path leading from the cam, scanning the brush and undergrowth, looking for anything that would indicate Ashael's passing. She could see each blade of grass with a clarity that was not given to her human eyes and marvelled that any creature could see so much. Scanning the ground, she spotted something and asked the hawk to circle this area. There! Some undergrowth was disturbed cutting away from the path, but still heading roughly in the direction of the river. I knew it! Bhearra thought, she did leave the path. Bhearra urged the hawk to follow the trail and the subtle signs she would never have been able to see without his help.

The hawk's head turned as he noticed movement below: a squirrel scampered over the ground between the trees. Bhearra nudged the hawk to ignore it, but his hunting instinct was too strong for her to overpower without going deeper into his consciousness than she was willing to attempt. He folded his wings and plummeted towards the squirrel, talons outstretched. As he reached the scurrying creature, it transformed into a woman. The hawk froze as her hand closed around his legs. Bhearra could feel his heart stuttering in fear and focused on trying to calm him. Bhearra herself was too shocked to even begin to understand what was happening. A brilliant golden glow surrounded the woman and a wave of peace flowed over the hawk, calming Bhearra too. The light around the woman was blinding and her form shimmered, denying Bhearra the opportunity to study her appearance.

'Bhearra, my most devoted one', a voice sounded in Bhearra's head though the woman's lips had not moved.

'Who are you?' Bhearra thought back.

'Don't you recognise me, my child?'

Bhearra would have laughed at being called a child at her age, if not for the exceedingly strange circumstances. Then the truth began to dawn on her. 'All-Mother?'

'Who else?' came the woman's voice again as she stroked the hawk's head and stared into his eyes.

Bhearra felt the gaze in the very core of her soul. How could this be? She was in the presence of the All-Mother!

'Time is short, dear one,' the All-Mother said, chunks of bloody meat appearing in her free hand, which she fed to the hawk.

'What do you mean?' Bhearra responded.

'A time of great darkness descends upon this land and all of my children.'

Although the words were dire, the voice in Bhearra's head had a musical quality, like bells were chiming just beyond hearing. Bhearra felt that she could listen to that voice forever.

'I feel something alien to this world spreading its evil tendrils through my land. Something that came here many years ago,' the All-Mother continued.

'What is it? How do we fight it?' Fear struck at the very core of Bhearra's being.

'Brave Sirion defeated them before, but they are more powerful than in the past. Their rage drives them to cause nothing but pain and suffering all around them. Already the land is dying beneath their feet.' The All-Mother fed the last chunk of meat to the hawk while she spoke.

The Zanthar! How can that be?'

'I know not; only that they are here and should not be.'

Bhearra felt panic rising through her, causing the hawk to start fluttering his wings nervously. *'Ashael! Ashael has gone to them. I have to save her!'*

'No, you must let her go.' The voice took on tones of command. *'Fear not, dear heart, I shall not forsake her, even in that blasted place, though my presence will be weakened by their dark magic. Young Ashael has her own part to play. I sent her to you to stand against these invaders.'*

'She's too young!' Bhearra wailed. *'She's not ready.'*

'Ready or not, the time has come. Ashael's path is not clear to me beyond this point, but we gave her all of the gifts we had to offer. Now we can only hope that they are enough.' The All-Mother looked steadily into the hawk's eyes, holding Bhearra with her gaze. *'I see that this pains you and I am sorry for that. We created Ashael to do what we cannot. It is time for her to take her place. And time for you to return.'* The All-Mother blew into the hawk's face and Bhearra felt herself coming unmoored from him. She was aware of the hawk taking flight as her consciousness was blown back, out of the hawk, drifting toward the cam, surrounded by golden light.

***

GEROD WATCHED AS Joren paced the small room, walking back and forth between the door, where he glanced at the position of the sun, and where Bhearra lay unmoving in the middle of the floor.

'It's almost noon,' he muttered. 'She should be back with us by now.'

'Let's give her a little more time,' Rana said from the stool where she sat weaving long grasses into baskets.

Gerod crouched by Bhearra's side, watching for signs of her waking. He had collected fresh water from the stream and had a full skin waiting for her, along with some nutcakes. Older than Joren, Gerod had been close to the young leader's father, Hymal, and had spent a great deal of time with Bhearra over the years. He was very fond of the old woman and knew how important she was to the well-being of the cam. He remembered when Joren had first been chosen as leader of their people, following his father's death. The young man had been little more than a boy at the time and seemed lost. Bhearra and Gerod had worked together to help Joren grow into his role as leader. *Thank the gods they chose Joren and not me,* he thought. *I would have no idea what do with all that's going on. Joren was the right choice.*

'We need to bring her back,' Joren said, drawing the hunting knife from his belt. He looked at it, then looked up in dismay. 'I don't know if I can do this.'

'You heard what she said,' Rana reminded him. 'Pain is an anchor. It could help to pull her back if she is stuck out there somewhere.'

Joren nodded tersely then strode over and knelt on the other side of Bhearra. He lay the stone blade of his knife across Bhearra's palm but then hesitated. Gerod watched, eyes flickering between Joren's face and Bhearra's. Joren's jaw was clenched and Gerod could see a muscle twitching in his neck. Gerod reached over and put his hand on Joren's, moving the knife away.

'Let me,' he said.

'I can do it,' Joren said between clenched teeth.

'But you don't have to. I'll do it.' Gerod drew his own knife from his belt. He gazed at Bhearra's face a moment, willing her to wake up. When there was no change, he laid the blade of his knife across her palm and prepared to cut her, as she had asked.

'Wait!' Joren grabbed Gerod's shoulder. 'Look, she's waking up.'

Bhearra's eyes were moving beneath her paper-thin lids. Suddenly she gasped and sat up, nearly knocking over the two men at her sides. Joren put his arm around her shoulders, supporting her, as Gerod offered her the water-skin. Bhearra took it and drank deeply before pushing herself to her feet.

'What happened?' Rana asked. 'Did you find Ashael?'

'No, I didn't find her. The All-Mother found me instead.' In a shaky voice, Bhearra told them how the All-Mother had appeared and captured the hawk she had been riding.

'The All-Mother appeared to you? Spoke to you?' Joren said in awe.

'I know. I can't quite believe it myself, and I was there!' Bhearra answered. 'She said that Ashael has to go, we have to let her go.' Bhearra ran her hands through her white hair.

'How can we?' Rana said, tears streaming down her cheeks. 'She'll die.'

'The All-Mother said she would be with Ashael, watching over her,' Bhearra said, moving to Rana's side and wrapping an arm around her.

'Is she going to keep Ash safe? Is she going to bring her home to us?' the younger woman sniffled.

'I hope so. We have to trust in the gods.'

Gerod looked at Bhearra from beside the hearth, where he was building up the fire for her. He knew it must be killing her to leave Ashael out there alone. Bhearra had taken a special interest in her ever since she was a baby. Who wouldn't, under the circumstances? He had been kept busy with his own boys at the time and he had still been fascinated by the baby that seemed to have come from nowhere. He caught Bhearra's eye and raised an eyebrow, asking her an unspoken question. *Are you alright?* She nodded at him, offering a strained smile.

'There's something else for us to worry about,' Bhearra said, addressing them all. 'And we should be very worried indeed. I know who these people are, though not what they want. The Zanthar have returned.'

***

MEEGRUM STRODE ALONG the corridor, boot heels thumping on the stone. The enchantress was on her way, and he knew his master would want to know at once. As he reached the door to the great hall, he heard voices on the other side and paused. Hairs rose on the back of his neck, alerting him to the magic being carried out within.

'What is taking so long? You should have had that world subdued by now.' The voice that spoke carried strange echoes.

'All is going according to plan, your majesty,' Daven responded, his raspy voice more difficult to hear through the wood.

'Then your plan is too slow!' the voice roared. 'Perhaps I should have sent someone else to deal with this. These barbarians defeated you before.'

'As a result of which, I know them better than anyone. I know how they think and how best to subjugate them, your majesty.'

'What of those bizarre, winged creatures that assisted them the last time?'

'I have a surprise for them if they show themselves, your majesty. I will not be taken unawares again.'

Meegrum could hear the frustration in his master's voice. No doubt he was speaking through gritted teeth. He hoped the king did not pick up on that; he could be petty if he decided he had been insulted.

'See that you're not. I will give you one more cycle of the moon, Daven. If you do not have that land under your control and the cattle ready for transport, I will send someone who can be trusted. Then I will separate your ugly head from your body. Do I make myself clear?'

'Yes, your majesty.'

Meegrum felt the power in the air slowly dissipate and knew the connection had been broken. *He'll be furious now. He hates having to speak to the king.* Meegrum briefly considered slipping away and coming back later but he knew the punishment would be severe if he withheld information. Reluctantly, he opened the door.

Energy still crackled in the air from the portal that had been opened, allowing the king to speak to them from Zan. Meegrum murmured a few words in the Old Tongue, drawing the energy into himself. His master stood at the far end of the hall, his back to the door. Anger radiated from every line of his taut body. Without warning, he turned and hurled a goblet at a wall, sending shards of stoneware flying across the room.

'Bastard!' he screamed. 'How dare he speak to me like that? We'll see whose head is separated from his body before this is over.'

'I have good news, my lord.' Meegrum desperately tried to control the tremble in his voice. His master was like a wild animal when roused; the scent of fear only incited him to greater violence.

'Must I drag it out of you?' Daven snapped.

'The enchantress is on her way, my lord. I felt her leave the protection of the cam and she is heading toward the river. She should be there by sundown.'

'I do not wish to wait any longer. Send a unit to get her now. Put Devorik in charge. Should he fail again, have him flayed. Slowly.' Daven paced as he spoke, his hands fisted at his sides. The harsh daylight streaming in through the windows only served to highlight his hideous scars.

'Yes, my lord. I shall send him at once. Is there anything else that you wish of me?'

'Have we heard anything from our spy?'

'No, my lord, not since I had the old woman in the mind-trap.'

'Could he have betrayed us?' Daven rasped.

'Not without my knowledge, my lord. I believe he must be dead. Perhaps some sort of accident.' Meegrum knew that if the spy had betrayed them, he would be held responsible. Sending slaves into the cams had been his idea. 'If I have your leave to go, my lord, I shall send Devorik and his unit now.'

'Yes, leave me,' Daven responded, turning to fill a fresh goblet with wine from a flask on a table.

Meegrum swiftly made his way towards the door, breathing a quiet sigh of relief. His master was always unpredictable and often brutal after speaking with the king. Meegrum preferred to give him time to calm down before having to deal with him. Just as he reached the door, his master's voice stopped him.

'Meegrum, send me a slave. A young one.'

'Of course, my lord. A boy or a girl?'

'Either. Both scream in the end.'

'Yes, my lord.' Meegrum hurried out of the door and about his tasks.

Chapter Seventeen

ASHAEL STUMBLED OVER A TREE ROOT AND FELL HEAVILY TO HER KNEES. *Why are you always so clumsy?* she asked herself as she leaned on the trunk of the tree and heaved herself back to her feet. The rough bark under her hand reminded of her home and she felt a stab of longing for that safe place. Cautiously, she moved toward the tree line, checking she was still heading in the right direction. Instead of taking the usual path to the river, across the plains, she had stuck to the forest, making her way over and under dense undergrowth in the hope that no one from the cam would find her if she went this way. *I wonder if they've realised yet that I'm not there. They might think I've just gone off to be alone.* Ashael realised that she was kidding herself. Bhearra would know. She seemed to know everything.

Satisfied she was going the right way, Ashael made her way back under the cover of the forest. A twig snapped somewhere behind her, causing her to jump in alarm. She peered back amongst the trees, looking for whatever had made the noise. She couldn't see anything. *Probably just an animal. Hopefully a small one.* Sweating from her exertion, she unhooked her travelling cloak from around her neck and folded it up, draping it over her arm. With a last glance behind, she set off again.

***

IWAN BREATHED A sigh of relief. *She didn't see me.* He had followed her through the forest for hours and, so far, had remained undetected. He still hadn't decided what to do. Should he try and talk her out of it? If she hadn't listened to the will of the cam, then why would she listen to him? Should he get ahead of her, reach the ford before her? He might be able to fight off the men who would come to take her. He'd never killed a man before, but an arrow could pierce a man's breast as easily as a deer's. But then the foragers would die, and she would never forgive him. He peeked around the tree he was hiding behind and saw that she'd created some distance between them. He set off again, slowly this time, being careful not to step on any more twigs.

***

ASHAEL EMERGED FROM the tree line and glanced at the sun: it was just after noon. Here, the tree cover veered away from the direction she needed to take to reach the river Donn. She would be out in the open for the rest of her journey. She paused and looked back at the trees. *I'll be there long before sunset. Maybe I should stop here and rest a while.* She made her way back into the shade and sat down at the foot of an evergreen.

She took some dried meat from her travelling pouch and nibbled at it though her stomach was in knots. So much had happened in the past few days; she felt overwhelmed just thinking about it. *Who are these people? What do they want from me? How can I make sure they release the foragers? What if they realise there's nothing special about me, that I'm not the one they want? Will they just kill the foragers?* With these questions swirling through her mind, Ashael did not immediately notice the change in the air. It was only when the hairs on the back of her arms began to rise that she came out of her reverie.

The air felt tense, threatening, like the moments before a thunderstorm hits. Ashael looked at the sky, which remained clear. Out of the corner of her eye, she noticed a shimmer in the air, similar to a heat haze. She thought that was what it was, until she noticed a circle of darkness in the centre of the haze. As she watched, the circle grew larger, until it was the size of a man. An arm emerged from the darkness, followed by a leg. Ashael's breath caught in her throat, fear flowing freely through her body.

A figure stepped out of the darkness. As he straightened up, she recognised the huge man she had seen the night before. Their eyes locked and for a moment Ashael considered fleeing. Whoever he was, this man terrified her. He stepped towards her, and she leapt to her feet. Her body was screaming danger at her, her breath coming in sharp gasps, her heart pounding. She was rooted to the spot as he stepped into the shade beside her.

'Enchantress.' That deep, cold voice from the night before. 'My master has been waiting to meet you.' Without any warning, he grabbed Ashael and spun her around, pulling her back against his chest. He wrapped a powerful forearm around her neck. 'Perhaps when he's finished with you, there will be something left for me,' he whispered into her ear.

The man started to press harder against Ashael's neck and she struggled for breath. She wriggled, trying to escape his grasp. *Surely they're not just going to kill me straight away? I have to make them free Colm and the others!* Spots began to dance in front of Ashael's eyes. She clawed at the arm around her neck, drawing blood, but he squeezed tighter. The man was dragging her backwards now, towards the darkness he had stepped out of. As they neared it, malevolent energy crackled over her skin and a deep buzzing sounded in her head. Once more, she tasted blood in her mouth and knew the darkness to be the work of the short man from last night. Just as she thought the buzzing would drive her mad, the man holding her tightened his arm once more. Ashael's vision went dark, and she slumped in the big man's arms, unconscious.

***

IWAN WAS CROUCHING in the undergrowth, fifty feet away from Ashael, when he felt the air change. Peering through a gap in the foliage, he could see Ashael turn her head to look at something, but the trees blocked his view of what she saw. *What's going on?* he wondered. Slowly, trying not to make any noise, he began to creep around to his left, hoping to get a view of whatever Ashael was looking at. She leaped to her feet as he moved, fear outlined on her face.

Then he heard a voice that made his blood run cold.

Devorik! Panic flooding his system, Iwan crawled rapidly through the undergrowth, aiming for a clear area of the forest floor. His bow, slung over his shoulder, caught on something and yanked him backwards. Carefully, he reached back to untangle his bow, praying to the All-Father that the string would not be broken. His fingers trembling, he finally managed to disengage the bow from the thorn bush it had caught on. *Let me help her, let me help her,* his thoughts ran in a mantra as he wriggled the last few yards to the clearing. Climbing to his feet, Iwan could finally see the circle of darkness floating in the air close to the tree where Ashael had been sitting. Ashael was being dragged backwards into it by a huge man with his arm around her neck, choking her.

Iwan swiftly raised his bow, pulling an arrow from the quiver strapped to his right thigh. As he prepared to take his shot, the man dragging Ashael gave a heave and pulled her most of the way into the darkness, only the lower half of her body still sticking out. Iwan could no longer see her captor, but he aimed carefully at a spot above where he believed Ashael's shoulder to be. *What if I aim wrong? I could hit her! But I have to do something, dammit!*

Iwan took a deep breath and held it for a second. Ashael was almost completely gone now, only her feet still visible. Releasing his breath at the same time as the bowstring, Iwan let his arrow fly. It flew true, straight into the inky void, just as Ashael's feet disappeared.

Leaping over fallen branches and undergrowth, Iwan raced toward the dark circle. Time seemed to slow down; he felt as though he was running through water, the air itself seeming to resist his forward progress. As he watched, the void shrank in on itself, getting smaller with every pounding heartbeat.

Gathering his strength, Iwan leaped towards what remained of the darkness. His outstretched fingers almost touched it before it disappeared, leaving him lying on his face on the ground where, moments before, Ashael had been sitting.

Groaning from the impact, Iwan rolled over onto his back. *I should have woken Joren last night. I'm so sorry, Ashael, I thought I could help you.* Pulling himself into a sitting position, he hung his head. His shoulder throbbed with his heartbeat, reminding him that he had pulled it when his bow snagged. He rolled it in the socket and it moved freely, though it was fiercely painful.

He walked heavily over to the tree where Ashael had been sitting. Her waterskin lay abandoned on the ground, sending a stab of longing through Iwan's heart as he reached down and picked it up, running his thumb over the smooth skin. *Oh, Ashael, why do you have to be so damned noble? Why did you have to go to them?* He had failed her. He had failed everyone.

He paced around, trying to figure out what to do next. *Should I go back to the cam? Tell them everything I know? The only way to tell them anything useful is to tell them everything. But once they learn of my betrayal, why should they trust anything I say? No. I can't go back.*

Iwan checked his bow and arrows. A couple of arrows had snapped but as long as he still had the stone heads, he could fashion new shafts. Wood was plentiful here. He still had his hunting knife strapped to his belt and a spare bowstring in his pouch. He tied Ashael's waterskin to his belt, next to his own, then stood, turning in a slow circle, trying to decide on his next steps.

The huge mountain range to the west, The Edge of the World, towered above the treeline. He could reach the foothills by tomorrow if he pushed himself. Turning his back on the spot where Ashael had disappeared, Iwan set off towards the mountains.

***

RANA LAY ON the pallet she shared with Joren. Her face felt puffy from crying. She shivered and pulled a blanket over herself. The sun had gone down a while ago and with it went the heat of the day. She knew she should get up and light the hearth, prepare some food, but she just didn't have the energy. She felt completely drained, like her tears had left her empty of everything. Her hand went to her stomach, and she curled herself around it, as if she could protect the life growing within. *All will be well, little one,* she thought. *I don't know how, but all will be well. You have a mother who loves you before she has even seen your face and a father who will always protect you. He's so strong, and brave. You just wait, he'll see us all through this safely.*

As if her thoughts had conjured him up, Joren stepped quietly into their home and made his way to her side. 'How are you feeling?' he asked, sitting on the pallet at Rana's side and taking her hand.

'Like a part of me is missing,' she answered, voice hoarse.

'I wish I could bring her back to you. I know Ashael is the sister of your heart, if not of your blood.' As he spoke, Joren stroked Rana's brow, pushing her hair back from her face. Rana sat up and rested her head on Joren's chest, breathing in the scent of him. He smelled like grass and fresh sweat and wood smoke. He smelled like home. She wrapped her arms around his broad chest, clinging to him.

'What happened after I left the meeting?' she asked, voice muffled by his body.

'We sent out messengers to the three cams closest to here. We need to let the others know that the Zanthar have returned. I've asked them to pass the message on to the cams closest to them, who should do the same. I want the leaders to gather here on Longest Day. That should give them long enough to get here and hopefully will give us enough to time to prepare. We need to come up with some sort of plan, but I don't even know where to start.'

'Doesn't Bhearra have any ideas?'

'She wants to speak to the other filidh, see if anyone knows any more about the Zanthar than we do. We've asked that the filidh all come to the gathering too.'

For a moment they just held each other in silence.

'I'm worried, Rana. I don't know how to face this threat. The Folk chose me to lead them when all they needed was someone to make sure that the cam functioned as a group; someone to organise hunts and resolve disputes. I'm not equipped to lead in a time of danger. How can I know how to lead if I don't know what we're facing? What if I can't protect the cam? What if I can't protect you?' Joren's voice cracked, and Rana could feel him shuddering as he tried to hold in sobs.

'There is no one in the cam who is equipped to face this. We're peaceful people. We know little about the Zanthar or why they are here. This is true for all of the Folk, Joren, not just you. You are strong and brave. You know when to take advice and when to make a decision. You care about every person who lives in this cam – even the ones you don't like. If anyone can lead us through this, it's you. I believe in you.'

Rana had tilted her head up to look Joren in the eyes while she spoke and now, he gently lifted her chin in his hand. The familiar feel of his calloused skin against her face stirred something in her.

'What would I do without you?' Joren said, his thumb tracing Rana's lips. He leaned down and kissed her, lighting a fire in her belly that sent warmth flowing through her body. *How can I be aroused at a time like this?* she wondered as her arms pulled Joren closer, seemingly of their own accord. Joren's body was responding to her need, but he pulled away from her, frowning.

'What about the baby? Is it safe?'

Rana laughed. 'Of course it is. Do you think people stop making love for three seasons?'

'I guess not. Are you sure you want this? It's been a tough few days.'

Rana remembered something Bhearra had said the day before, at Nela's farewell rite. *In the face of death, we affirm life.* She answered Joren by pulling him to her and kissing him hard.

For a time, they found peace in each other.

Chapter Eighteen

ASHAEL CAME TO SLOWLY. THE ARM AROUND HER NECK WAS GONE AND SHE was lying on stone, the chill from its rough surface seeping through her clothes. The scent of burning wood overlaid the mustiness of this place. She opened her eyes, looking up at a stone ceiling. Torches positioned on the walls cast a flickering light over everything. There was a groan from behind her and she twisted around to look. The man who had grabbed her was lying on the stone a few feet away, an arrow sticking out of his right shoulder. Behind him was the other man from her vision, the one with the power.

'How did this happen?' the mage shouted. He saw that Ashael was awake and gestured to someone behind her who hauled her roughly to her feet.

'You thought to betray us?' the mage spat, stepping close.

He stood almost a head shorter than Ashael and had to look up at her. She could see that the hair was thinning on top of his head. Despite his meagre appearance, Ashael's skin crawled from the power coming off this man.

'I don't know what you're talking about,' she said through gritted teeth. Her stomach roiled and bile crept up her throat. She twisted, trying to see who was holding her. A young man was behind her, a jagged scar running over his face and across an empty socket where an eye should be. Behind him stood three others, all powerfully built and wearing similar clothing: loose fitting trousers and tunics with some sort of leather vest over the top. It looked like kyragua hide but Ashael didn't have time for a good look before the mage grabbed her head, jerking it back round to face him.

Staring at Ashael's face, he spoke to one of the men behind her. 'Get that arrow out of Devorik's shoulder then take it to the dungeon and shove it into one of the prisoners.'

'No! Leave them alone!' Ashael tried to shout but her voice came out hoarse. 'I did what you said. You have to let them go.'

'You don't seem to understand your position here,' the mage said as the man he had spoken to carried out his orders. 'But you will.'

The one called Devorik screamed as the arrow was pushed through his shoulder and yanked out the other side. Bright red blood pulsed from the wound left behind. Ashael struggled, trying to free herself from the grip of the man behind but he caught both of her wrists in one hand and pulled them upwards, forcing her arms into a painful and unnatural angle that prevented her from moving.

'Meegrum, sir, please help me,' Devorik gasped, sweat beading his brow.

The mage stepped towards him. 'Help you? Why would I waste my power on you?' he sneered.

'I carried out my mission,' Devorik groaned. 'I brought the enchantress.'

'Yes, you did. So, what need do I have of you now?' Meegrum lifted his foot and placed it onto Devorik's wound. 'If you're stupid enough to get yourself shot then you are of no use to me,' he said, as he applied pressure with his foot. Devorik let out a high-pitched scream before passing out. Meegrum stared down at him the way a man might look at animal droppings he had just stepped in.

Meegrum turned to the man holding Ashael. 'Take her to the great hall but do not enter until I arrive – the master doesn't like to be disturbed when he is at play. You two,' he motioned to the remaining men, 'take Devorik to the barracks. If he survives, I might still have a use for him. If he dies, give him a sky burial. The vultures may enjoy him.'

The man holding Ashael let go of her wrists, giving her a moment of relief before he wound her long braid around his hand and yanked her along the corridor.

***

MEEGRUM HURRIED ALONG the stone passages. Being in the presence of the enchantress had affected him more than he would care to admit. *She's so much more than I thought. How can she be unaware of her power?* He wrapped his arms around his torso, trying to stop the trembling. Until this moment, he had never doubted his lord's plan to overcome this woman but now, having been close to her, felt her power, all of his instincts were telling him to flee. *It'll have to be another world,* he thought. *The king will have our heads if we go home, and there is nowhere on this world that would be safe from her. I don't have enough power to open a portal to another world on my own.* He was moving so quickly he didn't even notice the slave boy cleaning the floor until he tripped over him, stumbling across the passage and bashing off the opposite wall.

'I'm s-s-sorry, sir,' the slave stammered, cowering next to his bucket of water. Meegrum slowly pulled himself to his feet. Fire ran up his spine and he focused on the boy who was trembling in fear, trying to hide behind his pitiful bucket. Meegrum stepped towards him, raising his hands and beginning to chant in the Old Tongue. The boy went rigid as a blue mist began to rise from his skin.

Meegrum drew a deep breath and the mist flowed into him. The boy began to convulse violently, limbs thrashing, leaving skin and blood on the rough stone, but Meegrum was only peripherally aware of this as the vitality of the boy's life force flooded his being.

The pain in Meegrum's spine faded until it was no more than a tingle. Strength flooded his muscles, making them twitch and dance beneath his skin. As the transfer ended, Meegrum fell to one knee, gasping. The shock of the disconnection was something that he could never quite prepare himself for. Shaking his head to clear it, he stood. He almost laughed aloud at himself. The fear that had sent him scurrying along this corridor was completely gone. *How could I have let her frighten me so much? She doesn't know her power exists, let alone how to use it. She can't even begin to threaten us!* Grateful that no one had seen him in such a state, Meegrum set off at a more sedate pace, heading towards the Great Hall and his master, leaving the body of the boy on the floor behind him.

***

ASHAEL CRINGED AS yet another scream rent the air. The guard, who she had decided to call One-Eye, was smirking at her obvious discomfort. 'Better get used to the sound of screams, witch,' he mocked. 'They'll be yours, soon enough.'

Ashael lay on the floor, curled around her stomach, which One-Eye had kicked when she had spoken to him. Obviously, she would find no help there. Her guard stood at ease, but she could see that his weight rested lightly on his feet – he was ready to spring into action should it be called for. She would not be able to out-run him. All she could think about was trying to get away and find the foragers

Another scream, this one weaker than the last. Ashael suspected that the screamer would not last much longer. Her heart ached with the knowledge that she could do nothing to help. She had never felt so weak and useless in her life.

Ashael's skin started to crawl, and her stomach tightened. Looking up, she saw the one called Meegrum coming around a corner. The hairs on her arms and the back of her neck rose. He seemed different, almost as if he had become larger in the short time since she had last seen him. Narrowing her eyes, Ashael tried to focus on Meegrum, examining him the way she would a patient. He moved differently, too. He seemed calmer, more confident, than he had been when she first arrived. His aura extended further from his body. As he drew close to Ashael and his energy overlapped with hers, Ashael became aware of another energy, a small pocket of it, that felt different from his. Young and innocent, this did not repulse Ashael the way Meegrum's usually did. *Strange. It doesn't feel like him at all.* Meegrum moved and the pocket did too, leaving Ashael's aura in contact with another part of Meegrum's. That peculiar buzzing sound started in her head

129

again and she pulled herself across the floor, tight against the stone walls, trying to escape his energy field.

The worst scream yet came through the door, a sound of pure anguish. Despite her situation, Ashael tried to pull herself to her feet, intent on helping somehow. One-Eye punched her on the side of the head, leaving her ears ringing. At first, Ashael felt no pain, only heat rushing to her left ear and cheek bone as her face started to swell. One-Eye lifted his fist again.

'Enough.' Meegrum's voice was firm. 'The master wanted her undamaged.'

One-Eye lowered his fist but continued to look at Ashael, his gaze cold. That was almost the worst part: he didn't seem angry or hateful, in fact he showed no emotion at all, as if violence meant nothing to him. Ashael shivered.

Meegrum lifted his hand and knocked on the huge wooden door in front of them then entered without waiting for an answer.

'My lord, I trust I am not disturbing you at your sport?' asked Meegrum, leaving One-Eye to pull Ashael into the hall by her hair.

Now Ashael felt pain; her face throbbed with every beat of her heart. As she was drawn further into the room, she became aware of a man at the far end. Not because she could see him – Meegrum blocked her view – but because she could feel him. She slowed, dreading the moment when she would face this… this… creature – whatever it was, it felt completely unnatural to her. One-Eye wrenched her hair again, yanking at her braid to speed her up.

'I have just finished. I see you have brought me a present.' A raspy voice came from beyond Meegrum, making Ashael's flesh prickle. The magical force of the voice hit Ashael, making her stumble, and she found herself on the floor, staring at a huge hearth with only a small fire flickering within. In front of the hearth lay a young boy. Ashael's vision tunnelled as her healer's senses began to catalogue the boy's injuries: broken bones, torn skin, fingernails that had been pulled off, burns to the soles of the feet. A sob burst from Ashael's chest at the sight of such suffering. She felt she should thank the gods that he was dead – he could be at peace now. Dully, she realised One-Eye had stopped dragging her. She raised her eyes, taking in first One-Eye and then Meegrum. They were both looking at her. The raspy voice sounded again but Ashael could not make out the words. Meegrum stepped back, bowing. The owner of the voice stepped forward and Ashael came close to fainting from the energy coming off of him. It tasted like decay. Like rot and ruin. The smell was like that of the peckara mushroom, whose flesh was fatally poisonous.

Taking deep breaths through her mouth, Ashael tried to pull herself together. She looked at the man who had put her so badly off-balance. She saw two images laid over one another and the effect made her dizzy. At one moment she saw a man of average height and build whose most remarkable feature was that he had severe scarring from burns covering most of his face and disappearing down into the neck of his tunic. His white hair grew in tufts because of the scar tissue. He had no eyebrows and, as far as Ashael could tell, no eyelashes surrounding eyes the colour of old ice. Then Ashael's vision would swim out of focus, and she would see another image beneath: a corpse – standing upright, walking and talking, but a corpse, nonetheless. She could see his tongue through a hole in his cheek and maggots squirmed in empty eye sockets.

Ashael could hear a panting noise and only slowly became aware the sound was coming from her: she could not catch her breath properly. She struggled to sit up as the nightmare creature came towards her, but fear had frozen her to the spot. A tinge of yellow began to creep into Ashael's vision and she gasped, trying to slow her breathing, knowing she would faint if she could not get control of herself. Gradually, she managed to calm herself and her vision sharpened. She would win the battle for consciousness. The creature was speaking but Ashael heard him as if through water and could not make out a word. He reached out a hand towards her.

A high chiming sound began in Ashael's ear, and without quite knowing what she was doing, she raised her hands and began to move them in a complex pattern in the air, muttering words she had never heard before. Flecks of silver light began to dance in the air between Ashael's hands, and the corpse-man stopped reaching for her, studying her warily. The flecks moved faster, whirling in a dance that left her eyes dazzled.

Meegrum and One-Eye stepped towards Ashael, but the corpse-man held up a hand and they both stopped. Ashael's eyes flicked toward them in time to see a flash of fear on Meegrum's face, though One-Eye stood as cold and disinterested as before.

How am I doing this? What *am I doing? Why did it make the corpse-man stop?* The thoughts flashed through Ashael's mind as her hands continued their work. The corpse-man spoke again, and this time she understood him.

'Your pretty little lights won't save you, you know,' he said, voice rasping as though he had difficulty speaking.

Maybe not, but none of you will touch me so there must be some power here.

'You cannot hope to stand against me,' he said, sounding confident though he still kept his distance.

Ashael's hands began to move faster, and she heard the strange words coming from her own lips. The lights danced faster in an expanding pattern. As they moved further from her body, the three men in the room took a step back.

They're frightened of the lights. How can I use that?

Ashael concentrated on the lights dancing before her, shutting off her awareness of the room around her. The lights felt like the stars to her – distant and alien yet also somehow familiar. She could almost feel the pattern, the connection between the movement of her hands and the movement of the light. She stared at them, fascinated, the connection becoming more familiar. One of the lights zinged into Ashael's hand, sending a shock into her, something akin to being close to lightning during a storm. Ashael snapped back to full awareness to see One-Eye approaching her, fist raised. Instinctively, she threw out her hands. The lights flew out from their swirling pattern, spreading over the room and towards the three men. Meegrum raised his hands, shouting as he did so, and a rippling shield appeared before him, stretching to cover the corpse-man too. As the lights hit the shield, they crackled and flared before disappearing. One-Eye wasn't so lucky. Several of the lights flew into him, singeing his skin. He fell to the floor, writhing as if trying to put out flames that were not there. The lights left singed holes wherever they touched his clothes, except for the kyragua-hide armour, which was unmarked.

Ashael looked on in shock, her hands dropping to her sides. She realised she should use the distraction as an opportunity to run but she couldn't tear her eyes away from the spectacle before her. Instead, she stepped backwards, moving towards the door behind her. There were only a few of the lights left; Ashael knew she didn't have long. She turned and ran for the door, fumbling with the unfamiliar handle before managing to pull the door towards her. Glancing back over her shoulder, she rushed through the doorway, only to be grabbed by the arm and spun round. The guard pressed her face against the wall, and twisted her arm behind her back. Ashael tried to see who had grabbed her. A face moved into her field of vision: one of the men from when she first came through the portal. He pulled her away from the wall and shoved her back into the hall. The last of the lights had gone out and Meegrum was lowering his shield. One-Eye lay on the floor, moaning.

'I believe this is yours, my lord,' the man holding Ashael said as he forced her to her knees in front of the corpse-man. Ashael could still see his double-image, but it no longer made her feel sick. Instead, she burned with anger. Anger for the boy whose body lay by the fireplace. Anger for the foragers still being held. Anger for Nela and for Faemon. Anger for her people. Ashael glared up at him, posture defiant.

'Whatever it is you want from me, you won't get it,' she spat at him.

'We'll see about that,' he said, looking at her thoughtfully. After a moment, he glanced to One-Eye who was climbing to his feet. 'Captain Zekinal, teach her a lesson.'

Chapter Nineteen

ASHAEL WATCHED A BAR OF SUNLIGHT CRAWL ACROSS THE FLOOR. IT WAS COMING from a window high in the wall above her. She lay in a heap on the stone floor, trying not to move; every time she did, something else hurt. Even breathing was painful. One-Eye had beaten her badly. Eventually the man who had caught her as she fled from the hall had to pull One-Eye away. The one they called Meegrum had been shouting something about how she must not die before Longest Day.

Ashael tried to think through the pain. *What do they want me for? Is it because of the lights?* She looked at her hands, trying to remember how she had moved them the night before. With at least three broken fingers and much swelling and bruising, she was unable to try and recreate what had happened. *What were the words I was saying?* By concentrating hard, she could feel the shape of the words in her mind, but she could not quite catch them.

The door opened and Ashael looked up from her place on the floor. The sight surprised her so much that she jerked to a sitting position, heedless of her injuries. Standing in the doorway was a being the shape and size of a man – but there the resemblance ended. It was wearing a floor-length robe of grey woven material. A long hood lay down its back, exposing a head and face that were covered in blue and white marbled scales. Its eyes were yellow with a slit pupil and two sets of eyelids which blinked independently. Small horns ran in two rows from the front of its head to the back. It had no nose that Ashael could see, and a long, thin tongue flickered from its mouth, testing the air, like a snake.

It moved further into the room and Ashael cringed. For a long moment they stayed like that, staring at each other, neither of them moving. The creature made no effort to touch her and Ashael relaxed a little. The creature opened its mouth and began to speak. Several voices were overlaid, all speaking the same words at the same time.

'We are here to tend to your injuries,' the voices said.

'We?' Ashael asked between cracked and swollen lips. 'I only see one of you.'

'We are of the Hive,' the creature answered, as if that explained everything. It took a step towards Ashael, and she raised her arms defensively. 'We will not harm you.'

'Why should I believe you?' Ashael asked, trying to count how many voices she could hear speaking as one. It sounded like a whole community, all in one creature.

'We serve.' Each time the creature spoke, a different voice was to the fore. 'We are mystics, not warriors. It is not permitted for us to cause harm.'

Ashael stretched out her senses, trying to feel the creature before her. There was no trace of evil, as with the men she had encountered here. Its aura was calm, contemplative. In fact, as alien as this creature was, something about its energy felt familiar. Like Bhearra. Ashael pulled her senses back and slowly lowered her arms. *I might be a fool, but I believe it.*

The creature stepped towards her again and Ashael stayed still, though she remained wary. Reaching her side, it knelt, and pulled its hands from its sleeves. The hands were covered in the same blue and white scales. The fingers were long and had an extra joint. They were tipped with claws that had been worn down to a softened point. It held bandages and a damp cloth. Ashael tensed as the creature placed the cloth on her cheek, washing away the dried blood. The cloth was cool against her hot and swollen skin, and for a moment she felt like crying over this small kindness. She was reminded of Bhearra and all she had left behind.

'We have a salve for your wounds, to speed healing. May we administer it?'

'No.' Ashael did not trust the creature enough to allow it to apply a salve to her; it could be some sort of trick.

'As you wish.' The creature finished cleaning her face and moved on, to her arms.

'Why are you doing this?' Ashael asked.

'We serve.'

'Who do you serve?'

'The great god, Alekiatorix, of course.' The creature began to bind Ashael's broken fingers together and she cried out in pain. 'We are sorry. We must bind the bones to allow them to heal.' Ashael panted, grinding her teeth against the pain. *Who is Alekiatorix? Is that another name for the All-Father?* Ashael used the questions as a focus to distract her from the pain in her hands. *Does it really matter? This thing is talking to me. Maybe I can get some answers from it.*

'Why am I here?' Ashael asked, as the creature cleaned and bandaged her other hand.

'It is not for us to speak of this thing. We serve.' The many voices issuing from the creature's mouth all shared the same tone and phrasing.

Ashael sighed in frustration. She thought for a moment before asking, 'What are you permitted to speak of?'

'We may speak of anything that has not been forbidden.'

'Well, that tells me a lot,' Ashael muttered. She had so many questions but no idea which of them were the most important, never mind which were forbidden.

The creature finished tending to Ashael's hands and arms and moved its hands towards her torso. Ashael flinched away and shook her head sharply. The creature sat back and rested its hands in its lap.

'We should check you for further injuries.' This time the voices sounded slightly disapproving.

'There's no need. It's just bruising.'

'Still, we should check.'

'Why? You can't treat it.' Ashael was beginning to grow suspicious. *Why is it pushing this?*

The creature cocked its head, as if listening to something only it could hear. 'Very well. Is there anything else that we may assist you with?'

'You could tell me why I'm here.'

'It is not for us to discuss this thing,' it repeated its answer from earlier.

'Then leave,' Ashael said with as much command in her tone as she could muster.

The creature touched its brow and then made a fluttering gesture with its fingers before bowing slightly and leaving the room.

***

MEEGRUM NURSED HIS wine as he stared at the fire. He had been taken completely unawares last night. How had she managed such a complex charm? She had no idea what she was doing; such magic should not be possible for these simpletons. At least he had managed to get a shield up in time – he hadn't failed his master in that. She was obviously starting to tap into her powers, but that didn't make sense. Everything he had learned suggested they would come to fruition in one moment, that she would change and at that moment she would be at her most vulnerable. If she could use her powers now, then would she ever be vulnerable at all?

A knock at the door interrupted his thoughts. He sighed before calling for the visitor to enter. The member of the Hive entered. These creatures did not consider themselves individuals, so they did not have individual names, but Meegrum had named this one Talak, meaning cowardly. The Hive were a non-violent race, and to the Zanthar, that made them cowards. The creature had accepted the name and would answer to it though it never used it to refer to itself.

'What news do you have, Talak?' Meegrum asked.

'The enchantress did not allow us to fully examine her, master,' the creature responded.

'What do you mean, "did not allow"? She's a prisoner! She has no say in the matter!'

'We do not use force, master. We serve.'

Meegrum threw his hands up in the air, exasperated. These creatures had their uses, but their ways were bizarre to him and beyond inconvenient. Anger simmered in the pit of his stomach.

'Did you learn anything useful?' he growled.

'We sense two sources of power in her,' Talak answered. 'She has her own, intrinsic power, separate from her destiny. We did not anticipate this – the lore does not mention any other power. Of course, the races on this world do not write, so stories may change over time. Much may have been lost before we started recording the lore.'

'So, what does that mean?' Meegrum asked, talking to himself more than to Talak. 'How does this change the plan?'

'It may be that there is more we do not know. I cannot offer useful advice at this point, master.'

'Then get out. And don't return until you have more information for me.'

Meegrum turned his back on Talak, walking to the window of his chamber. He heard the door close as the creature left. The window looked out onto a rocky slope, the land bereft of anything living. The magic that Meegrum and his master used had sucked all of the life from this place. Their magic was getting weaker. They needed the plan to work.

***

THE PAIN OF her broken fingers distracted Ashael from her meditation. Sighing deeply, she re-positioned herself, trying to ease the pain enough to focus. She sat cross-legged, backed into the corner of the room. The rough stone caught at her long braid, so she pulled it over her shoulder, letting it hang down in front of her. She turned her face, letting her hot cheek rest against the cool wall. She could feel the history of the stone – the generations of life that had formed it: the tiny fossils within; the goats that had climbed upon it when it was still part of a mountain, before it was ripped from its home to become a part of this building. She let herself linger in the memories of the stone. For a time, people and their troubles seemed insignificant. Such short lives. Barely worth the notice of the stone.

Reluctantly, Ashael came back to herself. She should not be so self-indulgent, she knew. The foragers still needed her. At least, she hoped they did. The one called Meegrum had ordered one to be hurt but hadn't said anything about killing them. *They need them alive*, Ashael realised. *If they kill them, they have nothing to hold over me. How can I help them? That's what I came here for. Nothing else matters.*

Ashael closed her eyes and tried to enter the meditation again but this time she focused on the foragers. She had to come up with a plan to help them. She couldn't afford to feel sorry for herself any longer. Ashael thought of how she had last seen them, in the vision before she came here. She remembered how sickly they had all looked, how they had been unconscious. She remembered how Colm's hair and beard were encrusted with blood. She remembered the smells of the place they were kept: blood, old urine, rot. The memory was so strong that the scents began to invade her nostrils once again. Gradually, Ashael became aware of the sound of breathing. Several people breathing. Surprised, she opened her eyes then drew in a sharp breath. She was no longer in her cell. Somehow, she had transported herself to the dungeon where the foragers were being kept. She leapt to her feet and turned in a circle, scanning the room. Colm, Tris, Erin, Ruraigh, Alayne. They were all here. Ruraigh had an arrow sticking out of his right shoulder. Ashael choked back a sob and ran to his side. Fortunately, it was just the tip of the arrow that pierced his skin, and not the full head. She reached for the shaft to pull the arrow free, but her hand passed straight through it.

She stared at her hand; she could see through it. *What? How?* Ashael reached for the arrow again and, once more, her hand passed through it. *This must be a spirit-journey,* she realised. *Bhearra told me about this. I'm not physically here.* She looked around at her friends and her heart sank. If she couldn't touch them, how could she help them? Maybe she could learn something while she was here and use it to help them later. Ashael began to walk around the room, examining everything she could see: the door, crawling with Meegrum's energy (Ashael gave it a wide berth); stone walls, much like those in the rest of the building; stone floor, closely fitted pieces; an indentation in the middle of the floor, soot and scorch marks on the stone – *a fire pit?* On a table at the far side of the room were some tools made of the same hard shiny material she had seen Meegrum and his companion carrying. She thought it might be metal, a material the Zanthar had brought here. There were still pieces of it around, or so she had heard, although she had never seen it for herself. She had never seen tools like these before, either. There was something like a knife, a club with spikes sticking out of it and a long stick with a pattern at the end. Ashael looked more closely. If she recalled it correctly, the pattern was the same as the mark on Iwan's chest, the one he had tried to cut off. Did that mean that Iwan had been a prisoner here too? Was that why he was always so evasive about his past?

Is there anything here they can use to escape? Ashael reached for one of the tools and again her hand passed through it. She leaned over the table for a better look. The club was bloodstained, a clump of hair hanging from one of its spikes. She recoiled in disgust, hand flying to her chest. The cold of her fingers against her skin made her realise there were no bandages on her hand, no broken fingers. Her spirit form appeared to be free of the injuries her body had sustained.

Can I make the lights come back? Ashael tried to remember how her hands had moved the night before. She tried to replicate the pattern, but nothing happened. Was it the wrong pattern? Or was the problem the fact that she was only here in spirit? She pinched the bridge of her nose and thought hard. *There must be something useful I can do here. Otherwise, why am I here at all? Think. I can't touch anything; I can't make the lights come back; I can't see anything that would help them escape, even if they did wake up.*

Can I wake them up? Ashael moved closer to the foragers. 'Wake up! Hello! Can you hear me? Wake up!' No response. She couldn't even be sure that she was making a sound that anyone except her could hear. Ashael flopped down onto the floor in the middle of the room. *I woke Bhearra. Where's that golden light when I need it?* Almost as soon as she had the thought, she began to see the golden light out of the corner of her eye. It surrounded and pervaded everything. *It's always there... It's in everything,* Ashael realised.

She took a deep breath, drawing the light into herself, as she had when Bhearra needed help. She breathed in for longer than seemed possible, the breath going on and on, the light infusing her body. Ashael held her breath, feeling the light flow through her. She felt connected to everything. It was overwhelming. Holding all of the foragers in her mind and heart, Ashael pushed the light. It exploded out from her, filling the room and dazzling Ashael with its power. As her vision cleared, she heard something hitting the floor and turned in the direction of the sound. The arrow had fallen from Ruraigh's shoulder. Through a tear in his clothing, Ashael could see that his skin was unbroken. The foragers began to stir. Ruraigh rolled his head, groaning. Colm's eyelids fluttered. Tris's fingers twitched. Erin mumbled. Alayne's eyes opened.

I did it! With that thought, the room faded and Ashael found herself back in her cell.

Chapter Twenty

MEEGRUM SWEPT PAST THE GUARD POSTED OUTSIDE HIS CHAMBER AND SLAMMED the door behind him. *How dare Daven blame this on me! Those ridiculous Hive things got the wrong information, that's not my fault. I've done everything he has asked of me, and more!*

His lord was demanding to know why the enchantress had been able to cast such a dangerous spell. Of course, Meegrum had no answer; she was supposed to be powerless until the solstice. He had to consider the possibility that this enchantress was not the one they were searching for. Daven had made it clear that Meegrum would be punished severely if he had brought the wrong person.

Meegrum stopped at the table against the wall and took a small apple from the tray in front of him, biting into it and enjoying the tart juice that filled his mouth. A knock came at the door.

'I do not wish to be disturbed!' Meegrum called.

Despite this, the guard poked his head round the door. 'Sir, it's the Hive creat –'

'I do not wish to be disturbed!' Meegrum screamed, throwing the apple at the guard, who ducked. The fruit smashed against the wall where his head had been only a moment before.

'You'll have to come back,' the guard said to the unseen visitor, pulling the door closed. Meegrum sank down into the hard, wooden chair by the empty fireplace. A copy of the prophecy lay on a table beside him, but he had no need to look at it; he had memorised it long ago:

In the year of the Dancing Flame will come the Vessel. When three moons rise on Longest Day, the soul of the land will enter the Vessel and she will become the embodiment of all. Strong she will be, to carry the soul, and powerful to protect it.

So little to base all of their futures on. If they failed and the king discovered their attempt, they would be killed. Slowly.

Daven's plan was bold; to drink the soul of the land as it entered the Vessel. With that much life force he would be restored to his past glory, or even beyond. Then he would make his way home and challenge the king, disposing of all of those who had benefited after his fall from grace centuries ago. Of course, Meegrum would be his executor, with all the power and privileges associated with the position.

Meegrum had put the Hive to work on detecting this Vessel, occasionally capturing creatures of this world to extract information. They had been waiting for nigh on eighty years before the Hive finally informed them, she had been born. That was when Daven had approached the king and started manoeuvring to get himself sent back to this cesspit of a world.

A tingling at the base of Meegrum's spine pulled him from his thoughts. *The prisoners,* he realised. *Something is interfering with my spells.* He rose to investigate but only made it halfway to the door. His spells rebounded, magic snapping back to him, the force throwing him across the room. He slammed into a wall, his head bouncing off the stone. Meegrum crumpled to the floor in a heap, unconscious.

***

Colm awoke with a start. He looked around at the unfamiliar surroundings, confusion clouding his thoughts. *Where am I?* Ruraigh, Tris, Alayne and Erin were also in the room, each looking as if they were just coming around. The last thing Colm remembered was sitting down to rest and share some food on the way back to meet Ashael. *Where are Nela and Faemon?*

'What's going on?' Tris was the first to speak. His voice was hoarse. He cleared his throat and tried again. 'Where are we?'

'How did we get here?' Alayne asked, pulling herself to her feet.

Colm saw her sway slightly before steadying herself against the wall. A stone wall. A stone floor. Small windows, high up in the wall, enough to let in a little light but too high to see out of. Or climb out of, for that matter. They were definitely in a room of some description, but it was like nothing Colm had ever seen before. On the wall facing him was an area that looked like an entrance but was barred by a huge slab of wood. Alayne had crossed the room to a table. Colm stood and started towards her when she jumped back.

'Oh, gods, where are we?' Her voice was now taking on a tinge of panic. 'This table's covered in blood! What is happening?'

Colm reached out to her. but she shook her head, straightening to her full height. Ruraigh put his hands on the floor to push himself to his feet. His fingers brushed against the shaft of an arrow lying beside him. He picked it up and rolled it in his hands, frowning.

'That's Iwan's arrow,' Colm said. 'I recognise the fletching. Could he be here somewhere?'

Erin looked at each of her companions in turn. 'How are you all so calm?' Her words came out in a rush, panic tinging her voice. 'We wake up in some mysterious room, with no idea how we got here, how long we've been here or anything, and you're all just talking as if there's nothing to worry about! We're not even all here! Faemon and Nela were with us, and they aren't now. Anything could have happened to them. Anything could have happened to us!' As she spoke, Erin jumped to her feet and started pacing the room.

Colm went to her and placed his hands on her shoulders. 'Peace. We'll figure this out, but we must keep our wits about us. Panic serves nothing.' He turned to the rest of the group. 'What is the last thing everyone remembers?'

'Filling our bags and baskets then heading back toward the cam,' Tris answered.

Ruraigh nodded in agreement. 'We sat down to rest and eat.'

They all looked at each other.

'Does anyone remember anything after that?' Colm asked. The other two men and Erin all shook their heads. Alayne looked at her hands and mumbled something.

'What was that?' Colm asked.

Alayne looked up but didn't meet his eyes. 'Darkness. I remember a cloud of darkness. And then some men. I think. I'm not sure about that part – it might have been a dream.'

At her words, a memory began to seep into Colm's mind. A terribly scarred face. A rasping voice, demanding to know where 'the enchantress' was. The scarred man grabbing his head and smashing it into a wall. Colm raised a hand to his head, questioningly. No pain. No sign of injury. Perhaps that, too, had been a dream.

'Was Ashael with us when we stopped to eat? Had she joined us?' Alayne asked.

'I don't think so,' Tris answered. 'Why?'

'I thought I saw her. Just as I woke up,' Alayne said. 'She's not here, though. I must be confused.'

'Faemon and Nela were definitely with us – where are they?' Erin asked, her tone still anxious.

'Perhaps they are in another room?' Tris ventured. 'With our bags and things. Iwan could be there too.'

'We need to make a plan,' Colm said. 'We've all been asleep for All-Mother knows how long. We have no knowledge of where we are or why we are here and two of our friends are missing. I think we have to get out of this room and try and find some answers. Are any of you opposed to this?'

When no one objected, Colm approached the entrance to the chamber they were in. Slowly, he pressed his hand against the wood and increased the pressure.

Nothing happened. The door didn't budge. He ran his eyes over the wood, looking for some clue. There was a sort of handle, made from an unfamiliar material. It was a ring hanging from a rod about halfway up the door. Colm glanced back at the others, who had crowded behind him, waiting to see what would greet them on the other side. Tris nodded.

Colm reached for the handle. The ring was cold and hard, like the strange, blood-covered items on the table. Colm paused for a moment and took a deep breath. His heart was pounding as if he'd just chased down an aurochs. There was no indication that anyone waited beyond but he wanted to be ready for anything. Gathering his courage, he pulled the handle towards him. Still no movement. Alayne and Tris moved up on either side of him and took hold of the handle too. All three of them pulled as hard as they could. Colm could see the cords standing out on Alayne's arm as she leaned her weight back. A grating sound came from inside the wood and Colm worried that someone might hear and come to investigate. There was nothing about their circumstances which suggested that anyone they encountered would be friendly. After a moment, Colm raised his hand and they all stopped, panting.

'I can help,' Ruraigh said.

'There's only enough space for three,' Colm answered. 'You and Erin stay back.'

The others paused to get their breath back.

'Let's try again,' said Colm. 'On the count of three. One… two… three!'

On three they pulled again, faces going red with exertion. This time the wood burst inwards in a cloud of dust and splinters. Gesturing to the others to stay back, Colm leaned his head through the gap between door and wall. He looked out into a stone corridor, stretching away from him. There was no one in sight but torches burned along the walls; someone had been here recently. He edged out into the corridor, Ruraigh close to his back, Alayne and Erin behind and Tris bringing up the rear. Silently, they crept along the corridor. They reached a junction. Off to the left the torches continued, but the path to the right was in darkness. The group bunched together, speaking in low murmurs.

'Which way?' Colm asked.

Ruraigh leaned into the centre of the group, his voice soft. 'Perhaps we are less likely to come across anyone if we take the dark path. Surely torches would be lit along that way if it was being used?'

'But it may be that no one goes that way because it's a dead end,' Erin whispered. 'We could be trapped.'

'We could be trapped whichever way we choose to go,' Alayne answered, a hint of exasperation in her tone.

'Show of hands,' said Colm. 'Who thinks we should go to the right?'

Ruraigh, Alayne and Tris raised their hands.

'Fine,' muttered Erin.

'To the right, then,' said Colm, reaching for the nearest torch – 'but let's take this with us.'

The right-hand corridor was not a dead end. It led to another darkened corridor and another after that. Periodically, the walls on either side would be interrupted by another wooden entrance. The foragers investigated each one, finding rooms full of broken furniture and ruined tapestries. So far, they had passed no accessible windows or passages to the outside. This building was large beyond comprehension.

'What happened here?' Tris asked in one room. 'So much destruction.'

'Whatever it was must have been a long time ago,' Erin answered. The room looked as if it had been undisturbed for many summers.

The stone beneath their feet grew thick with dust as they ventured further. Clearly, they were in a part of the building that was no longer in use. Colm worried about the trail in the dust they were leaving behind. *It's too late now. If we turn back, we could run straight into a pursuer, if there are any.*

In the next room that they checked, Ruraigh picked up several pieces of wood that appeared to be from a broken chair. Colm raised his eyebrow, questioning.

'We'll need another torch soon,' said Ruraigh, nodding towards the flame that was already starting to gutter.

'Good thinking, Ru,' Colm said, clapping the younger man on the shoulder.

Ruraigh opened the next door they passed. Nothing but dust and cobwebs. Three rooms on, they found moth-eaten clothes of peculiar design scattered on the floor. The foragers began collecting these and wrapping the cloth around the wood they had found. Now they had a supply of torches, all they needed was tallow to make them burn better.

As they made their way along the latest corridor, Colm realised there was less dust here. He was wondering if they were nearing parts of the building that were in use when Alayne put a hand on his shoulder, stopping him where he was.

'Can anyone smell that?' she asked in a murmur.

Colm sniffed the air and shook his head. He looked at Tris, who had raised his head and was still sniffing.

'Fire. Meat. Roasting meat… What do we do?' Tris said.

'We have to turn back,' Erin said in an urgent whisper. 'Find somewhere to hide.'

'We can't hide forever, Erin,' said Ruraigh. 'We have to try and find a way out of here. Where there's food, there may be an entrance nearby.'

Alayne sighed. 'Maybe we should split up. One of us can try to find a way out. The others can wait back in the last room we passed. One person is less likely to get caught than five.'

Colm didn't like the idea of splitting up, but he saw the sense in what Alayne said. One could move faster than five and hide more easily, too.

'Alayne is right,' he said. 'I'll go.'

'We'll all go back to the last room,' Alayne said. 'We can decide there, with less chance of being seen.'

The foragers backtracked to the last room they had passed. This one had a huge frieze hanging from the wall, torn in places, a table with the legs at one end broken off and some broken dishes. After shutting the door, they moved to the far-side of the room to reduce the chance of anyone hearing them if they passed.

'Colm, I know you offered to go, but I'd like to be the one to look for the way out,' Alayne started. Colm began to speak but Alayne held up a hand. 'I'm the best tracker of us all. I can move quickly and quietly and spot signs of others well in advance to actually running into them. It makes most sense for me to go.'

'You have a young child at home,' Ruraigh pointed out. 'You should stay here. I'll go.'

'You have a mate at home. For all you know, there could be a baby on the way,' Alayne retorted.

Erin looked between the two. 'I have young children too.'

'Yes, you should stay here, as well,' Ruraigh answered.

'All of you should stay here,' Colm interjected. 'I'm the oldest, my children are grown and though Sola, All-Mother bless her, will mourn for me, she'll manage without me. Probably better than she does with me, truth be told.' The last was said with a sad smile.

'This entire line of thinking is wrong,' Alayne said. 'If we don't get out of here then what will it matter who has children or is needed at home? None of us will be getting there. Now, I am the best equipped for the task. Do any of you dispute this?' She looked around as each of her companions shook their heads. 'Then I'll be going. It's hard to gauge time in this dark, gods-forsaken place but, if you can, wait no more than a notch for me. If I'm not back by then, I've been captured.'

'Are you sure about this?' Colm asked, his voice gruff with emotion.

'I'm sure. You should use that table to bar the entrance. I'll scratch at the door when I return so you'll know it's me.' With that, Alayne gave them all a brief kiss on the cheek and slipped from the room.

Chapter Twenty-One

ASHAEL PACED THE ROOM, FAR TOO ENERGISED TO MEDITATE ANY LONGER. When she had returned to her body, her injuries had been completely healed. *Somehow, I must have healed myself when I healed the foragers. So, I'm still connected to my body when I'm spirit-walking. I wish Bhearra and I had studied this more. I need to know how to control it. Why did I get pulled back?* Ashael paused in the middle of the stone floor, thoughts drawn to the foragers. She had seen enough to know she had healed any visible injuries and they were waking up, but she had no idea what happened after that. She could only pray they would find a way to escape. She had tried to get back to them, but without knowing how she had done it the first time, she hadn't been able to.

Ashael heard voices close to her door and hurriedly sat down in the corner she had been in before. She pulled her knees up to her chest and wrapped her arms around them, putting her forehead to her knees. If she could stay in this position, she might be able to hide the fact that she was healed. As the door opened, she slowed and deepened her breathing, feigning sleep.

Between slitted eyelids, Ashael saw the Hive thing enter her cell, robe sweeping the floor. It paused, waiting until the door swung shut behind it before speaking.

'How is it that you are healed?' it asked in its many voices.

Ashael sighed and straightened. 'How did you know?'

'We can feel when others are in pain. You are no longer in pain,' it responded.

'Will you run and tell those men so they can have me beaten again?'

'We do not condone violence. We take no part in that. How did your healing come to pass?'

'I don't know,' Ashael answered, her words true, though she hid her suspicions. *This thing is not like the men who brought me here. Perhaps I can befriend it. Win it to my cause.* 'What's your name?'

'We are of the Hive. We do not have a name, such as your people do.'

'Then what should I call you? Amongst my people, it is customary to have a name for those that help us,' Ashael answered.

'Lord Meegrum calls us Talak. You may use that name if it pleases you.'

'Very well, Talak. Why did you come to see me?'

'We came to check on your injuries. Those that you no longer have,' Talak replied.

'Why do you check on me? I can't imagine it matters to those men if I suffer.'

'They do not care if you suffer. We do, so we serve,' the voice at the fore now was gentle, soothing. Talak moved towards Ashael, sitting on the floor beside her.

Ashael's thoughts raced. This thing seemed to be open to conversation. *I need to get it to tell me things, without revealing anything about myself.* The thought made her heart sink. She had never before had cause to be duplicitous and she hated the thought of doing it now. *Careful. Don't let your guard down.*

'Why do you serve men such as those?' Ashael asked. 'I feel the evil pouring from them. But not from you.'

'Many generations ago the Zanthar came to our land.' Now the voice at the fore sounded like an elder, preparing to explain something to young ones. 'At first there was war and many of the Hive died. The Zanthar could not defeat us, but neither could we banish them from our world. You see, our greatest strength is also our greatest weakness: we of the Hive, we are all a part of the whole. We are but one in many. The knowledge of one is the knowledge of all, there is no confusion between us, no delayed orders, but each death is felt by all of the Hive. There was so much fear and pain in those years.' Talak trailed off, staring into space.

Understanding washed over Ashael. Somehow, these creatures had one consciousness. *That's why it always says 'we'. Why it has all of those voices.* Her throat tightened in empathy. Deep waves of sadness rolled off Talak. Ashael gently put a hand on its arm, offering what little comfort she could.

Talak patted Ashael's hand with its own then resumed speaking. 'After a time, Our Glorious Father, Alekiatorix, showed us the way to peace. We made a deal with the Zanthar. We would be useful to them and be their servants. This will continue as long as we are able to live according to our code.'

'I'm sorry for prodding at old wounds,' Ashael said in a soft voice.

'It is not for you to apologise,' Talak answered, climbing to its feet. 'We must go. The guard outside will become suspicious if we stay too long. Then we may be forbidden from tending to you.'

'But I have no injuries to tend.'

'Still. You may have further need of us.'

Ashael flinched as the door flew open and crashed against the wall. The scarred man stood there, breathing heavily. His scars stood in stark relief against his flushed face.

'What did you do to him, you bitch?' his spat, his gravelly voice strained.

Ashael cowered in the corner. She wanted to be defiant, to stand before this thing disguised as a man, but instead her knees trembled, and her stomach roiled.

With her failure to answer, the scarred one stepped forward and grabbed her hair, pulling her head back. 'I know you did something to him. Tell me what or I will make you suffer.'

'My lord, what has happened?' Talak asked tentatively.

'Meegrum has been injured.' The scarred one answered without turning around. 'Go to his chamber and tend to him immediately.'

Talak wrung its long fingers and shifted from foot to foot. 'My lord —'

'Go. Now.' Although the scarred one spoke in a strained whisper, his words had the effect of a roar. With an apologetic glance at Ashael, Talak turned and fled, robe billowing behind it.

Ashael felt like a deer staring down an arrow. Her limbs would not move, and she could find no words. She watched, terrified, as the scarred man pulled something from his belt. He held it in front of her eyes – it appeared to be a knife made from metal. *What sort of people would rip the minerals from the earth to make such things?* He bent down and pressed the blade against her cheek bone until Ashael felt a trickle of blood run down her face.

'Tell me what you did,' he said, moving the blade up to rest it beneath Ashael's eye.

'I don't know what you're talking about.' Ashael forced the words past numb lips.

The scarred man pressed the blade of the knife against Ashael's lower eyelid. Her breath caught in her throat as she felt the skin split. Her pulse thundered in her ears and heat rushed to her skin.

'Meegrum lies injured in his chamber though none entered the room,' the scarred man rasped. 'I may need you alive, but you don't have to be in one piece. Now tell me what you did, or I'll have this eye out.' He pressed harder on the knife to emphasise the point.

'I didn't do anything! I don't know *how* to do anything!'

'My lord!' A voice came from the doorway. 'My lord, the prisoners – they're gone!'

Relief flooded through Ashael. The foragers had escaped. It didn't matter what happened now – she had saved them.

Rage twisted the already hideous features of the scarred man. 'You did this,' he hissed, twisting his hand in Ashael's hair and pulling her head further back. Spittle flecked his lips. He turned to the man at the door. 'Find them and kill them,' he snapped.

'No!' Ashael cried out, her terror rising once more. 'You got what you wanted. Just let them go. Please.'

'On second thoughts, bring them to me,' the scarred man called after the guard. He turned back to Ashael. 'I think I'll make you watch as I feed on them. You should know what you're going to help me do to your world.' He moved the knife away from Ashael's eye and straightened up a little.

'I'll never help you, no matter what you do!' Ashael spat.

'Oh, you won't be able to stop me, no matter what you do,' the scarred man chuckled, the sound like rocks grating against each other. 'Of course, you'll only need one eye to see what happens to your friends.' Before Ashael could respond, the scarred man yanked her head back and flicked the point of his knife at her eye.

Ashael's vision took on a red hue that turned partially black. *I can't see the knife!* The scarred man moved back, and the knife was once again visible to her. The pain was enormous and came just as Ashael saw the jelly-like blob on the tip of the blade.

Chapter Twenty-Two

COLM PACED THE LENGTH OF THE ROOM AS THEY WAITED FOR ALAYNE TO RETURN. It was almost impossible to judge how long she had been gone. Colm felt no hunger or thirst or the need to relieve himself; none of a body's cues that time is passing. There were no windows to see the sky through. They had found a few tallow lanterns mounted on the walls and had lit them from the torch they carried. Colm glanced at one and saw that half of the tallow was now gone. At least this was an indication that time was indeed passing; the sun could have stopped in the sky, for all they knew.

Colm glanced at Erin, who had been sitting in the corner, muttering to herself, ever since the argument they had had a short time ago. She thought they had waited long enough and wanted to leave. Colm and the others thought they should give Alayne a little longer. The atmosphere between Erin and the men was becoming increasingly fraught. *I'm too old for this,* Colm thought. *I should be home, getting under Sola's feet. I miss you, dear heart.*

Colm paused his pacing and leaned against the rough stone wall. Until now, he had been so focused on finding a way out of this strange place that he hadn't taken much time to consider where they were. The building was like nothing he had ever seen before. Even the bigger homes in the cam had only two or three rooms, and most had only one. His own home would likely fit inside the room he stood in now. He had never heard of a building made of stone, either. As far as he knew, all of the cams used wood to build with.

'What do you think happened to us?' Ruraigh asked, crossing the room to stand beside Colm, Tris close behind.

Colm heaved a deep sigh. 'I wish I knew, Ru.'

'Don't you have any idea?' Ruraigh pressed. 'You can't be friends with Bhearra for as long as you have without picking up some knowledge of magic, surely?'

'Some, aye,' Colm responded. 'Nothing like what's happened to us, though.'

'You think it was magic then, whatever it was?' Tris asked, nervously drumming his fingers against his leg.

'I can't see what else it could be,' said Colm, frowning.

'It would need to be pretty powerful magic, wouldn't it?' Ruraigh asked. 'To bring us all here, keep us unconscious, make sure we don't remember anything. Could Bhearra do that?'

'I'm not sure.' Colm shrugged, getting frustrated, though whether it was because of the questions or his inability to answer them, he couldn't say. 'I can't see why she would try.'

'Let me be sure I understand,' Erin said, climbing to her feet and stalking towards the three men. 'You think that whoever did this may be stronger than Bhearra – the most magically gifted person any of us has ever met – and you *still* want to wait longer before we try and get out of here?' Erin's voice had risen as she spoke until she was almost shouting.

'Keep your voice down,' Ruraigh hissed urgently. 'Someone could hear you.'

'So, you have at least some survival instinct then,' Erin lowered her voice grudgingly. 'It's past time you three accepted that Alayne isn't coming back. Either she's been captured, or she found the way out and she's long gone. We need to go.' Erin strode over to the table blocking the door and began hauling at it. Colm went to her and placed a hand on her shoulder.

'I know you're scared, Erin,' he started.

Erin whirled round, batting his hand away. 'Don't you treat me like a child, old man. Of course I'm scared. I'm terrified. We all should be. I have children at home who still need their Mama. I don't know where I am or how long I've been away or how to get back to them. I need to see my children. I need to know they're safe and well.' Her voice broke on the last word and her fury turned to sobs. Colm gathered Erin into his arms and smoothed her hair, wishing there was something he could say to reassure her. He had been so busy trying to figure out what had happened to them that it had not occurred to him that something could have happened back at the cam. *Sola, dear heart, please be safe. All-Mother, I beg of you, protect her.*

Colm started as he heard a sound near the door. Swiftly, he pushed Erin behind him and stepped in front of her, Tris and Ruraigh taking up position on either side of him.

Scratch, scratch, scratch.

Colm motioned to Tris and Ruraigh to take either end of the table. Erin had backed away to the wall at the far side of the room. Colm lifted one of the table's broken legs. He held his hand up and counted down with his fingers. When his hand formed a fist, Ruraigh and Tris lifted the table and stepped back with it, as quietly as they could. Colm stepped behind the door, took a deep breath and held his weapon ready.

He threw open the door.

'Alayne,' he breathed in relief as she brushed past him into the room. He hurriedly closed the door, allowing Tris and Ruraigh to barricade it again.

'I would have been back sooner, but I stumbled across a lot of activity. I had to hide until things settled down.' As she spoke, Alayne rummaged through a woven bag she had tied to her belt. 'I found a storeroom. I got us some dried meat and fruit, a couple of waterskins and these. I think they're knives but they're not like any I've ever seen before.'

Alayne handed one to each of them. Colm examined the strange but familiar weapon. It was similar to the flint hunting knives they used at home, but it was made of the strange material they had seen elsewhere. He stuck the thing through a loop on his belt just as Ruraigh tested the blade of his own with his thumb. Immediately, blood began to well along a shallow cut.

'Just as well I also got these,' Alayne quipped as she pulled some strips of hide bandage from her bag. 'Here you go, Ru; try not to use them all up before we get out of here.'

Erin looked at Alayne, shame written all over her face. 'I owe you an apology. I wanted to leave. I thought you wouldn't be back. I did you a disservice.' A flush crept up her neck.

'Never mind,' Alayne shrugged, rummaging in her bag again. 'You're still here.' She tossed a clay pot to the other woman. 'Tallow, for the torches.'

Colm watched as Erin moved to prepare the torches. Some of her tension seemed to have been released with her earlier outburst. Now she looked exhausted. *Maybe we should try and get some rest before we leave,* he thought, looking at each of the others in turn, seeing the toll this was taking on them all. *No. We would get no true rest here. We'll all feel better outside of these walls.*

He turned to Alayne. 'What did you find?'

'A way out, though it won't be easy.' Alayne replied, taking a rawhide cord from her wrist and using it to tie her hair back. 'Through the cooking hall, there's a large room that appears to be for storage. There's a sort of pulley system, with a wooden platform attached to a rope, it seems to be for raising and lowering supplies from a room below. I could see light and feel air moving from down there so there must be an entrance. I couldn't reach the rope from the platform though, so I couldn't get down to check it out properly.'

'What was the activity you mentioned?' Tris asked, shifting impatiently from foot to foot.

'Groups of armed men moving about the halls,' Alayne answered. 'Looking for us, I think. I overheard someone mention five prisoners. They think some woman is responsible for letting us out and injuring a man called Meegrum. It sounded like he's someone important but not well liked. One man said he hoped

Meegrum would die and one of the others hushed him – said the walls may have ears, whatever that means.'

'Are we ready to go?' Tris asked, almost before Alayne had finished speaking.

'More than ready,' Erin muttered.

Colm and Tris moved the table from the back of the door while the others made sure they had gathered everything they could use.

They eased out and started along the corridor, single file. Alayne led, followed by Tris, Erin and Ruraigh, with Colm bringing up the rear. They shuffled along, each holding the shoulder of the person in front, no torch lit so as not to draw attention to themselves. There was still the smell of a fire burning, though that of roasting meat had faded. The fire smell grew stronger and there was a glow of light ahead. Colm peered over the heads of the others and saw that they were approaching a junction with a well-lit corridor. Alayne paused and they huddled together.

'A cooking place is to the right,' she said in a low voice. 'We have to pass through it to get to the storage room. I'll check if the way is clear.'

They all murmured their agreement and Alayne set off at a quiet jog.

Colm tried to stifle his impatience. Now that they were on their way, the further delay filled him with frustration. Tris shifted his weight from foot to foot, the constant motion grating on Colm's nerves. It appeared to be bothering Erin, too; she lay a hand on Tris's arm to stop him.

Colm's heart leapt into his throat when a face appeared around the corner, until he recognised it as Alayne's. He let out a slow breath, letting go of the adrenalin, then moved after Alayne as she gestured for them to follow her.

The corridor they stepped into had torches at regular intervals along the walls. There was no dust on the floor here, but spiders' webs hung from the ceiling and sconces. They followed the smell of fire past two barred entrances, walking in a tight group, hands on their weapons. They came to an opening in the wall. The cooking space beyond was vast, with two massive fireplaces both pouring out heat. In the centre of the room was a huge table with half-prepared food littering the surface. Alayne swiftly crossed the room to the rear corner. She leaned through a doorway then turned and gestured for the others to follow. Colm waited to watch the corridor as the others crossed the expanse of the cooking hall.

When the others were all safely in the storage room, Colm began to cross the kitchen. Just as he passed the table in the centre of the room, a young woman appeared in a doorway. Both of them stopped in their tracks, staring at each other. The young woman was the first person Colm had seen in this place. She looked like she could have come from the cam, although he did not know her. She wore simple clothing and had her long hair tied back. She looked thin and malnourished. Bruises marred the side of her face and her lip showed signs of having been split lately. Colm could see her pulse flutter in her throat. *She's scared*, he realised.

'I don't want to hurt you,' he said in a soft voice, raising his hands in what he hoped was a non-threatening gesture.

'You're one of the prisoners?' she asked, voice trembling.

'Why do you think that?' Colm responded.

'You're not a slave and you're definitely not Zanthar, so you must be one of them.'

Colm's heart stuttered. *Zanthar! All-Mother save us!* He stepped towards her, and she immediately stepped back, gaze flicking between the doors into the room.

'I don't want to hurt you,' he said again.

'You think I haven't heard that before?' she challenged, tilting her chin defiantly.

'I don't know what's going on here,' Colm said. 'Or even where "here" is. I just want to go home to my mate. Will you let me do that?'

'Take me with you,' she said, the last thing Colm expected to hear.

'What?'

'Take me with you. Please.'

'I don't know where we are or how we're going to get home. I couldn't promise to keep you safe.'

'I'm not safe here.' She looked at her feet and Colm realised just how young she was. Barely more than a child.

They both jumped as they heard footsteps approaching along the corridor. Colm looked at the girl in panic.

'Go!' she hissed.

He turned and ran into the storage room. The torches in here had been extinguished and the room was full of hulking shadows. Heart pounding, Colm made his way towards the nearest shadow and crouched behind a large crate full of some sort of supplies. He held his breath, trying not to make a sound. He heard a man's voice coming from the cooking hall.

'What have you been up to then, little one?' The voice was gruff, full of hard edges.

'Uh, what do you mean, sir?' the girl answered.

'You're all flushed, girl. Have you been up to no good?' The voice was moving closer now.

'I… I was organising the supplies, sir. They be heavy crates, sir.'

'Are you sure that's all it is?' The voice grew menacing. Colm peered around the edge of the crate that he hid behind. He could see the girl's back and, in front of her, a man in unusual dress: trousers and a tunic of a style Colm had never seen, with what appeared to be a kyragua-hide jerkin over the top. He loomed over the girl's tiny frame. He was missing an eye, which added to his threatening demeanour.

'Of course, sir.' The girl sounded terrified.

Just tell him I'm here, Colm thought, easing the knife from his belt. He would rather escape without confrontation, but he would not sit here and hide if that man lifted his hands to the girl.

'If one of the others has been having his way with you then I'll geld him. And it'll be worse for you,' the one-eyed man growled, grabbing the girl by the arm.

Colm tightened his grip on the weapon and shifted his weight, ready to spring to his feet.

''Course not, sir,' the girl squeaked. 'None but you, sir.'

'See it stays that way.' The man let go and stepped back. 'Make sure you're in my chamber just after moonrise. Don't be late or you'll have bruises on the other side of your face to match last night's.'

Colm eased himself to his feet as the man swept out of the kitchen. The girl began to weep. *I can't leave her here*, Colm thought. *She'll be safer with us, whatever happens*. His eyes scanned the room as he thought, looking towards the light coming through gaps in the floor at the far end. A soft voice took him by surprise.

'The others have gone below. I waited for you.' Ruraigh stepped forward, out of the shadows. 'We have to take her, don't we?'

Chapter Twenty-Three

JOREN TOUCHED HIS FINGERTIPS TO HIS HEART, LIPS AND FOREHEAD. DANLIV RE-turned the gesture then embraced Joren in a powerful hug. He was powerfully built, though his once-fiery hair and beard were showing some silver and a layer of fat was starting to form over his muscle. Danliv was leader of neighbouring Trout Cam and a force to be reckoned with. Joren remembered nights from his youth when his father and Danliv would sit by the Heart-Fire long into the night, drinking lacha. Joren would stay quiet and watch them, listening to their stories and bawdy jokes until his mother scolded them and chased him to bed.

'It's good to see you, Joren.' Danliv clapped the younger man on the back. 'You look more like your father every year.'

'Thank you, Danliv.' Joren responded. 'I'm sorry we're not better prepared for your arrival. We didn't expect to see you for another three days. Did you travel alone?'

'When I got your message, I thought it foolish to wait. I came as soon as I could. The rest of my party should catch up tomorrow.' Danliv turned as Rana approached. 'Rana! Look at you, child. Ever more beautiful.'

'Thank you,' Rana answered with a smile. 'Would you care to join us for some food? You must be weary from your journey.'

The group entered Joren's and Rana's home. Bhearra was waiting by the hearth. Danliv greeted the old woman warmly and the two exchanged news of shared friends for a few moments.

'So, are you going to tell me what's been going on?' Danliv finally said, settling himself on the floor with a bowl of stew.

Joren started explaining about the missing foragers. Rana's eyes filled with tears when he told of Faemon's and Nela's return; Joren took her hand. Bhearra took over the tale, explaining how Ashael went against the wishes of the cam to exchange herself for the foragers, and of her own contact with the All-Mother when she went looking for Ashael.

By the time the tale was finished, evening had fallen, and the room was filled with gloom. Joren stood and lit some tallow lamps, stretching his tall frame as he did so. It was unusual for him to sit for so long and it had taken a toll on his muscles. He waited, apprehensively, for Danliv to speak.

'This is... hard to accept,' Danliv said, staring into the fire pensively. 'If it was anyone else telling this tale, I would question their mind or their motives. Maybe both. But Bhearra, you're the steadiest person I know. Like a rock, you are. And Joren, you were never one given to flights of fancy, even as a child. I just... I don't know what to make of it.'

'I understand how you feel,' Bhearra said, her voice gentle. 'The All-Mother herself appeared to me. I lived through it, and I can still scarce believe it myself, so you must feel no shame for doubting. Think of it this way: if all is true and the Zanthar have returned, we must prepare to defend ourselves against being taken as slaves again. If I am wrong, the preparation will still benefit us against whatever foe has taken some of our number.'

'You speak true, Bhearra, as always. I need some time to take this all in, though. I think I shall go for a walk.' Danliv hauled himself to his feet, joints creaking. Rana moved to offer her hand, but Danliv waved her off. 'It's no fun getting old, girl, but it's better than the alternative.' He chuckled and made his way to the door.

'The guest hut has been prepared for you,' Rana said, walking at his side. 'There is fresh water, food and blankets. The hearth has been set. Let us know if you need anything else.'

Danliv bent down and kissed the young woman on the forehead. 'I'm sure you've thought of everything.' With that, he headed outside.

Joren added more wood to the fire. 'Do you think he believes us?' he asked, turning to face Bhearra and Rana.

'I think he'll give our words serious consideration,' Bhearra responded. 'Danliv is not one to make hasty judgements. Our cams have been closely tied for generations. It is well that he was the first to arrive.'

'If we can persuade him that what we say is true, he'll be a powerful ally in convincing the others,' Rana stated, beginning to brew some tea.

'And if we can't persuade him?' Joren asked. 'What then?'

'We do our best to persuade the others ourselves. If need be, we prepare to defend ourselves against the Zanthar alone.' Rana rested her hand on Joren's arm as she spoke. He covered it with his own, wondering at how small and fragile she seemed. It belied the strength that lay within her, lifting everyone around her. Especially him. She turned back to the tea and Joren saw her hand go to her belly. The sight strengthened his resolve. *I will find a way to convince them. I will keep you both safe.*

***

'BHEARRA!' THE CRY came from outside. 'Bhearra! We need you!'

Bhearra hurried to the entrance of Joren's home, throwing back the leather curtain that kept the cold out. 'I'm here,' she called out. 'Who needs me?'

Gerod was almost at Bhearra's home. He switched direction and headed towards her. 'It's Faemon. He's having some sort of fit. Hurry!'

Bhearra followed Gerod towards the other side of the Heart-Fire, Joren and Rana close behind.

'Tell me exactly what happened,' she puffed. Full dark had fallen and the light from the flames dazzled her, making it hard to see anything else.

'Some of us were gathered at the fire,' Gerod explained. 'We were sharing food and chatting. Faemon was saying how well-recovered he felt. Then his eyes went strange, as if he was staring at something no one else could see. He went rigid. I spoke to him, but he didn't respond. He didn't seem to have heard me.' A group of people parted as she approached, revealing Faemon, lying motionless at their centre.

'What else?' Bhearra asked as she went to her knees beside Faemon.

'His left side sort of slumped. He fell to the ground, and I ran for you.'

Bhearra checked for a heartbeat and breathing. Both were there but faint. The left side of Faemon's face was slack, his mouth and eyelid turned down, but his eyes were open, and he appeared conscious. As she worked, Bhearra spoke to him in a soothing voice.

'N-n-n-n-n,' Faemon's right eye focused on Bhearra as he tried to speak.

'Hush now, save your strength.' Bhearra squeezed his shoulder. 'We're going to take care of you.'

'N-n-n-n-n,' he tried again.

'What is it, dear? What's so important?'

'H-h-h-h-huh,' he exhaled.

Bhearra crouched, waiting for him to try again. No inhalation came. Bhearra took a deep breath and closed her eyes, trying to centre herself, to slow the rapid beating of her heart. She reached out with her senses, searching for Faemon's essence, just as she had that day with Soraya's baby, Bhearrael... There. It was still in his body. Bhearra tried to touch the essence, to soothe it, encourage it to stay. She was peripherally aware of Gerod loosening Faemon's clothes, propping him up, while Rana spoke in a soft voice, encouraging Faemon to breathe.

Bhearra watched helplessly as Faemon's essence began to rise out of his body, a soft golden mist escaping into the night air. She reached out to smooth his passage when something caught her attention. The mist rising from Faemon's head was not the golden colour of the rest. It was black and smelled of rot. A buzzing sound, like a cloud of angry bees, filled Bhearra's mind. As the golden mist evaporated, the black stain remained, floating in the air above Faemon's body. It swirled, growing ever tighter, until it was no more than a spot. Bhearra reached towards it with her senses, probing and examining. This darkness felt familiar. *Where have I encountered this before?*

The black spot disappeared with a pop that sounded in Bhearra's mind. She came back to herself, opening her eyes to see Rana bent over Faemon's body, crying. Joren knelt behind her, head bowed. The crowd around them had grown as more people had learned something was wrong. Many of the Folk were crying while others mumbled prayers. Bhearra saw Danliv at the back of the crowd. His eyes met hers and he nodded. Bhearra knew then that he would stand with them.

***

THE REST OF Danliv's party arrived the following day. They entered the cam solemnly, having met scouts who informed them of Faemon's death. Angus, the young filidh of Trout Cam, offered to assist Bhearra in preparing the body for the farewell rite which would take place that afternoon, and Bhearra graciously accepted. As much as she hated to admit it, moving a body around was a young person's task. It would also give her a chance to get to know Angus better, try to gauge his support. Danliv took the other men and women of his cam on a hunt, boasting that he would catch a deer for the traditional guest's gift.

Bhearra led Angus to her home, where Faemon's body rested. Gerod and Bran had already undressed him and covered him with the fibre shroud he would go to the earth in. Bhearra paused at his feet and swallowed the lump in her throat. She knew death was merely the next stage of life. Faemon would join the ancestors in the Summerland, where he would rest for a time before being reborn. Although she felt sorrow over his loss, she carried no guilt that she could not prevent his death. Missing his last words, though: that weighed her down.

Angus cleared his throat and Bhearra started – she had forgotten he was there. 'I'll start heating some water,' she said, turning to face the young filidh. 'Would you like to prepare the herbs? Everything is in those baskets.' She gestured towards the wall.

'Of course,' Angus replied, moving to where she had pointed.

Bhearra watched the young man as he worked. He was small for a man, both in height and stature. *He looks like a strong wind would blow him away.* He had the black hair of their people, but his skin was very light and his eyes blue-green. Very unusual. His skin had reddened from the sun. Summer would not be kind to him.

Bhearra prodded the fire, causing the flames to dance, before hanging her cauldron in place.

'How did he die?' Angus asked, his voice soft.

'I don't rightly know,' Bhearra sighed. 'I haven't seen the like before.'

'Really?' Angus looked surprised.

'Really. It seems that even at my age there are new things to learn.' Bhearra gave a wry smile.

Angus blushed. 'That's not what I meant.'

'No shame in being old, or in acknowledging it,' Bhearra reassured the lad. The water was coming to a simmer, so she removed the cauldron from the fire and carried it carefully to Faemon's side. She collected a goat-hide cloth and dipped it into the warm water. 'I think it was something to do with the head. He seemed to lose function down one side of his body. He wasn't able to speak, though he was trying.' She looked over at Angus. 'Sometimes, if a person takes a bad blow to the head, there are similar problems. I've never seen it without an injury, though.'

Angus brought over the herbs they would use to anoint Faemon's body and began crushing them in a pestle and mortar that had been stored next to the herb baskets. He knelt at Bhearra's side, eyes on his work as she removed the shroud and began to wash the body.

'Could he have had a head injury no one knew about?' Angus asked.

'It's possible. There's no sign of one but no one knows what happened while he was gone. Not even he did.' Bhearra continued to wash the body as she told Angus of all that had happened.

'So, there could be a magical cause then?' Angus asked when Bhearra had finished her story. He helped her to roll Faemon onto his front, allowing her to wash his back. Angus carefully began to melt some beeswax, mixing in the crushed herbs as he did.

'Possibly, yes. Perhaps even likely.' Bhearra explained about the black spot she had seen as Faemon's essence left his body.

'Could the Zanthar do this? Kill from a distance, I mean?' Angus sounded close to panic.

'We cannot be sure that's what happened. Even if his death is something to do with the Zanthar, it's just as likely to be something they did while he was there.' Bhearra said soothingly. The young man's face had gone grey, except for two spots of colour high on his cheekbones. He stared at Faemon's body in horror.

'I... I'm sorry. I can't be here,' he stammered before rushing from the hut.

***

ASHAEL DRIFTED IN a grey fog. She knew something was dreadfully wrong, but she couldn't quite bring herself to care. That strange creature, Talak, had given her something. Something that had clouded her mind and dulled her pain. *What pain? Why was I in pain?* She hadn't wanted to take anything from it at first, but she couldn't remember why not. *It doesn't seem to mean any harm. I wonder if it's male or female. I don't want to keep calling it 'it'; that seems rude. Would it be ruder to ask?* Ashael snorted laughter. *I shouldn't be laughing. Why shouldn't I be laughing?*

Ashael tried to roll over onto her side, but something stopped her. She lifted her hand towards her face, but it stopped short. She opened her eyes. Something was odd. She couldn't see properly. What was different? It was hard to think through the fog. She tried to sit up, but something still stopped her. With great concentration, Ashael managed to focus on her torso. Some sort of rope was holding her down. It pinned her to the bench she was lying on. Ashael let her head fall back, limp. Even that brief effort to focus had left her dizzy. She panted and tried to think. *I can't feel the rope holding me down. Why is that?* As she concentrated on her restraints, she became aware of the sensation of being held down. *Ok, so I can feel it if I pay attention. This is so strange. I have to try and think. There's something... something important.*

Ashael turned her head to the left and started when she saw the one-eyed guard standing within arm's length – or at least, he would be if she could move her arms. *Why didn't I see him before? How did he get so close without me noticing?* Ashael turned her head upright again, watching how the guard disappeared from view. *I can't see past my nose! Why can't I see past my nose?* She let her head fall to the left once more. The guard smirked at her. He pointed to the drooping eyelid that covered an empty socket then leaned forward.

Ashael felt his breath wash over her cheek, hot and foul, as he whispered in her ear. 'How do you like it, witch?' With that, Ashael's memory came flooding back and she screamed.

Chapter Twenty-Four

COLM STIFLED A SIGH AND SLOWED HIS PACE, ALLOWING THE GIRL TO CATCH UP. It had been six days since they escaped. Six days of travelling through unfamiliar land, not sure where they were going and constantly looking over their shoulders. Six days of Erin complaining they weren't moving fast enough and giving the girl, Gert, disgusted looks. Six days of short rations and no campfire. *Thank the gods it's summer.*

As far as they could tell from the position of the sun and stars, they were somewhere in the mountain range known as The Edge of the World, so they were travelling east, hoping to find familiar land and figure out how to get back to the cam. There was plenty of small game in the hills, but they were scared to draw attention to themselves with a campfire, which meant they couldn't cook anything. Instead, they rationed out the dried meat Alayne had brought with them and foraged what greens they could find.

Colm thrust out a hand as Gert stumbled beside him, catching her just in time to prevent a fall. Unlike them, the poor girl was unaccustomed to walking for any distance and her feet were suffering. While the Folk from the cam wore only thin hide slippers, Gert had some sort of hardened leather footwear. Colm had no idea how she managed to walk at all, being so disconnected from the ground. He had encouraged her to discard these things and go barefoot but she looked at him like he was soft in the head, so he didn't press the issue.

He'd been getting a lot of those looks since they'd escaped. Alayne and Tris did not entirely trust Gert, even though she had distracted the guards at the outside entrance to the storeroom, helping them get away without bloodshed; and Erin resented being slowed down. *They probably would have left her on her own by now if it wasn't for Ru backing me up about the one-eyed man,* he thought. She had been able to give them some information about their captors and what she had told them left Colm deeply troubled. She had claimed that the men in control were Zanthar – a name from the past that Colm never thought to hear outside of stories. If it was true, then his people were in great peril. Gert claimed she had not always been here; she had distant memories of another place before this one, when she was very young. She didn't know any details of why they were here, after all this time, but she did know the Zanthar were expecting something big to happen on Longest Day and that it involved a young woman who was also being held captive.

Colm was anxious to get Gert to Bhearra – let the filidh decide what to make of the girl's tale. The trouble was, judging by the length of time the sun was in the sky, Longest Day would be in the next four or five days. Last night, the sun had only been down for a short time – barely long enough for the sky to get truly dark. They would not reach the cam before whatever happened that the Zanthar were waiting for.

Erin turned and glared at Gert. 'How do we know you're not slowing us down deliberately?' she asked.

Colm sighed. 'We've discussed this before. If she was going to betray us, then why would she help us escape in the first place?'

'I don't know,' Erin huffed. 'But there must be some reason that she's so slow.'

'I'm sorry.' Gert looked at her feet and increased her pace a little, wincing. She was limping, her feet rubbed raw.

She's tough to keep going when her feet are causing so much pain, thought Colm. 'When we get out of these hills, we should be able to find a willow, get you some bark for the pain,' he said, voice gentle.

Tris, who had been scouting ahead, came hurrying back towards them. Colm saw him stop and speak to Alayne and Ruraigh. Colm gave Gert an apologetic look then sped up to find out what was happening.

'… the embers were still warm,' Tris was saying as Colm arrived just a moment behind Erin.

'Was there anything to say whether this was a friend or a foe?' Alayne asked, tension clear in the line of her shoulders.

'No.' Tris shook his head.

'Maybe we should look for somewhere to hide, just in case,' Ruraigh said, looking around. 'There's bound to be caves in these hills. Maybe we could find one?'

'Could you tell how many people had been there?' Colm asked.

'Not for certain but there was little disturbance, and it was only a small fire so I would guess not many. Why?' Tris said.

'I think we need to keep moving.' Colm met Erin's eyes and she nodded at him, relief crossing her face. 'If it's only a small group we should be able to overpower them if need be.'

At that moment, Gert drew up to them. 'What's going on?' she asked.

Tris explained that he had found a sign that someone else was in the area.

"Far as I know, if anyone needs go farther than a day from the keep, Lord

Meegrum sends them through a portal. Not like' to be any of them wandering about here,' Gert told them.

'A portal?' Alayne asked.

'I'm not rightly sure what it is. I never seen one. Meant to be a kind of hole in the air that takes you out wherever you be needing to go.' Gert looked at her feet as she spoke.

'Magic doesn't work like that,' Erin scoffed, though she looked uncomfortable as she did so. 'Someone's been having you on.'

Gert blushed and shrugged. 'That's just what they say.'

'Don't be too quick to dismiss it, Erin,' Colm said thoughtfully. 'It would explain a few things. Like how we got there.'

'Perhaps we could discuss this after we've decided how to proceed?' Ruraigh interjected.

'I think we should keep moving, with caution,' Colm said.

Erin nodded her agreement, as did Alayne. Ruraigh looked at the two women then also nodded.

'I agree,' Tris said.

They all turned and looked at Gert.

'What?' she asked, looking confused.

'What do you think we should do?' Tris asked her.

'She's not one of us,' Erin snapped. 'She shouldn't get a say.'

'Enough of this,' Colm said, voice sharp. 'Would you treat someone from another cam with so little courtesy?'

Erin looked sheepish but did not back down. 'She is not from another cam; she is from the place we were taken against our will. A place filled with Zanthar, if she is to be believed. Why should we give her a place?'

'She no more asked to be there than we did,' Colm said. 'She helped us to get away. She has given us no reason to distrust her. This has to stop.' Colm looked around the group. No one voiced disagreement so he turned to Gert. 'Do you think we should continue or look for somewhere to hide?'

'Um, just the same as you, I guess,' she answered. 'Why do you care what I think?'

'Everyone gets a say in important decisions. That's how we do things.' Alayne looked at Gert with a frown. 'As long as you're travelling with us, you get a say.'

'No one ever asked what I think before,' Gert said. 'I'm just happy you let me come along. I'll do whatever you all want.' She looked at her feet again. Out here, in the daylight, she looked even younger than she had before.

Colm hadn't asked but he suspected that she had not yet come of age by the cam's standards. His flesh crawled to think of that giant one-eyed man brutalising this girl who was little more than a child. If Joren and Bhearra allowed her to join

163

the cam, he would ask Sola if she could stay with them. He was sure she would agree; Sola had a soft heart.

***

THE GROUP MADE their way along a narrow trail – a steep cliff face rising to their right and another dropping off to their left. Colm watched anxiously as Gert stumbled in front of him, letting his breath out only when she had regained her footing. In his mind's eye he could see only too clearly what a body would look like broken on the rocks below.

'I've been wanting to ask you something,' Colm said to the girl, 'but I don't want to cause you any pain.'

Gert snorted. 'It'd take more than a question to cause me pain. Ask.'

'You have a scar on your arm – looks like a broken pattern. How did that happen to you?'

Gert looked down at her upper arm and the scar that Colm had asked about. 'The original pattern was my slave-brand. All the slaves have them, somewhere on their body. The Zanthar use them to control you, to find you, to hurt you.'

'They can find you with that?' Colm asked, alarmed.

'When it was whole, they could have. Zek didn't want his bed-slave used to spy on him, though, so he cut my arm down the middle of the brand; broke the pattern. Hurt real bad when he did it but I guess he did me a favour. I never would have been able to run away otherwise.'

'You're sure they can't track you now?'

'I'm sure. Lord Meegrum tried to use the brand to hurt me once. I faked it so he would think it still worked.'

Clever girl, Colm thought.

A pebble bounced past his face, startling him so that he, too, stumbled. He reached out a hand and caught himself against the jagged rock of the cliff to his right. Another pebble tumbled past his face. Colm craned his neck, looking for the source of the disturbance, but he couldn't see anything past the shape of the rock looming above. Gert looked back, realising that Colm was no longer behind her. He lifted a weathered finger to his lips, hoping that she would understand his signal for quiet. She watched, eyes wide and frightened, as Colm leaned away from the cliff, trying to see further up.

Just as Colm reached the limit of his balance, a face appeared above the rocky overhang, startling him. For a moment he teetered, struggling to keep his footing. He heard Gert scream, but the sound seemed far away. He recognised the face above at the same moment that he overbalanced and fell off the side of the cliff.

Colm twisted as he fell, grabbing for handholds, desperately trying to stop his descent. His left shoulder jarred when he caught the trunk of a sturdy bush that brought him to an abrupt halt. He managed to get his right hand around the bush, taking some of his weight off his injured shoulder. A voice called from above, but he couldn't make out the words over the pounding of his heart and the rush of blood in his ears.

'Colm!' Gert cried, 'Colm, can you hear me?'

'Yes,' Colm muttered.

'Colm!' Gert called again.

'I hear you.' Colm struggled to raise his voice, his chest and throat restricted by the awkward position he was hanging in.

'Oh, thank all of the forgotten gods, I thought you were dead.' Gert's voice was thick with emotion.

'Colm, where are you? We can't see you,' Alayne called down.

'Hanging from a bush.' He tipped his head back, looking up. 'It has red leaves. Very thick.'

'I see it,' Alayne shouted back. 'We're coming to get you. Hang on.'

Colm grunted, saving his breath. He could hear what sounded like arguing above but the words weren't clear. He flexed his elbows, moving some of the strain to his back. Colm was still strong for someone his age, but he was under no illusions that he would be able to hang here for long. He twisted his head, looking around as much as he could from his awkward position... There: a ledge that looked wide enough to support his weight. He tensed his abdominal muscles, lifting his legs then stretching them out towards the ledge. He growled with the effort, toes scrabbling for purchase. The ledge was just beyond his reach. The burning in his shoulders and upper back told him that he wouldn't be able to dangle where he was for much longer.

He let his legs fall back and tried to catch his breath.

'Dammit!' said Alayne from above. 'Colm?'

'Still here,' he answered. *So far.*

'The rope we have doesn't reach you. We'll think of something. Just keep hanging on.'

Colm couldn't wait. 'I can see a ledge; I'm going to try and reach it.' He was struggling to talk now. He knew that he had to reach the ledge, or he would fall, soon. He swung his legs back and forth until his whole body began to swing. If he could work up some momentum, he might just be able to jump to the ledge. Of course, he could miss. Or reach the ledge only to topple off. But if he didn't try, he was definitely going to fall. His muscles were screaming in pain. He took as deep a breath as he could manage. *All-Father, give me courage.* He swung towards the ledge and let go of the bush.

Time seemed to stop, suspending him in the air. He had time to think of Sola.

He saw her face, every line and contour of it familiar to him. His body filled with warmth and a smile came to his face. *I love you, Sola.*

Then he landed on his back. He skidded along the ledge, his tunic bunching up, exposing skin, rock scraping furrows in his back. He came to a halt, lower legs dangling over the side of the ledge. *Thank you, All-Father. When we get back to the cam, I'll be sure to make an extra special offering in your name.*

'What's going on?' Erin was almost screaming when Colm became aware of his companions again.

'I got to the ledge,' he called up. 'I'm alright.'

'Someone's coming to get you. Colm, you won't believe this, it's –'

'Iwan,' Colm finished for her as the man in question appeared on the ledge next to him. 'What in the All-Mother's name are you doing here?'

Chapter Twenty-Five

COLM AND IWAN INCHED THEIR WAY UP THE CLIFF FACE. ON THE WAY DOWN, Iwan had used his knife to gouge out hand holds. Now, the two men, tied together with the rope that Alayne had been carrying, used the holds to climb back up to the path.

Sweat trickled down Iwan's forehead, into his eyes. He rubbed his face against his upper arm as best he could, reluctant to lift a hand away from the rock before he had to. The rope around his waist tightened.

'How are you doing back there, Colm?' he asked.

'Tired. How much further?' Colm answered.

Iwan craned his head back, trying to gauge the distance to the path. Alayne peered over the edge, anxiously watching their progress.

'Almost there. About my height still to climb,' Iwan said.

'I can make it,' Colm muttered behind him, but he didn't sound sure of that at all.

Iwan's fingers cramped from clinging to the rock. He stretched for the next handhold, hauling himself up a little further. He was impatient to get to the top and find out what the foragers knew about Ashael.

It seemed a long time had passed before he finally reached the top of the cliff. As soon as he was within reach, Ruraigh and Tris leaned over and grabbed his arms, pulling him up onto the path. As Iwan lay panting, Tris and Ruraigh hurried to help Colm. Alayne handed Iwan a waterskin and some dried fruit, which he took gratefully. He pulled himself into a sitting position and sipped at the water, stretching his arms and shoulders, trying to prevent stiffness from setting in.

'Now that we're all safe, maybe you can tell us what's going on,' Alayne said. 'Did you come looking for us?'

'Yes and no,' Iwan replied. He looked along the narrow path where they were all spread out. 'Let's move from here, first. It's not the safest place to have a meeting. I camped a short way from here last night. Why don't we head there? Then I'll tell you everything I know.'

'Very well. I suppose we'll have to stop for the night soon, anyway.' Alayne went to tell the others the plan.

Iwan spotted a dark head looking down at Colm as he rested on the path – the young girl with the group. She wasn't from the cam but she looked familiar. That could mean trouble.

Iwan led the group to the remains of his campfire – the one Tris had found earlier. They were reluctant to light another fire and risk drawing attention to themselves, but Iwan assured them that he had come across no one else in the days that he had been travelling. What really convinced them, though, was the thought of a hot meal. None of them could remember when they had last eaten hot food. Gert and Erin set the fire while Iwan and Alayne set out in search of game.

Alayne was an excellent tracker, and it wasn't long before she spotted signs of a goat. Iwan nocked an arrow on his bow string, ready to shoot when they found the animal. He could see Alayne was desperate to ask questions but instead she concentrated on the task at hand. Iwan followed her as she tracked the goat, trying to figure out how much he should tell the foragers. They rounded a bend in the path and saw the goat in front of them. On silent feet, Alayne moved aside, giving Iwan a clear line of sight. The goat was facing away from them, nibbling at a sparse patch of grass. Iwan lifted his bow and sighted down the arrow, waiting. His shoulders twinged as he pulled the bow string tight; he would be feeling that climb for a few days. Iwan stood perfectly still, careful to avoid startling the goat. Alayne seemed a statue at his side. The animal finally lifted its head. Iwan let out his breath as he released the arrow. It flew straight and true, embedding itself in the goat's neck. The animal collapsed, blood seeping out onto the dry soil beneath it. Iwan stepped to its side and quickly drew his knife across its throat, finishing the job.

'I thank you for your sacrifice that we may eat,' Iwan said as he rested his hand upon the goat's still-warm body. 'As you feed us, so we too shall one day feed the land. Blessings of the All-Mother upon your spirit.' He then hoisted the goat onto his shoulders, and he and Alayne headed back to camp.

As the goat roasted over the campfire, Iwan finally began his story. He told the foragers of how they had gone missing and the cam's search for them. He told them of Bhearra's illness and Ashael's intervention. When he got to the part of the story where Faemon returned to the cam with Nela's body, Erin began to weep and Alayne comforted her, tears shining in her own eyes. Iwan saw Colm's body tense up and sensed his distress. The only one who was completely unaffected by the news was the dark-haired girl who Colm had introduced as Gert. She studied Iwan's face from the other side of the campfire. It made Iwan uncomfortable. *Does she know me?* He broke eye contact, hoping it was not recognition he saw on her face.

Iwan related the message Faemon had brought from their captor. He refrained from mentioning the vote to keep Ashael at the cam; it could do nothing but cause hurt. When he told them of Ashael giving herself over to save them, he did not mention the portal. Nor did he fully explain how he got here himself. He did not tell a lie, but he did phrase things to suggest that he had been following a trail left by those who took Ashael. *Now is not the time to try and explain how I know where to go,* he justified to himself. When he had finished his account, Iwan paused and took a sip of water. Looking around the faces of the foragers, all he saw was confusion.

'So now it's your turn. Where's Ashael? What did you find out when you were released?'

The foragers all looked at each other, sharing some silent communication.

Finally, Colm spoke. 'Iwan, we weren't released. We escaped. We don't know anything about Ashael being there.'

Iwan's heart fell. He had suspected this, but he hadn't been able to stop himself from hoping they would know something. Even just that she was alive, that there was still a chance he could save her.

'There was one odd thing,' Ruraigh said. 'One of your arrows was on the floor of the room that we awoke in. Colm recognised the fletching. How would one of your arrows have got there?'

'I shot after them when they took Ashael,' Iwan answered. 'Maybe I hit someone.' *Please, All-Mother, don't let it be Ashael.* Iwan's stomach clenched. The smell of roasting goat was not as appealing as it had been a moment before. *Pull yourself together!*

'Do you know anything, Gert?' Colm asked, suddenly.

'There was a girl. Don't be knowing her name, though,' Gert said, drawing her knees up to her chest and wrapping her arms around them.

'What do you know?' Iwan demanded.

'Not much,' Gert mumbled into her lap. 'Lord Daven, he be wanting a girl. Some enchantress, I heard tell. They was holding her prisoner. Meant to be something big happening on Longest Day. Something to do with the girl. That's all I know.' Gert raised her eyes, looking straight at Iwan. 'Might be some as know more,' she said with a hint of defiance.

'Why didn't you tell us any of this before?' Erin asked, her voice harsh. 'What else have you been keeping from us?'

'Didn't know it was anything to do with you,' Gert answered. 'Not like Lord Daven drops into the kitchens to tell me all his plans! I only know what I do from overhearing things. That and Zek's idea of pillow talk.' Gert's voice was heated now.

'How did you come to be here?' Iwan asked her, trying to defuse the tension rising between the two women.

'She helped us escape,' Colm explained.

He told Iwan how they had made their way to the room she called a kitchen, how she had kept his presence secret from the one-eyed man called Zek. 'When we got down to the room where the supplies came in, Gert warned us about the two guards outside. She ran out, screaming about a fire in the kitchen, calling for them to help. As soon as they left their posts, we ran. After that, they would have known she helped us and they would have killed her; we had to bring her with us.' Throughout the story, Erin had tutted and huffed, making it clear that she hadn't agreed with the decision to bring the girl along.

'The food is ready,' Alayne said, pulling the meat from the flames. 'Let's eat. We can all take some time to think, then figure out what to do from here.'

After the meal, Iwan headed into the bushes to the relieve himself. As he finished and adjusted his clothing, a voice sounded behind him, making him jump. He turned around to find Gert standing close by, although she had turned away to allow him some privacy.

'I won't tell,' she said. 'You don't have to hurt me. I'll keep quiet.'

'What are you talking about?' Iwan asked, heart pounding.

'I won't tell them you're from the keep,' she said, turning to look at him.

'You're confused,' Iwan said, but his voice lacked conviction.

'Maybe I am,' Gert said, 'but I still won't say anything. Please don't hurt me.'

Iwan looked at the girl, saw how she trembled. She was terrified of him. 'Of course I won't hurt you. Whatever you think I am, you're wrong. You're safe now.' *How can I reassure her without saying too much?* 'Ashael, the girl who was taken, I care for her. I just want to find her and see her home.'

Gert examined his face as if she could read his soul there. Maybe she could.

'I believe you,' she said. With that, she turned and headed back to the campfire.

Iwan let out a slow breath, trying to calm his pounding heart. He needed to compose himself before going back to the others. The dishonesty was wearing on him but now was not the time to unburden himself. He had to get to Ashael. If he managed to get her to safety, he would tell Joren and Bhearra everything and accept their judgement.

Back at the campfire, Colm was speaking. '... can't just leave him alone.' He broke off and they all turned to look at Iwan as he approached. Although the sun was still in the sky, even this late into the evening, it had moved to the other side of the mountain, casting them in shadow. The flickering light from the fire revealed concern on their faces.

'Is there a problem?' Iwan asked, sitting on a rock close to the fire.

'We were discussing how to proceed,' Ruraigh said. 'We're all anxious to get home, and from what you've told us there's still several days travelling ahead, but we don't want to leave you alone.'

'You should go home,' Iwan said. 'I can handle this.'

'Iwan, you haven't seen that place,' Colm reasoned. 'It's massive. Bigger than any cam I've ever been in. If Ashael is there, it'll be difficult to find her and difficult to get her out. Surely it makes sense to have more than one person searching?'

'It does make sense, and I appreciate the offer,' Iwan replied, hoping they would not see through his attempts to put them off, 'but Ashael gave herself up to save you. I can't ask you to endanger yourselves now. If you went back in and something happened to you, then Ashael's sacrifice would have been for naught.'

'What if we split up?' Tris suggested. 'Some of us can continue back to the cam and tell them what we know, and some of us can go with you to help Ashael.'

'She's there because of us. We can't just leave her,' Alayne agreed.

'If you insist.' Iwan knew any further protest would be suspicious, so he agreed. *This changes things. I can't just walk in with them in tow. As if this wasn't all complicated enough!*

***

IN THE END, they decided Colm and Tris would go with Iwan, while the others would head back to the cam and tell Bhearra and Joren everything they knew. Colm was anxious about leaving Gert with the others, but Ruraigh had been in favour of taking her along from the start, so she had a supporter in him.

Colm was bone-weary. The fall and ensuing adrenaline rush had really taken it out of him. Iwan wanted to push on through the night, stopping to rest only when the sun was down. It would take everything they had to get back to the keep before Longest Day. There were still a couple of notches of light so they would move on as soon as they had said their goodbyes.

Alayne came over and hugged Colm, wishing him a safe journey. 'You make it home, Colm. Be safe.'

'I'll do my best,' he answered, stepping back to look at her. 'Keep an eye on Gert for me, will you? She needs taking care of.'

'Of course. Is there anything you want me to tell Sola?'

Colm thought for a minute. What words could he send to explain all of this? How could he let his mate know that he loved her when the words seemed so inadequate?

'Tell her I had to go back. That it was the right thing to do. And I'll be back under her feet before she knows it. She'll be wishing I was gone again.'

Iwan and Tris wandered over, ready to go. With a last wave to the others, Colm turned and began retracing his steps back towards the prison he had only recently escaped from.

Chapter Twenty-Six

RED. EVERYTHING WAS RED AND PULSING. ASHAEL SCRUNCHED HER EYES CLOSED. Eye. How long would it take to get used to the fact she had only one eye? Whatever they had given to her to dull the pain was wearing off and the entire left side of her face throbbed with every heartbeat. She would take the pain over the fog though. She would wrap herself around the pain and make it her own. She would not give that monster the satisfaction of watching her suffer.

Ashael had tried to heal herself as she had inadvertently done before, but it hadn't worked. She had failed several times before she remembered Bhearra explaining how their magic could only work with what was there. If her eye had been damaged, she should have been able to heal it, but it had been removed; she couldn't grow another one. That was when she had given up.

She heard voices approaching. It sounded like One-Eye and Talak. Ashael tried to relax the muscles of her face, to give them no sign of her pain. She opened her eye a tiny bit. She watched Talak speak softly, gesturing towards her with a bottle in hand. One-Eye tutted and went back to his place by the door. Ashael let her eye fall fully closed as Talak approached. A cool cloth touched her face, soothing some of the pain. She lay passively, trying not to betray her consciousness. Talak hummed as it worked, a mother's voice, soothing a little one. The tenderness touched Ashael, and her throat grew tight. *I will not cry. I will show no pain.* Despite her determination, tears leaked from her right eyelid and trickled down her temple into her hair. No tears came from the space where her left eye used to be. Ashael felt Talak's fingers on her brow. Its skin was warm and dry, similar to a snake's. She tried to concentrate on the sensation, block out thoughts of her eye. Something small, cool and hard, pressed against her lips. The bottle she had seen? She tightened her lips, shaking her head slightly.

'Just a little?' Talak spoke quietly, its voice cajoling. 'For the pain.'

Ashael shook her head again. After a moment the bottle was withdrawn and Ashael relaxed. She heard fabric rustling as Talak retreated, leaving her alone with her pain.

Sometime later, Ashael heard voices again. Someone had come to relieve One-Eye. *Will the taunting start again?*

'Lord Meegrum is still unconscious,' the newcomer said. 'Lord Daven is furious. Best stay out of sight if you can.'

'How is Devorik?' One-Eye asked.

'Hanging on. His wound isn't healing, though. Samarak thinks there might be an infection.'

Good! Ashael thought. *I hope he dies. Painfully.* Part of her was shocked at this desire for vengeance but it was there all the same.

One-Eye's voice moved closer. 'That Hive thing tends to the witch's injuries, but Devorik must live or die alone? It's not right.'

'It'll all be over tomorrow,' the newcomer said. 'Then we'll be able to go home. Lord Daven has promised to reward us all handsomely. I'm sure he'll be in favour with the king again, after he takes this land.'

So soon? I need to do something. I need to stop him. Ashael groped for the strength to move, to fight, to do something. *Stop him? You couldn't stop him taking your eye when you were free and whole. Now what good could you possibly do?* Bitterness flooded Ashael until she felt she would choke on it. *At least the foragers got away. I saved them. I did what I came here for.* She listened to the guards chatting a little longer before One-Eye left and silence settled over the room again.

***

A ROCK MOVED under Iwan's foot, clattering down the steep slope they were climbing, narrowly missing Tris, who scrambled up the slope a short way behind. Colm watched from closer to the bottom, his muscles burning with fatigue. Iwan had set a swift pace, barely stopping to rest, for three days. They had been on the move for notches now, and Colm was exhausted. He heaved a sigh and started pulling himself up again, using the sporadic, straggly bushes to steady himself. The land beneath his feet was dry and growing more desolate. It didn't seem natural. Other areas in the mountains were teeming with life, but here death reigned. He pulled himself to the top of the slope where Iwan and Tris lay, heads poking over the edge, looking down the other side. He sprawled next to them.

'What are we looking at?' he asked in a low voice.

'Checking for patrols,' Iwan answered, without turning his head.

There's something strange about him, Colm thought. *Something I can't quite put my finger on, but he's not himself.* Another part of Colm's mind piped in; *He obviously cares for Ashael. Maybe it's just concern for her.* That voice always sounded like Sola, often mildly chiding him. And maybe it was right. Maybe Iwan and Ashael were closer than he had realised, and that was all that was making Iwan tense. Still, it seemed like there was something the young man was not telling them.

The other side of the slope led down to the trail that Colm and the others had followed in their escape. They had shaved time from the journey by travelling in a straight line instead of following the trail around obstacles. In the distance, a smudge of smoke marred the sky. Colm pointed it out to the others and Iwan turned to look at it.

'It must be the cook fires at the keep that Gert told us about,' Iwan said, his voice tight. 'It's too far. We're not going to make it in time. Dammit!' He punched the ground, leaving some skin from his knuckles on the bare rock. He lifted his arm as if to do it again, but Colm caught him.

'Take heart,' Colm said. 'Gert didn't know what the plan was, or even that it definitely involved Ashael. Just that something big was happening on Longest Day.'

'Something big to do with the girl,' Iwan snapped, pulling his arm away.

'We still don't know enough to give Ashael up for dead,' Tris said, voice reasonable. 'She's in there because she came to save us. We have to keep going.'

Colm studied Iwan's face. The younger man looked like he was caught between taking off running towards the keep and giving up altogether. Colm put his hand on Iwan's shoulder and squeezed. Iwan looked up, face haunted. He seemed on the verge of saying something but looked away and shook his head.

'We'll rest here, eat something,' he announced. 'Then we push on.' Iwan's voice was steady though his body trembled.

***

BHEARRA SAT ON the floor, beside the hearth, gazing into the smoke rising from the embers, seeking a sign. *How do I reach the hearts and minds of the cam leaders who assemble even now? How do I convince them that what we say is true, that we must prepare to fight for our existence?* The smoke danced in the breath of air coming in through the entrance. Bhearra watched with unfocused eyes, trying to let go of expectations, be open to possibilities. For a moment the smoke shimmered, creating a shape almost like a face. As soon as Bhearra drew her attention to it, the face was gone, the smoke nothing but a ribbon. The old woman groaned and pushed herself to her feet.

'You can bring me home to the Summerland any time you like,' she muttered to the All-Mother. 'My old bones grow weary.' She knew, however, that her time had not yet come. Her people still needed her.

Bhearra glanced towards Ashael's empty alcove and sadness rose to the surface, threatening to overflow in tears. In Bhearra's long life she had watched people die; some even from violence, though not many. Friends, lovers, family members. But none under circumstances even remotely like these. There was a chance that Ashael was alive and well, but neither she nor the foragers had returned and Bhearra held out little hope that she would see any of them again.

From outside came the hum of many people speaking in low voices. The last of the other cam leaders would arrive this afternoon, according to the scouts. The Folk of Oak Cam would provide a feast for their guests, as was traditional. After everyone had eaten, the meeting would begin. Whatever the outcome, at sunset the filidh would join together to conduct the closing ritual of Longest Day, bidding the sun a good journey as he entered into the waning half of his cycle. This year was especially propitious as all three moons would join their brother in the sky tonight, a celestial phenomenon that occurred only once in a generation or so. Bhearra prayed that the night would bring good fortune to the Folk.

***

MEEGRUM BECAME AWARE of the pain first. His head pounded as if a blacksmith was using it as an anvil. He opened his eyes, but the light stabbed into them like a hot knife; he quickly closed them again.

'Lord Meegrum?' the many voices of the Hive creature spoke close to his ear.

Meegrum grunted in response, lifting his hand to cover his eyes before attempting to open them again.

'Lie still, master.' Talak spoke again. 'Do you have pain?'

'Of course I have pain,' Meegrum growled. 'What happened?'

'We do not know, master. You were found several days ago, on the floor of your chamber. You had suffered a head injury. Do you remember anything?'

Meegrum searched his memory. The last clear image was of throwing an apple at a guard and hitting the wall instead. The fruit had exploded, spraying juice and flesh everywhere. After that there was nothing.

'No,' Meegrum answered, slowly taking his hand away from his eyes. The pain in his head flared again but not to the same extent as before. 'Where am I?' he asked, realising for the first time that he was not in his own chamber.

'Lord Daven insisted that you be moved for your safety. You are in the room adjoining my own,' Talak answered.

Meegrum grimaced to think that he had been so close to this creature for several days... Wait! How long? There was something... 'What day is it?' he demanded.

'The solstice, master. Just after noon,' Talak answered, the hint of a smug tone in its many voices.

'The solstice!' Meegrum shouted, pushing himself up with his elbows. His head swam and a cold sweat broke out on his forehead.

'Slowly, master. You really should rest.' Talak leaned over, holding a goblet with water to Meegrum's lips.

'Get Lord Daven – now,' Meegrum growled, then allowed himself to slump back onto the bed.

***

ALAYNE LED THE group through a narrow defile, followed by Gert, Erin and Ruraigh at the rear. Iwan had described this path to them: if they turned left upon reaching open ground, it should bring them out of the foothills only two days' walk from the cam. Alayne was anxious to get home, to hold her son and her mate. Gethyn would be worried. *If only there was some way to let him know that I'm well and I'm on my way home.* She was so lost in thoughts of her family that she didn't realise how quiet things had become until Gert tapped her on the shoulder.

'Might be I'm talking out of turn, but is it always so quiet around here?' the girl asked, bringing Alayne back to the present moment.

'No... It's not,' Alayne said slowly.

The birdsong that had accompanied them for days had now stopped, leaving an eerie silence. Alayne slipped the strange knife from her belt. 'Tell the others to be ready,' she said in a low voice. 'Something isn't right here.'

Alayne wasn't sure whether she heard the low rumble first or felt the vibrations in her feet. 'Stay together!' she cried, pulling Gert close to her as pebbles and small rocks bounced down around them.

A grinding sound filled the air and Ruraigh threw himself over the top of Alayne and Gert, pushing them to the ground. Alayne lost track of what was happening. There was noise and dust and darkness, and she couldn't breathe properly. Ruraigh suddenly weighed twice as much and Alayne worried about Gert, pinned beneath them both.

The noise stopped and gradually the air cleared.

'What happened?' Alayne asked.

'Rock slide,' Ruraigh answered, voice strained. He lifted his weight a little, allowing Alayne to push herself up though not freeing her completely. Gert wriggled out from beneath her.

'Erin? Where are you?' Alayne coughed as she spoke, dust clogging her throat.

'Over here,' Erin said from somewhere to the left.

Alayne heard rocks shifting and then Erin appeared through the haze.

'All-Father save us,' Erin said in a rush. 'How bad is it, Ru?'

Alayne twisted around, trying to see, but her movement made Ruraigh curse so she froze. 'Tell me,' she said, trying to stay still.

'My leg. It's trapped under a rock,' Ruraigh answered through gritted teeth.

'A big one,' Erin said, sounding worried.

'Can you two move it?' Alayne asked, looking from Erin to Gert.

'We can try,' Erin said, moving out of Alayne's field of vision.

Alayne tried to suppress her frustration at being unable to help, pinned beneath Ru. If Erin and Gert couldn't move the rock, she would have to slide out, even if it did hurt him. She craned her neck but couldn't see past Ruraigh. She heard Erin count and then Gert and her both grunting from exertion. Ru let out a high-pitched scream.

'It's no use,' Erin said, panting. 'The rock is too heavy. We can't move it.'

'Ru, I'm going to slide out from under –' Alayne began, but she was interrupted by a scream from Gert.

'What? What is it?' Alayne cried.

There was a sound similar to grating rock but not quite the same.

'Who are you?' Erin shouted. 'Stay back!'

Alayne tried again to twist around so she could see what was going on. A shadow fell over her and then the weight that was holding her down disappeared. Alayne rolled over and pushed herself up on her elbows. Standing over her was something that looked like the mountainside come to life. Taller than any of the Folk, the man-shaped creature had grey skin that looked hard, like rock. Its eyes glowed violet and a sac pulsed over its lower face.

It held an unconscious Ruraigh in its arms, hoisting him as easily as if he were a child.

'What are you doing?' Alayne asked, panic making her voice high-pitched.

The sound like grating stone came again. The rock-man turned and started walking away. Then it stopped and turned to look at them, motioning with its head.

Erin hurried to Alayne's side and helped her to her feet.

'Do you want us to follow you?' Alayne asked the creature.

Again, the sound of stone. Alayne realised that the sound was the rock-man talking.

'We can't just follow it!' Erin screeched. 'Are you mad?'

'If it wanted to hurt us, it could have already,' Gert spoke in a low voice.

The rock-man started walking away again and Alayne started after it. 'I don't think we have much choice.' She looked at the other two women. 'Keep your wits about you.'

Chapter Twenty-Seven

ASHAEL COULD FEEL THE TENSION IN THE AIR. WAS IT LONGEST DAY ALREADY? How long had she been here, trapped in this awful place? She tried to piece together everything she had overheard. *There has to be a way to stop them.* Ashael tested the bonds that kept her restrained. No give. She wasn't going to be getting up without help.

'What do you think you're up to, then?' The guard moved into her view.

This one looked young. Maybe even younger than her. He was tall and broad of shoulder, but his eyes betrayed his innocence. Without really meaning to, Ashael reached out with her senses, trying to get the measure of the young man before her. She sensed pain and a great deal of fear. There was none of the cruelty that surrounded One-Eye or the soul-crushing evil that flowed from the master of this place, the one they called Daven. There was something else about this boy… Shame. He was ashamed of his own people. Ashael reached further, looking for anything she could use to get through to him.

The guard checked Ashael's restraints, pulling them even tighter. 'It's more than my life's worth to let you escape,' he muttered, justifying his actions though Ashael had said nothing. 'I'm sorry,' he said, giving the ropes one last pull and moving back to his station by the door.

His mother. There were memories of a woman, someone brave and kind, who had taught him a different way of looking at the world than others of his race. Ashael realised how much she was intruding in this young man's mind, and she broke off, embarrassed. *He wants to help me. All I need do is give him the opportunity. But how?*

Her thoughts were interrupted when Talak entered the room. The guard stayed at the door, allowing the Hive creature to approach Ashael alone.

Talak leaned down, speaking into Ashael's ear. 'It is almost time. We cannot help you to escape; our people would be killed for such disobedience.'

'I wouldn't ask you to risk your people for me,' Ashael murmured. 'You have been kind to me, and I thank you.'

'But there is something that may help to protect your people.' Talak pressed a small vial into Ashael's hand. 'If you drink this, you will fall asleep and not awaken.'

'I'll die?'

'Yes. But in death, you will not be used to harm your people.'

Ashael tried to swallow past the lump in her throat. 'I will think it over.'

Talak leaned over and pressed its cheek to hers. Ashael was absurdly touched by the gesture. 'Be well, Talak.'

***

MEEGRUM SHUFFLED ALONG the hall, two guards hovering behind. They had attempted to support his arms – guide him like an old man! – but he had made it clear that he would not tolerate this. He would rather they left him altogether but Daven had insisted they accompany him. A wave of dizziness washed over him, and he swayed for a moment. *I have to get my strength back. I have to be ready for the ritual tonight. All that we have done for years comes down to this night.*

Meegrum pulled himself straighter by sheer force of will. 'I want a bath and two slaves in my chambers immediately,' he called over his shoulder. 'One of you go and see to it.'

'Yes, sir,' one of the guards answered, hurrying off to do as he was bid.

Talak had informed Meegrum of the prisoners' escape and Daven's subsequent punishment of the enchantress. Without the drain of the spells keeping the prisoners, he would be able to channel more energy into healing himself. *How was she able to break the spells, though? And why did they rebound on me that way?*

When he reached his chambers, two slaves were hauling the tub across to the hearth where there was water heating over the flames.

'Wait outside,' he barked at the guard still following him.

As the slaves filled the tub, Meegrum made his way across the room to the table, where food had been laid out. He broke a chunk off a loaf of bread and dipped it into some broth. Suddenly, his body reminded him he had not eaten for days. He devoured the food, washing it down with copious amounts of wine. His belly cramped, causing him to double over. He looked wistfully at the platter of cheese and meat still on the table, deciding to keep something for after his bath.

'Help me undress,' Meegrum commanded the slaves.

The girl moved to his left while the boy moved to his right. Both were young – just how he liked them. They worked together to remove his clothing. When they had stripped him to his undergarments, he placed a hand on top of each of their heads, wrapping his fingers in their hair. He began to chant in the old tongue, already feeling his strength return. The slaves went rigid, the spell paralysing them.

Fear flashed across their eyes. Meegrum stood in the centre of the blue mist arising from their bodies, breathing it in, absorbing it through his pores. Sparks danced on his skin, energising him further.

In a few moments the mist was gone and the slaves were limp. Meegrum allowed their bodies to fall to the floor. He strode across the room on legs that no longer trembled. He threw the door open. Both guards were outside now. Meegrum beckoned for them to come inside.

'Get rid of them,' he said, gesturing to the bodies.

The guards each lifted a slave and carried the body from the room. When the door closed, Meegrum slipped out of his undergarments and into the still-steaming water.

***

ASHAEL'S THOUGHTS WERE spinning. She rolled the vial between her fingers. Should she drink it? If she died there would be no hope of escape, no life with Iwan, no more dreams of tomorrow. But her people would be safe.

Or would they? How did her imprisonment put her people at risk?

It could be a trick. She did not believe it was; Talak had given her no reason to doubt its intentions. Still, she had to consider the possibility. Perhaps it had been commanded to befriend her so she would drink poison at its suggestion.

The door crashed open against the wall and Ashael flinched, dropping the vial in her fright. She scrabbled about, trying to find it, her fingers grazing it before knocking it to the floor.

'It is time,' One-Eye said, strutting across the room. He leaned over, rotten breath in her face. 'Let's see what you're made of, witch.'

He cut the ropes that bound her and hauled her to her feet. The room spun and sounds seemed distorted, as if they were travelling through water. Ashael stumbled, her balance defeated by the sedative they had forced upon her. One of the guards grabbed her arm and twisted it, forcing her into a hunched posture. They shoved her into the corridor, laughing when she tripped and hit the floor face first.

After an interminable period of time that probably only lasted moments, Ashael was pushed through a door that led outside. For the first time in days, she felt the kiss of the sun upon her skin. A breeze lifted her long hair, soft as a caress, and sighed past her ears. Ashael's head cleared as if she had never been drugged and she felt the embrace of the All-Mother.

The guards shoved Ashael forward again and she deliberately stumbled, wanting them to believe she was still incapacitated. She moved over dead ground, toward a massive boulder which she was forced to lie on top of. The young guard looked at her apologetically as he tied a rope around her torso and arms, securing her to rings hammered into the stone.

Ashael looked around as much as she could. Walls rose on all sides of the area she was in. Withered stalks of dead plants spotted the ground. The sun had started his descent, light shining at an angle, illuminating the wall opposite Ashael, casting her shadow on it. Ashael squinted, trying to see her shadow more clearly. There was something odd about it – a haze around her. She closed her eye and reached out with her senses. There was definitely something surrounding her, but it was elusive, and she couldn't quite catch the edges of it.

Her senses touched Meegrum, moving in her direction. She recoiled in disgust as the buzzing sound she had begun to associate with him sounded inside her head. Seeking solace, Ashael unconsciously plunged her awareness into the ground. There was still life in this seemingly barren place; it was just buried deep, hiding. Ashael touched seeds, waiting for the right conditions to grow; she touched insects passing through, deep below the surface. Deeper still there was water flowing, carrying life in its very existence. Even in her pain and fear, Ashael was reminded of the bounty and power of the All-Mother and she was awed.

The arrival of Meegrum and Daven jolted Ashael back to awareness of her body. First Moon was now visible in the sky above her. *How long have I been here? How long do I have left?* Talak appeared in her field of vision, its robe flapping in the breeze. It was wringing its long, thin fingers, as if distressed. Ashael felt sorry for it. She had come to feel a certain fondness for the strange creature.

The small outdoor space was filling up with men in armour. Ashael recognised some as guards; One-Eye was there, also Devorik. Sickness radiated from him, a smell of rot and despair. He must be expecting something of great importance to have dragged himself here. He leaned against a wall, glowering at Ashael. For a moment, she felt his breath in her ear and his arm around her throat again, and her stomach clenched. *I hope you're suffering*, she thought at him. The cool breeze blew over Ashael's face, sweeping away her memories and grounding her in the present. *I'm missing something*, she thought. *There's some lesson here. Something I can use. To do with hidden life… No, that's not it. Dormant life?*

Other people began to make their way through the crowd, people in clothing like hers but not quite the same. Slaves. Ashael felt mostly pain and fear from them; however they had come to be here, they were no more free than she was. Their suffering angered her. *Someone needs to help them. I need to help them.* She only realised that she had clenched her fists when she became aware of pain from her nails digging into her palm.

Meegrum and Daven stepped up to either side of Ashael, looming over her. She closed her eye, refusing to look at them, to let them see her fear. She went inside again, looking for the answer she felt was there. Again, she felt the life that passed through this seemingly dead place. Her mind kept being pulled back to the seeds – life, but not alive.

The breath in her face was foul and brought Ashael unwillingly from her reverie. Daven leaned over her and, once again, she could see beyond the face on the surface to the corpse beneath. There was nothing but death here, with the appearance of life.

'Not long now,' he rasped. 'As soon as the third moon rises, you and your land will be mine.'

Ashael turned her face away, as far as she could. *Think! Life, but not alive. What does that mean and how does it help me? There's not enough time! If only Bhearra were here, she would know what to do.*

Energy was building. Ashael could feel it fluttering at the edges of her consciousness. She had no idea what was supposed to happen when the Baby, the smallest of KalaDene's three moons, joined the others in the sky, but she had no doubt that it would be big.

Power over life itself. That's what Bhearra said about the prophecies. The one who came would have power over life itself.

Ashael's thoughts circled. She was getting close; she could feel the answer just beyond her reach, but panic was making it difficult to concentrate.

'I will suck the life from this land,' Daven rasped, his mouth close to Ashael's ear, his hand resting lightly on her neck. 'Not even the tiniest insect will be left when I'm through. And you're going to make it possible.'

Don't react. Don't let him distract you. Life is the key.

Ashael opened her eye. The golden light surrounded everything once more. Ashael let her gaze wander over the gathered people. She began to see the lines of connection between them – threads of energy joining them to each other, reflecting their relationships. A thick, black rope emanated from Daven, surrounding everyone here. A thin, violet thread ran from Talak to Ashael, drawing her eyes down to her own body. More threads than Ashael could count led from her into the land beneath her. Instinctively, she followed a green thread, the colour of summer leaves.

It led to an acorn, buried close to the boulder upon which Ashael was bound. She recognised the feeling of this acorn. The oak it contained was a child to the very tree that provided her home. In her mind's eye, Ashael saw the bird that had carried this acorn so far from home before dropping it here. Again, the breeze lifted her hair and Ashael could smell a hint of herbs and smoke. That touch of home was all Ashael needed. She inhaled deeply, letting the golden light fill her, then breathed the light along the green thread connecting her to the acorn. *Grow.*

Grow, Ashael thought again, pushing more light toward the seed. First a sprout, then roots, found purchase in the ground beneath her. Daven still rasped in her ear but that seemed to be happening very far away. It was unimportant. She watched in awe as a shoot formed from the seed, pushing its way through the barren soil, growing by the second.

'My lord, beware!' Meegrum cried. 'She uses her power!'

Ashael felt the light and life surging through her being. Now she realised that when she had healed Bhearra and then the foragers, she had only touched the edge of what she was capable of. Now, it all lay open to her. Ashael directed her mind to the ropes that bound her. Woven from once-living plant fibres, they were of her domain. With a breath, they returned to their living state, green, healthy fibres falling away from her. Ashael stood and beneath her feet, grass started to grow.

She looked at her captors and the fear writ large upon their faces made her heart sing with a savage sense of triumph. Meegrum was chanting, a cloud the colour of rot building around him.

Grow. Ashael aimed more light at the sapling that was forcing its way through the ground beside the boulder. A fully-grown oak burst from the soil and knocked Meegrum backwards, a branch hitting his head hard enough to stun him.

A part of Ashael watched what was happening to her, separate from it. She looked through her own eyes as if seeing into another room. She watched as she placed her hand on the boulder to which she had been bound moments before. The living rock violently expelled the dead rings that had been hammered into it – they flew through the air.,

Daven stalked toward Ashael, hatred on his scarred face. Ashael circled the boulder warily, wondering why none of the soldiers rushed to help their master. Many had their hands up, shielding their eyes. That was when she realised that she was glowing. All the colours of the rainbow swam across her skin. Ashael held her hands in front of her and looked at them in wonder. The ground beneath and around her was now covered in lush grass and meadow flowers. Saplings appeared all around, some causing damage to the walls as they burst up underneath the stone work.

Daven moved closer and Ashael stepped back again, her focus returning to her opponent, heedless of the soldiers who were now behind her. She smelled the rot a fraction of a second before a baking arm was thrust around her neck.

'We must stop meeting like this,' Devorik panted in her ear.

Daven smirked. 'Good work, Devorik. Perhaps I'll let you live after all.'

Devorik yanked Ashael off of her feet. As fear settled over her, the colours left her skin and her glow faded.

Chapter Twenty-Eight

BHEARRA JOINED THE OTHER FILIDH AT THE HEART-FIRE. THE SUN, FIRST MOON and Little Sister were in the sky. The Baby should be visible soon. In the light of all four celestial children, the filidh would conduct the Longest Day ritual in front of the gathered Folk. Bhearra looked over the crowd and started to feel nervous. Her heart sped up and beads of sweat popped out on her brow. *Why am I nervous? I haven't felt this way since I was a young apprentice.* Bhearra turned to speak to Ravena, filidh to the Folk of Forked River Cam but before she could open her mouth, she was overwhelmed with the sense of pressure building. A gale that touched not a single leaf seemed to blow through Bhearra's core, leaving her shaken and breathless.

The gathered filidh all seemed to feel something, some of them growing pale while others bent over, gasping for breath much as Bhearra had. At first Bhearra thought that the trembling she felt was her own legs but then a pebble bounced past her feet. The earth itself was shaking.

Bhearra fell to her knees as the tremors became more violent. She heard cries of fear, saw people stumble and fall. She gathered all of the strength she could muster and put it into her voice.

'Be calm!' she called over the tumult. 'All will be well.'

A branch fell from one of the trees surrounding the clearing with a great cracking noise.

'Move into the centre of the clearing if you can,' Joren's voice rang out.

Bhearra searched the crowd for him. Her eyes caught movement above and to her left, another branch starting to fall. Soraya and Bhearrael were beneath it. *The baby!* Bhearra threw out a hand and sent her will to the tree, thrusting her consciousness into the wood itself. The branch was almost completely detached from the trunk of the tree. *Hold on, hold on,* Bhearra thought, willing the wood to stay together.

'Soraya!' Bres screamed his mate's name just as Bhearra lost her battle and the branch came crashing down.

***

BHEARRA CRAWLED OVER ground that was still shaking, though the tremors were smaller. Soraya was on the ground, hunched over the baby. Joren reached them at the same time as Bhearra. He wrapped his arms around Soraya and helped her to her feet. She and Bhearrael were safe. Bhearra knelt next to Bres, unconscious and pinned under the fallen branch.

A deep gash to his temple leaked blood across his face. Gently, Bhearra probed his skull; it was intact. He was breathing, slow and steady. Angus appeared at her side and began wiping the blood from Bres' face with a rag torn from his tunic.

Soraya, realising that she and the baby were safe, had finally spotted her mate. She lunged towards them, but Joren held her back.

'Let her go,' Bhearra said. 'He's unconscious but not too badly injured.'

Joren offered Bhearra his hand and she took it gratefully, pulling herself to her feet. She left Angus to continue tending to Bres so she could check on the rest of the Folk. The ground had finally stilled, and people were clustered together, some crying, others praying.

'Rana?' Bhearra asked Joren.

'Over there,' he nodded towards his mate, who was moving through the crowd, calming people. 'She seems unhurt. The baby...' Joren trailed off, a question in his tone.

'Your baby is in the safest place possible right now,' Bhearra assured him, patting his arm.

A scream rang out and Bhearra and Joren turned in unison, seeking the source. Elwa, one of the young women of the cam, stared in horror, arm outstretched.

'The Heart-Fire!' she cried in anguish. 'It's gone out!'

Chapter Twenty-Nine

ASHAEL STRUGGLED TO GET AWAY, BUT DEVORIK'S ARM CLAMPED TIGHTER around her neck. *Not again, not again, not again!* Her thoughts beat against one another on wings of panic.

'Look, it rises, my lord,' Devorik breathed against Ashael's ear.

The gathered crowd all turned their faces to the sky as the Baby began to peek over the walls. Daven grabbed Ashael's long hair, wrapping her now unkempt braid around his fingers. He jerked her head back while Devorik forced her to kneel. Daven chanted, words like nothing Ashael had ever heard before. The sounds wriggled into her, burrowing beneath her skin.

The rainbow that had played over Ashael was entirely gone now, though she could still see the lines of connection between the onlookers. A hooked thread, the colour of pus, snaked from Daven towards Ashael, growing thicker and longer with each alien word. Disgust sank deep into Ashael's stomach, and she flinched away from the questing thread, looking down to the ground beneath her. The lines of energy that connected her to the earth had multiplied to a number beyond her ability to count. *Go! Go away! It's not safe!* Ashael directed these thoughts at the earth connections, willing them to let go.

The chant coming from the scarred lord grew louder, the hooked thread finally meeting Ashael's skin and burying itself in her bare arm. Ashael howled in pain and revulsion, frantically trying to brush it away, but her hand went right through it.

Daven tipped his head back and roared in triumph before the sound was choked by his jaw snapping shut. Cords stood out on his neck and arms. Ashael watched in horror as the line connecting her to Daven began to pulse. One of the threads connecting her to the earth lost its light, withering and dying in a matter of seconds. Then another. And another. Ashael felt each connection severed, the living energy funnelled to Daven. Fury overtook fear in her heart. *How dare he do this!* Ashael understood his plan now, or at least enough of it to be enraged. Energy surged in her and her glow returned but it was unlike the rainbow light of a few moments before. This time her light was blinding.

'No!' Ashael shouted in a voice that echoed from the walls around her and the mountains beyond. 'You will not!' Ashael threw out her hands and a wall of power exploded forth. The people who had not run inside were thrown from their feet, many hitting walls and crumpling to the ground. Daven was thrown against the boulder Ashael had been tied to. The living vines that had formed the rope binding her now snaked their way around Daven, drawing tight, tying him to the massive rock. Those who were not unconscious fled, some crawling, their breath knocked from them by the blast.

Ashael blazed, flames dancing over and around her, brighter than the sun. She stepped towards Daven, oblivious to Meegrum pulling himself to his feet and chanting on the far side of the courtyard. Devorik lay behind her, unmoving. Hatred contorted Daven's features as he looked at Ashael, the corpse-face swimming below the scarred surface.

'You do not belong here,' Ashael said, her voice full of ancient power. 'Leave and never return.'

'Who are you to command me?' Daven screamed, flecks of spittle flying from his lips.

Blue-black darts of energy flew at Ashael only to fizzle out when they touched the flames surrounding her. She turned and spotted Meegrum, the darts flying from his hands as they formed complex patterns in the air. Ashael's hands formed their own patterns – she called up the lights that had come to her aid when she first arrived here. With a flick of her wrists, Ashael sent them zooming at Meegrum. He managed to neutralise some with his own darts, but a few got through his defences. They sizzled when they came into contact with him, and a smell of cooking meat filled the air. Meegrum screamed, beating at his clothes.

From the corner of her eye, Ashael saw movement coming towards her, fast. She threw more lights as she turned to face this new danger. The young guard, the one who hadn't wanted to harm her, was struck in the neck by a band of her lights. He collapsed, frothing at the mouth with his limbs thrashing, before going completely still. Ashael ran to his side.

'No, no, no! I didn't mean to,' she moaned, kneeling beside him.

The guard's hand fell to the side and opened, a hide package falling from it. Ashael recognised it as the travelling pouch she had carried at her belt. Her throat tightened as she realised that he had been trying to help her. *He's little more than a boy*, she thought, her vision doubling as tears swam in her eye. His chest stopped moving and Ashael choked back a sob.

Daven was still struggling with the vines but Meegrum stood dusting himself off, looking ready to attack again. Only the three of them remained conscious. Ashael felt her power falter. The fierce glow around her started to sputter. Her rage had disappeared with the life of the young guard and Ashael knew she would not survive another confrontation. With the last of her strength, she called to the water she had sensed earlier, rushing below them on its own secret course. It came shooting out of the ground like a geyser, knocking Meegrum to the ground .

Ashael grabbed her travelling pouch and fled, her only choice to go back into the castle.

***

INSIDE THE HUGE stone building, Ashael ran in panic, stumbling with the lack of depth perception from her missing eye. She was exhausted. Her leg muscles ached though they drove her on through this unfamiliar place. The combined effects of her injuries, the conditions she had been kept in and the confrontation she had just escaped all crashed down on her at once and she fell to the floor, sobbing.

She knew she couldn't stay there but she couldn't bring herself to move. She gave a breathy scream when hands touched her back.

'Come with us, quickly.' Talak helped Ashael to her feet and guided her down the corridor at a brisk pace. After several turns, it pushed open a door and ushered Ashael inside.

The way Talak kept looking over its shoulder suggested it would not turn her in and Ashael was too exhausted to fight if it did. Instead, the creature closed the door and pulled a heavy chair over, jamming it closed.

'That won't keep anyone out for long, but it'll give us some time if need be,' Talak said, hurrying to Ashael's side and putting a long, scaly arm around her shoulders.

'They'll kill you if they find you've helped me, won't they?' Ashael asked, her sobs trailing off to sniffles.

'We have prayed to Alekiatorix and he has shown us the way,' Talak answered, giving Ashael's shoulders a squeeze before striding to the other side of the room and sweeping back a curtain to reveal a shelved alcove. Talak took down a bundle and shook it out. It was a robe, identical to the one it wore. 'Quickly, put this on.'

Ashael pulled the robe over her head. It trailed the floor and the sleeves were so loose she could slide the hands of her folded arms inside them as Talak did. With the hood up, she would be completely covered. Shouts and pounding footsteps sounded along the corridor. As they drew closer to the door, Ashael pulled the hood up and held her breath, letting the air out with a whoosh when they passed by.

'Can you defend yourself?' Talak asked.

Ashael shuddered and covered her face with her hands. Her voice came out muffled. 'No. Never again.' She looked up at Talak through red-rimmed eyes. 'I killed a man. A boy, really. It was an accident, I thought he meant me harm, but he was bringing me this.' She held out her travelling pouch then bowed her head in shame. 'I will not risk such a thing again.'

Talak bowed his own head. 'Oh, great Alekiatorix, in your wisdom, guide the soul of the boy to his next life. Let him know peace. Please soothe the pain of this young woman, who had no ill intent. Always in your service.' Talak stayed still for a moment before gently shaking its head and moving to a table. It lifted a goblet of water and offered it to Ashael who took it gratefully. She gulped the water, oblivious to the stream that was running down her chin. She cared not at all at this lack of dignity – water had never tasted so good.

'I know a way out of the keep that is unlikely to be guarded, but it will be unpleasant.'

'All of this has been unpleasant,' Ashael muttered; then, louder, 'What do I have to do?'

***

ASHAEL HELD UP the bottom of the robe and hurried along the corridor. She heard voices approaching from around a corner and quickly slowed down to a more sedate pace, dropping the robe and tugging the hood forward. With her head bowed, none of her skin would be visible. Talak had told her that the guards paid little attention to it – as long as she did not speak, they would be unlikely to notice anything different.

The owners of the voices rounded the corner and strode on past Ashael with barely a glance in her direction. She let out a breath and, when she was sure they were out of sight, lifted the robe again and scurried on.

Dear gods, why did I listen to it? Get into Daven's rooms? This is insane! Talak had told her how to find the lord's chambers and where she would find her exit. It had hurried off in the other direction to tend to the injured, knowing that it would arouse suspicions if it was not seen soon.

'How can you be sure he won't be in his room?' Ashael had asked.

'There was a transmission scheduled from Zan tonight. The portal always opens in the great hall. Not even Daven will fail to keep an appointment with the king,' Talak had answered. Ashael understood little of this, except that Talak was certain the lord's rooms would be empty. And it seemed that Daven answered to someone.

Footsteps approaching from behind pulled Ashael from her thoughts and again she dropped the robe and slowed her pace.

'Oi, lizard!' a hoarse voice called.

Oh no! One-Eye! Ashael recognised the voice of her tormentor. He had taken great delight in taunting her when she lost her own eye to Daven's rage.

'I'm talking to you,' he called as Ashael kept the same sedate pace.

What do I do?

His footsteps picked up speed behind her. Panic fluttered in Ashael's breast as she felt him get almost close enough to grab her.

'Zekinal!' a voice called from further back.

'What is it?' One-Eye growled in frustration, stopping and turning around.

Ashael forced herself not to run, her pulse pounding in her ears, almost drowning out their words.

'Lord Daven wants you immediately. Devorik is dead. The woman killed him. You're to be promoted.'

'It seems the witch has done me a favour. Perhaps I'll just kill her when I catch her, instead of taking her other eye first.'

Bile rose in Ashael's throat at his words. When his footsteps faded, she was careful not to increase her pace. If she sped up, panic would have her and soon she would be running without control. If Talak's directions were right, then Daven's chambers lay just ahead. She would be out of here soon.

Chapter Thirty

D AVEN SCREAMED WITH RAGE, THE SOUND ECHOING THROUGHOUT THE BUILDING. Meegrum watched from the other side of the Great Hall, careful not to get too close. In a mood like this, his lord could lash out at anyone. Already, the life he had taken from the enchantress had started to fade, used up by the fire of his anger. He may decide to feed on anyone who caught his attention.

'Why am I waiting for that impotent fool to contact me when I should be drinking this land dry?' Daven shrieked, throwing his hands into the air.

Meegrum knew better than to speak; anything he said would only enrage his lord further. Daven paced the far end of the hall, muttering to himself. There was a knock at the door.

'Enter,' Meegrum called, hoping it was the soldier returning with the slaves he had sent for. Instead, the Hive creature stuck its head around the door.

'Master, I have the information you requested about the injuries.'

'Well?' Meegrum asked, gesturing for it to come into the room.

The creature approached, its eyes focused warily on Daven at the far end of the room, although it spoke to Meegrum. 'Fifteen soldiers injured, all from being thrown against the walls. The worst was a dislocated shoulder. We've fixed it but he won't be much use for at least a moon's turn. Devorik was the only fatality.'

'What of the slaves?' Meegrum asked.

'Most had fled inside the building before the blast but two were injured. One with a broken arm, which we have splinted, and one with a knock to the head.'

'Are they able to work?'

'No, master, not for some time,' Talak answered.

'Put them out, then. Them and the one with the dislocated shoulder.'

'Master?'

'You heard me. I want them gone before first light or I won't be so merciful.'

'Yes, master,' Talak said, bowing its head and moving back towards the door.

Why am I being merciful? Meegrum thought. *Why not have their life force?* He frowned, drawing in breath to call Talak back, when a black mist started to form at the other end of the hall. *I can always use their brands to kill them later.*

'My lord,' Meegrum said, inclining his head towards the mist which was even now swirling and solidifying.

Daven turned, straightening his tunic and composing his scarred face. The king must not know what had happened here. Daven took several deep breaths as colour started to form in the blackness.

'Is this thing working?' the king's voice boomed through the portal to someone out of view, before the image resolved itself in the centre.

Meegrum slid along the wall, making sure he would not be seen by the king.

'Yes, your majesty.' The weary voice of Grimwold the king's chief advisor, came through.

The centre of the portal revealed the image of the king, a grossly fat man with jowls hanging from a ruddy face, his shiny head topped with a poorly fitting crown. Grimwold had been advising him for generations to have a new one made, but he insisted on wearing the crown of his predecessor. Sweat left a sheen on his brow and beaded around his mouth, and he licked his lips in a tic that disgusted Meegrum.

Daven bowed, but Meegrum noticed that he did not go as low as his position in the court dictated.

'Have you subdued the indigenes yet?' the king barked in greeting.

'Almost, your majesty,' Daven answered, his tone respectful.

'I grow tired of waiting, Daven.'

'Of course, your majesty. I will have good news for you soon.'

'I know you will, Daven. I'm feeling generous so I'm sending you some help.'

'There's no need for such generosity, your majesty,' Daven said, his voice alarmed.

'I am a generous king, am I not?' The king's tone was silk over steel.

'Of course, your majesty. I simply meant I am not worthy of your generosity.'

Meegrum tensed; he could hear Daven's teeth grinding from here. They must tread carefully for now, or the king would see them both beheaded.

'Worthy or not, my daughter's husband, Cenric is leading a party of warriors to the World-Gate as we speak. He should be through first thing in the morning. You will meet him there.'

'I will send a welcoming party, your majesty,' Daven answered, his voice growing taut with anger.

'*You* will meet him, Daven. Your pet, Meegrum, will also be there. Am I making myself clear?'

'Yes, your majesty.' Daven's bow was deeper this time and, to Meegrum's relief, concealed the contempt on his face.

'Very well.' The king sat back, the oversized crown slipping to the side on his sweat-slicked brow. 'You will give Cenric every assistance until that cursed land has been brought to its knees.'

The portal began to dissolve around the edges, turning back to black mist before dissipating. Daven held his bow, an obeisance that the king would appreciate, and which also served to hide his fury.

Just before his image disappeared, the king called, 'Tell Cenric I will be in contact tomorrow evening, after the feast you will be offering him.' The king's chuckle echoed after his image had dissolved.

***

ASHAEL SLIPPED THROUGH the door to Daven's personal chambers, her pulse pounding in her ears. This area of the building was quiet; probably the last place anyone would think to look for her. She leaned against the door, letting her heart rate return to normal, taking a look around. The room was neat and clean, with no sign of any instruments of torture or evidence of violence. There was nothing about the room that would suggest the nature of the man that called it home, other than the thick, cloying smell of rot. Ashael relaxed her eye, looking for the golden light that she had come to realise was the life force of the world, present in and around everything. Except for this room. Here she saw a thick sludge, the colour of putrescence. It hung, stagnant, in the air, unlike the golden light, which flowed and swirled. It reminded Ashael of swamps, filled with hidden dangers and decay. Sickened, she let her sight return to normal, and crossed the room in purposeful strides.

At the far side of the chamber, a small door was tucked into the corner. Ashael stepped through it into a small room with a very narrow window from halfway up the wall to the ceiling. Breathing deeply, she filled her chest with fresh air, immediately feeling somewhat restored. Before her was a bench with a hole in the middle. Talak had called this a garderobe, explaining that this was where the lord relieved himself. Holding her breath, Ashael peered into the hole. She could see the rough stone wall descending to a very narrow strip of rocky ground between the wall and the edge of a cliff. The way was thought to be impassable and so the guards did not patrol this section of the keep.

The sun had set but twilight lingered long at this time of year and Ashael still had sufficient light to attempt the climb. She took off her hide shoes, tucking them into a pocket of the robe, which she also removed. The loose robe that Talak had given her would impede her climb but leaving it behind would ensure his death so she tied it around her torso, failing to notice the hide slippers falling from the pocket.

She panicked when she realised that the hole was too small for her to go through it. A child might have managed but not a grown woman. She pulled at the boards around the hole, straining to lift them. No give. She pulled again, putting as much strength into it as she could muster. Still no movement. Ashael had no idea how long she might have before Daven returned. *Maybe I could do something with the wood, like I did with the vines. Speak to the life in it somehow.* She shook her head. That power had cost lives. Not just that of the guard she had unwittingly killed but Nela, who had been killed just to get Ashael here. She couldn't use it. Not until she knew more about it.

The edge of the wooden bench stuck out a little beyond the stone it sat on. Ashael lay down on the floor of the room, positioning herself next to the bench with her knees pulled up to her chest. She tucked her feet under the lip of the bench and then pushed with her legs. This time she felt a little give, though not much. She pushed again, shoving with all her might, until spots danced before her eyes. The wood gave way with a loud crack that echoed off the stone walls. Ashael lay panting, listening anxiously for the sound of anyone coming to investigate the noise. After a moment, she got to her feet and pulled the bench up. Now she had space to get out. Ashael took a moment to remove the rawhide from her hair, smoothing it as best she could before tying it back again. She briefly wondered if her loss of an eye would make the climb more difficult. Her throat tightened and she clenched her fists, fighting the emotional pain and the phantom ache in her eye socket. *It doesn't matter. If I fall, at least I'll die free. All-Father, please guide me in this climb. Make me swift and sure as a goat. Let it be.* Ashael took a last deep breath before swinging a leg over the edge of the wall, seeking her first toehold.

Ashael made her way down the crud-encrusted wall carefully. The smell was awful, and she tried hard not to think of what she was climbing over. Her fingers and toes began to ache with the tension of clinging to the rough stone and her head pounded with her heartbeat. The dying light of the day cast confusing shadows on the stone; between that and her missing eye, Ashael struggled to see clearly. Eventually, she closed her eye and continued her climb by touch alone.

After what felt like several notches, Ashael's foot touched the ground, the ledge she had stepped onto barely wide enough for her feet. She would have to sidle along the wall. She took a few moments to catch her breath, resting her forehead against the castle wall, irrespective of the grime coating the stone. *If Daven comes to relieve himself now, he'll see me. I have to move.* Ashael carefully edged her way along the wall, arms out to either side, running along the stone, ready to grab for purchase should she slip. Gradually, the ledge widened, until she was able to turn and walk normally. Beyond the ledge, the ground fell away to a river rushing far below. Across the ravine, mountains rose against the twilight, their sides in shadow. Talak had told her the castle was in the mountains her people called the

Edge of the World. If she travelled east, she should eventually find herself back in land she recognised. *That's the way they'll expect me to go. It would be easy for them to find me.* She took a few moments to think, trying to get her bearings. Little Sister and the Baby were still in the sky, but they were on the way down behind the peaks across the ravine, so that was west. The river looked to be running roughly south. *Rivers run downhill. If I can follow the water, I should be able to find my way out of the mountains. Then I can figure out how to get back to the cam.*

Ashael got moving again, this time looking for a way down the steep cliff face to the water. She had almost reached the corner of the building and was starting to worry about running out of cover. The slope had grown less steep, but it still looked dangerous. She leaned over for a better look. Voices sounded nearby, making her jump and almost lose her balance. She leaned back against the wall and looked around frantically for the source of the voices. Footsteps crunched over the rocky ground, somewhere close to the corner of the building, and they were coming closer. Two men, at least. It was now or never.

Ashael sat down and dangled her legs over the side. Although no longer a sheer drop, the grade was still far too steep to descend on her feet. Adrenaline coursed through her body, making her hands tremble. Ashael took a shaky breath, closed her eye and slid over the edge.

***

IWAN CROUCHED IN a gully, watching the activity around the keep. There were far more patrols than usual; obviously Gert had been right about something big happening.

'What do you want to do?' Colm breathed in Iwan's ear, his voice so low even a rabbit wouldn't have heard him from any further than a few inches away.

'There's no way we'll get passed them,' Iwan answered. 'There are too many.'

'What do you think is going on?' Tris spoke from behind Colm, his voice a little louder.

Iwan and Colm shared an exasperated look, before the older man motioned for Tris to be quiet. There was a reason Tris was a much better forager than a hunter.

Colm pointed. 'Look – something's happening.'

The three men watched as the people in the open space outside the keep moved together, clearly falling into defined places. A few men walked back and forth, shouting orders and pointing. A large gate at the front of the massive stone building opened, allowing a brief view inside, where people scurried about unknown tasks. Two men came out, riding on the backs of horses. Colm and Tris looked stunned and Iwan tried to echo their surprise. The Folk hunted horses on occasion when a herd entered their territory, but it would not have occurred to them to use the beasts in any other way.

'What in the All-Mother's name…?' Colm murmured.

'Are they on horses? What are they doing?' Tris asked.

Colm hushed Tris again but only half-heartedly. Given the commotion, it was unlikely they would be discovered now.

It was clear the men on horseback were important, as all eyes were on them. They moved to the front of the gathering, one of them shouting something that Iwan couldn't quite make out from this distance. The men turned the horses and trotted forward, the crowd moving off in formation behind them.

Iwan, Colm and Tris watched until the people were out of sight. When they were sure they were alone, they started picking their way carefully towards the keep, taking a circumspect route to keep to as much cover as possible. Iwan glanced at the sky and saw a band of lighter purple in the east. Longest Day was over.

Chapter Thirty-One

JOREN STOOD WITH BHEARRA AND THE OTHER FILIDH WHERE THEY WERE GATHERED around the extinguished Heart-Fire, dusk heavy in the air.

'If I leave now, I can make it to Trout Cam and be back by sundown the day after tomorrow,' Angus said, looking around the group.

'You shouldn't travel alone,' Ravena said.

'One or two people could join me but any more would only slow me down.'

'What are you going for?' Gerod asked, approaching the gathered filidh.

'I can bring back a flame from our Heart-Fire. It keeps the line of the promise. Each new Heart-Fire is lit with a flame from another.'

'So, the Heart-Fire will remain unlit until your return?' Gerod asked, shock colouring his words.

'That is the way it must be,' said Bhearra. 'Who will go with Angus?'

'I will,' answered Eislyn, mate of Ravena.

Eislyn carried a long bow over her shoulder and moved with the easy grace of a hunter. Ravena frowned at her mate, but none could deny that she was the perfect one to accompany Angus, being known for her skill with the bow she carried.

'Then I will come too,' Ravena said.

'No, my love,' replied Eislyn. 'I can travel more swiftly without you and your wisdom will be of use here in the cam.' Eislyn took Ravena's hand in hers and kissed the palm.

'We should leave at once,' Angus said, shifting from one foot to the other.

'Wait but half a notch,' Bhearra insisted. 'I shall gather some supplies for you. It is the least I can do.'

'Very well,' Angus agreed reluctantly.

Bhearra walked off towards her oak and gestured for Joren to follow. 'How is Bres?' she asked when they were alone.

'He has not yet woken,' Joren answered. 'Soraya fears for him but Rana is there, keeping her calm.'

Bhearra snorted a laugh. 'Rana could calm an aurochs bull during mating season.'

Joren laughed, imaging his diminutive mate standing in front of an aurochs, talking calmly to a creature with horns as long as her arms. She would barely come up to its shoulder. 'She has a gift,' he agreed.

'Tell me, Joren, does anything strike you as a little odd about Angus?' Bhearra asked, looking back to the gathered filidh.

'Truth be told, something strikes me as odd about most filidh, Bhearra. I sometimes believe that's what *makes* a good filidh.'

Bhearra turned to Joren, eyebrow raised, a smile playing at the corners of her mouth.

'Not you, of course,' he added hastily, winking at the old woman. Joren looked back at Angus, struck by how dark the cam seemed without the Heart-Fire shedding its light over everything. 'You don't trust him?'

'I don't know him.' Bhearra sighed, starting to walk again. 'But there is something I can't quite put my finger on.'

***

THE SKY WAS starting to lighten in the east when Angus and Eislyn left, carrying torches lit from Bhearra's hearth. Many of the visitors now made their way to the temporary shelters that had been set up between the trees ringing the cam, hoping for a few hours' rest. After the events of the night, Joren had asked them to gather at midday to finally have the meeting that should have followed last night's interrupted ritual.

Although her weary bones prodded her to rest, after Bhearra saw Angus and Eislyn off she settled herself by the extinguished Heart-Fire. In ones and twos, the Folk approached her, looking for reassurance that the gods had not forsaken them. Again and again, Bhearra told people that the All-Mother would not abandon them as long as they kept their faith.

Over the course of that long morning, Bhearra supervised the re-building of the Heart-Fire. She placed offerings of herbs and food in amongst the branches and twigs that would feed the flames. Some of the Folk brought items of clothing and jewellery to be offered in the fire. She checked on Bres several times though his condition remained the same. At last, there was nothing else for Bhearra to do. With about two notches until midday, Gerod finally convinced her to rest. She made her way home and sank gratefully onto her pallet without undressing.

Bhearra lay on her back and sighed, tense muscles loosening, though the ache in her back that came from old age still nagged, reminding her that she was past the prime of her life. She remembered the sensation of being in the hawk. The power and speed and freedom. She longed to feel that way again and understood why some became lost in the experience. *Perhaps when my time is done, the All-Mother will grant me a lifetime as a hawk.* Her thoughts drifted in the between-place, neither sleeping nor awake. *Ashael, wherever you are, I hope you are safe.*

'Bhearra?' Ashael's voice sounded in Bhearra's mind, startling the old woman.

'Ashael? Ashael!' Bhearra called aloud, sitting up so fast the room spun a little. She listened, every muscle in her body taut, desperate for a response.

Silence.

Just your tired mind, conjuring what you want to hear, Bhearra told herself as she lay back again. Her pounding heart didn't quite believe her logical thoughts.

'Bhearra?' This voice was not in her head, coming instead from the doorway. 'Are you there?'

'Come in, Ravena,' Bhearra called, sitting up again with a sigh. So much for a nap.

'Oh, I'm sorry to disturb you at your rest,' Ravena said, entering and seeing Bhearra on her pallet. 'I'll come back later.'

'Not at all,' Bhearra said, climbing to her feet despite the protestations from her back. 'Have you eaten recently?'

'Not since Eislyn left,' Ravena answered.

Bhearra looked carefully at the middle-aged woman before her. Tall and somewhat imposing, Ravena's dark colouring suited the bright cloth that she wore. She carried a staff carved with images of animals, birds and plants, a work of devotion that had taken her many seasons to complete. Fork River Cam lay distant enough that the two filidh saw each other only rarely, but Bhearra had come to like and respect Ravena over the years. Now, she saw a woman who looked worn beyond the events of the past few days.

'Is there something wrong, my friend?' Bhearra asked, moving into the main living space and gesturing for Ravena to take a seat.

'I am filled with foreboding,' Ravena answered, 'but I do not know its source.'

'When did the feeling start?'

'I can't be exactly sure. I think it came and went over the winter, but I put it down to my usual impatience during the earth's long sleep. However, it has been a constant companion since the equinox. That is when I truly noticed it, as my heart usually warms with the earth but instead, I have been frightened.' Ravena looked down at her hands, clasped in her lap.

'What have you been frightened of?' Bhearra asked, her voice gentle.

'I know not. Some darkness that I cannot fight.' Ravena lifted tired eyes to Bhearra's wizened face. 'This fear has grown urgent and agonising since Eislyn left this morning. I do not believe she will return.' Her voice cracked on the last word and Bhearra wrapped her in an embrace as she wept.

Bhearra's mind raced. For generations this land had been safe, the only threat coming from accidents. Even encounters with predators, such as killed Joren's father, were incredibly rare. Now, Bhearra could not be so sure. If the Zanthar had truly returned, no one would be safe. She wanted nothing more than to offer comfort to Ravena, to assure her that she would see her mate again soon, but she couldn't.

'We can speak to Joren, ask him to send somebody after them,' Bhearra suggested.

'I fear they would be too late,' Ravena answered, her voice muffled by Bhearra's shoulder.

'Do you think something has already happened to them?' Bhearra asked, alarmed.

'I don't know. I think I will feel it if something happens to Eislyn, but I cannot be sure.'

Bhearra pulled back and studied the other woman's face. Fear had drawn Ravena's features tight, and her eyes pleaded with Bhearra for help.

'Let's speak to Joren anyway. Then we'll see what can be done.'

Joren had been sceptical at first, but Bhearra had asked him if he would be so quick to dismiss it if she were the one with the feeling of something wrong. So, he asked Bran and Gerod to go after Angus and Eislyn. Ravena was grateful but her agitation increased, nonetheless. Bhearra drew Joren aside.

'We must take this seriously, Joren,' Bhearra said in a low voice.

'I respect your judgement but what more can we do?'

Bhearra looked towards the baskets of herbs that lined the walls of her home. Joren followed her gaze.

'The blackweed?' he asked. 'Do you mean to ride the hawk again?'

'It would let me check up on them. The hawk can travel much faster than Bran and Gerod.'

'I thought it was dangerous to do often?'

'It can be. I know what I'm doing.'

'When?'

'Now would be best.'

'I'll delay the meeting then. Let me get Rana and Danliv.' Joren walked over to the entranceway then turned back. 'You're sure?'

'Yes, I'm sure.' Bhearra worked to keep her face calm although her heart leapt in eager anticipation.

The hawk had been circling close to the cam when Bhearra had called. He often stayed close; he too had been changed by their encounter. Bhearra slipped into his mind easily, urging him to take flight immediately, eager to feel the wind in his feathers again. *Oh, it was glorious, flying. If only man had been given wings!* The thought drew Bhearra's mind to the stories of the Flores – those people from beyond The Edge of the World, who were fabled to have wings and had come to the aid of the Folk when last the Zanthar set their feet upon this land. *Perhaps we should send someone beyond the Edge of the World. If we can find them, the Flores would make powerful allies.*

The hawk dived and Bhearra's thoughts broke off as she revelled in the freedom of flight. For a time, she just existed in the hawk's mind, without guiding him, before she remembered her task. They were high over the forest now and Bhearra took a moment to get her bearings before nudging the hawk towards Trout Cam. Everything looked so different from up here. Bhearra marvelled again at the detail the hawk could see. A splash of bright red on the ground caught her attention and she urged the hawk down to investigate. He swooped as if coming in for the kill and Bhearra's heart sang with the speed of it. The hawk landed on a branch just above the red thing and peered at it, head cocked. It was a headscarf, one that Ravena had been wearing the night before. *She must have given it to Eislyn.*

The area around the headscarf was trampled and disturbed, the ground showing signs of a struggle. Drag marks led off back towards Oak Cam. Bhearra urged the hawk to focus his eyes on these marks and saw splatters of blood, soaking into the dry ground. She pressed the hawk to follow the drag marks. He was reluctant. He did not enjoy staying close to the ground where his prey could see him coming and other predators may decide that he would make a tasty snack. He wanted to soar again, but Bhearra exerted her considerable will and the hawk responded. He skimmed above the ground, his shadow flowing over the strange scuffs and marks.

They rounded a bend on the path, and there was Eislyn. She was bleeding profusely from a wound in her leg, the belt she had wrapped around it doing little to staunch the flow of blood. She was on hands and knees, dragging the injured leg behind her. There was no sign of Angus. Had he been taken? Had he gone looking for help?

Bhearra tried to call to Eislyn, but all that came out was the scream of the hawk. Eislyn needed help if she was going to make it back to Oak Cam before her wound weakened her too much. *Why didn't I check where Bran and Gerod are?* Frustration rose in her, quickly followed by shame. She had been too busy enjoying her time in the hawk. She had failed to take an obvious course of action. Bhearra quickly cast her senses about, looking for traces of the two men. Nothing. They were too far away. Something was close, though. A stag. *Perhaps he could carry Eislyn on his back... All-Mother guide me,* the filidh thought desperately as she threw her consciousness out of the hawk, aiming for the stag. There was a moment when she thought she wasn't going to make it: it was the longest moment of Bhearra's long life. Her consciousness felt completely untethered, as if she might disappear in the slightest breeze. Then she thudded into the stag. He reared onto his hind legs, pawing at the sky. Bhearra sent out a feeling of calm, trying to soothe the beast. It was completely ineffective. When his front hooves came back to the ground, he began shaking his large head from side to side, trying to dislodge the alien presence in his mind.

The stag's heart pounded faster as his distress increased, his feeling of panic beginning to influence Bhearra. His body felt heavy and dense, suffocating in comparison to the light-boned hawk. He was immensely powerful and Bhearra could feel his strength as he fought to be free of her. Again, she tried soothing him as she had the hawk, and again she failed. *I must calm him! Eislyn needs my help!* Frothing at the mouth, heart thundering in his chest, he continued to savagely shake his head back and forth, his antlers catching in the brush around him, ripping away great chunks of greenery. His heart missed a beat and eventually Bhearra admitted defeat. She must leave him, or his distress may kill him.

Bhearra called to the hawk, who remained nearby. *I'm sorry* – she aimed the thought towards the stag and then leaped for the hawk. She slipped into him as she would slip into a tunic she had worn for years. The hawk was perched in a tree above where the stag had struggled. As she watched, the deer came back to himself. His powerful chest heaved, and his eyes rolled in their sockets. He reared once more before bounding over some bushes and crashing off through the forest. Bhearra felt sorrow at the pain she had caused such a magnificent creature, and relief that he would recover from her clumsy attempts. Taking flight, Bhearra and the hawk headed back to check on Eislyn.

The injured woman had crawled a little further along the path but looked to be nearing the end of her endurance. Her normally dusky skin was ashen, her mouth drawn tight in pain. The hawk screamed Bhearra's frustration as he swooped just above Eislyn's head. She looked up, startled. Bhearra saw the fear in Eislyn's face and wanted to weep for her inability to help. *There has to be something I can do. Think!* Bhearra knew if she went back to her body, it would be too late. No one from Oak Cam could travel here quickly enough to help Eislyn before she lost too much blood. Bhearra reached out with her senses again, hoping to find someone close enough to help, but only the forest animals were within her reach. She had two options. She could hunt for Bran and Gerod and hope that she could make them follow the hawk, leading them back to Eislyn to help her, or she could head for Trout Cam and hope she could find someone there, and that they would pay enough attention to follow a hawk. It had to be Bran and Gerod. The hawk needed no urging to take to the air again.

***

BHEARRA HAD COVERED around half the distance back to Oak Cam before she found the men she was seeking. The two of them were ambling along the path with the air of people who expected to be walking all day. They carried no sense of urgency. Bhearra urged the hawk to swoop down over their heads, close enough that the draft from his wings fluttered the men's hair. Bran yelped in surprise and pulled the sling from his belt. He was pulling a pebble from a pouch in his tunic when Gerod put his hand on the younger man's arm, stopping him. The hawk swooped again, and this time he screamed at them before wheeling around and flying part-way down the path.

Gerod and Bran stared. Bhearra asked the hawk to repeat his actions, swooping close to the men, screaming and then heading down the path.

'What in the All-Mother's name is it doing?' Bran asked.

Bhearra urged the hawk to fly to Gerod, but the bird balked at being asked to do something so far outside his nature. Bhearra sank her will a little deeper and the hawk obeyed. He flew directly at Gerod and settled on his shoulder. Bhearra could feel Gerod's shoulder tense beneath the bird's talons. She made the hawk stare into her friend's eyes, willing him to see her.

'Bhearra?' Gerod asked, voice full of wonder.

'What are you talking about?' Bran asked.

At long last! Bhearra urged the hawk to fly down the path again.

'Quickly!' Gerod cried. 'I think Bhearra is in there. We have to follow that bird.'

The hawk could fly much faster than the men could run so Bhearra had to keep asking him to double back, screaming at them in the bird's voice, trying to hurry them. By the time they reached Eislyn, she was unconscious and Bhearra was exhausted from exerting her will over the hawk for so long.

As soon as they saw the injured woman in the path, Bran and Gerod forgot about the hawk. Bhearra settled him on a branch and watched as Gerod bound Eislyn's wound with a strip of cloth ripped from his tunic while Bran dripped water into her mouth. Bhearra knew they would do everything they could and then carry Eislyn back to the cam. She thanked the hawk and asked him to take her home. As he beat his powerful wings to take off, Bhearra relaxed her grip on him, letting him control the journey now.

Chapter Thirty-Two

ASHAEL PICKED HER WAY AMONGST THE ROCKS LITTERING THE FLOOR OF THE gorge. The noise of the fast-flowing river drowned out all other sound as it echoed off the steep sides. The sky above had brightened but little light made it down here. The shadows and uncertain footing meant that Ashael had to move slowly. Her back and legs were battered and bruised from her bumpy journey down here and the phantom ache had settled in where her left eye used to be.

Head down, thick braid hanging over her shoulder, Ashael trudged on, bone-weary. *Just a little further, then I'll rest.* She squinted up at the top of the gorge, looking for some landmark, or a glimpse of the sun, something to help her work out how far she had gone. Nothing. Just blue sky. She knew that she couldn't have travelled far but she had lost all sense of time and distance in her exhaustion. Spray from the river made everything damp and many of the rocks were covered in moss and slime. Ashael placed her feet carefully, using her bare toes to grip the rocks she clambered over. She shivered, her tiredness adding to the chill of the water and shadows.

Up ahead, she spotted a narrow cleft in the rock wall, a dark spot in the otherwise light-coloured stone. *If there's enough space for me to squeeze in, I can rest there for a while.* Ashael hurried as much as she could over the slippery rocks. The cleft in the rock was narrow and dark. Ashael peered inside but could not see the back. She crouched down, examining the ground at the entrance. No sign of anything passing this way for a while. Ashael looked up at the sky again. If she went in, she would be hidden from anyone looking down from above and if she could squeeze far enough back, she might be hidden from ground level too. She could sleep. With that thought, Ashael turned sideways and pressed into the space.

A short distance in, the cleft narrowed further until Ashael's back was against one wall and her breasts brushed the other. Just beyond this point, there was a gap in the wall facing her. If she could get in there, she would be invisible from the entrance. She pressed forward, holding her breath. The rock wall pressed harder against her breasts, digging in painfully, catching at her tunic. *This is foolish. If I keep pushing forward, I could get stuck in here. Better to back up a bit and just crouch near the entrance.* As she started to wriggle back out, Ashael pressed against the rock before her and felt something move. There was a loud click followed by a rumbling and vibration through the stone. The noise was deafening in the constricted space and Ashael screamed. She struggled to free herself from the rock as dust filled the air, coating her mouth and nostrils, making her cough and splutter, and blocking out what little light was coming from the entrance. Bits of rock rained down, bouncing off Ashael's head and shoulders. Her tunic had caught on the rock in front of her and it ripped when she finally managed to pull herself free. She fell back towards the entrance, arms up to deflect the falling stone.

Finally, she had enough space to turn her head towards the entrance. She could see nothing, not even a glimmer of light. Panicking, she raised a hand to her face, pressing her fingertips against the lid of her remaining eye. There was no injury that she could detect. Breathing a shaky sigh of relief, Ashael thanked the All-Mother that she had not lost her sight completely. *Why can't I see anything then?* Ashael pressed forward, an arm extended before her until her fingertips brushed stone. *How did I get turned around?* Her mind refused to accept what her body was telling her. The entrance was gone.

As the truth dawned on her, Ashael scrabbled madly at the rock before her questing hand. Broken, sharp-edged chunks of rock ripped at her skin but in her panic, she barely registered the pain. Her breathing quickened until the dust filling the air began to choke her, and she coughed until she retched. Ashael cried with deep, heaving sobs that shook her whole body. To escape from the Zanthar, only to be trapped in a cave so close to their stronghold! Ashael wept from the futility of it all, for the loved ones she would never see again, for the life unlived.

At last, no more tears came. Ashael leaned her head back against the rock wall, drifting in an exhausted haze. She thought of Bhearra; of the older woman's seemingly inexhaustible supply of energy and warmth, her wisdom and kindness, her strength and the sheer force of personality that made her appear to take up so much more space than her tiny frame accounted for. For a moment she could smell the aroma of herbs that always accompanied her mentor.

Ashael, wherever you are, I hope you are safe, Bhearra's voice sounded in Ashael's head.

'Bhearra?' Ashael croaked, her voice weak from tears and dust. 'Bhearra, where are you?'

Nothing.

'I must have imagined it,' Ashael spoke to herself, her voice bouncing off the rock all around her.

Gradually, Ashael became aware that she could see. There was light coming from somewhere. She peered at the blocked entrance but there was not so much as a chink between the rocks that had fallen. She turned her head and realised it was coming from the back of the cave, beyond the narrow section where she had got into difficulty. *I can't go that way; I could get stuck.* Ashael snorted at her own stupidity. She was already stuck. She might as well try.

She edged her way back to the point where the cleft narrowed. The light was coming from the passage she had spotted earlier. It was a violet glow, steady like daylight, but no day she had ever seen had been this colour. Ashael paused for a moment, listening. There was no sound other than the river, which she could still hear muffled through the stone walls. A faint draft blew over her hot, puffy face, refreshing and welcome. *Maybe there's another way out.*

Ashael pushed herself into the gap, the rock again pressing against her breasts, the rip in her tunic catching a rough edge of stone that scraped the delicate skin beneath. As panic began to beat at her chest again, she took a few deep breaths then slowly let all of the air out of her lungs, making her chest as small as possible. Then she pushed hard. At first it didn't work. Just as she thought she would be trapped like this until she died, Ashael burst through the narrow section, her momentum carrying her to the back wall of the cave, which she bounced off painfully.

Ashael rubbed her shoulder and breathed deeply, thankful for the space that had opened up around her. Facing her was a passage through the rock; smooth walls lined with crystals emitting the violet glow that she had noticed before. A light but steady breeze blew down the passage towards her, suggesting there must be a way out somewhere along it. She took a few steps toward the entrance of the passage. Her legs shook with exhaustion and her vision swam. She sank heavily to her knees. She needed to rest. That was why she had come in here in the first place.

Ashael unwrapped Talak's robe from around her torso and lay it on the ground. She sat down on it and nibbled at some of the strange food that Talak had given her – the thing it had called bread. It didn't seem like food at first, but after a moment her stomach decided it was and demanded more. She ended up eating half the bread and a little bit of the other thing - cheese - sipping water between bites. At least she had managed to fill the waterskin from the river before she came in here.

She used a splash of water to wash the dust and grime from her hands and to clean her cuts. She still didn't feel clean, but she had done all that she could until she got out of here. Hunger sated for the moment, she could stay awake no longer. Ashael lay down on the robe and gave in to her body's need for sleep.

***

'IT LOOKS CLEAR,' Iwan said, standing and gratefully stretching his limbs. There had been no movement from the keep since the huge party had set out before dawn.

The three men had been watching from their hidden vantage point ever since, trying to decide what to do next. None of them wanted to leave without Ashael but they had no idea what had happened last night; indeed, if she even still lived.

'Let's circle around, look for another entrance,' Tris suggested. 'There might be something less conspicuous.'

'Very well,' Iwan said absently. He had to find a way to leave the other two behind. He had a much better chance of getting in and out again if he was alone. How to do it without raising suspicion: that was the thing.

Moving through bushes for cover, they circled around the east side of the keep. Colm had told Iwan how the foragers had escaped through the kitchen storeroom. Iwan wondered if he might be able to sneak in that way, but he was sure it would now be heavily guarded. Still, it was on this side of the keep so they could always check as they passed.

To stay hidden, they had to follow the curve of the land, losing sight of the keep for a few minutes before hooking back around to face the east side of the massive stone building.

'That's where we came out.' Colm pointed to a wide entrance through the thick stone outer walls. 'I don't see anyone around. Do you?'

'No,' Iwan answered. *Which worries me*, he added silently.

'Maybe we can get in that way,' Colm pressed.

Tris didn't say anything, seeming content to let the other two make the decisions, but he looked like he agreed with Colm. Iwan made a fist by his side then forced himself to relax. How could he convince them this was a bad idea without revealing that he already knew that there was no way it would be unguarded? The sound of footsteps echoing from stone saved him from trying. The three men melted back into better cover, Colm and Tris behind some rocks while Iwan lay on the ground, shielded from view by some low-growing bushes. He parted the branches in front of his face so that he could see who was coming. A robed figure led three others outside of the walls. One of them stormed off, shouting curses back at the walls, spittle flying from his lips. His arm was in a sling, his face ashen.

Iwan's brow furrowed as he watched, so focused on the man making all the noise that he barely spared a glance for the other three. The injured man spat in the direction of the walls before staggering off.

Iwan turned his attention back to the others. All three stood for a moment with heads bowed, before the robed figure headed back to the keep and the other two turned around. Iwan ducked his head down as they turned in his direction, praying that he hadn't been seen. He heard quiet voices murmur to each other but no sound of alarm, so he risked another peek.

The two people were walking away from the keep on a diagonal from Iwan, the taller one – a man, he could see now – blocking his view of the other. The man's left arm was in a splint of some sort. *What's been happening here?* Iwan craned a look back over his shoulder, trying to make eye contact with Colm or Tris. It was no good; he couldn't see either of them. He turned back and as the second person came into view, what he saw drove him to his feet, not even pausing to consider that it could be a trap.

Iwan ran towards the two people leaving the keep. The second person, a woman with a headscarf, looked towards him, her eyes widening in shock.

'Iwan?' she said in a breathy whisper.

'Mother!' Iwan cried, racing to lift the woman into his arms.

Chapter Thirty-Three

BHEARRA FELT A SHARP PAIN IN THE TIP OF HER WING THAT SWIFTLY MADE ITS way up to her shoulder. How could she have been injured mid-flight? She turned her head, searching for the source of the pain, but there was nothing. She soared through the sky, despite her aching wing… Arm. Her aching *arm*: the wing was not hers. Bhearra gradually remembered that she was not the hawk but only a passenger. The pain moved again, insistent, demanding her attention. It took some time but eventually she realised she must have been gone too long. Joren was calling her home. With a deep pang of loss, she bid farewell to the hawk and let her consciousness slip out of him. *Home. I must go home.*

When she opened her eyes, Joren was bent over her, his face bearing the stamp of his worry.

'Thank the All-Mother!' he exclaimed. 'I thought we'd lost you.'

Bhearra lifted her hand and saw a shallow cut across her thumb. Blood had pooled and now ran down her arm.

'Don't move,' Rana said from Bhearra's side. The young woman took Bhearra's injured hand in her own and gently washed away the blood before applying a mild salve and wrapping the wound with a hide bandage.

'Thank you. Both of you,' Bhearra croaked. Her throat was parched.

Joren helped her to sit up and Rana brought her some water. It was only after she had drained half a cup that she realised Ravena was gone. She had expected the other woman to be waiting for news of her mate.

'Where is Ravena?' she asked.

Joren and Rana exchanged a look.

'Has something happened?' Bhearra demanded.

Joren looked at his hands, clasped between his knees as he squatted next to her. 'Do you know how long you were gone?' His voice was soft, concerned.

Bhearra looked around, noting the quality of the light; it must be close to dusk. She had left before noon – she must have been gone for at least four notches. She had lost a considerable amount of time.

'It seems I was absent much longer than I meant to be,' Bhearra answered. 'That would be why you had to bring me back.' She raised her injured hand.

'We tried everything else we could think of to wake you,' Rana said.

'I have no doubt,' said Bhearra. 'Now tell me, please, what has happened?'

'Gerod and Bran brought Eislyn back.' Joren got to his feet and began to pace as he spoke. 'She was badly injured – unconscious when they got here. Ravena is tending to her in the guest house. Some of the other filidh are helping her.

'Gerod said they saw no sign of Angus, so Danliv has gone searching for him. Until Eislyn wakes up, we won't know what happened to them. And the Heart-Fire remains unlit. People are frightened and I have nothing to tell them, no comfort to give.' Joren stopped pacing, his back to Bhearra, the tension in the lines of his body showing the strain he was under. 'Bres awoke and seems none-the-worse for his injury. Bertrand checked him over. What happened with you?'

Bhearra explained how she had found Eislyn and then attempted to take over the stag, with some notion of being able to carry Eislyn on its back. As she remembered the stag's fear, Bhearra felt sorrow for the pain she had caused it but beneath that feeling was a desire to feel the strength of the great creature again. *If I'd had more time, I may have been able to soothe him.* She put the thought aside for later examination and told Joren and Rana how she had used the hawk again to find Gerod and Bran, leading them to Eislyn.

'And then I'm not sure what happened. I remember asking the hawk to bring me home and being tired. Then nothing until the pain brought me back.'

'Do you think Angus was taken?' Joren asked.

'That seems the likely explanation,' Bhearra answered, pulling herself to her feet.

'Where are you going?' Rana asked. 'You need to rest.'

'Not until I've seen Eislyn,' Bhearra said, moving towards the entrance.

Joren stepped in front of her, blocking her way. 'When was the last time you slept?'

'I will sleep after I have seen Eislyn.'

'Bhearra, you've been through –' Joren began.

'I know better than you what I've been through,' Bhearra snapped, interrupting. 'I am old enough to be your grandmother and I know my own limits. I will check on Eislyn and Ravena and then, and only then, I will rest.' Bhearra looked up at Joren, her strength of will taking up more space than her petite, stooped frame.

Joren held his ground for a time, a silent battle of wills raging between them. Bhearra stared at him, head held high, until he stepped back.

'Forgive me,' Joren said, bowing his head. 'You know what you need better than I do.'

'Of course,' Bhearra touched his arm, and the tension went out of the air. 'Would you care to accompany an old woman?'

'Gladly,' Joren answered, smiling.

***

A FIRE BLAZED in the hearth, making the air in the guest home hot and close. It was stifling after the cool of the evening air outside. Sweat formed on Bhearra's skin when she stepped into the single-room hut. She peered through the haze of smoke to where Eislyn lay, bundled in blankets, on a pallet against the far wall. Ravena was kneeling at her side, head bowed, speaking under her breath.

Bhearra and Joren stood silent, waiting for Ravena to finish her prayers.

When she quiet murmuring stopped, Bhearra made her way across the room, placing a hand on the other filidh's shoulder. 'How is she?'

'She's so cold,' Ravena said without turning. 'I can't seem to make her warm. The wound to her leg is deep; she has lost a lot of blood.' Ravena squeezed Bhearra's hand. 'If you had not found her, led the men to her...'

'Is there anything I can get for you, Ravena?' Joren asked from near the entrance.

'No, thank you.'

'May I examine her?' Bhearra asked, kneeling beside Eislyn.

'Of course.' Ravena got to her feet and moved back, giving Bhearra space.

Bhearra gently peeled back the blankets, revealing Eislyn lying in her undergarments, her flesh ashen and clammy. The wound to her thigh was deep and ragged, the edges inflamed. Bhearra sniffed, checking for the scent of infection, but all she could smell was the lavender of the salve that Ravena had spread on the wound.

Bhearra reached out, searching for Eislyn's essence. The huntress was there, fighting for survival. Bhearra concentrated on feeling the energy around her. She sank roots into the earth, channelling life force through herself and into Eislyn. She stayed like that for a time, doing what she could. Eislyn's breathing eased a little and Bhearra slowly came back to herself.

'We have done all that we can,' Bhearra said. 'It's up to her, now.'

***

IT WAS ALMOST noon when Bhearra was awoken by a commotion outside. Stiff from sleep, she struggled into clean clothes then headed outside.

Folk were all milling around the extinguished Heart-Fire, looking toward the far end of the cam expectantly. Bhearra saw Rana with a group of stoneworkers who were making blades. She wondered over to them.

'What's happening?' Bhearra asked as she approached the group.

Rana stepped away from the stoneworkers and answered Bhearra in a low voice. 'Danliv's son, Falen, arrived ahead of the rest Danliv's party. They've found

215

no sign of Angus, but Danliv is on his way with a flame for the Heart-Fire. Joren has gone out to meet him. They should return soon.'

'Well, a flame for the Heart-Fire is good news, at least. I'm sure we will all feel better when it has been relit.' As she spoke, Bhearra looked around the gathered people, seeing an unusual lack of purpose in many of them. 'How is Eislyn?'

'The same. I checked on her a while ago,' said Rana. 'One of the other filidh was sitting with her to let Ravena sleep. I can't remember his name…' Rana blushed. 'The older man, from Blossom Cam, I think.'

'Bertrand?' Bhearra asked.

'Yes, that's it!' I can't seem to remember things the way I normally do.' Rana absently put a hand to her belly which was starting to swell.

'Many women become forgetful during pregnancy. It's perfectly normal.' Bhearra smiled and squeezed Rana's arm. 'Tell me, how are you feeling? I haven't been paying you enough attention with everything that's been happening.' Bhearra studied Rana's face. She was a little paler than usual, her face drawn.

'I'm fine. Tired, mostly. At least I can keep some food down now – except rabbit; I can't even look at it just now!' Rana looked down and her face creased with sadness. 'I miss Ashael so much. I wish I could share this with her.'

'I know, dear. I miss her too.'

'Do you think she's…'

'I think we would know if she was gone. I'm sure she's out –' Bhearra broke off as people started to murmur and move towards the far end of the cam, to the path that most people took in and out of the clearing.

Joren and Danliv strode through the cam, side by side, Danliv holding a torch, its flame fluttering in the wind created by his movements. Bhearra hurried over to him and gave the welcome gesture. The big man passed the torch to Bhearra, his face serious.

'I thank you, Danliv,' Bhearra said. 'All of Oak Cam thanks you for the flame that binds us, Heart-Fire to Heart-Fire.'

'It was my pleasure, Bhearra, filidh of Oak Cam.' Danliv returned the traditional greeting, touching his fingertips to his heart, lips and forehead before bending down and kissing Bhearra's forehead, making the old woman laugh.

'Gather the Folk,' Bhearra called. 'It is time to light our Heart-Fire!'

***

THE CROWD GATHERED around the centre of the cam was swollen by their visitors but, despite the larger numbers, a hush covered them all. Even the babies seemed to sense the importance of what was happening, giving quiet coos and gurgles but not a single wail.

Bhearra stood at the centre, before the Heart-Fire, eyes closed, senses extended. She could feel the essence of each member of her cam, as well as those who visited. She saw the bright lines of energy that connected them to each other and to this place that served as their home. Bhearra stretched her vision further, looking for the connection that led from the Heart-Fire to each of them and to their gods.

A glowing thread led from each of the Folk of Oak Cam to the centre of the unlit Heart-Fire. There, the threads wound around each other, forming a rope of energy that pulsed with life. The rope climbed into the sky, disappearing above the treetops. As Bhearra gazed upon this rope made out of the faith of her people, the love and life and devotion that they poured into the Heart-Fire, she noticed a few threads were blackened. She focused her abilities on those, trying to understand why they were different. It was as if the life had gone out of them. Bhearra touched the dead threads with the core of her being and felt a deep sadness wash over her. For all her strength and wisdom, Bhearra did not know what had caused these threads to die, or what it meant, but she was certain that it signalled the end of something, a great loss.

The touch of a hand on her shoulder brought her back to herself and Bhearra turned to see Joren on one side of her and Rana on the other. The visiting filidh had arranged themselves in a crescent behind them, Danliv and the other cam leaders in the same formation on the other side of the fire. Bhearra ran her eyes over the wood and kindling one more time, checking that the offerings were still in place. If anything, there were even more now, almost every log and stick draped with precious items; food, tools and jewellery stuffed into every space. The gods could not possibly doubt their devotion. She shook herself, trying to shake away the sadness.

'My people,' Bhearra spoke in a voice that carried clearly to all gathered. 'We keep the eternal flame of the Heart-Fire as a sign of devotion to the All-Father and All-Mother. As we tend the flame, we tend our bond with them and with this land, created in the ecstasy of their union. We give offerings to them in the flame to renew them, so that they may continue to give us life.' Bhearra paused and scanned the crowd, meeting the eyes of many of the Folk.

'Our Heart-Fire was extinguished through no choice of ours. The time has come to bring it to life again. Please, join me in prayer.'

Some of the gathered Folk closed their eyes, while others looked to the sky. Some murmured and others stayed silent, but Bhearra knew, whatever their actions, at this moment the Folk of Oak Cam were of one heart. She took the torch with the flame from Trout Cam and raised it above her head.

'All-Father, we beseech you. See the flame of our devotion and know we keep faith with you. All-Mother, look upon our Heart-Fire and see it burn in your honour. As you provide food for the Folk, we take no more than we need.

As you provide shelter, we tend the forest that provides our home. As you take joy in each other, so too, do we. See that we walk in balance with you, treading lightly on this land. As this flame burns eternally, so does our devotion to you.' With this last, Bhearra lowered the torch to the waiting wood. The fire took hold surprisingly quickly, leaping from kindling to log to offering, reaching for the sky.

'It is a sign,' a voice called from the crescent behind her.

Bhearra looked around to see who had spoken.

'The gods are pleased with your offerings,' Bertrand spoke again. 'Oak Cam remains in their favour.'

The Folk of Oak Cam looked to Bhearra for confirmation. Inwardly, she groaned. She was not so quick to see signs, preferring to ponder and consider matters, but if she were to disagree with Bertrand now, her people would lose the look of hope that shone on their faces.

'Our Heart-Fire is as strong as our devotion,' Bhearra answered, smiling. She hoped that no one noticed she hadn't actually agreed with Bertrand.

The Folk were talking amongst themselves now, small groups forming, some people moving away towards their homes.

'Wait,' Joren called, his voice carrying across the hubbub. 'Our Heart-Fire has been returned to us, but that is not our only purpose here today. We must discuss matters of some import.'

The Folk returned to their positions, some looking at Joren warily.

'You all know of the strange events over this early summer. You all know that a group of our own were taken and that Ashael left the cam seeking to help them. Bhearra discovered some information about these events, and I have asked you to be patient, to wait until we could gather with our friends from the other cams. Well, now we are gathered. It is time to tell you all that we know or suspect.'

Bhearra watched the Folk as Joren spoke, saw many exchange worried glances, saw arms tighten around little ones. They were scared. Bhearra wished she could tell them they had no cause to fear but as Joren gestured to her to begin, she knew she must do the opposite.

'Ashael left the cam to try and save the people that were taken. On that day, I used old magic to try and locate Ashael. Instead, I found the All-Mother.' A few startled gasps sounded and Bhearra waited as a murmur ran through the crowd. 'I know that it is difficult to believe but it is true. The All-Mother told me to let Ashael go and that we face a grave danger. An old enemy has returned to our land: the Zanthar.'

'The Zanthar have been gone for generations, ever since Sirion and the winged ones defeated Daven,' a voice called from near the back of the crowd. 'Why would they return now?'

'We do not know,' Bhearra answered. 'Only that they have.'

'What do we do?' another voice called.

'We must assume they mean to enslave us again,' Joren answered. 'We must prepare to defend ourselves.'

'How can we do that?' Soraya spoke from the front of the group, Bhearrael clutched tightly in her arms. 'We do not know the ways of violence.'

'Perhaps we must learn,' Joren grimaced as he spoke.

'This is madness!' This time it was Olim, the leader of Blossom Cam, who spoke. 'I've heard all the old stories. If the Zanthar have truly returned, then we cannot possibly defeat them. We should flee. As far and as fast as we can.'

Bhearra saw people nodding in agreement, while others jeered.

'This is our land! Why should we run?'

'Should we give them our children as well as our homes?'

'If we stay here, they'll surely take our children!'

'Wait!' Sabien, the leader of Fork River Cam called out. 'We are getting ahead of ourselves.' He stepped forward, drawing all eyes to himself. 'I mean no disrespect, Bhearra – we all know of your wisdom – but how can you be sure it was truly the All-Mother? After all, I have never before heard of the gods speaking to people in so direct a manner.'

Bhearra heard murmurs of agreement and knew this would be the most difficult part for the Folk to believe. 'There is nothing I can say that would prove it to be true. I have searched within myself, questioning this experience, but I have no doubt in my heart. It was the All-Mother.'

'So, all we have is your word that the All-Mother herself spoke to you and told you we are under attack from the Zanthar, a people gone from our land so long that they have settled into legend?' Sabien looked around the gathered Folk, clearly seeking support. 'You will forgive me if I am not convinced that we need take any action.'

Bhearra nodded. 'I understand your concern, Sabien. Just know that I would not bring this before you all were I not absolutely certain.' She looked over the crowd, waiting for the next question or challenge. A disturbance started at the back, the crowd parting to let someone through. Two figures moved through the Folk until they reached the front. Ravena had her arm wrapped around Eislyn's waist, supporting the smaller woman, who limped on her injured leg. Eislyn's face was pale, her hair dishevelled. Rana rushed to them, linking her arm through Eislyn's, taking some of her weight.

'Eislyn, I am so very glad to see you awake, but you should be resting,' Bhearra said.

'This is important,' Eislyn panted.

Ravena held Eislyn up, worry for her mate etched across her face. Gerod appeared next to the women, carrying a stool which he placed behind Eislyn. The injured woman sank onto it gratefully.

'You need to know what happened,' Eislyn said, pain colouring her voice.

'Please, tell us,' Bhearra answered.

'Angus and I were making our way to Trout Cam for the flame. Without warning, three men I have never seen before appeared from between the trees and blocked our path.' Eislyn paused, gritting her teeth. Bhearra saw beads of sweat pop out on the young woman's brow and hurried to her side with some water.

'Gerod, please get some willow bark from my home,' Bhearra said in a low voice, holding the waterskin to Eislyn's lips.

'No willow bark until I've finished,' Eislyn said when she had drunk enough water.

Gerod looked to Bhearra, and she gestured for him to get the bark anyway.

'Tell us what you need to,' Bhearra said to Eislyn, kneeling in front of her, to be of any assistance that she could.

'Angus knew the men. One of them grabbed me and Angus said to let me go, that I didn't know anything that would be a problem. The man that seemed to be their leader said someone called Lord Daven wanted to see Angus. Angus seemed terrified. He was shaking but he told them he would go and asked them again to release me.' Tears stood bright in Eislyn's eyes, reflecting the firelight. Ravena was weeping and Bhearra's own throat tightened in empathy.

'Can you describe the men?' Joren asked.

'They were all large; powerfully built. All three had light colouring – much lighter than any of the Folk. They wore strange clothes and carried weapons I didn't recognise, like long knives made from a material I've never seen before. Incredibly sharp.' Eislyn gestured at the wound in her leg.

'What happened next?' Bhearra asked.

'The one that did all the talking grabbed Angus, pulled his arms behind his back. The man holding me pulled a knife made of the same strange stuff as the longer weapon. I struggled, pulled my legs up, thrashed about. I was kicking at him, clawing at whatever I could reach. He stabbed me in the leg, and I collapsed. He wanted to finish me, but Angus was shouting about how there were hunters coming behind us with bows and I would die from the wound anyway. I passed out. I don't know how long for. When I came to, they were gone, and I started trying to get back here. You know the rest.'

There was silence from everyone in in the cam, no sound but the crackle of the flames. Bhearra climbed to her feet, knees creaking. Many of the faces she could see had paled, tears tracking down many cheeks.

'Thank you for going to so much trouble to tell us all of this, Eislyn,' Bhearra said, taking the willow bark from Gerod, who had returned while Eislyn spoke. 'Chew this for the pain. It's a little bitter but it will help until we get you back to bed and make you a proper draught.'

'You mentioned a name,' Joren said. 'Can you say it again, please?'

'Lord Daven,' Eislyn said, accepting the willow bark. 'They said Lord Daven wanted him.'

'Daven. The leader of the Zanthar.' Joren looked around the crowd, meeting as many pairs of eyes as he could. 'Do you need any further evidence, Sabien?'

'How could it be the same Daven? It's been generations!' Sabien protested.

'Perhaps it is another Daven. But only the Zanthar would use that name,' Joren answered, his voice impatient at this refusal to accept reality. 'Does anyone still doubt Bhearra's vision?'

'This only further convinces me that we need to flee,' called the leader of Blossom Cam. 'Did you see what direction they headed in, Eislyn?'

'Not where they went, but they appeared from the west.'

'Then we will travel east as far as the sea and then turn south. My party will leave at dawn. Any who wish to may join us.' With that he stalked away toward his tent, gesturing for Bertram to join him.

A babble of voices cried out at once, everyone vying to be heard. Bhearra could feel the fear rising from them in waves. She sent out as much soothing energy as she could, but she was exhausted and could offer little comfort.

Joren raised his hand and waited for quiet before he spoke again. 'I will bind none of you to action. You may leave if you wish. I only ask that you do not rush to a decision but let us meet again tomorrow to discuss this further.' Joren turned then, and Rana took his hand, the two of them heading towards their home.

The crowd broke up, people moving off in smaller groups. Bhearra helped Eislyn to her feet, allowing Ravena to take her mate's other side. As they prepared to take the injured woman back to the guest house, Bhearra looked over her shoulder and saw Joren hold open the entrance curtain to his home for Rana, and for a moment envy struck her heart. They had each other to lean on, to fight for. Bhearra had no one to share her burden with. For the first time in years, her heart ached over the loss of her mate. She had shared her bed with others, but never had she shared her life the way that she had with Arlen. *I'm just a lonely old woman.* She shook herself and continued on her way.

Chapter Thirty-Four

MEEGRUM REINED IN HIS HORSE BESIDE HIS LORD, NEITHER MAN BOTHERING to dismount. They would not be here for long. Ahead of them, filling the narrow gap between two cliff faces, was the World-Gate, the semi-permanent portal between Zan and KalaDene. At the moment it was merely a black cloud; the way was not yet open. Zekinal arrived beside them, panting.

'Do you have any orders, my lord?' he asked.

'Make sure the warriors are in perfect order,' Daven responded without looking around.

'Yes, my lord,' Zekinal said, turning to head back to the men who were still arriving on foot.

'And make sure no one speaks of the Vessel.' Daven turned to look at Zekinal. 'Tell them any man who makes mention of her will end up looking like me.'

The warrior swallowed audibly. 'Yes, my lord.' He hurried off.

'What shall we do about Cenric, my lord?' Meegrum asked. 'We cannot move forward with him poking about.'

'Do you think me unaware of that?' Daven asked, his voice cold.

'Of course not, my lord.' Meegrum knew that Daven's rage over what had happened ran deep.

'We must arrange an accident for him. One which the king cannot question.'

Before Meegrum could answer, colours started to swirl within the blackness before them. Meegrum nodded to Daven, knowing sound could be transmitted before they would be able to see through the portal.

As the colours began to coalesce, Meegrum heard the many sounds of horses and men milling about. Cenric's voice could be heard, laughing at the punchline of some bawdy joke. Meegrum's fingers tightened on his reins, anger on his master's behalf pulsing through him. For the king to have sent Cenric, of all people, was a clear insult to Daven. Cenric had been raised to believe Daven an incompetent fool, a has-been who no longer had any power or deserved any respect.

At last, the portal was fully open and Meegrum could see the young man astride a beauty of a horse. *I hope the horse survives Cenric's accident. Magnificent beast.* Dust filled the air on the other side of the portal, kicked up by feet and hooves.

Cenric moved forward, bringing his party through the portal. He shimmered for a moment, appearing to have been cut in half and shifted to the left, much as an arm appears when held in water, then he was through. Meegrum and Daven stayed still, making Cenric come to them; a subtle insult.

'Lord Daven, my mother sends her greetings,' Cenric called, his voice coloured by the smirk on his face.

'Welcome, Cenric,' Daven rasped. 'The king bid me to inform you that he would be in touch this evening, after the welcoming feast.'

'A feast! I did not expect such a welcome; I understood you were poorly provisioned here.' Cenric's horse tossed its head, impatient to be off.

'Not so poorly provisioned that we cannot extend the usual courtesies.'

'My men and I thank you. I trust you have barracks enough for five hundred?'

Meegrum almost gasped at this. Five hundred men! Travelling with so many was clearly intended to intimidate Daven, a display of Cenric's wealth and influence.

'Of course,' Daven answered through gritted teeth. Meegrum could see a vein throbbing in his lord's temple.

'Lord Cenric, shall we go ahead?' Meegrum said. 'Captain Zekinal can see to your men and I'm sure you must be eager to refresh yourself.'

'Not at all. I am more than happy to wait here until all of my men are through the portal.'

'Then we shall go ahead and make arrangements for them,' Meegrum said.

'I thought you had courtesy enough to escort a guest yourself, but if that is not the case then by all means, go back to your keep. I'm sure I can find the way.'

'We shall wait, of course,' Daven answered. 'We thought only of your comfort, Cenric.'

The handsome young man raised an eyebrow at Daven's failure to use his title. 'Well, Daven, my comfort is with my men.' With that he turned his horse to watch the long procession passing though the portal.

***

THE SUN HAD passed its zenith by the time they arrived at the keep, and Meegrum was stiff and sore. That was the longest he had been in a saddle for years; the journeys he took these days were usually made by portal but Daven wanted him to conceal the extent of his abilities from Cenric.

'That insufferable little peacock thinks he can waltz in here and insult me without consequence,' Daven fumed as soon as they were alone in his chamber.

'If we were ready to move against the king I would duel him, man to man. I'd like to see him hanging off the end of my sword.'

Meegrum poured wine for them both, passing a cup to Daven and, as usual, waiting for him to drink before draining his own cup.

'He believes himself untouchable because he is the king's pet. He does not yet realise how fickle our king can be in his affections.' Meegrum poured again as he spoke.

'How soon until we can kill him?' Daven asked.

'Well, my lord, the wisest course would be to wait; let him report to the king that we are co-operating fully, lull him into a false sense of security.' Meegrum paced, stretching out his legs. 'Then, when he has an unfortunate accident, the king will have no grounds to accuse us of anything, suspicious as he might be.' *And perhaps I will be able to convince Merelle that I had nothing to do with the death of her son.*

'Are you suggesting we delay our plans even further?'

'No, my lord, simply that we proceed very cautiously. Disguise the groups searching for the enchantress as scouting parties or some such. We must find her before we can move forward, at any rate.'

'If the prophecy was correct then the opportunity to feed from her has passed. She is worth nothing to us now. I would see her dead.'

Daven opened the door to his garderobe and, over his shoulder, Meegrum saw the bench propped against the opposite wall and a pair of soft hide slippers on the floor.

'What?' he asked in confusion, moving towards the door.

Daven turned towards him, face puce except the heavy ropes of white scar tissue. 'I will have that bitch's other eye!' he screamed. In his rage, Daven released a blast of power that scorched the walls. Meegrum only just managed to get a shield up in time to lessen the blast, but he was still pressed against the wall by the force.

All at once the force dissipated and Daven collapsed.

***

ASHAEL AWOKE SLOWLY, stretching, eyes still closed. She had dreamt of home, and for a moment she thought herself on her pallet, expecting to hear Bhearra moving about in the other room. Then everything came back to her, and she sat up with a start.

She was still alone, thank the All-Mother. She had no idea how long she had slept but it had done more good than she could say. Not only did she feel less exhausted, but she almost felt... good. Peaceful. Getting to her feet, Ashael stretched and looked around. Behind her was the neck of stone that she had forced her way through while in front was the smooth-walled passage, lit by glowing crystals.

Ashael took a couple of steps into the passage and ran her hand over the walls. *Who could have made this place?* She let her eyes travel over the rock, admiring the beauty of it. *This must have taken a long time. It must have been important to someone.* She knew that, this close to the Zanthar stronghold, the likeliest explanation was that this was their place, but it felt completely different. She felt safe here, for no reason she could explain. With a brief glance back at the way she had come in, she gathered her belongings and began to make her way along the passage.

She hadn't gone far when she came to a branch in the path. Without being able to see the sky, she had no idea which direction she was travelling in. *How do I figure out which way to go?* As she stood at the intersection, a breeze ruffled her hair. *Follow the air. Hopefully that will lead me to a way out.* She turned into the passage to her right. As she walked, she studied the glowing crystals. They emitted their own source of light, something she had never seen before. She pressed her fingers to one; it was cool to the touch, its sides smooth and polished. *How do you get light without heat?* That was when Ashael realised that the cuts and scrapes on her hands were gone.

She looked at the deeper scrape to her chest. Only a scab was left, looking almost ready to fall off. *How long was I asleep?* Ashael felt a trickle of discomfort at that but then she remembered how she had inadvertently healed herself while spirit-walking. *Maybe I did something similar in my sleep.*

Not entirely happy with that explanation, but not quite willing to consider the implications of anything else, Ashael continued, reaching another branch in the passage. Again, she turned toward the breeze, as best she could tell. She had only gone a few paces along this passage when she thought about what she was doing; wandering around some sort of cave system with no idea of where she was going. She could easily get lost. If she didn't find a way out by following the way the air seemed to be coming from, she might want to retrace her steps.

Ashael dug through her travelling pouch, looking for some way to mark the path she had taken. At the bottom of the pouch her fingers brushed something solid. Wondering what it was, she pulled it out and her throat tightened with emotion immediately. It was the chalk that she had found for Rana, to help her sickness. She hadn't had a chance to make the remedy for her friend before she had left the cam. After a brief prayer of thanks to the All-Mother, Ashael headed back to start marking her path.

Ashael stepped into the passage she had started off in and moved to the left a little, to show the direction she had come from originally. Crouching down, she made an arrow on the floor, pointing back towards the passage she would now be taking She stood and glanced around, ready to head on. *What in the All-Mother's name is going on?* The passage she had just stepped out of was gone. Only smooth wall remained, as far as she could see, the only branches on the other side of the passage. *Did I get myself turned around?* She stepped over to the nearest passage on the wall facing her and looked down the path leading from it.

I don't think that's the way I went. The stone looks different – darker. But then I was looking at the crystals more than the stone. Ashael took a few steps down the corridor, seeing that it turned just up ahead. This definitely wasn't the way she had come before. Frowning, she stepped back into the first corridor and turned in a slow circle, examining the walls, floor and ceiling. When she came to face the passage with the turn just ahead, she gasped. The entrance was gone. *I definitely didn't get confused that time. This place is changing round about me! How is that even possible?* Stepping up to the wall, Ashael ran her hands along it. When she touched the section where she thought the entrance had been, the hair on the back of her arms stood up. Waves of coldness swept over her from head to toe, making her shiver violently. She stumbled backwards, away from the sensation, and her body calmed almost immediately. Digging about in her travel pouch once more, Ashael took out some of the cheese that Talak had given her. She broke a piece off and looked at it thoughtfully, before throwing it straight at the wall she had just been touching. The cheese sailed right through. *So, the passage is still there, just concealed somehow. Clever.*

She approached the wall, putting her hands on the concealed entrance again. Knowing what to expect, the coldness was lessened but still unpleasant. Ashael pushed forward. There was some resistance, but it was like pushing against tightly-drawn fabric rather than a solid surface. Clenching her teeth against the waves of cold, she pushed harder and all at once stumbled forward, through the concealment.

For a moment she stood gasping at the shock of passing through. It was akin to standing beneath an icy waterfall; she even touched her hair and clothes to confirm that she was not soaking wet. *So, it's possible that the first disappearing passage is just hidden, too.*

From where she stood, the original passage was still clearly visible. Steeling herself for the icy shock, Ashael stepped through the concealment again. This time, she felt nothing. She turned and looked back, again seeing only solid wall. It appeared that the entrances concealed themselves after she had passed through them.

Ashael let her eye relax, letting go of focus. This place was entirely suffused with the gentle life force that she was used to. Looking at the wall, she could see a shimmer, like a heat haze, over the wall where she knew the entrance to be. Turning, she examined the wall on the other side. There was a shimmer a few paces away, close to the arrow she had drawn on the floor. Ashael let her vision return to normal, drumming her fingers against her lips. *Someone has gone to a lot of trouble here. Why? What is the purpose? Is it something similar to the charm that Bhearra weaves to disguise the cam from large animals?*

She sensed this was something close to the truth. She felt no danger here. In fact, despite this mystery, she still felt more peaceful than she had at any point since leaving the cam. She approached the wall next to her chalk arrow and ran her hands along the stone until she found the place where her hair raised. Taking a deep breath, she pushed through and began to retrace her steps, this time keeping one hand on the wall. She followed the faint breeze, hoping it would lead her outside.

Chapter Thirty-Five

'**M**OTHER,' IWAN CRIED AGAIN, HUGGING THE SMALL, MIDDLE-AGED WOMAN and spinning her around.

'Iwan, my boy, my beautiful boy,' the woman sobbed.

It was only when she raised her hand to her head scarf that Iwan saw that it was blood-stained, wrapped as a bandage rather than a scarf.

'You're hurt! What happened?' Iwan asked.

'I'm fine, just hit my head on a wall. The Hive said I should rest but I'm fine. Where have you been?'

The man with the splint was standing nearby shifting his weight from one foot to the other. 'I sure am pleased to see you, lad, but we best be going. Quick, like.'

Iwan turned to regard the man and realised that it was Luca, a friend of his mother's who'd been like family to him. Iwan took Luca by the shoulders and hugged him tight.

'What's going on here?' Iwan asked.

'We'd best away before catching up,' Luca answered, his voice gruff.

'Very well. There are some places we can get out of sight – back this way,' Iwan said, taking his mother's arm and leading her back the way he had come. *Where are Colm and Tris?* Iwan looked around for the others, before glancing back at the keep. *I'll be back, Ashael.*

'Colm! Tris!' he called. 'It's not what it looks like. I can explain.'

There was no response. They must think he was with the Zanthar.

'I am no threat to you,' he tried again.

'So, you didn't bring us here to hand us over?' Tris spoke, his voice coming from Iwan's left.

Iwan looked around and saw his companion standing in the brush a short distance away, holding Iwan's own bow, the string drawn and an arrow pointing straight at him.

Iwan moved his body between Tris and his mother, shielding her from the arrow. He held his arms out to his sides, hands open, posture relaxed.

'I did not trick you into coming here.'

'Iwan, what's going on?' his mother asked, trying to see around him.

'Just stay there, Mother, everything will be fine.'

'So, you've been perfectly honest with us, have you?' Tris asked, sarcasm dripping from his words.

'I did not lie to you. I came here to help Ashael.'

Tris made a scornful sound. Iwan could see his muscles starting to tremble from keeping the bowstring drawn. Iwan was larger than Tris, with a longer arm span, and he had made the bow for himself. It would not be an easy weapon for the other man to handle.

'Tris, I didn't ask you to come with me. You and Colm insisted. The last thing I want is for you to be caught again. It would make everything Ashael has done pointless.'

'That's true, Tris,' Colm's voice sounded from further off. Iwan's eyes flicked to the movement as the older man stepped out from behind some boulders. 'He tried to talk us into going back to the cam, remember?'

'That doesn't mean anything,' Tris answered, the tremble in his arms now more pronounced.

'He could have handed us over when we first arrived and all those men were gathered outside,' Colm said.

'If he's not one of them then why is his mother here?' Tris asked.

'A very good question, and one that I think we need him to answer. Preferably out of sight of this gods-forsaken place.'

Tris stared at Iwan, the point of the arrow jittering as Tris strained to hold the draw. At last Tris breathed out and lowered the weapon. 'Very well,' he muttered, 'but there had better be a good explanation.'

'I'm sure Joren will be interested in your explanation too, after you took his hospitality and swore to Oak Cam,' Colm said, his voice hard.

'I will gladly explain everything to Joren and accept whatever punishment he sees fit. As soon as I get Ashael out of there.'

'The enchantress? Is Ashael her name?' Iwan's mother asked.

Iwan nodded, turning to face her now the danger from the arrow had passed. 'She's gone. Escaped last night.'

'What? Are you sure?' Iwan took her by the shoulders.

'Positive.'

'What happened?'

'It seems there's a lot to discuss. But not here,' Colm said.

'Let's go back to that dry riverbed we spotted earlier,' Iwan suggested. 'It's well hidden. We can rest there.'

'I don't think you should get a say in how we go from here,' Tris said, voice tight with anger. 'We can't be sure it's not some sort of trap.'

Iwan's mother gave Tris a withering look. 'My son is a good man. You would do well to listen to him.'

Colm pinched the bridge of his nose between weathered fingers. 'We passed a cave a little way back. Do any of you know anything about it?' He looked between Iwan and the two who had just left the keep.

'Used to be a kyragua den,' Luca said, rubbing at the stubble on his chin. 'Devorik's men killed it. Cave should be empty now.'

'Then that's where we'll go. Tris, make sure we're not followed.'

***

THE CAVE STILL smelled of kyragua. Iwan wrinkled his nose in distaste. At least they would be out of sight here, safe to work out their next move. Iwan moved towards the back of the cave where there was the sound of dripping water. Tris watched him suspiciously over Colm's shoulder while the two spoke in low voices.

Iwan found a small pool of clear water with an opening in the rock above it. Iwan knelt and filled his waterskin before going back and sitting beside his mother. With great care, he unwound the scarf from her head and examined her injury. A large lump rose from her temple, the skin badly bruised. Iwan poured some cool water onto the scarf and held it to his mother's head.

'We came for Ashael,' Colm said, turning to look at them all, 'so let's start with what happened to her.' Tris looked displeased but did not interrupt.

'Thank you,' Iwan said softly. 'Mother, what do you know?'

Between them, Iwan's mother and Luca told of the young woman who had been held prisoner in the keep. Much of it was only rumours, they said, but both had been serving refreshments in the courtyard when the three moons joined the sun in the sky. They told of how she had glowed and called upon the earth itself to save her. They told how Daven almost won but then the enchantress had somehow defeated him.

'She was like a volcano, such force,' Luca said. 'We were both thrown into the wall. Your mama hit her head and I broke my arm. I passed out for a few moments. When I came to, she was gone, and the lords – they was furious about it all. I played dead for a while; I was so sure they would kill us out of spite.'

'How she could have gotten out? Do you know where she went?' Iwan asked urgently.

'No, son. Only that she couldn't be found,' his mother answered, patting his arm as she spoke.

'How did you come to be leaving the keep?' Iwan asked.

'It was the strangest thing; the Hive said Lord Meegrum ordered us put out on account of we couldn't work.' Luca frowned. 'I never heard of them putting anyone out before. Usually, they just kill anyone they don't need anymore.'

Iwan took his mother's hand in his, gripping it tightly. 'We need to get you away from here before they change their minds. Come with us, back to the cam –'

'Who said you're going back to the cam?' Tris interrupted. 'We still haven't heard any reason not to believe you're one of them.'

'I do believe it's time to hear your story, Iwan,' Colm said. 'Is that even your name?'

'Yes. My name is Iwan ap Moyna,' Iwan gestured to his mother as he spoke. 'This is my mother, Moyna verch Gwen. I will tell you all you wish to know. Where would you have me start?' Iwan glanced toward the rear of the cave. He thought he had heard a rustle back there. Colm looked, too, but the others didn't seem to have heard anything and there was no further sound.

'Start at the beginning,' Colm answered.

'And hope you convince us of your honesty,' Tris said in a growl.

Iwan took a sip of water, swirling it in his mouth for a moment before swallowing and beginning to speak. 'You grew up with tales of the evil Zanthar and all they had done to your people. I grew up with the Zanthar. We,' he gestured to his mother and Luca, 'we are of the same descent as you. We share ancestors. But where your people followed Sirion and were freed to form the cams, our people were still enslaved. When Daven was facing his final days here, some of the other Zanthar fled back to Zan, taking their slaves with them.

'My family were amongst those taken. There, some were fed upon, their life force stolen to extend the lives of the highest castes of Zanthar. Others were kept as slaves. The Zanthar keep slaves from many worlds but with each generation our numbers diminish. Something about Zan is hostile to other races. And so every few generations, the Zanthar travel to yet another world to enslave another people. Many women are taken as bed-slaves.' At this, Moyna coloured, a flush rising up her neck to her face, and she stared at the floor.

'You mean they are forced?' Colm asked through gritted teeth.

'Yes. Forced then often killed.' Iwan wrapped his arm around his mother's shoulder.

'It is an abomination! All-Mother strike them from this place!' Colm moved across the cave and knelt at Moyna's feet. 'I am so very sorry for your pain.'

'Get to your place in all of this,' Tris said impatiently.

'I was born on Zan, but my mother and I were brought here 20 summers ago with Daven's group. They did not confide in slaves, but we often go unseen; I managed to pick up some of their plans. There was some prophecy that had Daven all excited. He believed it would let him defeat this land once and for all, avenging his defeat here and providing him with enough power to challenge the king back on Zan.

'In his search, he realised that his slaves could serve as spies and I was sent out to join your cam. I was told to claim that I was a traveller. They said that if I tried to warn you in any way, I would die before I could finish speaking and they would kill my mother too. Meegrum was able to use our slave-brands to access our memories, see whatever we saw. He didn't contact me for more than a moons' cycle and I thought they had forgotten me until the night I was invited to join Oak Cam. After that, I tried to cut off the brand.' Iwan lifted his tunic and showed his smooth chest. 'Ashael healed me. Somehow she took away my brand.'

Moyna gasped and ran her hand over her son's unmarked skin. 'How?'

Iwan squeezed his mother's hand and shook his head. 'I do not know. But we need to be aware that they can track you and Luca by your brands. They will be distracted at the moment, but we have to figure out a way to shield you before they change their minds and decide to look for you.'

Colm rubbed his chin. 'Gert had such a brand, but she told me that Zek had cut her, breaking the pattern, and the brand no longer worked. I wish no harm to either of you, but if what Iwan says is true, then we cannot risk taking you with us as things are.' Colm held out the knife from his belt. Moyna looked at Luca and he nodded and reached for the knife. Moyna held out her arm and Iwan squeezed her hand as Luca pulled the blade across the brand, making a shallow cut that broke the lines of the pattern. Iwan wrapped the wound with a piece of cloth torn from his tunic.

Luca lifted his own tunic and turned his back. 'I can't reach the brand. Will you do it?' he asked, holding the knife out to Colm.

Colm nodded and accepted the knife, swiftly cutting across the brand. He took a rag from his travelling pouch and held it to Luca's back, turning his head to speak to Iwan.

'Why didn't you say anything after Ashael healed you?'

'I had no idea what would happen: after I discovered she had made the wound vanish, I was going to tell her everything. But she left before I got the chance.' Iwan took another drink of water.

'Why didn't you tell *us* what was happening? Or at least tell Joren and Bhearra?' Tris challenged. 'You say you're not one of them, but you haven't acted like one of us.'

'They still had my mother. I was terrified they would kill her. Or worse. It was an impossible situation.'

'We could have helped you!' Tris shouted.

'How?' Iwan kept his voice low, calm, though his own temper was fraying. 'Could you have got my mother out of there? Would you even have believed me?

Or would you have thought me mad?'

'You're right, to an extent,' Colm said. 'When you first arrived at the cam, we may not have believed you. But we took you in, Iwan. We made you one of us. Joren took you into his closest group. Your troubles became ours. You should have trusted us.' Colm's face betrayed the injury to his feelings.

'You should have trusted me,' came a voice from the back of the cave.

They all tensed, looking to the shadows further in. Tris pulled the knife from his belt, but Colm touched his arm, holding him back.

There was a shuffling and the sound of footsteps and then Ashael stepped out of the rock, gingerly stepping around the pool of rainwater.

Iwan wanted to run to her but was frozen to the spot, staring at this familiar yet strange woman. She raised her head and Iwan saw that she had lost an eye, her left eyelid sunken over an empty socket. Iwan's throat tightened, along with his fists. He vowed to himself that he would find the person who had done this to her and make them regret it. Ashael raised her chin defiantly, staring at Iwan with her good eye. She seemed taller, though that was surely a trick of perspective. Her long, dark hair was braided but untidy and full of dust. She wore a robe like the Hive's, hanging loose on her lean frame. Her face and hands showed scabs and the fading yellow of bruises

'I would have believed you.' She held his gaze with her good eye, her strength of will shining through.

Iwan dropped his gaze, ashamed.

Colm stood, breaking the moment. 'Ashael, what has happened to you? Your eye…'

'I will tell you all, but not now.' Ashael's voice was full of pain.

Colm took hold of Ashael's hands. 'Iwan told us what you did. That you exchanged yourself for us. We owe you our lives.'

Ashael smiled at Colm, her face lighting up. 'You owe me nothing.' She wrapped her arms around Colm, giving him a warm embrace, before doing the same to Tris. 'Now, if none of you minds, I would really like to go home.' Ashael's voice cracked on the last word.

Chapter Thirty-Six

Daven's eyes fluttered open, water dripping from his face. Meegrum breathed a huge sigh of relief, putting down the jug he had just tipped out over Daven.

'What happened?' Daven asked, voice barely above a whisper.

'You went into the garderobe and saw that the enchantress had escaped through there.' Meegrum answered, holding a goblet of wine to Daven's lips as he spoke. 'In your fury, you forgot about your injuries, my lord. You let the force erupt from you. Then you passed out.'

'How long?' Daven asked, pushing himself into a sitting position.

'Just a few minutes, my lord.'

A knock came at the door, making Meegrum jump and almost spill the wine.

'Who's there?' Meegrum called.

'Lord Cenric is here to see Lord Daven,' called a guard.

'Damn him,' Daven rasped, trying to stand.

'We cannot let him see you now, my lord.'

'I'm fine.'

'My lord, half of your hair has gone grey and one of your eyes is filled with blood. You do not look fine. Cenric will see weakness to exploit.'

Daven's jaw clenched, the only sign of his anger as he nodded.

'Lord Daven is indisposed just now,' Meegrum called towards the door, helping Daven to his feet and moving towards the garderobe.

'Then, I must assist him, of course,' Cenric called back.

'He has no need of assistance,' Meegrum said, supporting Daven and guiding him to the garderobe. 'In here, my lord,' he said under his breath.

'Well, if he has no need of assistance then how can he be indisposed?'

As soon as Daven was safely in the garderobe, Meegrum strode to the main door of the room and threw it open in frustration.

'I was attempting to be discreet, Lord Cenric, but since discretion appears to be beyond you, my Lord Daven is in the garderobe. It would appear that he has eaten something that disagreed with him.'

Cenric gave a disbelieving laugh. 'You mean he has the trots?'

'Yes. Although that is not how it is normally phrased in polite company.'

'Fortunately for me, I'm not in polite company.'

'Cenric,' Daven called from the garderobe, his voice weak but better than it had been moments before, 'I hope you will excuse me. I am in no condition to receive guests at the moment.'

'You must have words with your cook, Daven. Preferably before dinner. I should not wish to suffer a similar fate.' Cenric walked out of the room, chuckling.

Meegrum stood in the doorway, watching him go, adrenaline making him queasy. Daven could have killed him if he hadn't had his shield up in time, and Cenric almost caught them out. If Cenric knew the full extent of Daven's weakness, he would not hesitate to exploit it.

'That was well handled, although I wish you had thought of something less… indelicate,' Daven said from behind him.

Meegrum bit back a retort, turning to face his master. Daven swayed on his feet. He had lost weight, looking like he was half-starved. His scars stood in sharp relief across his face and neck, twisting his mouth into a perpetual sneer.

'Bring two slaves, immediately,' Meegrum barked through the door to the guards standing outside. 'In fact, make it three!'

Meegrum moved to Daven's side and steadied him, guiding him to the bed. 'Sit, rest, my lord.'

Daven sat on the edge of the bed, a tremble running through his body. Meegrum stood, looking down upon him. His lord looked close to death. *What if I didn't help him? What if I walked out of here, sent the guards away and barred the door? Would he die?* Meegrum's mind raced through the possibilities, weighing up the risks against the benefits of letting Daven die. *It's too soon. I do not yet have enough power of my own.*

One of the guards knocked and quickly entered with three slaves: two adults and a child. The guard stared at Daven, eyes wide, until Meegrum grabbed the young man by the shoulder and shoved him out of the room, muttering a quick incantation that would paralyse the slaves and prevent them from fleeing. He pulled the child, a young girl, to the side of the bed. Children had always been Daven's favourite; so much life yet unused, so much possibility ripped away in a moment.

Daven put his hand on the girl's head, smoothing her hair before wrapping his fingers in it and jerking her forward. Daven began to chant, the mystical words of the Old Tongue filling the air with their power. The child sobbed but no blue light escaped her. *Where is her life force?*

'Meegrum, what is happening?' Daven rasped, the magic in the air dissipating as he broke off his chant.

'I have no idea, my lord. Try this one.' Meegrum pushed the woman forward.

Again, Daven began chanting, trying to pull the life force from the woman before him, and again nothing happened.

Panic rising in his breast, Meegrum thrust the last slave in front of his master; a pale, middle-aged, hunched man. This one would have little life force left. Daven was struggling now, the effort of calling up the life force taking a toll on his already depleted state. This time, the blue essence rose from the man immediately and Daven sucked it up greedily. It was not long before the slave fell, lifeless, to the floor.

'More... I need more,' Daven gasped, breathless.

'Bring more slaves,' Meegrum called to the guards. 'As many as you can.' *We must find out what was different about these two,* he thought, looking at the woman and child cowering on the floor. *What magic protects them?*

Chapter Thirty-Seven

ASHAEL WASN'T SURE WHETHER SHE WANTED TO HUG IWAN OR SLAP HIM. HE had come all this way, risking his own life to try and save her, but he had been lying to her since they met. Lying to them all. How much of what he said could she believe? She watched him with Moyna, saw how tender he was with his mother. Surely that was the sign of a good man? He had been in a terrible position. The night they had spent together had been real. Hadn't it?

'You said the tunnels extend through the mountains?' Colm asked.

'As far as I could tell,' Ashael responded.

'Perhaps we could use them to get away from here without being seen,' the forager mused. 'Do you think you could find your way back, even with the changes you told us about?'

Ashael held up the piece of chalk. 'I marked my path. I can definitely get back to the tunnel I started out in. I'm not sure how that helps us though.'

'Seems as good a place to start as any. We know it's further away from the Zanthar keep than we are now.' Colm stood and squeezed Ashael's shoulder. 'I can't tell you how glad I am that you escaped. If you had died… Well, I'm not sure I understand all of what you've told us, but the cam would have been a poorer place without you.'

'Thank you,' Ashael said.

***

THE PLAN WAS simple: choose the paths that would lead them downwards, doing their best to travel east. Ashael chewed her lip. Iwan was directly behind her; he had tried to strike up conversation, but she had made it clear that she didn't want to talk. She needed time to work out how she felt about all of this. Iwan's hand rested on her shoulder, exactly as she had suggested they proceed, nothing more. Still, the warmth spread through her skin and made her flush. Every so often, her clothing would shift as she moved and Iwan's thumb would brush against her skin. She found herself utterly focused on that contact until her entire awareness was centred on the inch of shoulder where their skin met.

Ashael was jerked back to the task ahead when she ran her hand over another concealed entrance. She stopped walking, jerking away from the wall as prickles raced across her flesh.

'What is it? What's wrong?' Iwan asked, concerned.

'One of the hidden passages,' Ashael said, rubbing her arms then shaking them to rid herself of the effects. 'Didn't you feel it?'

'I wasn't touching the wall,' Iwan said. 'Where is it?'

Ashael pointed and Iwan reached out his hand to the wall in front of her.

'I feel only wall,' he said, frowning.

One by one, the group touched the stone at the point where Ashael could feel the charm. None of the others felt anything out of the ordinary.

'As far as I can tell,' Colm said, 'we're travelling roughly southeast. Branching off here suggests the hidden passage will be moving more eastward.'

Ashael took a deep breath, then pushed her upper half through the concealment so that her feet were in the passage with the others while her head and shoulders leaned beyond. She heard a muffled cry and turned back to see Moyna staring at her, eyes wide, a hand over her mouth. Ashael leaned back.

'Are you well?' Ashael asked.

Moyna nodded. 'That was the strangest thing I ever saw. It was like you were sticking through the wall.' The older woman shuddered.

'My apologies, I didn't think how it would look. I should have warned you,' Ashael said. 'It looks as though the passage through there does go roughly east. Unless we've misjudged, being underground.'

'How will we get through, if the rest of us can only feel rock?' Tris asked.

'We've already passed through several from the other side; the concealment doesn't show from that direction. This is just the first time that you'll be passing through from the concealed side,' Ashael responded, gesturing towards the wall.

Tris put his hands on the spot Ashael indicated and pushed. He looked like he was trying to push a mountain.

'I don't understand,' Ashael said, biting her lip. 'Why would you be able to move through in one direction and not another?'

'Perhaps it is to do with sight,' Luca spoke hesitantly. 'We could not see the other charms we have passed through. Might be the eyes convince the arm there's nought there but stone.'

'That makes sense,' Ashael mused. 'Bhearra taught me that the mind is powerful enough to shape the word around it. That could be the answer. Try with your eyes closed.'

Tris closed his eyes and leaned against the wall again, to no avail.

'We can always carry on down this way and hope for another path leading off the way we want to go. We're bound to come to one sooner or later,' Colm said.

'But there might be more places like this. What if we come to one that blocks our path completely?' Ashael asked, the worry clear in her voice.

'We were holding on to each other,' Iwan offered. 'You can go through; maybe you can take us with you.'

Iwan put his hand on Ashael's shoulder and put his other hand on the wall. He instantly jerked back, the dark hairs on the backs of his arms standing up straight. Ashael didn't need to ask if he'd felt it that time.

One by one, Ashael led them through the wall.

***

ASHAEL WASN'T SURE how much time had passed but she was starting to get hungry when Iwan spoke.

'I know you're upset with me,' he said, 'and I understand that, but I need you to know that I never meant for anyone to get hurt.' They had passed through another concealed entrance and were still walking in single file. Iwan's hand rested lightly on Ashael's shoulder.

Ashael didn't answer for a moment, pausing for so long that it felt difficult to break the silence that stretched between them.

'Did you know the Zanthar were going to take the foraging group that day?' she asked at last, her voice low.

'Of course not.'

'Would you have told us if you had?'

'I... I don't know. I probably would have tried to stop them going out.'

'Why didn't they just come into the cam and get me?' Ashael asked. 'Taken by surprise, we would have been no match for them.'

'Something to do with Bhearra's charm. They can't find the cam, despite knowing where it is. The day I arrived, I had to wait for someone to cross my path and invite me in.'

The reminder of how Iwan had taken advantage of them made Ashael's shoulders tense. He must have felt the change.

'I'm sorry. I've wanted to tell you the truth for so long.'

'I want to understand. I want to forgive you. But if you had told us, given us some warning, Nela might still be alive. I might... My eye...' Ashael began to sob silently, her shoulders shaking beneath Iwan's hand.

'I wish I could have made different choices, but I made them because they had my mother.'

'You keep saying that. You couldn't act against them because they had your mother and because of the brand. So, what changed? You say you came to stop Devorik taking me but, surely, if you had succeeded that would have made them hurt your mother. What was it Iwan? What made you decide to act when it had all gone too far?' Ashael only realised that she was shouting when she stopped and heard her voice bouncing back to her off of the stone walls.

The group had come to a halt, Ashael and Iwan facing each other in the violet light, all trace of its peace gone from Ashael's mind. Rainbow light began to dance on her skin.

'Don't you know?' Iwan asked, his voice soft. 'I fell in love with you, Ashael. That's what changed.'

The moment of tenderness was shattered as a voice like stone grating against stone came from behind Ashael. 'Seize them!'

Ashael whirled around as two creatures stepped out of the tunnel wall. She heard Moyna cry with fear and looked behind her, only to see another two of the creatures blocking their path. All four were very tall, with mottled grey-and-green skin and hair that looked like moss. They each wore only a loin cloth, and their eyes glowed with the same violet shade as the crystals. Where a mouth and nose might go, the creatures had a pulsing sack, similar to a frog's throat.

Their body language was not overtly aggressive, but they did each hold a spear, similar to those the Folk used for hunting but much larger. Ashael stepped forward and the creature closest to her raised its spear to block her path. *What are they? Something else the Zanthar brought with them?* A fifth creature stepped out of the wall into Ashael's path. This one was shorter than the other four, with a less impressive physique, but was otherwise similar in appearance except he wore a white sash as well as a loin cloth. He stopped dead when he saw Ashael.

'We must bring them to the council,' he said.

'We apologise if we have intruded,' Ashael said, addressing the creature with the sash, who seemed to be in charge. 'We did not realise these caves were occupied.'

Their captors looked at each other in confusion, the sash-creature frowning at her.

'How is it that you come to speak?' he asked in a deep rumble.

'Ashael! What are you doing?' Colm asked from behind her.

'I'm sorry, I don't understand,' Ashael said to White-Sash, before turning to answer Colm: 'I'm trying to get us out of this.'

'Your kind cannot usually speak the true tongue, but only make babbling noises,' the sash-creature answered.

'Are you speaking to it?' Iwan asked.

'Of course. What do you think I'm doing?' Ashael snapped.

'How can you do that?'

'I don't know what you mean,' Ashael said. 'Why are you all acting so strangely?'

'How can you understand them?' Iwan asked.

Ashael looked at him, confused. She turned her attention to Iwan, trying to understand what he meant. No longer concentrating on White-Sash, when he next spoke, she heard what her companions did: the sound of a rockslide with no words; grumbling and grinding that hinted at speech but was unintelligible. She looked back at White-Sash and concentrated on him again.

'We must get them back to the council with all haste. Tchalikila will know what to do,' he said to his companions, gesturing at Ashael. Now she understood him again.

One of the larger creatures brandished its spear at them and indicated the wall. White-Sash waved a hand and the entrance to a passage became visible. Ashael's group bunched tight at her back, tension radiating from them.

'They want to take us to their council,' she told her companions. 'I think we're safe for the moment.'

'As long as they don't use those spears,' Iwan muttered.

'Let's not give them cause to,' said Colm, moving up beside Ashael.

***

As THEY TRAVELLED through the tunnels, Ashael studied their captors, trying to learn more of them. One of the spear-carriers had started to speak but White-Sash had hushed him, looking pointedly at Ashael.

'By my reckoning, they're taking us deeper into the mountains,' Colm said quietly. 'We're going in the wrong direction for getting home.'

Ashael sighed. 'I suppose we'll just have to walk further once we've convinced them to let us go.'

'How did you speak their tongue? Is it part of the filidh training?'

'No. I didn't even realise I was doing it. I have no idea where that came from.' Ashael thought it must be something to do with her new powers, but she didn't want to talk about that until she could speak to Bhearra. She still didn't really understand what was happening to her.

Sweat started to trickle down Ashael's back and dampen her hair where it lay against the back of her neck. 'Is it getting warmer or is it just me?' she asked, pulling off the robe she had taken from Talak, revealing her stained and damaged clothing beneath.

'It's warm,' Colm answered, sweat beading his brow.

Ashael turned to check on the rest of the group and saw flushed, sweat-slick faces. Moyna started to cough and Iwan, who was walking beside her, patted her back. Before she could get the coughing under control, Iwan started to cough, too, then Luca, Colm and Tris. Ashael was the only one unaffected.

One of the spear-carriers gestured to Ashael, putting his hand over his mouth. The others were all covering their mouths as they coughed.

White-Sash turned and spoke to Ashael, 'Your kind have trouble breathing the air here, near the heart of Agni. Breathing through these things that you wear seems to help.'

Ashael started ripping strips of cloth from Talak's robe for each of them. 'Why can't we breathe here? Where are we?' she asked.

'Tchalikila will decide how much you should know,' he answered, turning away to resume the march – but first waiting until Ashael and her companions each had a piece of cloth tied over their mouths and noses.

'Thank you,' Ashael said, instinctively bowing her head.

White-Sash only nodded but Ashael could sense that he was pleased.

Pools of steaming water lay in some of the passages they took, a foul smell rising from them. Ashael leaned close to look at one of the pools, but White-Sash put a hand on her shoulder and pulled her back.

'That is the devouring-water. One drop would eat through you,' he said.

Ashael noted that his skin was smooth and tough. He was cool to the touch, almost refreshing in this sweltering place. *How can they stand this heat?*

From up ahead came the sound of many voices – the grating, booming sound of these rock people. The passage they were in opened out into a huge cavern that soared high overhead. Ashael let her eye follow the walls upwards until she had to crane her neck back. Far above them, she saw the suggestion of blue sky. Not that they would be able to get out that way. The walls were smooth as far up as she could see.

The spear-carriers in front of her moved to the side and Ashael had trouble believing what she saw. There were more of the rock creatures here than she could count. In the middle of the cavern was a huge shaft filled with a pool of roiling red-and-black liquid. The heat and the rotten smell were overpowering and for a moment Ashael fought to stay conscious. Colm took her elbow and she leaned against him gratefully.

'What is this place?' he hissed.

Ashael could only shake her head in response. The spear-carriers took a few steps forward then turned and gestured for Ashael and her companions to follow them as they set off around the edge of the cavern.

Ashael desperately wanted to dawdle, to take in everything around her and figure out what it all meant. Instead, she was forced to hurry, stealing as many quick glances as possible.

They approached a brightly coloured canopy, something like the hide shelters the Folk used for working under during the rainy season, but much lighter. The fabric rippled in the faint breeze that moved around the cavern. The group stopped a short distance away and White-Sash went up to speak to people under the canopy. Ashael watched as he approached a large, seated figure with its back to them. Long, white hair swung as the figure turned to look at them and then stood abruptly, striding to their group on powerfully muscled legs. She was the largest woman Ashael had ever seen, towering over even the spear-carriers. Her eyes were milky white, unlike the others' violet colour. At first, Ashael thought she might be blind, but the woman stared straight at her. Under her scrutiny, Ashael felt herself laid bare, as if this woman could see to her very core.

'Bow! You must bow to Tchalikila,' White-Sash called, hurrying up to Ashael.

'No,' the woman held up her hand. 'I bow to the Vessel.' With that, the woman fell to her knees in front of Ashael, coming face-to-face with her. 'You honour us, Vessel.'

***

A SHORT TIME later, they were all seated under the canopy. Drinks had been brought to them and cool water to wash in. Despite Ashael's pleas for information, none was immediately forthcoming. Tchalikila had left White-Sash, whose name was Faruse, to see to their needs, and had promised to return shortly with answers for them.

'Where is she?' called a voice from outside. 'Tchalikila told me the Vessel is here. I must see to her comfort!'

A small, wiry rock creature entered the canopy and immediately fell to his knees in front of Ashael, placing his head upon her feet. 'Oh, Vessel, how may I serve you?'

'You can start by telling me what in the All-Mother's name is going on,' Ashael snapped. 'And stop calling me Vessel. My name is Ashael.'

'Of course, Ves... Ashael. But first let me see to your comfort.'

The creature before her sat with his legs folded under him, closed his eyes and began to chant. Despite her unexplained fluency in their language, Ashael did not understand these words. He stood and made a symbol in the air with his hand directly before Ashael. He moved around her group, making the symbol several more times, stopping only when he faced Ashael again. A cool breeze sprang up from nowhere, circulating around the hot and weary travellers.

'Better?' he asked.

'Yes, thank you,' Ashael answered, tipping her head from side to side, allowing the breeze to cool her neck. It felt wonderful.

'You should be able to breathe comfortably now,' the creature said, gesturing at the cloth around Ashael's mouth.

Cautiously, she pulled the cloth down and took a breath. The air was as fresh as straight after a rainstorm. Ashael smiled and breathed deeply before asking, 'What is your name?'

'I am called Sanvari, if it please you.'

'Thank you, Sanvari. Now – where are we?'

'We are in the Heart of Agni, he who is the body of the world.'

Ashael waited, hoping for something more. Something useful. Sanvari just stood there, seemingly waiting for her next question.

Luca and Moyna had fallen asleep, despite the strange circumstances. Ashael supposed that their injuries weakened them. Tris sat beside them, guarding them as they slept, while Iwan and Colm sat to either side of Ashael. They had agreed that she would try to find out all she could, translating for them as they went along.

'Why are we here?' Ashael tried.

'This is our home. The Agnikant have always lived here. We are the beloved of Agni and so, we live in his heart. Faruse found you in a place where only Agnikant should be, so he brought you here to Tchalikila, for guidance.'

'Why do you all keep calling me the Vessel?'

'Because you are the Vessel, whose coming has been foretold. Long and long have we waited for you.'

Ashael rubbed her head where a dull ache was beginning to settle. This was getting her nowhere.

Tchalikila appeared, glancing over her shoulder to someone walking behind her. When she stepped aside, Ashael could not believe her eyes. Alayne, Erin and Ruraigh stood there, huddled together, with a young girl she did not recognise. *That must be the girl Colm told me about. What was her name again?* Ashael stood and when Alayne saw her, joy broke over her face and she raced towards her friend, followed by the others. The girl stood off to the side as the others shared a tearful reunion.

'Gert! Where's Gert?' Colm asked suddenly. When he saw her standing on her own, he scooped her into a tight embrace. 'Are you alright, lass?'

Gert nodded and hugged Colm tighter.

'What are you all doing here?' Iwan asked.

'We were caught in a rockslide after we left you. Ruraigh was pinned beneath a rock. One of these creatures got him out and brought him here. They have strange magic; his leg is almost entirely healed.'

'We haven't been able to communicate with them, though,' Alayne added.

'Ashael can talk to them,' Iwan said.

The newcomers all turned to look at Ashael.

'I don't know how,' she said, 'but it seems that I can. I'm trying to find out why they brought us here.' Ashael felt a lump form in her throat as she saw Ruraigh looking at her face and then quickly away, a grimace flashing across his features. She knew she had lost what little beauty she had with her eye, but it hurt to be confronted with that fact so soon.

Tchalikila spoke and they all hushed so that Ashael could hear what was said.

'We shall give you some time to get reacquainted. Sanvari will stay to tend to your wishes, you need only ask. I shall return soon and bring with me a meal that we might seal the bonds of friendship with food.'

Chapter Thirty-Eight

MIST CLUNG TO THE GROUND, WRAPPING AROUND THEIR ANKLES AS JOREN AND Bhearra made their way across the cam in the pre-dawn light. They spoke in hushed voices.

'How many of our people are leaving?' Bhearra asked.

'Ten, so far: two families.'

'I hate the thought of them leaving with that coward,' Bhearra grumbled.

'What can we do? The Folk must be allowed to choose their own fate. You know that.' Joren stopped walking and looked around before speaking again, his voice even lower. 'I'm just surprised that more people haven't asked about Angus and the implications. Where there is one spy...'

'...there may be others. Makes me wonder why Iwan disappeared at the same time as Ashael.'

Joren frowned. 'Surely you don't think... Iwan is always so helpful.'

'How much do we really know about him?'

Bhearra studied Joren's face and saw the thoughts flashing across his eyes. He trusted Iwan, allowed the stranger to join the cam, brought him into the circle of confidantes. If he could spend so much time with someone and be wrong about him, then who else could he have misjudged?

'Neither of us saw any reason to doubt him, Joren. Maybe that's because there is no reason. I hope that's the case, but I think we need to keep an open mind. If he returns, he may come as one of them rather than one of us.'

Joren stared at Bhearra for a moment, jaw clenched, then gave a curt nod. He was startled when Rana placed a hand on his arm, having silently approached him.

'I didn't hear you,' he said.

'I know. You two were obviously pretty deep into something. Why didn't you wake me?'

'I thought you might need the rest.'

'There will be plenty of time for rest when I'm as big as an aurochs,' she said, smiling and absently rubbing her belly. 'For now, I should be with you to see off the ones who have chosen to leave. We should hurry.'

Joren kissed Rana's forehead and took her hand, and the three of them walked over to the shelters that had been used by the Folk from Blossom Cam.

Bertrand appeared as they approached, taking Bhearra's hands in both of his and kissing them. 'I am sorry to be leaving you like this, my friend.'

'You have no choice, I know. Your duty is to the people of Blossom Cam,' Bhearra answered, embracing her old friend.

'I have tried to counsel Olim to stay a little longer, to listen before making any decisions, but his mind is set.'

'What are his plans?' Joren asked.

'Return to Blossom Cam to get the rest of our people, then head east

'Will you just run forever?' Rana asked. 'What about when winter comes?'

'We should have found somewhere to settle for the season by then,' came a voice from behind them.

Bhearra, Joren and Rana turned to see Olim joining them. A small, wiry man, he had a permanent scowl, caused by poor eyesight. It could make him appear unapproachable but whenever Bhearra had dealt with him before, he had been very pleasant.

'When spring comes we'll push on. Maybe the Zanthar won't follow us.'

'I wish you would stay, Olim,' said Joren. 'We're stronger together.'

'Then come with us. This plan of yours to fight them is madness. The last time the Zanthar came we were enslaved. Don't let it happen again.'

'This time we know more. They won't take us unawares again.'

'They'll take us all the same.' Olim looked sad. 'Perhaps we should have spent more time learning how to fight instead of building homes. Maybe then we would have a chance.'

'Is there nothing I can say to persuade you to stay?' Joren asked.

'I wish you the best of luck, Joren, but I owe it to my people to get them as far away from the Zanthar as I can. The gods know it still might not be enough. If you'll excuse me, I have to make sure we're all ready to go.'

'Be safe, Olim,' Joren answered.

'Oh no,' Rana said, looking towards Bres and Soraya, who were walking towards them.

'We're sorry,' Bres said, not quite able to look them in the eye. 'We have to think of Bhearrael. It seems safer to go with the others.' Soraya stood slightly behind her mate, the baby wrapped in a sling. Tears gleamed, unshed, in her eyes.

Rana embraced Soraya and the baby. 'I understand, but I'm so sorry to see you go.'

'You must do what you judge right for you,' Joren said, his voice soft.

'It is time,' Olim called.

'May the All-Mother sustain you and the All-Father lend you his strength,' Bhearra said, voice raised to include all of those who prepared to leave. 'May they keep you safe on your journey. With their blessing, we will see each other again.'

Bhearra, Joren and Rana stood there together for a long time after the small group had passed from their sight.

***

TCHALIKILA HAD REFUSED to discuss anything until they had all eaten together. Faruse and Sanvari had joined them in their meal, as had a newcomer: an old man who had been introduced as Rashveda of the Far-Sight. He was bent with age, and Ashael thought that he might be even older than Bhearra. Unlike the other Agnikant that they had met, he was bald, though he shared the violet eyes of the others.

As they ate, Sanvari told them a little about the making of each dish, Ashael translating for the rest of her group. They were served fish wrapped in nettle leaves, followed by spicy goat with an unfamiliar tuber. The food was flavoured very differently to what the cam Folk were used to, but they enjoyed the meal, which was accompanied by cool, clear water and a drink made from fermented fruit. Ashael avoided that one; she wanted to be sure she had a clear head when she was finally allowed to ask her questions.

Ashael tried hard not to stare at the Agnikant as they ate, food disappearing somewhere behind the breathing sacs that covered their lower face. Their voices seemed to come from there as well, despite the fact that she could see no mouths. These creatures were fascinating. *I can't believe I've never heard of them before. How can we live so close to each other but have no bonds?*

At last, the food was finished, and the dishes cleared away. Sleeping places were arranged around the edges of the canopied area and some of the foragers took them gratefully. In the end, Ashael, Iwan, Colm and Alayne sat with Tchalikila, Sanvari and Rashveda.

'Now that we have shared food and drink, our people are friends. We may speak freely. What would you know?' Tchalikila asked.

'Everything,' Ashael answered at once. 'The problem is, I don't know enough to understand which questions are the most important.'

Rashveda gave Ashael a look full of warmth. 'You are wise to recognise what you do not know, young one. Let us begin with the prophecy.' He looked to Tchalikila for her approval, continuing when she nodded.

'Many cycles ago, the leeches – the ones who call themselves Zanthar – walked upon the body of Agni, stealing the life of he who is the body of the world. Before the leeches came, the Agnikant and the Folk were friends, but I'm ashamed to say that when the Zanthar arrived, we hid inside the body of Agni. We failed you and have long been too ashamed of that failure to seek you out. While we remained hidden inside Agni, the Folk were defeated. I'm sure you know that part of the history?'

Ashael quickly recited what she knew, how her people had been slaves until Sirion's rebellion.

'Indeed. After the leeches were removed from the body of Agni, he, along with his brother Saulas and sister Kala – those you know as the All-Mother and All-Father – made a pact. You see, they are our gods, of this land only. They have no power over these leeches, who belong to a different world. Kala was sure the leeches would return, and the gods did not wish to leave their children defenceless. And so they agreed to join forces to create the Vessel.

'From the bones of Agni, the blood of Saulas and the breath of Kala was the Vessel created. One to hold the soul of this world and the souls of all living creatures upon it. One with the power of life to counter the death that the leeches bring. One who can heal where the leeches destroy. You are that Vessel.'

'What in the All-Mother's name makes you I'm the Vessel? You're suggesting I'm a god?' Ashael spluttered, shock and indignation vying for prominence.

Rashveda and Tchalikila exchanged a look. 'That may be best shown. Perhaps you would accompany me?' Tchalikila asked.

Once Ashael had translated for the others, they insisted she didn't go alone. Colm stayed behind to watch over their sleeping friends, while Iwan and Alayne accompanied her. The Agnikant had given them no reason to think they were in danger here, but after everything they had been through the group was still on edge.

Tchalikila led them from beneath the canopy, around the cavern, now dark except for a fierce red glow coming from the crater at the centre. They turned into a small and dusty passage.

'Where are we going?' Ashael asked.

'I think it would be better for you to see first,' Tchalikila answered without looking back.

They followed the passage only a short distance before coming to a small cave. Tchalikila made a pattern in the air over the cave entrance with the flame of her torch, then entered. Walking to the centre of the space, Tchalikila held her torch to a fire pit set with wood. The flames caught surprisingly quickly, the light dancing on the walls of the small cave.

Ashael gasped and put her hand to her chest. Before her, on the far wall, was a life-size image of herself. The only difference was that the image had both eyes.

'What? How? I can't...' Ashael couldn't find the words she needed.

'Look over there,' Iwan murmured, pointing to another image further along the wall. This was an Agnikant, bearing Ashael's face.

Examining the walls, Ashael saw herself with wings; another creature, squat with webbed hands and feet, also shared her appearance. Her vision swimming, Ashael dropped to her knees, hanging her head and taking deep breaths.

'What is the meaning of this?' she asked at last.

'These images have been here since the Vessel was made,' Tchalikila answered from where she waited near the entrance to the cave. 'For generations, those of the Far-Sight have been maintaining this room so that we would recognise the Vessel when she came to us. Agni has instructed that we must help you in your transformation. It is a sacred duty that falls to me.' The Agnikant leader's white eyes glowed, casting their own light before them.

Ashael translated for Iwan and Alayne, who knelt at either side of her, offering what support and comfort they could.

'I knew you were special, since the first time we met,' Iwan said, brushing the side of Ashael's face with the back of his hand. Part of Ashael longed to lean into his touch but she was still angry with him for his deception and so she held herself still until he removed his hand.

Ashael looked at Tchalikila and said again, in the tongue of the Agnikant, 'There's been some confusion. I cannot be this Vessel that you speak of. My resemblance to these images must be a coincidence. There is much that I do not understand but I cannot possibly be a god, whatever new powers I seem to have.'

'Tell me, have you ever met the Agnikant before?' Tchalikila asked, voice amused.

'No, never.'

'Then how is it you speak our tongue?'

'I... There must be some explanation.'

'There is. You are the Vessel. Created to bear the essence of all of the major races that make Agni their home. Humans, Agnikant, Flores –' here she gestured to the image with wings – 'and Ponto.' She tapped the version of Ashael with webbed hands and feet. 'I understand it is a lot to take in, but it is true.' Tchalikila looked at Ashael with sympathy on her face. 'Perhaps it would help to sleep on it?'

Ashael nodded, though she did not think she would be able to sleep.

The area under the canopy was refreshingly cool, Sanvari's charm still working to create a breeze that allowed the humans to be comfortable and made it possible for them to breathe freely. Iwan and Alayne filled Colm in on what they had seen, while Ashael spoke quietly to Rashveda.

'I have seen your face many times in my dreams,' the old man was saying. 'I am honoured to finally meet you, child of Agni. Many of us here have a little magic but Tchalikila is our sage, and she will be your guide in the ways of the Agnikant.'

'What do you mean?' Ashael asked.

'It is your destiny to learn with Tchalikila, as you will learn with the Flores and the Ponto, as you must learn with your own filidh. You will only be complete when you have learned how all of those pieces fit together.'

Chapter Thirty-Nine

ASHAEL ROSE FROM HER SLEEPING MAT, WHERE SHE HAD SPENT THE NIGHT awake. She stretched, working out the knots that had formed during her restless night, and looked around her companions. Ruraigh was sitting up, back against the wall and injured leg sticking out in front.

'How are you?' Ashael asked, keeping her voice low so as not to disturb the others.

'Surprisingly well,' he said, flexing his foot. 'I'm certain my leg was broken after the rock-slide. The pain was overwhelming.' He looked up at Ashael. 'I don't know what magic they have here but surely it comes from the gods. It has only been a matter of days and already I can walk, though not without a little pain.'

'May I?' Ashael asked, gesturing at the leg.

'Of course.'

Ashael knelt beside Ruraigh and examined his leg, looking for the signs of his injury. There was slight bruising; yellow, fading. She placed her hands around the leg and stretched out her senses. Ru's leg had definitely been broken, and badly, as far as she could tell. This injury appeared to be at least a season old, not just a few days.

'Even Bhearra couldn't have healed this break that fast,' she said, sitting back on her heels. 'I think you should be able to walk on it, as long as you give yourself lots of chances to rest.'

'You'll be able to make sure he's well, won't you?' Alayne said, sitting up. 'When do you think we can leave?'

'I will speak with Tchalikila about getting you home as soon as possible but... I'm going to stay for a while. If they'll have me.'

At that moment, Tchalikila entered the canopied area as if she had been summoned when Ashael mentioned her name. 'Your friend should be strong enough to walk home, and any who wish to leave may go, with our blessings.'

'I thank you for your hospitality. My friends have been away too long from their families,' Ashael said.

'And you, Vessel? Would you stay with us?'

'For a time, yes' Ashael said. 'It would seem I have a lot to learn.'

'May I stay?' Iwan asked, approaching from behind.

Ashael translated for him and Tchalikila answered, 'Any friend of the Vessel is a friend of the Agnikant. Any of you are welcome to remain here.'

'Afraid to face Joren?' Tris asked Iwan, an edge to his voice.

'Someone should stay with Ashael,' Iwan answered. 'If she wishes me to leave, I shall return to Oak Cam and explain myself to the Folk.'

Ashael looked from one man to the other. Tris gave Iwan an angry stare while Iwan looked at Ashael with longing and trepidation.

'He can stay,' Ashael said eventually.

'Let us break our fast and arrangements can be made,' Tchalikila said, clapping her hands together.

Over food, it was decided that Iwan and Moyna would stay behind while the rest travelled back to the cam. Ashael had expected Luca to want to stay with Moyna, but he said he had knowledge of the Zanthar weapons and would be able to help the Folk prepare. Sanvari would lead them through the tunnels and out of the mountains, to the edge of the River Donn. They could be home in three nights if they could move swiftly enough.

The travellers gathered in the cavern, carrying food and travel packs given to them by the Agnikant. Ashael moved around, hugging each of them and wishing them a safe journey. Now that the moment of separation had come, she was sad to see them go. She unconsciously raised a hand to her sunken eyelid, thinking of all that had happened, all that she had been through to free these people.

'Are you sure you won't come home with us?' Colm asked, squeezing her tight.

'I'm sure. The Agnikant seem to know so much about who I am. I have to stay here and learn how to fight the Zanthar.'

'I could stay with you,' he said. 'If you need me...'

Ashael felt a lump rise in her throat. 'Thank you, my friend, but no. Go home to your mate. Sola will be so very glad to see you.'

Colm's face lit up at the mention of Sola, and Ashael glanced at Iwan, standing off to the side with his mother.

Alayne stepped up, the last to say goodbye. 'Be safe, Ash,' she said, pulling her friend into a warm hug. 'I love you.'

'I love you too.' Ashael sniffed back some tears then straightened up. 'Give Rhys a hug from me.'

'Of course. Anything else?'

'Tell Bhearra everything you know. Tell her I'll be back as soon as I can, and that I miss her. Look after Rana for me; she's always so busy taking care of everyone else.' Ashael's heart felt like an aching ball in her chest. She missed them so much.

Sanvari clapped his hands. 'It is time to make a start, if you wish to make good progress this day.' With backwards glances and a few more farewells, the foragers, accompanied by Luca and Gert, set off for the final phase of their journey home.

***

ASHAEL SAT CROSS-LEGGED on the floor of the small cave with her images on the walls. She stared, trying to understand. Made by the gods? Did that mean she wasn't really human? What about the images of her as each of the other races? The questions beat around her mind like wings, giving her no respite.

'May I join you?'

Ashael looked up. Iwan stood in the doorway, looking anxious. 'Come in.'

Iwan sat beside her on the floor, not saying anything.

'Where is your mother?' Ashael asked.

'With Faruse. It's amazing, she can't speak to him and yet she somehow makes herself understood. She got some fabric from him to make us clothing.' Iwan snorted a laugh.

The two sat in silence for a few moments until at last Iwan raised his head and looked Ashael in the eye. 'I meant what I said, in the tunnels. I love you, Ashael. Is there any place in your life for me?'

Ashael's answer caught in her throat as she took in his earnest face. He was handsome, strong and, despite his dishonesty, she was sure that he was a good man.

'I do not know what the future holds for me. Right now, I'm not even sure who I am. Or what I am. I can't make any promises.'

Iwan dropped his head, the muscles around his jaw working as he fought his emotions. 'I understand.'

'I can't make any promises,' Ashael said again, putting her hand on Iwan's arm, feeling the taut muscle beneath his skin, 'but I care for you. I don't know how any sort of relationship will work but I'm willing to explore the possibilities, if you are.'

Iwan pulled Ashael into a tight embrace, resting his head atop hers.

Chapter Forty

IT WAS LATE AND MOST OF THE CAM FOLK WERE IN BED. BHEARRA STOOD BY THE Heart-Fire, feeding wood to the flames. Tonight, it was her turn to tend the eternal flame. She cherished this time of closeness to her gods, especially at night when all was peaceful.

Almost as soon as that thought passed through her mind, a voice she hadn't heard in what seemed an age came from the entrance to the cam. She looked up and her hand flew to her chest as she saw Colm striding across the clearing.

'Joren! Rana!' Bhearra cried, seeing the other foragers appearing behind Colm.

A few sleepy faces peered out of windows before rushing outside. Bhearra hurried over to the returning foragers, spotting Alayne just behind Colm. The young woman veered off, heading towards her home, calling for her mate and son. Gethyn burst out and grabbed Alayne, lifting her clear off her feet.

Bhearra felt joy bubbling up in her chest, emerging as a laugh.

'Colm, my friend, it is so good to see you!' Bhearra exclaimed through the laughter.

'What's going...? You're back!' Rana came running up. 'Ash!' She looked around, her delight turning to a frown. 'Where is Ashael?'

'She did not return with us,' Colm answered, 'but she is well.'

'What do you mean?' Rana demanded. 'Where is she?'

'Colm...? Colm!' Sola ran up and threw herself into her mate's arms, sobbing. 'Oh, thank the gods!'

'What about Ash?' Rana persisted, though the reunited mates did not seem to hear her.

Bhearra stepped back and put an arm around Rana. 'Give them a moment, dear. We will soon know all.'

***

'... AND SO she decided to stay, learn more about this prophecy and her abilities,' Colm concluded. He sipped some water then squeezed Sola's hand.

'Iwan and his mother stayed with her,' Alayne continued. 'Ashael is safe, I think. The Agnikant seem to hold her in high regard and they were nothing but kind to us.'

'It's a lot to take in,' Bhearra said, pushing herself to her feet with a groan. 'It is almost dawn and you all must be exhausted. Let us retire. We can meet again later today.'

Joren stood and helped Rana to her feet. 'I am glad to see you all returned to us. We will meet here at midday, share a meal and consider our next steps. Luca, you are welcome here. You may stay in Iwan's hut for tonight.'

'I'll show him the way,' Alayne said.

The group broke up, talking quietly. Bhearra, Joren and Rana walked together towards the two trees that were their homes.

'When will Danliv return with the rest of Trout Cam?' Bhearra asked.

'It depends how long it takes for them all to pack up.' Joren rubbed his face as he spoke, stifling a yawn. 'Less than a moon-cycle, I would think. Why?'

'I was thinking he would be the best person to work with Luca on the weapons.'

'So Iwan was a slave, his mother held hostage, and still he tried to save Ashael,' Rana said, taking Joren's arm. 'He must have been so frightened all the time, pulled in two directions.'

'It is likely,' Joren agreed. 'Although I'm not sure how much that excuses the betrayal.'

'That is a question with no easy answer, I fear,' Bhearra said with a sigh. 'My old mind is too tired to contemplate it any further right now. Sleep is calling to me.'

Joren patted Bhearra's shoulder. 'Go, sleep. We shall speak more after some rest.'

Bhearra bid the young couple good night and hobbled to her tree, her hips stiff from sitting on the ground for so long. Entering her home, she looked towards Ashael's empty alcove and sighed. She understood why Ashael had stayed away but her heart was heavy nonetheless.

She headed to her own alcove, stripped down to her undertunic and lay down on her pallet. She started to drift towards sleep almost immediately, exhaustion overcoming her. She saw Ashael's face before her, missing an eye. Her apprentice was saying something, but Bhearra was too tired to work it out. The face receded and Bhearra sank into a dreamless sleep.

***

'I SAW HER!' Ashael exclaimed. 'Just for a moment, but I think she saw me too.'

'Well done,' Tchalikila said from the other side of the glowing stone that they meditated over. 'You are making excellent progress.'

'I just wish I could speak to her. I miss her so much.'

'Keep practising and you will, Vessel. The Heart-Link is one of the gifts of the Agnikant. With time, you will be able to use it to communicate with those you love over great distances. But I think that is enough for today.'

'So soon?'

Tchalikila laughed, the sound like pebbles bouncing over each other. 'It has been half a day already. It is time you eat.'

Ashael was surprised so much time had passed but then her stomach rumbled and she, too, laughed. She headed back to the smaller canopy set up for her own use and discovered that Moyna was there, setting out food for her.

'Thank you, Moyna, but you do not need to serve me.'

'You set my Iwan free. Feeding you is the least I can do,' Moyna said, looking at Ashael in awe.

Ashael studied Iwan's mother thoughtfully and rainbow light began to dance over her skin.

'I removed Iwan's slave-brand without realising,' Ashael said. 'I may not be able to do it again, but I would like to try.'

Moyna gasped and looked up. 'You mean me?'

Ashael nodded. 'I cannot promise it will work. Would you like me to try?'

Moyna nodded, tears shining in her eyes.

'Lie down, here,' Ashael said, indicating the bundle of furs she slept on.

Moyna lay down and pulled up the sleeve of her tunic. Ashael looked at the brand, the same one that Iwan had tried to cut from his chest. Anger rose in her belly, but she choked it back down, taking deep breaths and finding her centre. The rainbow light spread, until it encompassed Moyna. For a few seconds, the light blazed. When Ashael's vision cleared, she saw unblemished skin where a moment ago there had been scar tissue.

'Take a look,' she said, softly.

Moyna squeezed her eyes tighter shut before opening them and lifting her arm into view. She sat up and embraced Ashael, their tears mingling.

'I'm free,' Moyna whispered. 'Free.'

Epilogue

'I THINK I KNOW THE ANSWER, MY LORD!' MEEGRUM SHOUTED AS HE BURST INTO Daven's chamber. 'I know what they have in common!'

'Out with it then,' Daven rasped. His eye was no longer filled with blood and most of the grey had receded from his hair, but even now, days after his loss of control, he was not fully recovered.

'The ones we can't feed on were all born here, my lord.'

'And those that still succumb?'

'All brought from Zan.'

'It's her. We missed our chance on Longest Day and now she's protecting them somehow.'

'I believe so, my lord.'

Daven sank into a chair and stared into the unlit hearth. Meegrum waited as Daven's eyes grew distant, but eventually lost his patience.

'My lord? What shall we do?'

Daven roused himself, turning a sharp gaze upon Meegrum. 'Kill her, of course.'

'But if the prophecy has come to pass then our magic will be no use against her.'

'Then we shall kill her the old-fashioned way, Meegrum. With steel.'

ACKNOWLEDGEMENTS

2017

To write these acknowledgements in as much detail as I would like would take almost another book, so I hope you'll forgive me if I try to keep this brief.

First and foremost, my thanks go to everyone who pledged their support and made this book possible. Quite simply, without you, it would not be here. I have been overwhelmed by the kindness and generosity of so many people, especially my family – those of my heart as well as those of my blood.

My thanks of course also go to the entire team at Unbound. Your vision of publishing is inspiring and I'm proud to call myself an Unbounder. In particular, I would like to thank Xander Cansell for answering all of my questions, Annabel Wright for overseeing the editing process and being so quick to offer her support, and Michael Rowley for providing an expert content edit and helping me to see the tweaks that were needed.

I owe a lot to many of the other Unbound authors who showed support and camaraderie throughout the entire process, and especially to Ian Skewis for helping me with my very first reading. I hope we appear together again. In no particular order my thanks also go to Natalie Fergie, Tim Atkinson, Stevyn Colgan, Amanda Lloyd Jennings, Helen Taylor, Stephen McGowan and Tabatha Stirling.

Thank you to all of the bloggers who hosted me during and after my campaign. It was lovely to work with all of you and I hope to write more for you in the future.

No list of thanks would be complete if I didn't mention my writing group, people who have become my friends and trusted advisors although we have never met face-to-face. So, for reading the first draft and helping me to shape this novel, my thanks go to Devin Shorey, Bryan Garret, Matt Clarke, Henry Sullivan, Joshua

Allen Tompkins and Andrew Burelson.

To my children – thank you for showing so much enthusiasm about this journey.

And last, but far from least, my thanks to my husband, Brian. He suggested that I write the book and then gave me the time and support to do so. Without him, Ashael's tale would still be in my head.

2021

MUCH HAS HAPPENED IN THE YEARS SINCE THIS BOOK WAS FIRST PUBLISHED BY Unbound. I attended my first Fantasycon in 2017, where I met so many wonderful people in the genre community. For the first time since I can remember, I felt like I had found my tribe. I have built many meaningful friendships since then, not least of which with Sammy H.K. Smith, author, editor and owner of Grimbold Books. I can't thank Sammy enough for republishing *Ashael Rising* and picking up the other two books in the trilogy. I'm so very glad that we found a home at Grimbold.

About the Author

SHONA KINSELLA IS THE AUTHOR OF EPIC FANTASY, THE VESSEL OF KALADENE series, dark Scottish fantasy *Petra MacDonald and the Queen of the Fae* and British Fantasy Award shortlisted industrial fantasy *The Flame and the Flood* as well as the non-fiction *Outlander and the Real Jacobites: Scotland's Fight for Freedom.* She was editor of the British Fantasy Society's fiction publication *BFS Horizons* for four years and is now Chair of the British Fantasy Society.

Shona is an avid reader with a love for language and is most often to be found with her nose in a book. She has worked in varied industries, from acting to the civil service, and has a degree in law from the University of Strathclyde.

Shona lives near the picturesque Loch Lomond with her husband and three children. When she's not writing, doing laundry or wrangling the children, she enjoys cooking, geocaching and nature walks with her family.

You can find her at www.shonakinsella.com

Also from
Kristell Ink Publishing

The Search of Gods and Heroes

By Sammy HK Smith

BOOK ONE OF Children of Nalowyn is a true epic of sweeping proportions which becomes progressively darker as the baser side of human nature is explored, the failings and ambitions of the gods is revealed, and lines between sensuality and sadism, love and lust are blurred.

Darkspire Reaches

by C.N. Lesley

HER BIRTH MOTHER left her as a sacrifice to the Wyvern, believing a second born twin had no soul. Her foster mother thought Raven possessed the magic of the First born. She believed she raised a slave. The emperor of all the lands believed she knew the secret of his birth and that he must silence her. Her tribe thought they could trade her for safe passage out of the emperor's lands.

The Wyvern knows better. He is coming for her. And his fury has no limits.

kristell-ink.com

Lightning Source UK Ltd.
Milton Keynes UK
UKHW012003020822
406760UK00008B/137/J